Ali McNamara a~~t~~ ... ~~gination~~ to one thing – bein~~g~~ ... ~~aming up~~ adventures when she was young has left her with a head constantly bursting with stories waiting to be told. When stories she wrote for fun on Ronan Keating's website became so popular they were sold as a fundraising project for his cancer awareness charity, Ali realised that not only was writing something she enjoyed doing, but something others enjoyed reading too. Ali lives in Cambridgeshire with her family and two Labradors. When she isn't writing, she likes to travel, read and people-watch, more often than not accompanied by a good cup of coffee. Her dogs and a love of exercise keep her sane!

To find out more about Ali visit her website at
www.alimcnamara.co.uk
or follow her on Twitter: @AliMcNamara

Praise for *From Notting Hill With Love ... Actually*:

'Perfectly plotted, gorgeously romantic, has some
great gags and leaves you with that lovely gooey feeling
you get at the end of a good Hollywood rom com'
Lucy-Anne Holmes, author of *The (Im)Perfect Girlfriend*

Letters From Lighthouse Cottage

Ali McNamara

sphere

SPHERE

First published in Great Britain in 2016 by Sphere

1 3 5 7 9 10 8 6 4 2

Copyright © Ali McNamara 2016

ISBN 978-0-7515-5863-0

Typeset in Caslon by M Rules
Printed and bound in Great Britain by
Clays Ltd, St Ives plc

Papers used by Sphere are from well-managed forests
and other responsible sources.

MIX
Paper from
responsible sources
FSC® C104740

Sphere
An imprint of
Little, Brown Book Group
Carmelite House
50 Victoria Embankment
London EC4Y 0DZ

An Hachette UK Company
www.hachette.co.uk

www.littlebrown.co.uk

For Scamp, Sam and Jake.
Gone, but never ever forgotten.

Dear Reader,

Life is never easy.

We all have many life-changing experiences every day. Some of which appear to us to be good, some we think of as bad.

Wouldn't it be so much easier if we had someone to help us along the way, to guide us on to the right path, to give us advice when we needed it, and to always be there looking out for us.

We do.

We just need to open our eyes and find them.

This is the story of what happens when that help comes to us in a very unusual way ...

Summer 2016

Sandybridge Hall is happy today. I know it is.

The house and its grounds are packed with visitors, all enjoying themselves on this beautiful July day. I'm amazed we've been able to attract so many people away from the delights of the local town and its beaches, which have been a popular seaside resort since Victorian times. But the hall, which stands a short distance from the centre of Sandybridge, is proving these days to be of equal value in the tourism stakes.

I gaze up at the Tudor manor in front of me; its golden yellow brickwork positively glows under the spell of today's warm sunshine. Sandybridge Hall was always happy when it had guests. When there were people walking through its beautifully manicured gardens, and exclaiming with joy at its perfectly restored interiors, the lattice windows lining the heavy brick walls shone that little bit brighter, and a warm, welcoming atmosphere radiated from the many corridors and furnished rooms the house contained.

Sandybridge Hall and its extensive grounds were made for people to enjoy, and people in turn had visited here in their thousands every year.

'Grace, there you are!' Iris, my young assistant, comes rushing towards me along the neatly trimmed grass. 'I have those papers for you to sign.'

'Thanks, Iris,' I tell her as she arrives next to me. 'Sorry to abandon you in the office alone, but I had to step out for a bit. I love to watch the house when it's in full flow. It always seems at its best then.'

'Well, we are pretty busy today.' Iris looks around her while I quickly squiggle my signature over the papers she's provided me with. 'In fact it's been like this all week.'

'That can only ever be a good thing.' I hand the papers back to her. 'This house has stood empty far too often in the past. I'm just happy to see it flourishing again.'

'All thanks to our glorious benefactor,' Iris says, winking at me.

'Indeed,' I say, thinking of him fondly.

'Oh, that reminds me ... ' Iris digs into the top pocket of her dungarees. 'Danny was trying to get hold of you earlier. He rang the office because he said you weren't answering your mobile. I guess this is why,' she says, raising her eyebrows at me and passing me my phone. 'You left it on your desk.'

'Sorry,' I tell her, taking the phone. 'I do that a lot.'

'So I've realised.' Iris wrinkles her nose and a tiny gold stud twitches. 'I don't know how you can leave it lying around. My phone is like my right arm.'

'That's because you're young,' I reply smiling. 'Mobile phones might as well be attached to you, you have to check them so often. But you have to remember, when I was your age the only telephones we used were attached to the wall, not ourselves. You couldn't take them anywhere!'

'Don't!' Iris places her hand on her forehead dramatically. 'I can't bear the thought!'

'And even when we did finally get mobile phones, they were only for making telephone calls, you couldn't use them like the little computers you do today!' I continue to tease Iris, who lives for her gadgets.

'You'll be telling me next you had one of those huge beige box computers in your house,' Iris says, playing along. 'I've seen them in museums. Did you play Pac-Man and Space Invaders on it? No, wait!' She waves her hand at me. 'I bet you didn't even have one of those – you probably had a type-writer to do your homework on!'

My stomach twists sharply. Iris has come a bit too close to the truth, and unknowingly hit a nerve – a particularly raw one today.

'More people!' I announce, glad of the distraction, as two large coaches slowly pass through the big black gates of Sandybridge Hall and pass along the gravel drive in front of us.

'Yeah, school trip,' Iris says, wrinkling her nose again. 'Teenagers. Doubt many of them will be interested in the history of the hall. Probably only here for the day out.'

'Nothing wrong in that,' I say, fondly remembering some of my own school trips. 'You never know, something they see today might spark an interest in history.'

'You think so?' Iris pulls a face.

3

I shake my head. 'Probably not. All I was interested in at their age was boys and getting away from Sandybridge.'

'Really?' Iris asks, genuinely surprised. 'I thought with your background you'd have been the school swot, nose deep in your history books all day.'

I laugh. 'Nope, definitely not. I hated history when I was at school. It wasn't until I was fifteen that everything changed.'

'Ooh, what happened when you were fifteen?' Iris asks, her interest sparked.

'Long story. I'll tell you sometime. Now I guess we'd better get back to the office – things to do and all that. Plus, I have to go out later.'

'Do you?' Iris asks as we set off towards the house. 'I don't have anything in the diary.'

'I have an important meeting,' I tell her without elaborating further. 'I'll be gone a little while.'

Iris shrugs her acceptance, and silently we walk along the gravel path, towards where the two coaches have dropped off their passengers.

A young teacher is attempting to gain control of his pupils, most of whom aren't taking the slightest bit of notice of what he's saying. As we pass by, I hear one particularly loud girl announce: 'I bloody hate history!' And immediately my mind is cast back to the summer of 1986 . . .

Part One

June 1986

One

'Grace!' my mother calls from the next room. 'Will you get in here and help me with this stuff, please. I've asked you twice already.'

I sigh, and stop gazing at the photos on the wall. Photos of places I've never been, but the person staring back at me from the photos had, and she looked like she was enjoying herself. The woman in the photos is as much a stranger to me as the places, but in the mad world I inhabit with my parents, I'm currently sifting through her belongings in the hope some of them might be worth something.

'OK, I'm here,' I tell my mother as I appear at the door of the sitting room she's busy clearing.

'About time. Now help me lift these boxes out to the van, will you? And, Grace . . . ?'

'Yes?'

'Stop daydreaming! There's a time and a place, and this most certainly isn't it. We need to get on!'

'Yes, Mum,' I mumble, and I begin carrying the cardboard boxes full of junk outside to our battered, pale blue van.

Harper's Antiques & Collectables

it states proudly on the side in ornate white writing.

Buy · Sell · Valuations · House clearances
4 Lobster Pot Alley, Sandybridge, Norfolk
02163 492445

This was generally my lot at weekends, either helping Mum and Dad serve customers in their little antiques shop, or helping them as I was today with a house clearance, which is where they got most of their stock. Occasionally we would go to an auction, which was a bit more interesting, but it didn't get much more stimulating than that. Sometimes – but only sometimes, mind – I was quite pleased when Monday came and school gave me an excuse to get out of dealing with old tat.

But old tat sold. It never ceased to amaze me how many customers Mum and Dad got in their shop, eager to purchase someone else's cast-offs – be it locals on the lookout for a bargain, or tourists visiting Sandybridge for a day out at the seaside. The customers kept coming, so my parents kept trading. Just as well really; they were hardly going to make their fortunes clutching mobile phones and Filofaxes to their chests, trading on the stock exchange. No, my parents were as far away from embracing the brash, colourful world of the eighties as I was from travelling the world. Mum and Dad preferred to remain very much in the past, and that was how they intended to stay.

'Can I go now?' I ask my mother, as we load what I assume is the last of the boxes into the back of the van.

'Go where?' My mother turns to face me, a puzzled expression on her face.

All right, don't rub it in! I think, just because I don't have the biggest of social lives here in Sandybridge. Actually, you could probably make that the whole of Norfolk, possibly even the world! No one could do less 'teenage' things than me – that I was quite sure of. I was fifteen and the most excitement I'd ever had was when I was almost caught bunking off school; except no one believed I was. The teacher who saw me popping into the corner shop to buy *Just Seventeen* magazine (in fact it was *Cosmo* too, but I hid it under the other) assumed I must be ill if I was taking a day off school, and offered me a packet of Lockets and a paracetamol from her bag.

My dealings with the opposite sex were virtually non-existent too. The most attention I'd ever had from a boy was the day Will Granger attempted to set fire to my crimped hair by dangling it, unbeknown to me, over a lit Bunsen burner when we'd been forced to do an experiment together in our chemistry class.

So while all the other teenagers in Sandybridge appeared to be constantly out partying, pushing the boundaries of life and the patience of their parents, I had barely left the pram, let alone the nursery.

'I said I'd watch the football later with some mates,' I tell Mum proudly. This was a very loose take on the truth. The 'mates' in question weren't really my friends, but I'd been in the classroom waiting for registration on Friday morning when it was being discussed by the 'cool' kids, and I'd kind of found myself included in the general invitation. This didn't happen often, and I was keen to make the most of it – even if it did mean watching overpaid men kick a ball around a field for ninety minutes, and topple over in performances worthy of a prima ballerina.

'Since when were you interested in football?' Mum asks, a hint of surprise in her voice.

'It's the World Cup, isn't it? How can you not be, it's everywhere right now?'

She narrows her eyes at me, and plants her hands firmly in the pockets of her blue dungarees.

I counter her suspicion with an innocent stare.

'Well, it's good to see you going out, I suppose,' she eventually concedes. 'Whose house are you going to watch this match at?'

'Duncan Braithwaite's,' I mumble, hoping Mum won't hear me.

Her eyes now do the opposite and widen in shock.

'Duncan Braithwaite? I'm not sure I want you hanging around with the likes of him, Grace. I heard he was trouble.'

'Mum, it's not just me; there's a whole gang of us. I'll be fine.'

Mum looks unsure, but nods her agreement. 'If that's what you want to do, I guess it's OK with me. But promise me you'll be careful, Grace. Fifteen is a difficult age, especially when boys become involved. I remember when I was fifteen I—'

'*Mum!*' I protest.

'Sorry, sweetie. You know I worry about you; you're my little girl, my only child. I'm allowed to worry a little, aren't I?'

I nod. 'But only a little, mind!'

She grins. 'Right, I think there's one more box left in the cottage, and that'll be it for now. I'm going to come back for the rest tomorrow when your dad is free to help me lift the heavy furniture. I wonder how he got on at that auction down in Fakenham? I wish I could have gone, but the family wanted this doing as soon as possible. Did I tell you Mabel especially requested we do her house clearance?' Mum tells me proudly, for the third time.

'Yes, Mum, you did. Isn't that a bit odd though, making arrangements for someone to clear your things?'

'I guess some people like to be organised. She seemed to know the end was coming, even though she was in good health when I spoke to her. I suppose that is a bit odd.' Mum looks away from the small cottage we've been clearing, up at the imposing lighthouse that stands next to it. 'What a shame there will be no proper keepers living at the lighthouse any more,' she says, looking fondly at the tall, white-brick cylinder that, at the angle we're viewing it from, appears to soar up into the clouds above, then disappear. 'Since they built that new one down the coast, our little lighthouse has been rendered useless. Mabel was the last keeper to live here in Lighthouse Cottage.'

'Things have to move on, Mum,' I tell her. 'Progress equals change.'

'I know, but I've never been very good with change. Maybe that's why your dad and I went into the antiques business – so we could hold on to the past a bit longer, eh?' She smiles at me, then turns away from the lighthouse and looks up towards the huge Tudor manor house that stands high up on the hill behind us. 'Do you know the hall is being sold too?' Mum says with a tinge of sadness. 'The owners can't afford to run it any longer, so they're being forced to sell and move elsewhere. Such a sad state of affairs; in the past the owners of that house owned the whole of Sandybridge – the houses, the shops, the lighthouse even' – she gestures up at the building next to us – 'but the years rolled by, and bit by bit they had to sell off the estate. Until the only thing they owned was the house, and now that's going too.' Mum shakes her head. 'I'm all for progress, Grace, but if it's at the expense of our glorious country's historical past, then I'll happily pass on it.'

I look up at Sandybridge Hall behind us. It suits its name well; even on this cloudy June day, the pretty golden yellow and terracotta red bricks make the house look warm and welcoming as it stands, stylishly surrounded by its own moat, at the top of a long tree-lined driveway.

'I bet you'd have loved to get in there, Mum, amongst all that antique furniture and paintings. You'd have been in your element clearing that one!'

'Oh no, that would never happen. The interiors of Sandybridge Hall are worth far too much to be sold in a house clearance,' Mum insists. 'Some of the paintings are of great historical significance, and they have odd bits of furniture in there dating back to the sixteenth century. There's even a rumour they have a quill pen that Mary Queen of Scots used to write a letter when she visited the manor.'

'Ah ...' I say, turning my gaze towards the house again. None of this interests me in the slightest.

'Anyway, I can't be worrying about that now.' Mum rubs

her forehead with the back of her h d, and a few strands of blonde hair fall out from under the s f she's earing to protect her hair from dust. 'I have my ow easures to sort through when I get this lot home. Mabel had some lovely pieces – we should do well from clearance.' She jumps up into the van. 'Grace, be a dear and get that last box from the cottage while I finish arranging these ones.'

'Sure,' I reply, pleased I won't have to talk about old things any more. History and preserving the past was definitely Mum's favourite soapbox topic, so it always came as a relief when she stepped down before getting into full flow.

I head through the gate of the white picket fence that surrounds the cottage's little garden, push open the wooden front door and go inside to find the last box. But it's not where I expect it to be, in the sitting room where we'd stacked all the other full boxes. So I go through all the rooms of the cottage to see if I can find it.

There's nothing in the old kitchen, only empty wooden cupboards with paint peeling from the doors, and an oven that looks like it's seen better days. The hall is too tiny to hide a box, so I run up the stairs, almost hidden in the hall by a curtain hanging at the base of them, to take another look upstairs. Nothing in the three little bedrooms, apart from some furniture that Dad'll come and collect later. The bathroom is empty too – save for an old white roll-top bath, and an old-fashioned toilet and sink. So I return downstairs for one last look in the sitting room in case I've missed something. But all I see is a wrought-iron fireplace standing magnificently at the end of the room, and some of Mabel's old furniture.

This could be quite a cosy little cottage if someone

were to buy it and do it up nicely, I think as I continue to search. I expect it will be sold to someone who will do it up to rent to the holidaymakers who are beginning to flood into Sandybridge. Since the town underwent a complete overhaul a couple of years ago and started putting money into the seafront and promenade, it's been attracting not only new businesses but people too. Now Sandybridge is re-establishing itself as a resort, almost as popular as it had been in Victorian times.

'Hmm, what's through here?' I ask as I turn the handle on a small door I'd not previously noticed, tucked away at the end of the hallway, near the front door. 'There you are!' I exclaim, as I find myself in a tiny room that the old lighthouse keepers probably used as an office. There are bookshelves, now empty of the books or papers they were built to hold, and a well-used writing desk that Mum and Dad will no doubt work their magic on, restoring it to its former glory before selling it on. But what I'm interested in at this very moment is sitting on top of the desk: my missing box.

I immediately head over to the desk and attempt to lift it.

Whoa! I hastily set the box down when I feel how heavy it is. What has Mum put in here? I wonder. I prise open one of the cardboard flaps and look inside.

'Oh, it's only a typewriter,' I say to the empty room. But the typewriter is one of those really old black ones, with long round keys. No wonder it's so heavy. These things were made to last. I'm about to close the lid and try to lift it again when I spot a typewritten sheet of paper wound on to the black roller. I reach into the box and unwind the paper so I can read it.

14

Dear Grace,

Congratulations on finding me. I knew it would
be you that did.

Please take Remy (that's what he likes to
be known as) home with you and look after
him well. He will be a great help to you in
the future, as he's been to so many people
in the past.

I must warn you, though, there are a few
rules to owning him:

You can't write letters on Remy, only read
them.

The advice Remy gives can only help guide you
in your endeavours; he can share no detailed
information. Dates and names, for instance, are
forbidden.

You are always free to choose to ignore him!
It does happen. But remember: he will always
have your best interests at heart.

When it is time to pass Remy on to a new
owner, you will receive instructions on how to
do so.

Good luck.

Love, Me x

'What on earth?' I mutter as I read the letter over again.
'Remy? Why would you name a typewriter, let alone call it
Remy?' I glance into the box. 'Oh, Remington! Now I get
it,' I say as I see the brand name REMINGTON etched in
ornate gold font across the top of the machine. 'But still ...
slightly weird. And why address the letter to me?' I shake my

head. 'I never knew old Mabel was a bit batty! What is she going on about? How can an old typewriter give you advice? And why write a letter to me on it? I suppose she must have known I'd help Mum with the house clearance.'

'Grace!' I hear my mother call from the hall. 'I've found that last box now. Time to go.'

But ...? I look suspiciously at the box sitting in front of me on the desk, then I hurriedly stuff the letter inside, close the lid, and with huge effort manage to lift the box out of the study and carry it out to the van.

'What have you got there?' Mum asks as I struggle to hoist the box into the back of the van with the others. 'I thought we had everything?'

'I found it in the study, it's a typewriter.'

Mum looks in the top, then wrinkles her nose. 'Beautiful as those old things are – and I'd say that one might be forty to fifty years old – we just can't sell them. People are only into those computers nowadays – you know, Amstrads, Commodores, that kind of thing.'

I do; there's a newly installed computer suite at school that we get to use once a week. There are even rumours that we'll be getting a Sinclair ZX Spectrum soon. But I'm speechless to discover Mum knows anything about computers, let alone the leading brands.

'What shall I do with it then? It's on the van now.'

'Would you like to keep it?' she asks. 'Could be worth something one day. Look on it as a thank you for helping me out.'

'As long as it's not instead of my wages, then fine. I guess it might still work. Maybe I could do some of my homework on it.'

'Of course it's not instead of your wages!' Mum puts her arm around my shoulder and gives me a hug. 'You do know how much Dad and I appreciate all your help, don't you, Grace? We couldn't run the business without you.' She kisses the top of my head. 'You're a good girl, always have been.'

Not for want of trying, I think, but I allow Mum her moment without making a fuss.

'Come on then, let's get this stuff back to the shop,' Mum says, releasing me and heading around to the driver's side of the van. 'Then you can get ready for your party tonight.'

'It's not a party,' I tell her. 'I'm just going to a mate's house to watch footie.'

'Yes, yes,' Mum says, climbing up into the seat. 'But you never know who you might meet, party or no party ...'

Two

Sandybridge's long seafront is home to many gift shops, which all seem to sell pretty much the same thing: picture postcards of Sandybridge in various guises, souvenir china, plastic buckets and spades, and brightly coloured children's windmills, which spin noisily round in the sea breeze this evening as I walk by. There's an amusement arcade, rows of bed and breakfasts that never seem to have any vacancies, two tea rooms – one of which is closed at the moment, but as I pass by I notice there's a sign in the window stating *Under New Management – Reopening Soon*. We have a really good fish and chip shop, which right now has a long queue of hungry people winding its way through the door and outside on to the pavement, and as I get a whiff of frying chips, I almost join it.

'No, Grace,' I tell myself sternly, 'you need to cut down. You'll never get into those size 12 jeans if you don't. Plus you

18

already had that chocolate bar this afternoon. Tonight you must be good.'

I'm always worrying about my weight, as are most of the girls in my class, judging by their conversations. While I'm not exactly fat, I'm too round to be happy, which is why I'm constantly having to fight my natural inclination to love and enjoy food.

With a growl of my stomach, I continue walking past the chip shop and on towards Duncan Braithwaite's house. To take my mind off my hunger I think about Sandybridge, asking myself why people would choose to come here for their holidays when there are so many other exciting places they could go in the world. True, we have two gorgeous beaches – a sandy one that lies a little way out of town, next to the lighthouse, which you have to cross a small bridge to get to – hence the town's name; the other, the one I am currently looking at, runs alongside the long concrete promenade and is completely covered in grey, white and brown pebbles.

It never used to be busy like this. Before the refurbishment, we'd been a quiet little seaside town, a bit run down, but charming in our own way. Now, we're what those travel programmes on telly would call a 'bustling little seaside resort'.

'When I'm old enough, I'll get away from here and see the world' – I tell myself the same thing every time I walk along the prom, gazing out at the never-ending horizon where sky meets sea. Although many people seem to be attracted by my home town's charms, there's no way I want to be stuck here on the north Norfolk coast, forever looking out at the same skyline the way some of Sandybridge's older residents have done all their lives. The world's a big place, filled with strange, interesting and exciting things, and I want to see and experience all of them.

But what could be stranger than the typewriter I'd brought home with me from Mabel's house earlier today?

When we'd got back to the antiques shop, I'd helped Mum offload the stuff from the van, as I always did, then I'd hung around outside while Mum checked in with Doris, the lady that helped us out part-time, to see what had gone on in the shop this afternoon and whether she'd sold anything.

I never spent any longer in the shop than I had to. Old stuff held no joy for me; the future was where it was at, not the past. The shop was cute, I guess, if you liked that sort of thing; 'quaint and cosy' we'd been described as when the local newspaper did a feature on us. But at fifteen, quaint and cosy wasn't my thing. So while Mum went in, I'd hung around outside the shop with one of those new chocolate bars, a Wispa, to keep me company.

When Mum had finished with Doris, we'd got in the van and driven home. Then Mum helped me lift the heavy black typewriter up to my bedroom, where I'd placed it on top of my chest of drawers – after pushing a load of unwanted rubbish I hadn't got around to clearing away yet on to the floor. Mum didn't even flinch; although she's super tidy around the rest of our little Victorian terraced house, she lets me do what I want in my bedroom and I'm grateful to her for that.

After Mum had left, I'd lounged around on my bed for a while, staring up at the *Back to the Future* and *Breakfast Club* posters I'd got from our local cinema, and my various pictures of A-Ha, desperately looking for some guidance from Michael J. Fox or Morten Harket about what I should wear tonight. I'd told Mum it wasn't a party, and that was the truth, but I still wanted to get my outfit right. Danny Lucas would probably be there, as he was mates with Duncan, and – as hard as I tried not to – I couldn't help fancying Danny.

I didn't want to. Danny wasn't really my type at all, if I had such a thing. He wasn't in any of my classes; I was in the top sets for all my subjects, and he always seemed to be put in the lower ones. So except for PE, where to my horror Danny would always see me at my absolute worst – bright red, out of breath and with my long brown mousey hair all over the place as I tried to keep up with the sporty girls who seemed to do everything effortlessly – I never got to see him much at school. But when I did, my tummy would fizz like a SodaStream, and my mouth would go all dry, and if Danny should ever look my way, to my annoyance I would feel my cheeks flush redder than Ferris Bueller's Ferrari. So tonight was my big chance. I wasn't sure to do what exactly, Danny probably wouldn't even look my way, but I'd be content just to get a smile from his gorgeous mouth, or even one of his infamous winks, that he usually reserved for the sporty girls who would prance and giggle in front of him.

It was after I'd taken a shower and returned to my room to get changed for this evening's festivities that I noticed it – a freshly typed sheet of white paper in the centre of the typewriter's roller.

'But how ... I mean what ...?' I stuttered as I stopped towel-drying my wet hair, and went over to the chest of drawers. Before I'd even had a chance to pull the paper out, I noticed the first line:

Dear Gracie,

What!

I quickly wound the rest of the paper out of the typewriter and began to read.

Dear Gracie,

    You don't even recognise this as being you, do you?

    At the moment everyone knows you as Grace. But very soon you will meet someone who will call you Gracie — and you will like it.

    Treasure this person, for he is the one who will make you happy, and who will always be there for you, no matter what.

    Love, Me x

I read the letter three times in total.

How had this happened? How could a typewriter type without anybody being in the room?

Ah, then I realised. 'Mum!' I called down the stairs. 'Have you been in my room?'

No answer. So I dropped the towel that had been wrapped around my body, pulled on my dressing gown and hurried down the stairs.

'Mum!'

As I entered the kitchen, I saw a note on the table.

Just popped to the shop to get milk – back in a few mins. Mum x

Weird . . . I dashed back up the stairs, picked up the paper and read it again. How could this have happened? And why was it calling me Gracie? This was mad; typewriters couldn't type on their own. If the first letter was typed by Mabel, then who'd typed this one?

I shook my head, told myself, 'Grace, you haven't got time for this now. However weird it is, you have to get ready.' So I tossed the paper on my bedside table on top of my Walkman, and began choosing the outfit that was sure to get Danny Lucas to notice me.

As I'm rounding the corner of Wendell Close where Duncan lives, I spot a young guy heading the same way as me. He's wearing tight black stonewashed denim jeans, a matching denim jacket, and a red-and-black checked shirt. Nothing wrong in that; stonewashed denim was a trend most of the boys went for, and on any normal occasion I'd have thought nothing of it. Except, to my absolute horror, his choice of outfit is an exact match for mine! The only difference being instead of jeans I'm wearing a short black denim skirt with opaque tights, and in the place of his Adidas trainers, flat black patent pumps.

I'm about to turn the other way, hurriedly trying to work out if I've got time to go home and change before kick-off, when the guy calls across the street to me.

'Hi, are you going to Duncan's to watch the football?'

I've no choice but to respond.

'Yes, are you?' *You idiot, Grace!* I cringe internally. Of course he is or he wouldn't have asked you.

'I am,' he says, nervously smiling at me. 'Do you know which house it is by any chance? I'm new here.'

I cross the road to join him. 'It's not far, just around the corner a bit. I'll show you, if you like?'

'Thanks, I appreciate it,' the boy says, looking at me as we begin to walk awkwardly next to each other in the direction I've pointed. 'Nice to meet you, by the way,' he says, holding out his hand, then he looks down at it with absolute horror, as if he's just done the stupidest thing ever.

Empathising immediately with this level of awkwardness, I quickly take hold of his hand and shake it.

He smiles gratefully at me, then he notices my clothes. 'Nice outfit.'

'Thanks, er . . . so is yours.'

'Well it would be, wouldn't it, twinnie?' he grins. 'And to think I nearly wore my football shirt too, but I thought that might be too obvious!'

'You like football then?' Oh, good grief, Grace – could your questions get any dumber? He must if he has a shirt!

'Actually no, I was going to borrow my brother's spare one, then I decided at the last minute not to. Between you and me, I hate football, but when they invited me tonight I thought it might be a good way of getting to know a few people.'

So I wasn't the only one using this as a way in with the cool kids. 'You've just moved to Sandybridge?' I didn't think I'd seen him before.

'Yes, about a week ago. My parents are taking over the tea rooms on the front.'

'I saw there was work being done. It looks like it's going to be nice when it's finished.'

'Yeah, I got roped into that, like I always do. Family business, see.'

24

'I know all about that – my family run the antiques shop in Lobster Pot Alley.'

'Ah right, I don't think I know that. I'll have to come and have a look one day.'

'Oh, it's nothing special. There's much better things to see in Sandybridge.'

'Really?' He raises an auburn eyebrow at me.

'Nah,' I reply. 'It's mega dull here.'

'Just as well I met you then!' His freckled face flushes a little, and he looks down at his feet.

'Look, we're here!' I say to cover his and my embarrassment as we arrive outside Duncan Braithwaite's and walk up the short drive to the semi-detached house. I ring the doorbell, and we wait awkwardly together on the doorstep.

Duncan Braithwaite eventually comes to the door; he's wearing an England shirt that says *Lineker* on the back. 'Oh hey ... er ... Grace,' he says, struggling to remember my name. 'I didn't know you were coming, and you brought a friend too?'

'No, we just met on the way, didn't we ... Oh, I'm sorry – I don't even know your name.'

'Charlie,' my companion says, not seeming to mind at all. 'Charlie Parker.'

Three

'Right, Charlie and Grace, come on in!' Duncan declares, throwing the door wide open. 'The match doesn't start for a while yet, but there's plenty of booze in the kitchen.' He looks expectantly at us.

Damn, I hadn't thought to bring anything.

But Charlie lifts a rucksack from his shoulder. 'Beer!' he says, holding it up.

'Good man!' Duncan says, patting him on the back. 'It's through there.'

We wander into the kitchen together, pushing through the kids already hanging out in there. 'Where did you get beer from?' I ask Charlie, wondering how he'd managed to buy alcohol.

'My brother got it for me,' he whispers, 'he's eighteen.'

Charlie puts his cans of beer down on the counter with the other alcohol, then pulls one from the plastic and offers it to me.

I hesitate.

'It's OK,' he says, whispering again. 'I don't really like it either.' He puts the can back down on the counter and looks around him. 'Fanta?' he enquires, finding some cans hidden behind the bottles and cans of booze everyone else is tucking into.

I nod gratefully, and take one from him.

Charlie takes one for himself, and we turn around and awkwardly watch our fellow 'footie fans' enjoying themselves. They don't even seem to have noticed we're here, and carry on laughing, chatting and swigging tins of lager in their own little gangs.

'Are you into this football lark then?' Charlie asks, removing the ring-pull from his can of Fanta. 'Or are you just here to socialise like me?'

'The latter,' I tell him, doing the same to my can. 'Can't bear football actually! But don't tell anyone here, will you?'

Charlie grins. 'Nah, your secret is safe with me. So, if you're not keen on football, what *do* you like?' he asks, as one of the cool girls from my class reaches past us for more beer.

'All right, Grace,' she says to my surprise as she retrieves a can. 'Nice shirt.'

'Thanks, Lucy,' I say, about to try and continue the conversation, but Lucy has already disappeared back to whatever clique she's currently inhabiting.

'Sorry . . . what did you ask?' I say, turning back to Charlie, my fleeting moment as one of the 'in' kids over as quickly as it had begun. 'Oh yes: what I like?'

Charlie nods.

'Erm . . . I like going to the cinema. There's one just up the road in Cromer, I get the bus to it sometimes.'

'What else?'

I think hard: what else do I like doing?

'That's it really,' I say, a tad apologetically. 'Most of my spare time is used up helping my parents with their shop. I mean, I like music, but doesn't everyone our age?'

'Nope, not me,' Charlie says matter-of-factly. 'I'm not into music at all.'

'Really?' I'm astonished by his honesty. Everyone our age always tries to fit in with whatever anyone else is into, whether they like it or not. 'What sort of things *do* you like then?'

'Nature,' Charlie says, again surprising me. 'Real things, things that live and breathe, not manufactured rubbish that someone else has decided for us we should like.'

I stare at him for a moment. Charlie is a bit shorter than me, so from here I can see the way his thick red hair tufts and forms into a cowlick at the crown of his head.

'What do you mean?' I ask, suddenly aware I've been staring a bit too long at his hair.

'How can you not know what I mean by nature? Plants, animals, the way things grow. I'm so excited to be living by the sea. I'm going to be able to investigate all sorts of marine life now. It's going to be great!'

I've never met anyone I thought might be weirder than me. But Charlie definitely is. He isn't cool, and he knows it, but he doesn't care. It's quite refreshing.

'I'm glad you're excited by the prospect of living here in Sandybridge. I can't wait to get away myself.'

'Why?'

'I want to travel the world, that's all. See stuff.'

'Nice.' Charlie nods thoughtfully. 'So, are you going on

this trip next week to Norwich? It's not exactly the world, but it will get you out of Sandybridge for a day.'

I wrinkle my nose. 'Nah, it's being organised by the youth club, and the youth club is run by the church, so it'll be all holy stuff and monuments.'

'Not necessarily, it might be fun.'

'So *you're* going then?'

'I may have signed up for it . . . '

'Well good luck with that! You won't catch me bussing it down to Norwich on a Saturday morning to look at old stuff – I get enough of that here in Sandybridge.'

Charlie smiles. 'I guess you do. But I thought you wanted to get away from here?'

'Yeah, but further afield than Norwich – I have my sights set on much more exciting places.'

'Cool.' Charlie nods. 'So what do you want to do when you leave school? If you want to travel the world then you'll either need to earn a pretty hefty holiday fund, or do a job that allows you to travel.'

Oddly, in all my daydreams about travelling the world, I've never actually considered how I'm going to fund it.

I feel silly.

'I haven't decided yet,' I bluff. 'Depends on how my exams go next year.'

'How do you feel about us being the last ones to do O-levels and CSEs?' Charlie asks, changing the subject to my relief. 'What is it they're calling the new ones?'

'GCSEs,' I tell him. 'They reckon it will be a lot easier to get the grades then too. Totally not fair.'

'Such is life, Gracie, such is life.'

'It's Grace,' I tell him. Then I stop. Wait, wasn't that what the letter said? Someone would call me Gracie? I look with suspicion at Charlie.

'What?' he asks. 'A slip of the tongue, that's all.'

'No, it's not that, it's . . .' Oh, how do I explain this? 'I was told earlier today that someone would call me Gracie.'

'And you didn't expect it to be me – right?'

I didn't expect it to be anyone. Let alone a ginger kid called Charlie who I didn't even know.

'I didn't know who it would be.'

'But you don't like to be called that?'

I shrug. 'It's just that no one has ever called me Gracie.'

'Is that your name – Gracie?' I hear a deep, sexy-sounding voice to my left. 'I always wondered.'

I turn around to find Danny Lucas standing behind me, lifting a can of Pepsi from the counter.

'I . . . I . . .' I stutter. Pull yourself together, Grace; this is your big chance! 'I mean, yes, my name is Gracie, you're right.' When Danny Lucas said it like that, it sounded like the most perfect name ever.

There's a shout of 'Football's about to kick off!' from the other room, and most of the kitchen dwellers begin mooching off into the lounge.

'Time to go!' Danny says, smiling at me. 'How do you think the match will go, Gracie?'

'Er . . .' Oh God, I know nothing about football. Then I remember Duncan's shirt. 'I think Lineker will score,' I say, trying to sound knowledgeable.

'And get the golden boot? Yes, you could be right.'

'Do they have golden boots?' I ask stupidly. It's as if I can't hear myself speak; all I know is that Danny Lucas is talking to me, and it feels fantastic! 'Isn't that a bit expensive?'

Danny's gorgeous face breaks into an even more gorgeous smile. 'And she's funny too! How have we never met before, Gracie?'

'I ... I really don't know.'

'Wanna come and sit next to me for the match?' Danny asks, like there was ever a choice.

'Yes please ...' I stupidly grin, then I remember Charlie and glance back at him.

'Oh, are you guys together?' Danny asks, surprised. 'Sorry, I didn't realise.'

'No!' I snap, seeing the chance I've been waiting for, for so long, slipping away with every word. 'I mean, we arrived together, but we're not ... well you know?'

'Even so, I don't want to step on anyone's toes.' Danny smiles, and begins to walk towards the door. 'I'll catch up with you two dudes later. Can't miss the most important match England's played in years, can I?' he calls as he disappears through the kitchen door with me forlornly watching him.

'Like him, do you?' Charlie asks innocently.

'*No* ...' I turn back towards him. 'Well, yes ... actually.' I sigh. 'Is it that obvious?'

Charlie grins. 'Just a bit. Come on, Gracie – as I'm sure you're quite happy to be known as now. Let's go through and endure this football with the others, shall we? We don't want to seem antisocial. Otherwise there was no point in either of us coming tonight!'

So Charlie and I sat and watched the football match. I tried to look interested, shouting, cheering and groaning when the others did. But it was quite a strain to maintain the charade for over ninety minutes.

All the good seats had been taken by the time Charlie and I went through to Duncan's parents' lounge, so we ended up squeezed together on some sort of gigantic double bean-bag, which – as all good bean-bags do – *looked* extremely comfortable, but was a complete bugger to sit in with any sort of elegance, and even harder to climb out of with any degree of dignity.

When Maradona – or Madonna as I thought he was called for most of the match – apparently scored with his hand instead of his foot, pandemonium broke out in Duncan's sitting room, with much derision and name-calling of the referee. But when he scored again a few minutes later there were begrudging mutters of 'pure class' and 'genius', so I was a little confused, to put it mildly.

I passed the rest of the match by surreptitiously eyeing up Danny Lucas at any moment I knew he'd be engrossed in the game.

God, he was gorgeous. His bright blue eyes flashed with intensity as he concentrated on the match, then they danced with delight whenever England did something well.

When Gary Lineker scored towards the back end of the game, the room erupted and everyone jumped around cheering and hugging each other. Charlie and I took so long to struggle from the beanbag that the hugging was all but over when we finally managed to get to our feet. So we turned awkwardly and gave each other a consolatory high five.

Then everyone settled down again, and where despair had filled the room before, hope now took its place as we all urged England to score again. Even Charlie and I were firmly caught up in the emotion of the game. But sadly it was not to be. Argentina won 2-1, and England were defeated once more.

Duncan stands up and gloomily turns off the TV pundits, clawing over every moment of the last ninety minutes – particularly Maradona's handball, which they seem intent on viewing from every angle possible.

'Well, that's that,' he sighs, reaching above the fireplace to pull down the giant England flag that has hung there throughout the game. 'Losers once again.'

The others nod miserably in agreement.

What's wrong with these guys? I ask myself. It's only a game!

Even though there's still plenty of alcohol to be drunk, the party never quite gets going again, as people mooch about dissecting the game, and in particular the referee's decision on the handball.

'Cheery, isn't it?' Charlie comments as we stand in the kitchen again, back in our positions from earlier, watching everyone.

'I know. You'd think someone died out there, not lost a football match!'

'I bet half of them don't even care that much,' Charlie says knowingly. 'They're only putting on the melancholy act to blend in with the others.'

I smile at him.

'What?' he asks, looking at me.

'Annoying, isn't it?' I say. 'When people do that. Don't they have any thoughts of their own?'

Charlie looks around the room, as if considering this.

'You know what, I don't think they do!'

I grin; I'm beginning to really like Charlie. He's different to anyone I've ever met.

'Looks like you were right, Gracie.' I hear the sweet tones of Danny Lucas next to me, so I immediately spin around.

'R-right about what?' I ask, desperately trying to make my voice coherent.

'About Lineker scoring and winning the golden boot! Clever girl!'

'Ah yes, I did say that, didn't I?'

'Well, technically Danny brought up the golden boot,' I hear Charlie mutter behind me. 'You thought they wore them.'

I choose to ignore him; I have more important things to think about right now, like Danny Lucas' gorgeous face right in front of me. Those blue eyes looking right into mine, and his perfect lips saying something . . .

Oh, what *is* he saying? Something about a trip . . .

'I'm going on that,' I hear Charlie say, 'but Gracie isn't.'

'I . . . I never said that.' I smile up at Danny. 'I said I was *thinking* about going.'

'You should,' he insists. 'The youth club trips are usually pretty good.'

'Well, in that case, I'll definitely sign up for it.'

And in that moment this whole night is made worthwhile, as Danny presents me with the most perfect smile.

'That's great, Gracie. I'll see you next Saturday then.'

'Yes, for sure,' I whisper, watching mesmerised as he drifts away, back to his customary territory of the in-crowd.

And for once I don't mind being on the edges of it, as I turn back to Charlie.

Charlie shakes his head at me. 'I don't know about *Great*

Gracie,' he says, grinning. 'More like *Gullible* Gracie, if you ask me.'

But I don't care. Danny Lucas has noticed me at last. He called me Gracie, just like the typewriter had said someone special would.

Danny Lucas is going to be important in my life, of that I have no doubt.

Four

Another letter is waiting for me in the typewriter when I wake up the next morning.

I don't see it at first, but as my eyes gradually begin to get used to the light that streams through my thin curtains on these bright summer mornings, I notice that the crisp white piece of paper I'd wound into the spool of the typewriter before I went to bed last night, in the hope something else might happen, has been covered in the old-fashioned black font again.

I jump out of bed and rush to the chest of drawers, then I carefully unwind the paper and read:

Dear Grace,

    Congratulations, you met him, your very own Mr Right! I hate to say I told you so, but I did! He called you Gracie and you liked it.

I'm so very pleased that you've decided to participate in the school trip this weekend with your new friends, as this day will be important to your future in so many ways. I only wish I could tell you why, but as you know, sadly I cannot.

Just trust in me that whatever happens, it's all for the good!

Love, Me x

How could a trip to Norwich be so important to my future? Unless I got off with Danny Lucas on the back seat of the bus, I couldn't see how taking a tour around a load of ancient monuments was going to benefit me in any way at all. So I let my mind wander to the Danny thought again . . . Mmm, if that was what the letter meant then I was all for it!

'Grace!' My mother's voice jolts me from my daydreams. 'Are you awake yet? Wilson is getting desperate for his walk before you go to school!'

'Mum, I'm on study leave! I keep telling you!' I call back, taking one more look at the latest letter. I've no idea how this is happening, or why, but I'm not about to turn my nose up at a typewriter that wants to give me advice about life; it's difficult enough being a teenager in the eighties. So if this little machine wants to help me through the next few years, then so be it! Getting letters on a battered old typewriter is hardly *Electric Dreams* or even *War Games* – two computer-based movies I'd enjoyed at the cinema. And I'm hardly going to turn into Matthew Broderick and start World War III now, am I?

'Oh that's right, I keep forgetting,' Mum calls from down-stairs. 'Do you have an exam today?'

'Mock exam,' I correct her. 'No, not today. I'll be right down for Wilson. Just give me a minute.'

I pull on some jeans, a sweater and my battered old trainers and head downstairs to find Wilson, our shaggy mongrel of a dog, looking agitated by the door.

'You'd think we didn't have a garden!' I tell him, ruffling his mottled grey brown fur.

'You know he won't use it for number twos,' Mum says helpfully as she puts toast on the table in the antique silver rack she always insists on using. 'Must have been where he lived before, perhaps they didn't let him.'

We'd adopted Wilson after one of Mum and Dad's house clearances. It had been for an elderly man who didn't have many relatives, just a nephew who came up from London to oversee the clearance of his uncle's home.

'His neighbours say the dog kept him fit,' he'd told us as Wilson lay curled up miserably in the corner on a blanket. 'But none of them want to take him – I've already tried.'

'So what will happen to him?' I'd asked, looking with concern at the obviously bereaved dog.

'I'll have to take him to a dogs' home, I guess. I can't have him; I live in a tiny flat in Chelsea. They won't allow any pets – let alone a dog as big as him.'

Wilson, not moving his head from the blanket, looked up at us sadly.

'Mum . . . ?' I'd begun to ask.

'No, Grace, we can't. He's so big! Where will we put him?'

'We can find a space in the kitchen for his bed, I'm sure, if not in the lounge.'

'But he'd need so much walking, Grace – look at the size of him.'

Wilson was pretty big; from my limited knowledge of dogs he looked like he might be a cross between an Irish wolfhound and an Airedale terrier. His coat was rough and looked like it needed a good brush, but he had the most gorgeous eyes that he had turned up to 100 per cent sad-dog mode as he watched us from his bed.

'I'll walk him,' I told Mum. 'I will!' I'd insisted before she could respond. 'Please, Mum, just look at him, we can't abandon him. And you do advertise a *full* house clearance, and Wilson is part of this house. We owe it to him.'

Mum had of course eventually agreed. Wilson had come to live with us, and I was proud to say I'd kept my end of the bargain and I walked him every day. Although I suspected Wilson missed his previous owner a lot, he fitted in with us quickly and easily, and even though he was a big dog, he wasn't the least bit of trouble – unless you forgot about his walk, then he'd wheedle and whine until you took him.

I grab Wilson's red leather lead from the hook in our utility room. 'I'll be back in a bit!' I call as I hook the lead to his collar.

'What about your breakfast?' Mum says, appearing at the utility room door.

'I'll get something later,' I tell her. 'We don't want Wilson peeing on the floor now, do we?'

'Make sure you do, Grace. You're looking far too thin these days.'

As if!

'Sure, Mum,' I appease her. 'I will.'

It's the beginning of a beautiful summer's day and there's not a cloud in the bright blue sky as Wilson and I walk along our street, and head for our favourite seafront walk. Wilson loves the sea, but bathing a dog as big as Wilson isn't the easiest of jobs. So I have to limit how often I let him splash around in the waves, because his thick coat always ends up soaking wet and matted with sand.

Most of the newer houses in Sandybridge are set back from the sea, with only the odd Victorian terrace sitting directly on the seafront, and most of those have been turned into B&Bs over the years, so Wilson and I have to walk through several streets, and along the high street a little way, before we can veer down towards the promenade and find our way to the beach.

It's still quite early, so although the high street shops are just opening up to customers, most of the shops along the seafront are still closed, preferring to start and finish their days later so they can cater to the majority of the holiday crowd. The B&Bs are busy serving breakfast though, and Wilson isn't the only one to pick up a waft of sausages and bacon frying as we pass by.

'I'll see what I can rustle up when we get back,' I tell him. 'Mum and Dad will have left for the shop by then. I'm sure we can do better than a bowl of Special K this morning, Wilson! Diet or no diet, I'm hungry!'

Wilson barks approvingly, and we continue on our way. We're about to pass by the empty tea rooms when I notice some people inside – one of them is Charlie.

As if he senses someone is watching him he turns around, then waves when he sees it's me.

'Hey,' he says as he runs over to unbolt the door. 'Who's this?'

'Wilson,' I tell him, as Wilson licks Charlie's hand in greeting.

'Hello, Wilson,' Charlie says, rubbing the top of his head. 'You didn't say you had a dog.'

'No, I didn't, did I? You can't really miss him either. Can I add him to my list of hobbies – he takes up enough of my time!'

'And who's this, Charlie?' A woman wearing white painting overalls, who I assume must be Charlie's mother as she has the same red hair as him, comes to the door to join him.

'This is Gracie, Mum, and Wilson. We met last night at the football.'

'Well hello, Gracie. What a pretty name,' she says, smiling at me. 'Won't you come in? We can't offer you much until we're up and running. But I'm sure I can find you a cup of tea from somewhere. Any friend of Charlie's is always welcome here.'

'That's very kind of you, Mrs . . . '

'Oh, call me Maggie, please,' she insists.

'Maggie. But I'm just taking Wilson for his morning walk. You really don't want him in your shop when he wants a walk, it'll be carnage.'

Maggie looks down at Wilson – who helpfully shakes himself at that very moment and removes several loose hairs in the process. 'Yes . . . I can imagine.' She looks at Charlie. 'Would you like to take a break now, Charlie, and go for a walk with Gracie?'

'*Mum* . . . ' Charlie flushes. 'Maybe Gracie doesn't want company.'

'I'm fine with it,' I say seriously. 'It's Wilson you need to worry about.' I wink at him, and he immediately grins back.

'What do you reckon, Wilson?' Charlie asks.

'Woof!' Wilson amiably agrees on cue.

*

41

To Charlie's obvious embarrassment, three pairs of eyes watch us with interest as we walk away from the tea rooms: Maggie, Charlie's father Peter, and his brother Luke.

'Sorry about them,' Charlie apologises. 'I don't get out a lot, so they get a bit over-excited when I do.' It's Charlie's turn to wink at me now.

Today Charlie is wearing casual clothes like I am – a pair of blue jeans and a navy blue hooded sweatshirt. I'm pleased to see that, like me, he isn't a slave to fashion, unless he needs to be.

'I know the feeling. My parents are much the same. It's worse for me though; there's only me for them to embarrass. At least your humiliation must be somewhat diluted between you and Luke.'

'Yeah, I guess there are some bonuses to having a brother.' He looks over at me. 'So you're an only child?'

I nod.

'Does it bother you?'

No one has ever asked me that before. People usually go along the lines of: 'It must be great not to have brother or sisters to argue with, or nick your stuff.' Or even: 'Your parents must spoil you rotten, you lucky thing!'

'No, I don't think so,' I tell him after I've thought about it for a moment.

'Good,' Charlie replies. 'That's good. Do you ever let Wilson off the lead?' he asks, changing the subject.

'Oh yes, he loves the beach. But it usually means a good wash when he gets home if I do.'

'Let's go down on to the beach then,' Charlie suggests. 'The sandy one over the bridge. I'll help you wash him if he gets too dirty.'

'You'll regret saying that!' I tease. 'But yes, let's do that. It's a lovely morning, and the beach won't be busy yet with holidaymakers. Wilson will love it!'

We turn off from the tarmacked promenade, along a paved street, then down the narrow road that leads up and across the little stone bridge that takes us on to Sandybridge beach.

As we begin to walk across the sand towards Lighthouse Cottage where Mum and I had been clearing yesterday, I unhook Wilson from his lead and let him run free across the sand.

'That's better,' Charlie says approvingly. 'I like to see animals doing what they do best.'

'You'll see what he does worst in a minute,' I warn him. 'Wait until he hits the sea!'

We watch Wilson take big lolloping strides down towards the waves, then he launches himself hard into the water.

'Wait for it!' I promise.

Like a small child digging a trench in the wet sand, hoping he can encourage the sea to flow up to his sandcastle's moat and fill it without the need for carrying buckets, Wilson begins to dig in the sand beneath the shallow waves.

Charlie watches open-mouthed as huge clumps of sand fly up over the top of Wilson, scattering sand all over him as he digs.

'I see what you mean,' he says, grimacing. 'Ah well, at least he's enjoying himself.'

'He is that! Come on, Wilson!' I call as we walk past him along the hard sand down by the waves. 'You can dig another hole further along the beach.'

'So you're not at school today then?' Charlie asks as we

eventually persuade Wilson to abandon his hole and he gallops along in front of us.

'No, study leave. I'm doing mocks at the moment.'

'Like I should be too right now.'

'Yeah, bad time to move schools. If you're bothered like ...' I add, not wanting to sound like a swot.

'Don't worry,' Charlie grins, immediately knowing what I mean. 'I think by now you probably know I'm not one of the cool kids. I want an education. But the opportunity of a shop here in Sandybridge came up suddenly, and Mum and Dad were looking for a new business. If it had been next year they said there was no way they'd have moved me, but missing mocks ... Well it just means I'll be thrown in at the deep end next year with no practice.'

'I guess ...' I didn't think I'd have been too happy if Mum and Dad had suddenly announced we were going to move. 'So what do you want to do after O-levels?' I swallow awkwardly. 'If you're doing them, that is?' I don't want to offend him if he's only doing CSEs.

'Yeah, I'm doing O-levels,' Charlie says, to my relief. 'There's a sixth form at the school, right?'

'Yes.'

'Then I'm going to do A-levels, I hope, in biology, maths, and either physics or chemistry.'

'Science bod, eh?'

'Only stuff I'm good at. How about you?'

'I'm not too sure yet – probably English, then possibly art or drama. Something like that anyway. Depends on my exam results.'

'You're the complete opposite to me then – Mrs Creative.'

'Only things I'm good at,' I mimic, and he laughs.

'So you're not going to follow in the family tradition then? Learn all about history and run an antiques shop?'

'No more than you're going to do Home Ec and end up running a café!' I tease. 'Nope, I hate history, bores the pants off me.'

'I couldn't follow in my parents' footsteps even if I wanted to,' Charlie says suddenly. 'I'm adopted.'

'Oh ... I ... I'm sorry?' I try, at a loss what to say to this.

'Don't be,' Charlie says matter-of-factly. 'I've had a great upbringing, both Luke and I have, he was adopted too – we're not related,' he adds. 'We were adopted at different times.'

'Ah ...'

'So I guess that's something we have in common. I don't like history either, because I don't have any of my own.'

Charlie is very pragmatic about all this. I'm not sure I would have been able to speak so rationally about it had it been the other way around.

We pause for a moment while Wilson begins digging yet another hole in the sand; only the sound of the gulls circling overhead and the ever-present sound of the coastal breeze breaks into our silence.

'So you hate history but you're going on a trip to a cathedral and castle on Saturday?' Charlie asks suddenly. 'You must really like Danny to do something you don't like to be with him.' He doesn't look at me while he speaks; instead he keeps his eyes firmly on Wilson's exploits on the wet sand.

'That's not the only reason I'm going. I—'

'So you admit it is *one* of the reasons!' Charlie interrupts triumphantly.

I decide to be honest. I like Charlie, and it isn't as if I have friends falling over themselves to come for a walk with Wilson and me, let alone offering to bathe him afterwards.

'So, maybe I do like him,' I reply, trying to sound casual. 'What's wrong with that? You must have had crushes on girls before?'

Two round pink circles appear on Charlie's pale freckled face as he stares out to sea.

'Oh, are you . . . I mean, don't you like girls?'

Charlie turns to me. 'If you're asking whether I'm gay, then no I'm not.' He hesitates. 'I just don't have much experience with the opposite sex, that's all.'

Another silence, this time a slightly awkward one, fills the gap between us on the sand.

'There's nothing wrong with that,' I tell him eventually, kicking at a piece of dry crisp seaweed with the tip of my shoe. 'Everybody's different.'

'My brother had his first girlfriend when he was twelve,' Charlie informs me with a worried expression.

'Seriously?' I reply, surprised to hear this. 'What did they do on a date, watch *Blue Peter*?'

Charlie's frown changes to a smile.

'No, let's give them a little credit,' I continue, pleased to see him smile again. 'Was it *Grange Hill*?'

'All right,' Charlie admits. 'So I'm being silly. Have you had many boyfriends then?'

'Nope. Not one. Not unless you count a quick snog on the back of the bus with Nigel Jefferson.'

'Really?' Charlie grimaces. 'The same one that was at the football game?'

'Yeah, I know, it wasn't pretty. He didn't even have the braces then. His buck teeth weren't easy to deal with, I can tell you.'

Charlie grins. 'You're funny.'

'Am I?'

He nods.

'It was only a dare, you know? That kiss with Nigel. I didn't fancy him or anything. One of the other boys dared me to do it.'

'And you did? I'll be careful about daring you to do anything in future then, just in case you go through with it!'

I'm surprised that the thought of Charlie in my future fills me with so much joy. I like him. It's been a long time since I've really liked anyone my own age. I usually just make friends with the girls at school for someone to hang out with in break time.

'So you haven't had a boyfriend, but you'd like Danny to be your first?' Charlie openly asks.

I'm the one blushing now.

'Yes . . . I mean, no. Oh, I don't know, he probably doesn't even like me.'

'Yeah right, what's not to like?'

I glance at Charlie. He has the same expression he'd had the previous night when he'd held out his hand to me.

But luckily for our awkwardness and us, Wilson saves the day. 'Wilson!' I shout, as he chases a terrified Yorkshire terrier along the beach. Never in my life have I been so pleased to see him misbehaving. 'Stop it now!'

We manage to catch up with Wilson, apologising profusely

to Mrs Chamberlain, who luckily I know through her visits to the antiques shop, and head off home to wash all remnants of sand from Wilson's coat, and hopefully all feelings of embarrassment between Charlie and me.

Five

Remy (even I was calling him that now) hadn't chosen to type me any more letters since the one the morning after the football game.

But this morning as my alarm goes off, and I try to force my eyes to stay open, I find myself wondering just why I've agreed to go on this stupid trip. It's a Saturday, and even when I'm helping Mum and Dad on a Saturday I don't have to get up this early.

It's as I finally persuade my eyes it's a good idea to stay open that I notice the now familiar piece of typed paper propped up in the spool of Remy. So I roll out of bed still rubbing my eyes, and go over to take a look.

Dear Grace,
    So the day has arrived for your trip to
Norwich.

I know the only thing you're excited about
is whether a certain boy will pay you any
attention, but please don't limit your enjoyment
of the day to only that. Today things will
happen to you that will change your life for
the good, Grace. I promise you.

Love, Me x

'What things?' I mumble, putting the letter safely into my top drawer with all the others I've had so far. 'We're going on a bus trip to Norwich, for goodness' sake. We're hardly flying by Concorde to New York!'

But secretly I'm quite looking forward to the day out. Not because I'll be spending it in the vicinity of Danny Lucas, I'm shocked to realise, but because I will be spending it with my new best friend, Charlie.

Charlie and I have seen quite a lot of each other in the past week. In between time spent helping his parents get their new shop up and running, he's been coming over to my house and helping me to revise for my exams. He's also taken Wilson for a walk a few times to give me a little more time, which is kind of him, but he says he enjoys it.

Even though Charlie says I'm the funny one, he makes me laugh with his dry comments and unusual take on the world, and I enjoy spending time with him.

The coach picks us up from the promenade, not far from Charlie's shop, and I'm surprised to see quite a crowd waiting at the stop. These youth club trips must be better than I thought.

I wave at Charlie as I spot him chatting to Duncan Braithwaite.

'Hey you,' Charlie says in his now customary greeting to me.

'Hey yourself,' I reply, grinning at him. 'What's up?'

'Not much, just talking to Duncan about the trip.' He gesticulates over his shoulder to where Duncan had been standing a moment ago, but finds he's already moved on to someone else.

'Ah, he's probably found someone with more exciting things to chat about,' Charlie says, making light of it, but I can tell he's hurt by Duncan's snub.

I feel for him. I know exactly how this feels, it happens to me all the time when I'm with the girls at school. It's like we're acceptable company until someone better comes along.

Guiltily I realise that I probably behaved the same way last week with Charlie at the party, when Danny paid me some attention.

'I think you talk about very interesting things,' I assure him. 'You always entertain me when we're together.'

'Even when I talk about the breeding habits of starfish?' Charlie winks.

On one of our walks with Wilson, Charlie had spent a good fifteen minutes talking about molluscs, starfish and crust-aceans, until I had pretended to fall asleep while we were walking along, and had rolled over on to the soft sand with my eyes closed, snoring loudly.

'Mmm ... maybe not the breeding habits,' I reply, wrinkling my nose. 'But the regeneration part was quite interesting. Imagine if humans could simply regrow their limbs when they lost them. It would be a medical miracle.'

It's as I glance over Charlie's shoulder that I spot Danny waiting with the other cool kids. How could I have missed him?

He's sitting on one of the wooden benches that line the promenade, looking cool, relaxed and totally gorgeous . . .

Danny notices me staring at him and gives a casual wave in my direction.

'Do you need me to hold you up?' Charlie asks. 'You're not going to faint, are you, because Danny Lucas waved at you?'

'Haha, very funny!' I chide, my expression not matching my terse voice as I try to give an equally casual wave in Danny's direction.

Danny smiles at me, and winks, and I do actually feel myself waver.

'Here's the bus!' someone suddenly shouts, and my moment with Danny is broken as I turn to see a burgundy coach pulling up next to us.

'Come on!' Charlie calls, as the doors open and people begin to pile on board. 'We want a decent seat!'

I follow Charlie up the stairs and take a seat next to him in the middle of the bus, while the cool kids all file immediately to the back.

'Glad to see you could make it today, Gracie,' Danny says casually as he passes by our seat.

'I wouldn't have missed it for the world, Danny!' I squeak in a voice so shrill I suspect only dogs can hear me.

Danny opens his mouth to speak, but is interrupted by another female calling, 'Over here, Danny!' in a voice a number of octaves lower than mine. 'I've saved you a seat.'

Danny shrugs, smiles apologetically at me, then carries on down the bus.

I desperately want to sit up in my seat and turn around so I can see who has stolen my moment, and more importantly who Danny is now sitting next to, but I daren't – it would be too obvious. So I sit and stare at the headrest in front of me, where the last inhabitant of my seat has kindly left their chewing gum stuck to the plush fabric.

'I wouldn't have missed it for the world!' Charlie mimics in a shrill girly voice. I turn to see him wildly fluttering his eyelashes.

'I do not sound like that!' I tell him sternly. 'Did I go a bit overboard?' I whisper now.

'I'm throwing you an invisible life jacket as we speak.'

I screw up my face. 'I can't help it. Whenever I speak to him my mind goes to mush, and I say stupid things.'

'They're not exactly stupid,' Charlie says sympathetically. 'They're just not very cool, that's all.'

I roll my eyes, and rest my head against the seat.

'Then I'm going to have to learn how to be cooler.'

'Easier said than done,' Charlie says. 'Why not just be you?'

'Because he's not going to notice me being me, is he?'

'I did.'

'But you're you, you're my mate, it doesn't count.'

'Cheers for that!' Charlie says. 'It's good to know I matter.'

'I didn't mean it like that, you know I didn't.'

Charlie sits up so he can see over the seat in front of him down to the front of the bus. 'Looks like that's everyone on board,' he says, sitting back again. 'We'll be off in a moment, then you can spend the next hour or so thinking about how you can become cooler, while I,' he says, taking a paperback book from his rucksack, 'will try and finish my new Stephen King novel.'

'Is that it?' I ask him indignantly, looking at the book.

'Yes, it is,' Charlie says, holding up the cover.

'Wha ... oh, I see: the book is called *It*. I meant—'

'I know what you meant, Gracie, but I think you're fine as you are. If you want to change, then it's up to you. But I'm not going to help you do it.'

And with that, he lifts up the book and begins to read.

'Fine,' I mutter under my breath. 'Then I'll just have to find a way of being cool on my own.'

During the coach journey, the youth leaders hand out our itineraries for the day. Charlie and I stop sulking – well, I do, Charlie has simply been engrossed in his book for most of the journey – and we read it through together:

Sandybridge Youth Club
Visit to Norwich: Saturday 28 June 1986

10 a.m. Arrival and visit to Norwich Cathedral:
You are free to wander as you please, but we urge you to spend time appreciating the beauty of this 900-year-old place of worship.

11 a.m.–1 p.m. Free time & lunch break:
Feel free to explore the rest of what this lovely city has to offer – not just the shops!

1 p.m.–3 p.m. Visit to Norwich Castle:
We are very lucky to have a guided tour of the castle. Please don't be late back from lunch.

3.30 p.m. Please return to the bus promptly:
We will depart for home at 4 p.m. sharp.
Thank you, and enjoy your day in Norwich.

'Organised, aren't they?' I comment to Charlie as we read through the itinerary.

'Wouldn't you be if you had this lot to keep under control? I'm surprised some of them are allowed off their leads.'

'Sorry about earlier,' I apologise. 'I wanted Danny to notice me, that's all.'

Charlie turns towards me. 'Gracie, you must know by now that he already has.'

'Honestly?' I ask, my eyes open wide. 'What makes you think that?'

'Male intuition,' Charlie says seriously.

'Really?'

'Nah, I can just see it. It doesn't take any special powers to work that out.'

'But what should I do?'

'Nothing.'

'Nothing? But what if he doesn't realise I like him too?'

Charlie laughs. 'He'd have to be an idiot not to know that. Although . . .'

'Stop it, Charlie!' I playfully punch his arm. 'Danny is OK, and you know it.'

'Yeah, I guess. For a cool kid, he's not so bad.'

I nod approvingly and sit back in my seat to think about what Charlie has said. Had Danny Lucas really noticed me, or was Charlie just teasing?

But I don't have long to think, because the bus is soon pulling up in a car park in the centre of Norwich.

We all pile off the bus, and the youth club leader, Barry, gathers us all around him.

'Right, gang!' he calls in a cheery voice, waving his clipboard in the air. 'If you all follow me in an orderly fashion, we'll set off on our first adventure of the day to the cathedral! Wagons roll!'

I raise my eyebrows at Charlie, who grins back. 'Come on, Gracie!' he mimics as he bows, then holds out his arm in a formal fashion for me to take. 'Shall we partake of our first adventure together?'

We all follow Barry through the narrow streets of Norwich as he bounds enthusiastically along, his clipboard held aloft so we don't lose him.

I try and keep an eye on Danny as we walk, but we've somehow ended up in the middle of the long line of kids snaking their way along behind the clipboard, and Danny is somewhere at the back, just before Glenda – Barry's sidekick (actually there was a rumour going along the snake that Glenda might be his girlfriend). So I can't look at Danny without turning around – and I don't want to be *that* obvious, whatever Charlie said.

'Righty-ho, gang!' Barry calls as we arrive outside the cathedral. 'Now, as the itinerary states, we will be viewing the cathedral independently at our leisure, but I urge you to take your time to look and appreciate your surroundings while you're inside. It really is an exquisitely beautiful place to behold.'

'Gee, has this guy swallowed a dictionary?' I ask Charlie, as we follow Barry into the calm of the silent cathedral.

Charlie grins. 'He likes getting value from his words, that's for sure.'

We wander through the cathedral, trying our hardest to appreciate the grand architecture, and the artistry of the colourful stained-glass windows. But this soon gets dull, and we begin to get bored. I feel it was a little optimistic for the organisers of this trip (even though it *is* a church youth club) to expect a bunch of teenagers to stay amused in a cathedral for long, and we soon start to hear hollers and shouts from some of the others as they try to test the echo capabilities of the large space.

Barry and Glenda hurriedly round us all up and usher us out on to the grass outside.

'I do hope you all enjoyed that brief glimpse of one of our county's truly splendid works of religious architecture?' Barry asks, still grinning broadly despite our swift exit.

'Do you mean the church?' someone pipes up, and there are a few sniggers.

'Yes,' Barry continues, looking flustered, 'the *cathedral*. Perhaps now would be a good time to take our lunch break?' He looks to Glenda, who nods her support. 'Please return back here at one p.m. prompt, and we shall continue with our tour. I'm sure *most* of you' – he glances at a small gang who are blowing huge pink bubbles of Hubba Bubba gum from their mouths and not listening to him at all – 'will find the castle much more interesting this afternoon.'

We all head off in our little gangs. The youth club recommended bringing a packed lunch on the trip to save us worrying about buying our lunches, but nearly all of us have ignored this advice and brought money. Even Charlie, whose mum had insisted on making him a packed lunch, had quickly ditched it, and was now heading off with the rest of us into the centre of town to find something more exciting to eat. We're all thrilled when we see the big yellow M of a McDonald's! We're used to Wimpys – even dull old Sandybridge has a Wimpy restaurant – but a McDonald's!

We may as well have travelled directly to New York, the thrill of finding something so American here in Norwich is so great.

Much to the manager's annoyance, we all queue up individually with our purses and wallets and order the cheapest thing on the menu – a Happy Meal. Then we all pile outside to find somewhere to eat it.

Charlie and I manage to find a vacant wooden bench to sit on, while some of the others head back to the grass outside the cathedral. Danny heads off with a small gang including Lucy Flanagan and Donna Lewis. I try not to watch them too closely as Charlie and I open up our cardboard boxes of food.

'Cool, a little race car!' Charlie says, pulling a tiny blue plastic car from his box.

'Is that it?' I ask with a tinge of disappointment. I'd heard great things about the free gift inside a McDonald's Happy Meal. I didn't call a car the most interesting of toys.

'It is meant for kids, Gracie!' Charlie says, holding the longest, thinnest chip I've ever seen between two of his fingers. He hungrily feeds it into his mouth, like he's munching on a potato-flavoured worm. 'It's not meant for young ladies trying to impress the local hunk!'

'I am not trying to impress him!' I protest, unwrapping my burger. It's a long time since breakfast; Charlie had had sweets on the bus, but I'd been good and refused them, so now I'm absolutely starving as I take a huge bite of the juicy burger. But at the same time as the taste sensation of a greasy cheeseburger hits my tongue, I feel the slightly less pleasant sensation of a large blob of red ketchup oozing from the bottom of the bun and hitting my chest.

'No!' I cry, gazing down in horror at my white T-shirt. I look like I've just been shot, and my blood is beginning to ooze from the bullet wound.

'Quick,' Charlie says, pushing a napkin into my hand.

'It will only make it worse if I rub at it,' I say, trying to stop the offending red blob from travelling any further down my front by leaning back and balancing it on my chest.

'Well you can't spend the rest of the day like that!' Charlie says, trying not to look at my boobs, even though I'm making that extremely difficult by poking them out towards him like some awful Page 3 model. 'Do you want me to try and remove it?'

I look doubtfully at him. The ketchup has landed in a particularly delicate area.

'I won't touch them, if that's what you're worried about.'

My cheeks feel as though they've turned the same shade as the ketchup. 'OK,' I say hesitantly. 'If you think you can get it off without it staining.'

'Gracie, we both know that's not going to happen,' Charlie says, sounding like a surgeon summing up the chances for a successful operation. 'All I can do is try and minimalise the damage.'

'OK, OK, just do it!' I tell him, closing my eyes.

I feel Charlie reach out and gently begin dabbing at my chest. How typical of me that my first experience of a boy coming anywhere near this area should not only be anything but sexual, but with my best friend.

'There – done,' Charlie says, almost as quickly as he's begun.

I open my eyes and look down at my chest, hoping that Charlie has somehow magically managed to remove any traces of the ketchup. But of course he hasn't. The blob has gone, but a nasty tomato stain still remains.

'Oh God, what am I going to do? I can't walk around Norwich like this!'

'Can't you arrange your hair over it or something?' Charlie suggests helpfully. 'It's long enough to cover it.'

I give him a withering look. 'I can't walk around looking like Neil from *The Young Ones*!'

Charlie laughs. 'Yes, you're not exactly the peaceful hippy type, are you?'

'Do you know, I'm really not right now!' I growl.

'Look, there's no point wasting our lunch,' Charlie says practically. He hands me a clean napkin. 'Good job I picked up a few of these, huh? They're coming in pretty handy today!'

I narrow my eyes.

'Tuck this in your top, Gracie,' Charlie says, sounding remarkably like my mother did when I was four. 'That will cover your ... *problem* for now. Eat up your lunch and then we'll go in search of a solution.'

'What solution?' I ask, doing as he says and tucking the white paper napkin over the top of my T-shirt so it covers the stain. 'I can't wear this all afternoon. I look like I'm wearing a bib!'

'Maybe you should get one,' Charlie says with a straight face. 'If you'd worn a baby's bib before you started eating, we wouldn't be in this situation now. Perhaps one of those plastic pelican bibs might be in order ... I bet there's a Mothercare here amongst the shops.'

'Do you *want* to wear the rest of your lunch?' I ask him. 'I bet I could do much more damage to your pale blue shirt with a whole greasy burger than I've done with a bit of ketchup to mine!'

Charlie grins and hurriedly stuffs what's left of his burger into his mouth while he shakes his head. 'See, Gracie, I said you weren't the peaceful hippy type, didn't I?'

Six

After we've eaten lunch, Charlie hurries me through the shopping streets of Norwich in search of an alternate top for me to wear.

Neither of us have a lot of money on us, but we head into Chelsea Girl where, to his credit, Charlie immediately finds me a perfectly good white T-shirt, which would have gone with my stonewashed cropped blue jeans and white leather pumps, but I had other ideas. Before we'd even entered the shop, I'd spotted in the window a short, pale pink bat-winged dress, with a thick white belt around the middle that hung seductively open over one of the mannequin's slender shoulders, and I loved it.

'I *need* that dress,' I tell Charlie as we hang around in the shop amongst the leg warmers and fingerless lace gloves. 'The one in the window.'

'Why?' Charlie asks, holding up the white T-shirt. 'What's

62

wrong with this? It's almost identical to the one you're wearing.'

'The dress in the window is different. It's sophisticated. People will notice me wearing it.'

Charlie eyes me suspiciously. 'When you say *people*, do you mean Danny?'

I feel myself blushing, but I shrug. 'Perhaps.'

Charlie sighs and looks into his wallet. 'Do we have enough money for it? Cos I only have four pounds fifty on me after lunch.'

I open up my purse. 'I have ... Six pounds and ... twenty-five pence. The dress is eleven pounds.'

'Twenty-five pence short. Sorry, Gracie, no can do. Looks like you'll have to take the T-shirt instead.'

I gaze longingly at the pink dresses hanging on the rail. 'It's in the sale too ... so cheap for what it is ... and they have my size, which is very unusual in sales.' I look at Charlie like a puppy asking its owner for a walk when they've already said no.

'I know where Wilson gets it from now,' he says, rolling his eyes. 'OK, OK, I'll see what I can do. Give me your money.'

Without questioning what he's about to do, I hand over my purse.

'What size are you?' Charlie asks.

I hesitate. 'Twelve ... well, maybe a fourteen. It depends.'

'OK ... what size are you today?'

I look at the dresses. They're quite loose fitting, which is why they have the belt to pull them in at the middle. 'A twelve,' I say confidently.

'Sure?'

'Yes. Sure.'

63

'Right.' Charlie heads over to the rail of dresses. He hoists out a size twelve, then he winks at me as he goes over to the till, where a young assistant who's been examining the state of her bright orange nail varnish looks wearily up at him.

I can't hear what Charlie says to her because the boutique has pop music blaring out at full blast all over the shop. But I see the assistant vehemently shake her head. Then Charlie says something else and the assistant shrugs. Charlie points to where I'm standing awkwardly waiting by a rail of T-shirts that have 'Choose Life' emblazoned across them, and the assistant's weary gaze follows his hand.

Then Charlie speaks again. His expression suggests he might be pleading with her. Suddenly the young girl's expression changes, she looks sympathetically at me, then she nods at Charlie, and to my amazement I see my dress being put in a plastic *Chelsea Girl* carrier bag while Charlie empties first my purse, and then his own wallet on to the counter.

Then the assistant counts up all the money, and runs it through the till, puts a receipt in the bag, and then hands the bag to Charlie.

A triumphant Charlie returns to my side, and hurriedly ushers me out of the shop and back out on to the street.

'How on earth did you manage that?' I ask him, looking inside the bag to check he'd really got it.

'Let's just say I have persuasive charms.'

'No, come on, Charlie, tell me: how?'

'I told her you were my girlfriend, it was our anniversary, and I wanted to buy you a dress but I didn't have enough money to get the one you wanted, and she took pity on me.'

I look at Charlie, but he doesn't look embarrassed like I expect him to. He seems quite happy with his explanation.

'That's so sweet of you, Charlie,' I tell him, feeling touched by his story. 'You didn't have to do that for me, you know.'

Charlie shrugs. 'I wanted to. Now go find a loo and get changed or we'll be late to the castle. And I don't think Barry will be in a very forgiving mood if we're late after this morning.'

I nod at him and dash over to Debenhams, where I quickly change in their ladies' loo. Then I tart my hair up a bit, so my unruly brown mane now sits in a high ponytail to the side of my head. I'm quite pleased with what I see as I take one last glance in the mirror above the sinks, before I head out through the store to find Charlie again, stopping on my way at a perfume counter to spray some Poison perfume from a purple glass bottle on to my wrists – to add a final sophisticated touch to my glamour.

Charlie is looking in the window of Our Price at the latest cassettes on sale, so I hurry over to him.

'Hey,' I say, suddenly feeling embarrassed. 'I'm back!'

Charlie turns around. 'So you are,' he says, standing back to take in the full new me. 'And you have legs too!'

I self-consciously cross one of my now bare legs over the other. I'm still wearing the white leather pumps I'd had on with my jeans before, but from my ankles up to my mid-thigh there's now much white leg to behold.

'Yes . . . but what do you think to the dress?'

'You look great,' Charlie says approvingly. 'But what's that smell?' He wrinkles up his nose. 'It's bloody awful.'

'That's Poison,' I tell him.

'It sure is. You could kill a dozen rats with that, no problem.'

'No, it's a perfume – a very sophisticated one. You probably wouldn't get it.'

'I don't want it!' Charlie says, pretending to back away. 'You smelt better before. What did you have on this morning?'

'Oh that was just Impulse,' I tell him with a wave of my hand. 'That was nothing.'

'It may have been, but it was a darn site pleasanter on the nostrils than what you have on now!'

'Charlie,' I say haughtily, 'I'm not going to say anything because you got me this dress to wear, and I'm extremely grateful to you for doing so, but I think our ideas of sophistication differ somewhat.'

Charlie nods slowly. 'Yup, you're probably right. *Although*,' he says pointedly, 'I would expect your ideas on most things would be different than mine, seeing as you're on an exchange trip from Russia and don't speak any English!'

'What?'

'That's what I told the shop assistant to get her to give me the dress cheaper.'

'But I thought you said I was your girlfriend?' I ask, half annoyed, half disappointed this wasn't the truth.

Charlie grins. 'Nope! I said it was your last day here, and it was all the English money you had left.' He begins to reverse away from me as he speaks. 'I told her back in your country you were very poor, and only had the option of second-hand clothes, so the dress would be the perfect way for you to remember the generosity of the English when you were queuing up for bread . . . Now now, Grace!' he shouts as he begins to edge away and I hurtle after him. 'Remember your dress!'

I chase Charlie back to the meeting point for the afternoon, and arrive a few seconds after him, panting heavily.

'Whoa!' Charlie says, holding his arms up across his face as I pretend to threaten him. 'Not my face! It could be my fortune one day! My ginger fortune!'

Under his red hair, Charlie's pale blue eyes sit in an even paler face covered in freckles. I laugh and give him a shove instead.

'You, Charlie Parker, are the biggest pain in the ar— Ah hello, Danny!' I recover as Danny Lucas strolls up beside us.

'Cheers, mate, you saved me!' Charlie says, uncovering his face. 'Who knows what she might have done!'

I smile at Danny while I calmly step on Charlie's toes.

'You look good, Gracie,' Danny says approvingly, looking me up and down. 'New dress?'

'Yes, I got it at lunchtime, do you like it?'

'Yeah ... especially this bit,' Danny says, lightly brushing my uncovered shoulder with his fingers.

I nearly faint on the spot.

Then he wrinkles up his nose. 'What *is* that stink?' he asks, looking around.

I see Charlie open his mouth, but I quickly jump in before he can speak. 'I know, it's odd, isn't it? Perhaps I can get rid of it?' I reach into my bag and pull out my can of Impulse. Then I spray it in the air as if I'm trying to get rid of the smell, but quickly walk through the mist at the same time so it covers me, and the Poison.

'That's much prettier,' Danny says, his nose in the air as he takes in the smell. 'Thanks, Gracie.'

I smile, but I don't look at Charlie who I just know will be grinning at me.

'Do you two want to join our group this afternoon to go and look around the castle?' Danny asks, glancing over to where Barry has reappeared with his clipboard. 'I don't know what this tour guide will be like, but I'm sure we can make it more interesting if he's rubbish – eh, Gracie?'

I nod so vigorously I feel my ponytail slide around my head.

'Charlie?' he asks.

'Whatever Gracie wants ...' Charlie says indifferently, sticking his hands in his pockets, 'is absolutely fine with me.'

Seven

Once Barry and Glenda have made sure we've all returned safely back from lunch, we head off towards Norwich Castle.

Barry joyfully recounts to us as we walk some of the history of the Norman castle, and I happily pretend to listen to him. Not because I'm the least interested in what he's telling us, but because I'm walking along next to Danny Lucas and he's talking to me!

We talk about school, and exams, and what we're planning on doing after our O-levels are finished, and I'm surprised to find Danny is thinking of taking an academic route like me.

'History, that's what interests me,' Danny says as we walk. He gestures to the old higgledy-piggledy buildings we're walking past, with their low thatched roofs that once were people's houses, but now contain offices and shops. 'Like, who lived in these buildings before they were banks and clothes shops?'

I shrug. I don't care who'd lived in them, to be honest, but I'm not telling Danny that.

'And *how* did they live?' he continues. 'I'm actually looking forward to this afternoon. I believe it's a great way to see how the Normans ran a fortress like the one we're going to see.'

'Uh huh.' I nod keenly. I hadn't expected this sort of thing from Danny. Even though I thought he was stunning, I kind of expected his looks were his main selling point. I hadn't expected him to try and engage me in conversation about Norman castles and their inhabitants.

'Do you like history, Gracie?' he asks as we arrive in front of Norwich Castle. 'You're not in my history class, are you? You must be in Miss Granger's.'

'Yes . . . Miss Granger's,' I confirm for him, without actually answering his question.

'She's supposed to be great at teaching it. I wish I'd had her, but I didn't quite make it into the top set.'

A look of disappointment crosses his face, and suddenly I see Danny in a completely new way. There's more to him than just being the local hunk; behind a pair of blue eyes that shine like sapphires, and hair as sleek and shiny as a horse chestnut, Danny Lucas has a brain – a sharp, enquiring mind that is interested in more than girls and football.

And I like him all the more for it.

'Never mind,' I tell him. 'I'm sure you're doing great in Mr Donaldson's class.' I look up at the imposing hill-top castle in front of us. 'I don't know much about the Normans – perhaps you can share some of your knowledge with me this afternoon?'

'I'd like that, Gracie,' he says, bestowing one of his

dazzling smiles I'd only ever seen him share with others, upon me. 'I'd like that very much.'

After we've climbed to the top of the hill the castle sits upon, we meet our guide in front of the castle entrance.

'Hey, guys, I'm Liam,' a tall, lanky, faired-haired chap tells us. 'And I'm going to be your tour guide this afternoon.'

'Fabbo!' one of the kids shouts, mimicking his enthusiastic tone.

But Liam doesn't look at all put out, 'Glad you're looking forward to it!' He grins. 'I like to have a keen bunch. Now, if you'll all just follow me.'

Liam leads us inside through a tall archway and we begin to tour the various parts of the castle.

I'm not sure if it's Liam's keenness, or my need to impress Danny, but I actually feel like I'm enjoying myself as we look at exhibitions showing how people would have lived, worked and defended Norwich during the time the castle was a working fortress.

'Watch it, Gracie,' Charlie whispers, when he finds himself standing next to me along the battlements outside the castle, as we take in the view across Norwich, while Liam tells us facts about battles, and stories about the lifestyle the soldiers that stood out here in all weathers would have had. 'You look like you might actually be enjoying all this history.'

'It's odd, but I think I actually am!'

Charlie glances at Danny, who's hanging on every word that falls from Liam's mouth. 'Yeah, right, enjoying it for Danny's benefit, more like! I have to hand it to you, though; you're doing a damn good job of making it look like you are! You should definitely go in for that drama A-level you spoke about.'

'No, I *really* am!' I insist. 'It's weird, I've never felt like this about history before, but I'm actually interested in hearing about all the stuff that went on here. Liam makes it sound so current.'

Charlie looks at me and pulls a face.

'Have you had too much sun?' he asks, putting his hand to my forehead. 'It is a pretty warm day.'

'Stop it, Charlie. I can change my mind, can't I? Anyway, this isn't like the stuff my parents are interested in. To me that's just other people's junk. This is real living, breathing history. We're standing in the actual place everything Liam is telling us went on. Isn't that amazing?'

'Yeah, fantastic,' Charlie says doubtfully. He looks at Danny, who, now that Liam has finished speaking, turns towards us and smiles.

I wave, and he comes over.

'Isn't Liam amazing?' he gushes. 'I'd love his job when I'm older.'

'Yes, he certainly brings the castle alive,' I agree.

'Barry says we've finished early, and we have forty-five minutes to entertain ourselves until the bus goes.' Danny looks thoughtfully at me. 'Do you fancy taking a walk, Gracie?' he asks.

'Er . . .' I glance at Charlie. I feel awful about even thinking of ditching him for Danny again.

'You go,' Charlie says, waving his hand at us. 'I'm going to get a drink or something.' He goes to pull his wallet from his pocket, then realises at the same time I do there's nothing left in it.

'Sorry, Charlie,' I apologise. 'Charlie helped me buy this dress at lunchtime, so neither of us have any money left,' I explain for Danny's benefit.

Danny doesn't hesitate. He reaches into the front pocket of his jeans. 'Here,' he says, handing Charlie a pound coin. 'I'll get Gracie something.'

Charlie looks at the money in his hand. Then he looks at me.

Please take it! I try to urge him with my eyes.

'Cheers, mate,' Charlie says, to my relief. 'I'll pay you back.'

Danny shrugs. 'No worries.'

'Shall we go for a wander then, Gracie?' Danny asks, and I jump a little as I feel his hand rest in the small of my back.

I swallow hard.

'Sure.' I try to say it casually, but it comes out as a squeak. 'Sure,' I repeat in a lower voice. 'See you in a bit, Charlie.'

Charlie just nods, and I'm sure he watches us as we walk down the hill together, towards the centre of Norwich. But I don't look back; I'm much too preoccupied with remaining cool and calm in the presence of Danny.

We walk down the hill and into a little park area, where we find an ice-cream van, and Danny buys us both a Mr Whippy ice cream with a chocolate flake on top. Then we walk over to a wooden bench and sit down.

'Enjoying it?' Danny asks, nodding towards my ice cream.

'Mmm, yes,' I manage, my tongue currently engaged in licking the soft smooth whip.

'Good,' Danny says. 'It's quite nice to get away from the others for a while, isn't it?'

I nod. I definitely feel that way, but I didn't expect he would.

'Not Charlie though,' I hurriedly say, not wanting to slight my friend in any way.

'No?' Danny asks, tilting his head to the side.

'No,' I maintain. 'He's my friend.'

'Ah ... I did wonder what the deal was with you two. So are you *just* friends, or more than that?'

I nearly splutter Mr Whippy all over Danny as the ice cream goes down the wrong way. 'No,' I try to say in between coughing.

Danny reaches over and pats me on the back, but instead of sliding away along the bench, he rests his hand on my shoulder.

I can't help but glance at it. I never expected to see Danny Lucas's hand anywhere near me, let alone resting there.

'Charlie and I are just good friends,' I manage to say, now I've finished choking.

'Good,' Danny murmurs, pulling himself even closer towards me. 'I'm very pleased to hear that, Gracie.'

I swallow hard. He isn't going to do what I think he is, is he?

But he is. Before I can think about it any further, Danny's face comes even closer, and in an instant his lips are on mine.

This is something I'd dreamt about happening so often; I thought I knew what it would feel like. But of course the reality of something is never quite how you imagine it's going to be, and this feels nothing like my dreams.

Danny's mouth is soft and surprisingly warm, considering he'd been eating ice cream, which is exactly how I imagined in my dreams it would be. I lean in towards him, actually managing to enjoy not only my first kiss with Danny, but my first proper kiss with any boy. I would never count Nigel Jefferson as my first kiss now, not after this. Forever more when I retell this story to my daughters and granddaughters, my first kiss will be this perfect moment with Danny Lucas. I'll remember the taste of him, the exquisite sensation of feeling his soft lips on mine, the warm glow spreading from my mouth right down to my toes. I'll remember ... a not quite so pleasant feeling of something wet and extremely cold falling into my lap ...

I pull away from Danny and look down at my dress.

'Oh no, not again!' I cry, as I see a large white blob of ice cream lying in my lap, with a half-eaten chocolate flake on top ...

Dear Grace,

Today you'll discover a place that's going to be very important to you in the future.

Look after it, Grace, because the events that take place there will shape your whole life.

Love, Me x

Eight

Strangely, Danny is not put off by the walking disaster that I am, and we continue to 'go out with each other' long after the bus has returned us safely to Sandybridge.

'Going out together' seemed to mean hanging around each other's houses watching TV, or very excitingly for me, a video on Danny's parents' new VCR that they'd recently bought, rather than actually going out on dates.

'You are so lucky being able to record things and watch them whenever you want,' I'd told Danny the first time we'd watched a recorded programme. It was only *The A-Team*, but that didn't matter. I'd been completely enthralled by the feeling of using such a magical piece of modern-day machinery. It was all I could do to get my parents to update to a colour TV a few years ago, and that was only because Mum had wanted to watch *Gardeners' World*, which without colour was left a little lacking.

But aside from lounging around in each other's sitting

rooms (neither of us was allowed to take the other up to our bedroom), hanging around the promenade with some of Danny's friends, and taking the occasional walk together – we couldn't take Wilson, because for some inexplicable reason he'd taken against Danny the moment he met him, and had to be shut outside in the garden anytime he came round to our house – we didn't actually do all that much. There was kissing, of course; plenty of that went on. One time Danny got a bit too enthusiastic and tried to fiddle with my bra strap when we were sitting on my lounge sofa and my parents were out. But I'd panicked and said I thought I heard Wilson barking, and I should probably go and check on him. When I returned to the sofa, it was as if nothing had happened, and we just went back to holding hands while listening to the rest of my Spandau Ballet album.

'It's my birthday next week,' Danny announces casually as we sit in his lounge on the sofa, this time watching a recorded episode of *Dempsey and Makepeace*.

'Is it?' I ask, surprised. 'You didn't say.'

'Just did, didn't I?' Danny grins, and his smile as always sends a very pleasant shiver right through me.

'Are you doing anything?' I ask, my mind already trying to work out what I might buy him. Maybe that Van Halen album we were looking at the other day in Woolworths?

'The lads are wanting to throw me a party, since it's the end of term as well. But we don't know where to hold it.'

'Can't you hold it at someone's house?' I ask, trying to be helpful. Ooh, what about a videocassette of the new *Rocky* movie? I think. I'm sure that's out now.

Danny gives me a withering look.

'What?'

'We could, if someone had parents who didn't mind their house getting trashed.'

'Oh.' I feel my cheeks redden. 'Will it be that bad?'

The last birthday party I'd gone to, we all sang 'Happy Birthday' while the birthday girl blew out the candles on her cake, then we all went home with pieces of the cake wrapped in a serviette, and a balloon and a pencil in a party bag.

'Most probably.'

'So you're looking for somewhere like a barn, or a big hall to hold it in?'

'Yeah, if we knew any farmers, or had any money to hire a place.'

'Hmm ... ' I try to think of somewhere, so I can impress Danny with my knowledge and party-planning skills. But I can't. I have little experience of teenage parties – big or small. Let alone places to hold them in. 'I'll keep thinking,' I promise him. 'Leave it with me.'

'Danny wants to hold a party for his birthday,' I tell Charlie the next day as we walk Wilson along the beach together. Charlie and I are still close, even though I'm seeing Danny, and I always make sure to find time for him. Luckily, with Danny and Wilson's issues, dog-walking is still something Charlie and I always do together.

'Where?' Charlie asks, watching Wilson chase along the beach after a tennis ball that Charlie now brought on all Wilson's walks. 'To keep him amused,' he'd said the first time it had been produced from his pocket.

'To keep him distracted from digging to Australia, you mean!'

'Well, there is that too.'

But the ball had been a great success, even after Wilson had lost the first one in the sea. Charlie had produced another, and now Wilson delighted in 'fetch' – well, his version of it. He would fetch the ball until something else on the beach took his fancy. Then it would be up to us to 'fetch' the ball, while Wilson chewed happily on a plastic bottle, or whatever else he could find washed up on the sand.

'He doesn't know yet where he's going to hold it. That's the problem. Apparently there might be damage if they hold it at someone's house.'

'*Apparently?* I think it's more than likely.' Charlie grins at me. 'For someone so keen to get out there and explore the world, you have quite a narrow view of it sometimes.'

'What do you mean?'

'You're an innocent, Gracie, an innocent in a big bad world.'

'I am not!'

Charlie raises his eyebrows at me in that annoying way he has when he thinks he's right.

'I'm no more innocent than you, Charlie Parker!'

'It depends in what sense we're talking.' Charlie reaches down and picks up Wilson's ball again. Wilson sets off across the sand before he's even had a chance to throw it. 'If we're talking relationships,' Charlie says, managing to throw the ball just in front of where Wilson eagerly waits, 'then I guess you are one step ahead of me now you're dating Danny "hotter than hot" Lucas. It's further than I've got with any girl.'

I nod in agreement.

'But if we're talking worldly wise . . . then I'm afraid I win hands down.'

'Why do you?' I snap. As much as I like Charlie, he can be quite infuriating sometimes.

'Because I've travelled . . . well, I've lived in lots of different places. My dad was a chef in the army so we went wherever he was stationed. It's only now he's retired we're settling down in one place. Where have you been?'

I'm annoyed, but I know he's right. The furthest I've visited is when my parents went to Cambridge for an auction. 'And that is exactly why I want to travel and get away from here when I can,' I tell him, not admitting he's right.

'And why *I* would be quite happy doing the opposite, and settling down here eventually. Change isn't always for the best. Sometimes it's good to put down roots somewhere and make it your home.'

'Perhaps, but I'm not ready to do that just yet! And neither should you be, you old codger!' I laugh as I race off up the beach in front of him.

We'd discovered one day that, even though we're in the same year at school, Charlie's almost a year older than me because of when our birthdays fall – mine in August and Charlie's in September.

'Less of that – you whippersnapper!' Charlie mimics, sounding like an elderly man as he chases after me.

I sprint off up the beach with Wilson bounding along next to me, and Charlie close behind. I've always been fairly fast, there aren't many of the girls who could outrun me at school, but I'm not expecting to outrun Charlie, who's small, thin and built like a whippet.

I keep running until I get to the end of the beach, then Wilson and I take the little footpath that leads up past the lighthouse away from the sand, and continues through a small thicket of pine trees that runs alongside the beach. When we emerge from the other side of the trees we find ourselves a few feet away from a high wall built with crumbling honey-and-terracotta-coloured bricks.

I stop to catch my breath, and to allow Charlie to catch up with me.

'You're fast!' he says, panting as he appears through the trees.

'Thanks,' I say. 'At least I can do something better than you!'

'Don't be like that,' Charlie says, sounding apologetic. 'I didn't mean anything by what I said. I'm quite jealous of you, actually. It must be nice to stay in one place for more than a year.'

I shrug. Charlie and I would never agree on this.

'It's like having curly hair,' I tell him.

'What?'

'Curly hair. If you've got it, you hate it and want it straight. And if you've got straight hair, you're always wanting to curl it.'

Charlie nods, and then he looks at me with an odd expression.

'You mean you always want what you can't have?' he asks quietly, almost as if he's saying it to himself.

'Yes, exactly that.'

'Yeah, I know how that feels.'

I look at Charlie. What does he mean?

'Do you know where we are?' I ask, deciding to overlook his strange behaviour. Charlie's often quite deep, and I don't always get what he means.

Charlie jumps from his contemplative state, and looks around him.

'Nope. Don't think I've ever been here.'

'We're on the border of the Sandybridge Hall estate. Behind that wall is the house and grounds. You can only see the house from the end of the beach because it's up on a hill.'

Charlie looks up at the mottled rusty red and golden yellow bricks.

'I've heard about the hall, but I've never seen it properly. Does someone live there?'

'Not any more,' I say, moving closer to the wall. I put my foot in a crevice in the bricks and hoist myself up so I can see the house properly. 'Come and see for yourself.'

Charlie does as I've done and finds a worn area of brick that he can get a foothold in. Then he lifts himself up so we're level.

'Whoa, big place,' he says, seeing the house for the first time. 'What is it, an Elizabethan mansion? Check out that moat, it's like a castle.'

'Close. It's Tudor,' I tell him. 'We came here to do a house clearance a while ago – only the gamekeeper's lodge at the bottom of the drive, not the main house. All the antiques from the house were put into storage when the owner had to move out. Apparently he's still trying to sell the place; it's too expensive to run.'

'Just look at the grounds,' Charlie says, gazing in awe at the acres and acres of lawns, trees and plants. 'There must be a whole colony of Sandybridge nature living here. Is that a lake I can see in the distance?'

'I think so. I've only ever been here the once, and like I said, that was only to the lodge. The owner of the main house was pretty private; it wasn't open to the public or anything. I think his family had lived there for years though; he's the last one, according to Mum. Seems a shame he has to sell.'

'So there's no one here now?' Charlie asks, jumping down from the wall.

'Nope,' I reply, doing the same. 'It's empty, as far as I know.'

'Then let's go explore!' Charlie says, his eyes lighting up.

'Why would we want to do that? It's only an old house.'

Charlie sighs. 'Ah, Gracie, now where's that sense of adventure that's going to take you around the world?'

'Not behind this wall, that's for sure.'

Charlie grins now. 'Maybe not, but what if we'd found somewhere for lover boy to hold his birthday party?'

I look blankly at Charlie.

'The house?' Charlie prompts, nodding back at the wall. 'You said it was empty.'

'Could we really hold it there, do you think?' I ask, my mind already turning over the possibilities for holding a party at Sandybridge Hall. 'Wouldn't we get in trouble?'

'Why don't we go and find out?' Charlie asks, pulling himself up on to the wall again. 'That's if you dare . . .'

'But what about Wilson?' I ask, watching Wilson sniff a patch of earth next to the wall. He then paws the earth, his usual ritual before he begins digging. 'He can't climb over a wall, and I can't leave him behind.'

Charlie looks at Wilson, then he smiles. 'For once, Gracie, I think you're going to be very happy that Wilson loves to dig holes!'

Nine

While Wilson continues to dig next to the wall, earth flying everywhere. Charlie and I manage to scramble up using footholds in the crumbling bricks, then when we are both balancing precariously on the top, we decide the only way to get down the other side is to jump.

Charlie goes first, landing sure-footedly on the grass below. Then it's my turn. I try to do the same, but I land on an uneven patch of grass and stumble into Charlie, who deftly catches me, and prevents me falling any further.

'Thanks,' I say to a red-faced Charlie, as he lifts one hand from my upper arm and the other from a rather delicate area of my chest.

'Anytime,' he replies. 'Oh, I don't mean that, I mean ... '

'Yes, it's fine; I know what you mean,' I reply hurriedly, to save further embarrassment. I brush some brick dust from my jeans. 'Now let's see if we can get Wilson through here too.'

I never thought I'd find myself encouraging Wilson to dig, but that's what Charlie and I do, and much quicker than I expect, we see a very grubby-looking Wilson appear on the other side of the wall. Looking extremely pleased with himself, he gives a huge shake, scattering clumps of earth everywhere, then looks up at me, wondering if I'm going to change my mind about this new hole and scold him.

'No,' I say, ruffling his head, 'you did good, *this* time!'

To begin with the three of us walk tentatively across the vast lawns. Well, two of us do; Wilson bounds along, stopping frequently to sniff or occasionally cock his leg. The grass below us, which in its day would have no doubt been kept neat and tidy by a gardener riding up and down on a large lawnmower, is starting to look quite dishevelled and overgrown already.

'I guess these lawns would have had sheep grazing on them in Tudor times,' Charlie says, obviously thinking similar, if probably more factually correct, thoughts to me. 'Either that or a lot of servants brandishing scythes. I bet they were pleased when the lawnmower was invented!'

'It's funny, isn't it, how you just take something like a lawnmower for granted,' I reply, hiding my embarrassment.

'I guess that's why a lot of people find history interesting: finding out how people did things differently to us, how they lived. How they coped before the gadgets we take for granted were invented.'

'I guess . . . ' I haven't ever thought about history like that. I've become a little more interested in it since I've been with Danny; his enthusiasm for the subject is contagious. But at school all they teach us is boring battle dates, and when monarchs had died. If they taught stuff about normal, everyday people, it might be a bit more interesting.

At Charlie's insistence we head towards the lake first, and he pauses to examine the water and any wildlife he can spot floating around in it. He informs me there are some newts, koi carp, and little water boatmen swimming around. There's almost a large shaggy dog to add to the list when Wilson tries to jump in too, but we manage to distract him by throwing a stick for him to chase. Then we head back through the grounds with Charlie spotting wildlife (a rabbit, and a tiny muntjac deer) and many varieties of birds, as we go.

'Isn't this place great!' Charlie says, turning full circle as we pause before the little stone bridge that leads across the moat to the front entrance of the house. 'Wouldn't you love to live somewhere like this, with all this nature on your doorstep, and the wonder of the beach only a few steps away?'

'No,' I say categorically, as I walk purposefully across the bridge and rattle one of the iron handles hanging from the double doors. 'When I have my own house it will be brand new, not old and crumbling like this.'

'I thought you were getting into all this history stuff since you've been with Danny?' Charlie says, following me across the bridge.

'Yes, I am. I don't know why I wasn't before really. I guess Danny makes it seem much more exciting.' But strangely nowhere near as thought-provoking as my conversation with Charlie about sheep and lawnmowers had been. While Charlie had been trying to educate me about all the flora and fauna at Sandybridge Hall, my mind had been full of other thoughts; thoughts about the past and the people who had lived there. Especially the occupants of this house I was now so desperate to get into.

'He makes it exciting, does he?' Charlie asks playfully. 'What does he do – dress up in costumes and re-enact battle scenes for you?' He pretends to brandish a sword as he dances across the bridge in pretend combat with an imaginary opponent. Wilson dopily follows him, sniffing at his legs.

'*No*, we just talk about stuff, and sometimes we watch documentaries.' It does sound a bit dull now I'm saying it out loud. But both Danny and Charlie seem to have awakened something inside me, something I never thought I'd find: an interest in the past.

I leave the door and walk past Charlie, wondering if I can see into one of the ground-floor windows. But because the house is surrounded on all sides by water, all I can see from this distance are empty rooms covered in different shades of heavy flocked wallpaper.

'It sounds absolutely thrilling!' Charlie mocks, as he follows me across the grass with Wilson in tow. 'Can I come round and join you sometime? I could do with some help getting off to sleep.'

'You're just jealous,' I say, giving him a taste of his own medicine.

'That's right, I am,' Charlie says before I can continue. But there's no mockery in his voice this time as he gazes down into the murky moat water. 'Very jealous . . . Now, about this door.'

As if nothing has happened, Charlie immediately heads back across the bridge towards the large wooden door, leaving me slightly bemused.

Charlie isn't jealous of Danny and me, is he? No, surely

not. He's only teasing me again. But he hadn't sounded like he was teasing ... Maybe he'd said he was jealous because I don't see him quite as often since I've been dating Danny. Yes, that must be what he meant.

Happy with my explanation, I follow Charlie. I find him and Wilson examining the door in great detail. While Wilson sniffs, Charlie feels all around the large and very intricate carved wooden door frame. When he finds nothing, he turns his attention to a couple of old stone plant pots that, by the look of the wilted plants inside, had once held geraniums. He lifts them up individually, and then replaces them with a shake of his head before turning to find me watching him.

'Look under that gargoyle thing,' he instructs, pointing to one of two grim-looking gargoyles guarding the entrance of the house.

'For what?'

'For a key, you numpty. What do you think I'm looking for?'

'Who would be stupid enough to leave a key to a big house like this underneath a— Oh,' I say as I tilt one of the grumpy-looking stone figures up. 'There is a key!'

'Told ya!' Charlie says triumphantly. 'Now let's try it in one of the doors.'

I take the large iron key over to Charlie and we try it in one of the locks. To my complete amazement it fits, and as we turn the key we hear the satisfying click of the mechanism unlocking.

'After you,' he says, holding out his arm.

I look at him suspiciously. 'Do you think I'm scared or something?'

'Not at all,' Charlie insists. 'But I might be! It's a big old house – it could have the odd ghost or two floating around.'

Scornfully I shake my head at him. 'Come on, scaredy-cat. I'll lead the way.' But it turns out it's Wilson that leads the way, as he bounds through the door in front of both of us.

As Charlie and I follow him into the gloomy, musty-smelling house, I jump as Charlie closes the door behind us.

'Not scared, eh?' he whispers, grinning at me.

The hallway we now find ourselves in is extremely wide, with an intricate dark mahogany panelled floor. There's a magnificent crystal chandelier above us, which would have sparkled and shone when it was required to provide light for grand balls and social occasions, but now it hangs rather gloomily from a dirty cream ceiling with elaborate plaster mouldings around the edge.

At either side of the hall two ornate wooden staircases glide gracefully up to the floor above, where we can see an open landing leading off to a number of upstairs rooms.

'Impressive,' Charlie says, as I gaze in awe at the staircase.

'Isn't it just? Imagine all the ladies who would have floated gracefully down those stairs wearing their beautiful long dresses, looking for their perfect suitor at the bottom.'

'Does my Gracie have a bit of a romantic streak in her?' Charlie asks, grinning.

'It would seem so,' I reply dreamily, still staring up at the staircase.

'So what's in the rest of the house?' he asks, walking over to one of the many wooden doors that lead off the splendid hallway.

We spend the next twenty minutes or so wandering around the house exploring. It would seem that the previous owners hadn't changed too much of the original features. But in amongst the Tudor architecture, I spot touches of Georgian, and quite a lot of Victorian I realise as we look around. I'd obviously learnt more than I thought from my parents.

As we wander through some of the upstairs bedrooms, even though they're devoid of all their furniture, I can still get a sense of what it might have been like to live here as one of the ladies of the manor. I'm particularly taken by one of the bedrooms which has been decorated in a gorgeous shade of Wedgwood blue, and it's as I spin around to try and take in the full effect of the flocked blue-and-gold pattern that I spy it sitting in an empty alcove.

'Hey, Charlie!' I call, peering inside the box. 'Come and look at this!'

Charlie appears at once in the doorway.

'What is it?' he asks, coming over to look.

'Paintings,' I tell him, gently tipping each frame forward so I can see the next. 'Good ones too, by the look of it.'

We look together at the abandoned paintings; there's one of some fruit and a jug of wine, a couple of landscapes, and a few portraits. One in particular jumps out at me, so I lift it from the box. It's a small gilt-framed portrait of a sandy-haired young woman sitting at a desk; in one hand she holds a quill pen, and in the other a letter.

'Why have you pulled that one out?' Charlie asks, looking at the painting.

'I don't know,' I reply, still looking at the picture. There's something about it I can't put my finger on, something famil-iar. Is it the fact the woman is holding a letter – something I'd recently become very interested in? No, it couldn't be that; my typed letters are nothing like the handwritten one in the painting. So what is it? I shake my head. 'Maybe I just liked it,' I reply to Charlie's question.

'Weird, these pictures being up here though. I thought you said the place was cleared out. Everywhere else we've been has been completely empty.'

'I expect the box was left behind accidentally. There's often so much stuff, it's easy to think you have everything.'

'Maybe.' Charlie shrugs. 'What should we do with it?'

'Well we can't exactly hand it in – people will know we've been in here. Perhaps we should just leave it where we found it,' I say, putting the painting of the woman back in the box.

'You're probably right,' Charlie says, and we push the box back into the alcove together. 'So, what do you think?' Charlie asks after we've left the bedroom and are heading down the stairs together.

'About?'

'Holding your party here, of course! That's what we originally broke in for.'

'We didn't break in,' I correct. 'There was a key, remember?'

'OK, *let* ourselves in then, if it makes you feel better.'

'It does, yes. I'm not sure if this is the right place, Charlie. It's a bit grand.'

'Too grand for the likes of Danny, eh?'

'No, I didn't mean that.' We've reached the bottom of the stairs now. 'I meant how can we hold it here? Who would we need to ask to get permission?'

Charlie tuts and shakes his head. 'This is what I meant earlier on the beach. You need to live a little, Gracie.'

'I don't know what you ... *Oh,*' I say as Charlie's meaning dawns on me. 'You mean we just use it anyway, without asking anyone?'

Charlie nods.

'I'm not too sure about that . . . '

'Come on, Gracie, it's not like you're going to host an acid house party. It's only a birthday party for your boyfriend. But of course, if you don't want to do it, if you're *scared* . . . '

'Yes, of course I want to, and of course I'm not!' I answer at once. The more I think about it, the more I realise the house would be perfect. We could hold the party in the large room that I'm pretty sure must have been used as a ballroom at some stage. 'I'm sure Danny would love to have a party here, it's just—'

'No buts, Gracie!' Charlie insists. 'We'll organise the best party Sandybridge has ever seen, then we'll be the cool kids for a change, instead of a couple of hangers on.'

I look at Charlie's eager face. He's very keen to do this.

'OK, you're on! Let's do it! Let's organise the best party ever!'

Dear Grace,

Tonight at the party you will argue with your best friend.

Don't go after him. It's for the best, I promise.

Love, Me x

Ten

'How do you think it's going?' I ask Charlie as we stand at the side of the room.

I feel a bit like Kevin Bacon in the movie *Footloose* as we watch people milling about in the middle of a hall festooned with balloons, and a Happy Birthday banner. In *Footloose*, Kevin's character organises a secret dance for his classmates, and before he starts the cool dancing, everyone is just hanging around looking awkward – which is pretty much what we're all doing right now.

In conjunction with Danny's mates and a few of the girls from school, I'd tried to organise the best party I could manage on our limited budget, in a venue we weren't really supposed to be in. OK, we *definitely* weren't supposed to be in.

I'd provided the banner and all the balloons, which Charlie and I had painstakingly stood in the hall and blown up earlier on this afternoon, and we'd requested all the guests bring some food and drink.

This had surprisingly worked very well, in that nearly everyone who came through the door had brought something. But not quite so well in terms of variety: we now had two tables laden with more crisps than Sainsbury's, four Viennettas that were melting pretty fast in the warm room, a frozen Black Forest gateau that wasn't thawing fast enough, and a pineapple-and-cheese hedgehog.

There wasn't a lot of variety on the drinks table either. There was more Coke than the pub in Sandybridge could probably get through in a week; a number of bottles of Hooch – which were disappearing rapidly; a bottle of vodka – no doubt 'borrowed' from a parent's booze cabinet – but luckily quite a lot of tins of lager and bottles of beer, which seemed to be very popular with the boys.

Charlie had borrowed his brother's boombox (I'm pretty sure without his knowledge) and we were blasting out tunes from the variety of cassettes and mix tapes that people had brought along.

'I think it's going as expected,' Charlie replies diplomatically as he looks out into the room. He turns to me. 'Cheer up, Gracie. Everyone looks like they're having fun. How about you join in?'

'I just want it to go well for Danny,' I tell him.

'Danny looks like he's enjoying himself,' Charlie says, looking over to where Danny is currently trying to down a can of lager in one, while his mates cheer him on. 'If anything, maybe a little too much,' he murmurs. 'Has he thanked you yet for doing this for him?'

'Not yet, but I know he's pleased.'

'Hmm ...' Charlie says. 'I think he should be thanking both of us – profusely. Blowing up all these balloons earlier nearly killed me.'

'Aw, has the poor baby not got much puff?' I say, ruffling Charlie's hair, which he hates me doing.

'Not any more,' he says, ducking away from my hand. 'Just as well I don't smoke, eh, like most of these others. Or I'd have probably keeled over after having my lungs abused by a thousand balloons.'

All evening a number of our 'guests' have been disappearing outside, I assume to get their much-needed nicotine fix. At least, I hope that's all they're smoking. But at the moment most people are inside; some of the girls have put on a Madonna tape, and are currently bopping around to 'True Blue', while the boys stand scornfully watching them, all except Tony Prentice, who is giving his all to Queen Madge with the girls.

I wish I was as cool as them, I think as I watch the girls gyrating around confidently on the dance floor in their short skirts and high heels, their perfect long hair being tossed like a Timotei advert over their shoulders while they laugh in a carefree manner.

I'm wearing what I thought was a fairly glamorous red-and-white dress. The top part is very fitted with long sleeves, and the bottom is a rah-rah-style skirt made up of many tiers of billowy red polka-dot fabric. Princess Diana was dressed in something similar on the news the other night, and I thought it was the height of sophistication when I left my house. But now, compared to the other girls, I feel a bit frumpy.

I spy Danny looking around the room, and I hope he's looking for me. At least that's something I have that the other girls don't – I'm going out with the coolest boy in the school.

Danny waves when he spots me and, to my delight, makes his way across the dance floor through the gang of girls, who all gyrate extra hard when he passes.

'My Gracie!' he says, dropping his arm casually over my shoulder as he arrives by my side. 'How's it going, sexy?'

Danny has never called me this before, and I'm not sure whether to like it or not. I've never thought of myself as sexy – awkward, self-conscious, a bit tubby maybe, but definitely not sexy.

'I'm very well,' I tell him. 'Are you enjoying your party?'

'Yeah! It's stupendous, and it's all thanks to my lovely Gracie.'

'I can't take all the credit,' I tell him, wriggling a little under his arm, which seems to be getting heavier by the second. 'Charlie helped me.'

'Ah, Charlie, good fella.' Danny swings me around, his hand still gripping my shoulder, to pat Charlie on the back. 'You're a good friend to Gracie, aren't you?'

Danny's words are starting to slur.

'I try,' Charlie says brusquely.

'You do more than that, fella. Gracie here talks about you all the time. If it weren't for the fact you're gay ... I'd be quite worried.' Danny lets out a huge guffaw, as though what he's just said is hilarious.

Charlie, his face flushed, glares at me.

'I'm not gay,' he quietly informs Danny. 'What have you been saying, Grace?' he asks, looking at me with a hurt expression.

'Nothing, I promise.'

98

'Come on, Charlie boy,' Danny says, putting his other arm around Charlie's shoulder now. 'We're all friends here, you don't need to be shy about coming out.'

'I'm not gay,' Charlie insists again, his face getting redder, this time with anger rather than embarrassment. He wriggles free from Danny's grip. 'I'm not sure why you would think that, or what Grace has been telling you to keep you happy.'

Charlie never calls me Grace. He must be very angry.

I shake my head at him. 'I haven't said anything, Charlie, honest.'

'Grace is my friend, my best friend, but that doesn't make me gay just because we're not anything else.' Charlie gives Danny a disdainful look. 'And if you can't handle that fact, then that's your problem, Danny, not mine.'

I watch Charlie storm away across the mahogany floor, pushing through the crowd of dancing girls.

I try to follow him, but Danny grabs my hand.

'Leave him, Gracie,' he says. 'He's probably tetchy because he hasn't admitted it to himself yet. It's clear he's batting for the other side, though. Everyone knows it.'

'But . . . ' My eyes scan the dance floor in search of Charlie but it's getting more crowded by the moment and I can't see him. 'Charlie isn't gay,' I tell Danny. 'At least, I think he isn't . . . ' I'm ashamed to admit even I have to think about it for a moment. Charlie's different to the other boys I know, there's no doubting that, but different doesn't make him gay. 'No,' I insist. 'Charlie likes girls, I'm sure of it. And even if he didn't, it wouldn't matter to me, he's my friend.'

'Really?' Danny asks.

'Are you suggesting I shouldn't be friends with him if he's gay?' I ask, pulling away from him.

'No! I'm not a gay basher!' Danny looks quite hurt at the suggestion. 'I only meant ... you two seem so close, it's hard to believe you're just friends.'

'Not jealous are you, Danny?' I ask, smiling at him, my momentary anger fading fast.

'Me? No, course not. It's a bit weird though, isn't it? A boy and a girl being friends and nothing else.'

'No, I don't think so. Anyway, Charlie doesn't think about me like that. We're mates, same as you and your friends are mates.'

'Yeah, right.'

'What do you mean?'

'Gracie, you're a pretty girl. If he really isn't gay then course Charlie thinks about you like that.'

I blush at Danny's words. That's the second compliment he's paid me tonight. But I'm not pretty, the other girls are pretty, the ones that wear high-heeled shoes and make-up to school, the ones that shop at Miss Selfridge. They're the pretty ones. I'm just Grace.

'Not Charlie. I've told you: we're just friends.'

'So he doesn't do this then?' Danny asks, leaning into me and kissing me on the neck.

'Definitely not,' I tell him, shivering with pleasure.

'Or this?' he asks, kissing me fully on the lips now.

Speechlessly I shake my head as he pulls away to await my verdict.

'Good, cos I wanna be the only one doing that to you. Shall we go somewhere quieter?' Danny asks suddenly, to my surprise.

'But this is your party,' I tell him. 'Don't you want to stay?'

'No, I mean somewhere quieter here in the house.'

'Oh ... yes, all right then.'

Danny escorts me out of the party and into the main hall. 'I don't suppose there's any furniture up there any more?' he asks, looking up the stairs.

'Er ... no, I don't think so.' I know Danny likes history, but it never occurred to me he'd be interested in furniture. I look around and wonder where Charlie has gone. I should really go find him and check he's OK.

'Right ... what about through here?' Danny asks, grabbing my hand and pulling me down the corridor.

'The servants' quarters are downstairs,' I reply, still looking behind me for signs of Charlie. 'Why do you want to go down there? There's nothing to see. The ballroom, where your party's being held, is the most fascinating room if you're interested in the history of the house.'

Danny pulls me down some worn stone stairs that, unlike their sumptuous upstairs counterparts, are uncarpeted, and we arrive in a long corridor that would have once bustled with the below-stairs staff. Danny pushes open one of the doors, and after he's felt around on the wall he pulls on an old Bakelite light switch, which most of the rooms still have. Suddenly a kitchen is flooded with harsh fluorescent light. I blink for a couple of seconds, my eyes used to the dim light in the hallway, then I look around as my eyes get used to the light.

Two of the long walls in the kitchen are lined with wooden cupboards; they have painted white doors and scrubbed wooden surfaces. Still hanging from one of the walls are the steel wall hooks that would have held the pots and pans used to cook sumptuous meals for the previous owner and his guests. On one side of the room is a large white Belfast sink with a wooden drainer, and opposite a forlorn-looking gap where a range cooker once would have stood. In the centre of the room is a long scrubbed wooden table where I can imagine vast quantities of vegetables being chopped, cakes baked, and other meals prepared in the kitchen's heyday.

'Ah, a table!' Danny announces, while I wander around the room. 'That will do.'

'For what?' I ask.

'Gracie, Gracie, don't be coy, we haven't stepped back in time, you know. I'm not the master's son trying to have his way with the housemaid!'

What on earth was Danny going on about?

'No, I know you're not,' I reply, thinking that Danny must be really drunk if he's confusing us with the people that lived here a hundred years ago. 'Isn't this place amazing though?' I continue, looking around me. 'You can almost smell a pig roasting in the oven, and hear the sound of the kitchen staff chattering away while they prepare food for the family.'

'Never mind that,' Danny says, as he moves towards me around the table. 'I'm only interested in you right now, Gracie.' Danny pulls me to him, wraps his arms around me, and we begin to kiss, then after a few seconds I feel him push against me, so I'm wedged up against the top of the table.

'Why don't you ... hop up ... on top of it,' Danny breathes heavily, as his kisses move from my mouth down on to my neck.

'OK,' I agree, moving away from him for a moment so I can pull myself up on to the table in the same way as we hopped up on to the tables at school, so we could swing our legs underneath.

'Great,' Danny grins, watching me. I don't know what it is,

102

but Danny looks different. His eyes, always so pretty, have an almost glazed look about them. Perhaps it's the drink.

'Are you OK?' I ask him as his hands slide up my thighs, pushing my dress with them.

'Sure am,' he mumbles, and as we kiss again I feel one of his hands go a bit too far.

I wriggle a little on the table, in case he's made a mistake.

But his hand doesn't move; if anything, it tries to probe further.

'Stop it, Danny!' I say, trying to make light of it as I pull away from his lips. 'What are you doing?'

'You know what I'm doing, Gracie,' he murmurs as he begins caressing my neck again. Except now it doesn't feel pleasant, it's starting to feel scary.

'No, I don't!' I cry, pushing him away.

Shocked rather than angry, Danny stands watching me from a few feet away across the floor.

'I mean, yes, I do know,' I try to say in a calmer voice. 'At least, I think I do.'

Danny looks as confused as I feel.

I jump off the table, and pull down my skirt.

'I'm sorry, but I'm just not ready for that sort of thing yet, Danny.'

'Of course you are, Gracie,' Danny says, approaching me again.

'No!' I put my hand out like I'm holding back traffic. 'No, I'm not. I'm not like those girls out there, Danny. They're all confident and grown-up, but I'm not them, I'm me. They might be ready to have sex, but I'm not.' I can feel myself breathing as heavily as Danny had been a few moments ago, but my shortness of breath is for a much different reason. I begin to move away from Danny around the table towards the door. 'I like you and everything, Danny, you know I do. But I'm sorry, I can't do that. Not yet anyway.'

Before Danny even has a chance to reply, I turn and run out of the kitchen, back along the hallway and up the stairs, my heart still pounding and my breathing shallow and fast.

I don't care if Danny ditches me because of what happened in the kitchen just now. I know some of the girls in my class have had sex already, I've overheard them talking about it, but I'm not ready for that sort of relationship yet, and if Danny can't deal with that, fine. I can't deal with him.

I pause in the upstairs hallway, not knowing where to go next. Music still booms from the ballroom as the rest of the party guests carry on enjoying themselves. But I can't go in there, not now.

Charlie – that's who I need to see, he'll make everything right, I know he will. Why didn't I go after him when we argued? If I had, the kitchen incident would never have happened. It's that damn typewriter's fault; I didn't push to go after Charlie because of what Remy had said. But was that really the reason I didn't follow him? Or was it more to do with Danny's persuasive powers? Whatever the reason, I need to apologise to Charlie as much as I need to see him right now.

As I stand in the hallway deliberating where he is, I wonder if he might have headed upstairs, but as I'm about to dash up one of the staircases to look for him there's a knock at the front door.

Instead of answering it to see who's there, I just stand staring at the big wooden door paralysed with fear. Who's out there? No one knows we're here tonight. At least, no one was supposed to know ...

'Gracie!' I hear my name called behind me as Danny catches up with me from downstairs. 'Gracie, I'm sorry.'

But I don't stop to listen; instead I throw myself at the door, and pull it open.

Whoever's on the other side has to be easier to deal with than Danny right now.

'Good evening, miss,' a large but fairly friendly-looking policeman says as I stand silently staring at him.

When I don't say anything, he looks past me into the house.

'Are you holding a party here tonight by any chance?'

I'm about to deny it, when 'Wake Me Up Before You Go-Go' comes booming through the hallway, as someone in the party decides that now would be a good time to crank up the volume.

'We didn't think we'd be doing any harm,' I protest, as thoughts of us all being banged up in jail for trespassing race through my mind.

The policeman holds up his hand. 'We'll deal with that later,' he says. 'Right now, I need to find out if any of you know a Charlie Parker?'

I'm not sure why, but I raise my hand.

The policeman nods. 'May I come in?' he asks.

As I stand aside to let him in, the policeman turns to summon his colleague from their car.

'Is everything all right, Gracie?' Danny asks while we're waiting for the second policeman to arrive.

'I'm not sure,' I whisper.

'Is it about the party?'

I shrug. I can't deal with his questions right now; I'm more concerned with what's happened to Charlie.

'Now,' the first policeman says when they are both standing safely inside and we've closed the door behind them. He takes off his hat. 'The reason I asked whether you knew a Charlie Parker before is there's been an accident . . .'

I gasp. 'Is Charlie OK?' I manage to squeak.

'He was hit by a car down on the main road at the front of the house and taken to hospital. We only know his name because it's written inside his trainers.'

That's so Charlie.

'We saw the lights on at the house, and guessed he'd come from here,' the policeman continues. 'We need to get in contact with his next of kin – do you know where we can find them?'

I nod. 'Yes, I can take you there. But is he . . . is Charlie OK?'

The policeman looks at me with sympathy.

'Let's just find his parents first, eh, love?'

As I leave Sandybridge Hall in a police car, Danny's words ringing in my ears about how he and the others will clear everything up, and how I'm not to worry, all I can think about is the last letter – the one that told me not to follow Charlie.

What if I had? I wouldn't be doing this now, that's for sure. I wouldn't be travelling in a police car with the siren blazing on my way to see Charlie's parents.

If I hadn't taken the letter's advice, my best friend wouldn't be lying in a hospital alone right now. He'd be with me, and more importantly, he'd be OK . . .

I'll never trust Remy again.

Summer 2016

Even with the age gap between us, Iris and I work well together in our little office. Sandybridge Hall employs a lot of people, but our office in one of the only wings of the house to be modernised is the hub of everything.

'Right,' I say once I've finished all my work for the morning, 'I'm going to disappear for a bit.'

Iris looks up from her computer screen, eyes me for a moment, then simply nods. Even though we have a great relationship, I'm still her boss, and if I want to slope off in the middle of the day to do something important, then that's up to me.

'I'll probably see you tomorrow, OK?' I add when she doesn't speak.

'Sure,' Iris says, obviously still a little put out at not being let in on my secret.

My mobile phone vibrates across the desk as I'm about to pick it up and put it in my bag.

'Hi, Olivia,' I say as I take the call. 'What's up?' Olivia's half of a brother and sister partnership that helps out at my parents' antiques shop. 'No ... ' I begin. ' ... No, Olivia, I can't, really.' I listen a bit more, and then I sigh. 'OK, sure, if it's *that* important. Yes, I'll go.'

'What's wrong?' Iris asks, looking intrigued.

'Apparently there's a rather large parcel for the shop that's arriving on a train today from Norwich. It needs collecting from the station in a vehicle; Olivia doesn't trust them to look after it properly if she leaves it there overnight. The shop's van is in the garage for its MOT, so now I've been volunteered to go and fetch it in the Range Rover.'

'And you can't *because* ... ?' Iris probes innocently.

'Nice try.' I wink at her. 'I'll probably just have enough time if I leave now,' I say, checking my watch. 'Right, I'd best get moving.'

Iris watches me as I gather my things from my desk. 'You sure you don't want to say where you're going?' she asks. 'It seems very cloak and dagger.'

'No, I don't,' I tell her purposefully, slinging my bag over my shoulder. 'Now I'll see you tomorrow, OK?'

Iris simply shrugs.

Sandybridge train station is on the other side of town from the hall, so I have to drive through the town centre to get to it. As I travel along the seafront I get caught in a small traffic jam, while a delivery vehicle blocks the narrow road dropping off its cargo – sacks and sacks of potatoes – to the fish and chip shop.

While I wait for the traffic to move again, I glance out of my window at the little coffee shop I'm pulled up next to, and remember what it looked like when Charlie's parents owned it back in the eighties, and how Charlie had worked behind the counter to learn the family business.

How things change, I think, as the traffic begins to move. How we've all changed since those happy, carefree days.

Finally I arrive at the station, and find the train carrying the package is delayed. 'Great, this is all I need!' I mutter. 'Today of all days ...'

So I return to my car, climb into the driver's seat, and wind the window down, hoping to hear the announcement of the train's arrival. I tap my fingers on the steering wheel impatiently, then to help me remain calm I reach for one of the sweets that I know my other half always keeps in the glove box – ooh, éclairs. Nice.

I pop one into my mouth and try to distract my thoughts away from what's supposed to happen later today – assuming I ever get there.

I look out of my open window at our little old station that doesn't seem to have changed in decades. It reminds me of one of those toy stations you might set up for a child's wooden train track. There's one ticket office, housed inside a small brick building, that leads out to just the one platform on the other side. The only modernisation the station seems to have undergone is the installation of automatic ticket barriers, replacing the elderly stationmaster I remember from my childhood, who would collect your ticket stubs at the end of your journey, and quite often know you by name too.

The entrance to the building is through an ornate brick archway, and it's as I gaze at this that I remember the time mistletoe hung from that same archway and I found myself caught underneath it ...

Part Two

December 1992

Eleven

Got it! I jump on to my train, that's minutes away from departing from Edinburgh's Waverley station, dragging my suitcase behind me. I find the carriage where I hope I have a seat reserved, then I heave my suitcase up on to one of the already overflowing luggage racks. Today there seem to be quite a number of people doing the same as me – returning home for the Christmas holidays. So in amongst the vast array of suitcases and bags stacked precariously on the luggage racks are even more bags filled to the brim with brightly coloured parcels decorated with ribbons and bows.

Suitcase safely stored, I make my way down the carriage of the train as it pulls out of the station, and find my aisle seat. I'm seated at a table opposite a lady who I'm pleased to see is already deep into her *Times* crossword.

She smiles politely at me as I sit down, then returns to her clues.

I sigh as I settle back in my seat. The long journey from Edinburgh to Sandybridge was never going to be an easy one, but it's one I've grown pretty familiar with after almost three and a half years of taking it. Whatever route I took home, several changes of train were involved, which usually meant rushing for my connections, so it was not a journey I undertook too often.

On the plus side, I love Edinburgh, the city I'd chosen to study my degree at; the university is great, the people are friendly and I love the city's rich and vibrant history, which I enjoy seeking out whenever I have some free time.

'Nearly miss the train, did you?' the lady opposite me asks, as my breathing begins to return to normal, and my flushed cheeks begin to cool.

'Yes, my taxi got caught in traffic on the way to the station. Only just made it!'

The woman smiles. 'Edinburgh is lovely, but if you get caught on Princes Street you're there for some time!'

'Yes,' I agree. I don't take taxis too often – as a student I can't afford them – but I'd had no alternative today with my large, cumbersome suitcase.

'On your way home from university for Christmas?' the woman asks, looking me up and down.

'Yes, how did you know?'

'I have a daughter about the same age as you. She's at Cardiff, studying English.'

'I nearly did English,' I tell her. 'But I changed to history.'

'Do you mind me asking why?'

'No, not at all, it's quite a long story though.'

I have until Newcastle,' the woman says, smiling, 'why not tell me?'

Over the next few minutes, I tell my new travelling companion how my academic change had come about. All about Danny, and how I'd tried desperately to show an interest in the subject he was so passionate about in the hope he'd feel the same way about me. Then I tell her what had really sparked my interest: the time I'd spent at Sandybridge Hall with Charlie. That was when I'd begun to think about the past as something I might be quite interested in, rather than something inherently dull. It was shortly after Charlie's road accident that I'd borrowed my first few history books from the library, when I'd been there getting fiction for Charlie to read in his convalescence.

'Your friend was in an accident?' the lady asks. 'How awful.'

'It was. He spent about three months in hospital, then quite some time recovering at home. Poor Charlie; it completely messed up his education.'

'Why?'

'He missed too much school, so when it came time for his exams he failed miserably – well, I say failed; to some people the grades Charlie got would have been pretty good, but to Charlie they were a definite failure.'

'Couldn't he retake them?'

'He didn't want to. He was too proud to stay back and retake his final year, so instead he started helping his parents out at their café.'

'He never went back to school or university?'

I shake my head. I still feel guilty about it, even after all these years. I can't help feeling it was partly my fault. If only

I'd gone after him instead of wasting my time with Danny. If only I hadn't listened to a stupid typewriter . . .

'So what happened next?' my travelling companion asks. 'Once you'd become interested in history, did you study it too?'

I nod. 'I never thought it would be one of my A-level subjects, but I loved it, and now I'm enjoying my degree so much. It isn't the battles that interest me, important though they are, or the kings and queens; it's the lives of the real, everyday folk – and, more importantly, how they lived. I'm particularly interested in the twentieth century, the years between and including the two world wars. My dissertation is going to be on the changing role of women between those years.'

'It sounds as though you make the perfect history student,' the lady tells me, as she begins to gather her things. 'I should know, I teach it. Only at A-level though, but that's why I was so interested in why you changed subjects.'

I smile at the lady as she stands up.

'Good luck,' she says. 'I hope you get a first next year.'

'Thank you,' I say as I watch her ease herself into the aisle of the carriage as we pull into Newcastle station. 'I hope your daughter does well too.'

'Thank you.' She smiles again one last time and begins to move towards the exit. 'It was lovely to meet you.'

Isn't it funny how we tell things to perfect strangers we meet on trains and buses, I think as I look out of the train window at Newcastle station. Sometimes it's so much easier to share with a stranger than with the people we're close to.

As new passengers get on to the train, another lady sits down in the seat that's just been vacated opposite me. She's

116

elderly, and she's carrying a small wicker basket. Once she's got herself settled, she opens up the leather catch on the basket and produces a tiny Yorkshire terrier, who immediately snuggles down into her lap.

'Are you OK with dogs?' she asks, noticing me watching. 'Dotty is quite friendly.'

'Oh yes, absolutely fine,' I tell her. 'I have one of my own at home, Wilson. He's a lot bigger than yours though, I'd never be able to bring him on a train – he wouldn't sit still long enough.'

Wilson hadn't taken too well to me leaving to go to university. Mum told me he pined terribly to begin with. But now he's grown used to the fact that I occasionally return home to see him, he isn't quite so bad and only sulks for the first day after I've gone.

'I prefer a little dog,' the elderly lady says. 'So much easier for me to deal with.'

'Yes, Wilson can be a bit of a handful.'

Mum had also told me how much help Charlie had been in looking after Wilson. Apparently, since I've been away, he's come around every day to walk him.

When Charlie had been recovering from his accident, I would push him along in his hospital wheelchair whenever I took Wilson for a walk, so he wouldn't feel he was missing out on our regular excursions. We couldn't quite manage the beach with the chair, but we could walk along the promenade, and then back through the town where the pavements were kind to Charlie's wheels. Then, when Charlie progressed on to crutches, he would hobble along next to us, pausing occasionally to have a rest while Wilson ran around doing his thing. When finally he was able to walk alongside

117

us like he used to, and we could at last return to our beloved sand, it was *the* best day – for all of us.

The lady and her dog change at York, and no one else takes the vacant seat as the train fills and the doors close.

We stop at York a bit too long for my liking, but nothing is said as to why. I look at my watch and realise we're now running late. Damn, I have a connection to make at Peterborough that was going to be tight even without this delay. But there's nothing I can do, except sit tight and hope we'll make up some time. As I gaze out of the window at the passing scenery my thoughts turn to Charlie; I've been so looking forward to seeing him again. Charlie still lives in Sandybridge with his parents. Unlike me, he'd chosen not to continue his education. He could have if he'd opted to retake his exams, but after the accident he seemed even more content than he had been before to stay in our hometown, helping his parents in their little coffee shop, which was still doing well, and was always filled with customers whenever I was there.

I still felt guilty about what had happened. If only I'd gone after him that night he wouldn't have got hit by a car, then his life would have turned out as he'd planned. Charlie would be doing what I was now: having a great time at a uni somewhere; partying, meeting new people, and generally enjoying himself while he studied and got a good education. But however much I fretted, Charlie seemed very happy doing what he was doing, and if Charlie was happy, then so was I.

Eventually we reach Peterborough and my earlier concerns prove correct: I'm too late to make my original connection, so I have to hang around at the busy station waiting for the next Norwich-bound train. Luckily it's not too long before one arrives, and I manage to squeeze on to it and find a seat before the whole train fills up. I close my eyes and lean my head back against my headrest as the train pulls out of the station; at last I feel as though I'm almost there, home again for Christmas.

Christmas in Sandybridge, I daydream happily, as memories of past Christmases there pleasantly fill my head. Like most seaside towns so reliant on holidaymakers, Sandybridge is always quiet in the winter months, and with the tourists gone, it's down to the locals to fill the void they leave behind.

Personally, I prefer it like that. I'm able to take Wilson for long walks on the beach without having to worry about him stealing picnickers' sandwiches, or running off with a beach ball. And even when the town's bereft of its holidaymakers, it's never drab or dreary – far from it. People come from all the surrounding towns to see Sandybridge's Christmas lights, we're famous for them, and I'm very much looking forward to seeing what the town has in store for Santa this year.

When I reach Norwich I make my final change, and as always I find the train from Norwich to Sandybridge is not only much smaller, but much quieter than my previous two mainline trains. The man opposite me smiles as I sit down, then returns to his book. So, pleased I'm not going to have to make conversation with anyone this time, I relax back into my seat for the last part of my journey. I pull my new Take That CD from my bag and place it into my portable CD player to keep me company. I smile to myself as I put the Tamsin Archer case that had held the boys' CD back into my bag. Now I'm on my way home to Sandybridge I don't have to pretend to be the type of person that listens to cool music. I can be myself again.

'Gracie Harper?' I hear a voice behind my headrest say, just as Gary Barlow is about to croon the first line to 'A Million Love Songs'.

I turn around and look up.

'Danny Lucas!' I say, a little dazed to see him standing above me. 'What are you doing here?'

'On my way home for Christmas; I just changed at Norwich from the London train to this one; you must be doing the same?'

I pull off my headphones to look at him properly, and see his familiar chiselled jawline – but now with a hint of dark stubble across it. His thick, dark mane of hair, but longer and more tousled than I was used to seeing it, and the same disarming smile – that was one thing that hadn't changed.

'Yes . . . yes I am.'

'I barely recognised you with your new hair!' Danny says, gesturing to my elfin crop. 'What happened to all your lovely tresses? What did I used to call you?'

'Rapunzel,' I murmur, slightly embarrassed.

'That's it! So why the short hair – you trying to be all cool and trendy at your fancy uni?'

'I fancied a change, that's all,' I tell him. This is a slight fib; what had actually happened was that one of my flatmates and I had tried to cut each other's hair to save money. Julia's hadn't looked at all bad when I'd finished with it, but my hair looked like a drunk Edward Scissorhands had got hold of it. So I was forced to go to a real hairdresser, who offered me the option of a bob to tidy it up, but I decided to go the whole hog and have it all chopped off, something I'd been toying with doing for a while, since I'd seen Demi Moore at the cinema in *Ghost*.

The man in the seat opposite me has set down his book and is watching our exchange with interest. 'Would you two like to sit together?' he offers. 'If you like, I can move to those free seats over there.'

'Yes, that would be great!' Danny says, before I can respond. 'Cheers, mate.'

The man collects up his book – according to the cover, it's *The Pelican Brief* by John Grisham, but earlier I'd caught sight of a page and discovered he'd wrapped the thriller's cover around a copy of *Men Are from Mars, Women Are from Venus* to hide what he was really reading.

Obviously I wasn't the only one trying to look cool. Maybe one day someone would invent a device that would prevent anyone knowing what you were reading or listening to. Then you could be uncool to your heart's content.

Danny sits down opposite me now the man has vacated his seat.

'So how are you?' he asks. 'It's been a while.'

It was actually the exact same length of time as I'd spent in Edinburgh. In all the times I'd been home to visit Mum and Dad, I'd never once bumped into Danny while I'd been back in Sandybridge. I was beginning to think he never came home to visit his family, but I knew that he did. Mrs Lucas had mentioned it to my mother, and Mum had relayed the fact to me when I'd casually enquired about Danny's movements.

'I'm good, thanks,' I say, looking across the train table at him, but at the same time trying not to catch his eyes, which seem an even deeper shade of blue today than they were the last time I looked into them.

'Uni going well?' Danny asks.

'Yes, very well. I'm in my final year now – degrees in Scotland are four years.'

Danny nods. 'Yeah, I know, couldn't be doing with all that extra study. Mine is just the three, I'm down in London.'

I knew that, but I don't let on. 'I'm surprised you wanted to tie yourself down with study at all. I would have thought that once you got out into the world, you'd want to keep on travelling.'

Danny had decided after his A-levels, which he didn't do as well in as he'd hoped, that he would take a year out and travel the world, which of course I was insanely jealous of. Partly because his parents were funding most of his trip, but mostly because he was going to leave me behind to do it.

After his disastrous birthday party at Sandybridge Hall, I'd not wanted anything to do with Danny and I'd deliberately kept my distance from him. Even though he tried desperately to apologise for his actions, saying it was the drink talking, not him, and could we try again, I would have nothing to do with him. Instead I devoted myself to helping Charlie get better. To begin with I would visit him at the hospital every day; when he was discharged, I would go over to his house to help Maggie look after him; and then, once we were allowed out on our own, came our walks with Wilson. I didn't know who I blamed more for Charlie's accident: me, Danny or the stupid typewriter – which still sat in my bedroom at home, though it hadn't been loaded with paper since that fateful day.

As Charlie got better, my annoyance with Danny began to wane, so much so that when Danny asked me out again just before we started sixth form together, I gave in and agreed to one date. But that one date ended up lasting for the next two years, with our relationship progressing slightly further this time than a quick fumble in a kitchen. Danny Lucas was my first, and I'd always remember him for that.

'I don't see it as tying myself down. I had a fantastic time travelling, but now it's time to get an education,' Danny says with the smile that used to send shivers of excitement down my spine when I was fifteen. Some six years later, to my annoyance, it's still having the same effect.

'Good for you,' I reply, trying not to sound bitter. Even though I'm living hundreds of miles away from Sandybridge, my longing to travel has not diminished. I'm determined to begin seeing the world as soon as my time at university is over.

Danny tips his head to one side. 'Not still bitter, are you, Gracie?' he asks. 'About me leaving you behind?'

'Ha!' I pretend to laugh. 'As if! I'm having a fantastic time in Edinburgh. Plus I only have a while left, then I'll be the one free to do as she likes!'

Danny grins. 'Good, I'm glad to hear it. Met anyone?'

I know he means anyone male.

'Yes, as a matter of fact I have,' I lie. There have been guys, but none who've lasted more than a few dates. They only ever seemed to want one thing; I was prepared to oblige a few of them on that score, but only for as long as it suited me. I was very firmly single these days, and I liked it that way.

'Oh.' Did Danny look a little put out? 'That's cool, what's his ... or *her* name?'

'*His* name is ...' I glance across at our friend with the book to gain a few seconds. 'John ... ny. It's John, but he likes to be called Johnny,' I add hurriedly.

Danny nods. 'Cool. Is he a history student too?'

'Zoology,' I reply, trying not to look at the book jacket again. 'He wants to work with endangered birds.'

Danny looks at me questioningly. 'Really?'

I nod with conviction.

'Well, I'm single,' he tells me with a hint of pride. 'Have been for a while.'

Knowing Danny, his idea of a while is probably a few days.

'Congratulations, what do you want – a medal?'

Danny laughs. 'Ah, you always did have a sharp tongue, Gracie. You know, it's a shame you're seeing someone – we could have hooked up while we're both back in Sandybridge.'

The audacity of him!

'I don't think so, Danny,' I tell him firmly, trying to ignore the excited butterflies dancing in my stomach. 'Even if I didn't have a boyfriend, I wouldn't just drop everything for you. I have plans while I'm home.'

Danny doesn't look in the least bit annoyed by my rejection.

'Plans with Charlie?' he asks, his eyebrows high in his forehead.

'Yes, amongst other things. It's Christmas, I have a lot of people to catch up with.'

'Fair enough!' Danny says, holding his hand up. 'I know when I'm not wanted.'

I'm about to respond when I realise the train is pulling into Sandybridge station.

'It's our stop!' I cry, leaping to my feet. 'I need to get my case down from the luggage rack.'

'Don't worry, I'll help you,' Danny says, standing up opposite me. We make our way along the carriage to the baggage area, and I point to my red case, which Danny pulls from under another two cases, then he reaches for a large rucksack stashed over the other side of the luggage compartment.

'Is that all you have?' I ask as we wait for the train to come to a stop.

'Yep. Travel light, me – backpacking taught me that. Unlike some . . . ' He smirks at my large suitcase.

'I have gifts inside that too!' I protest.

'Yeah, yeah,' Danny says, grabbing hold of my case as well as his own bag and alighting from the train now the doors are open. 'Come on, Gracie, or you'll end up in Cromer, and no one wants to be there at Christmas!'

I reprimand him as we both get off the train, partly for the Cromer comment – our two towns have always had a slight rivalry – and partly for carrying my case, which I quickly take hold of myself as we head into the little ticket office.

'How are you getting home?' Danny asks as we exit the station.

'Walk, probably.'

'But your house is a long way from here.'

'So? I like walking.'

'We could get a cab,' Danny says, glancing at a lone taxi driver in front of us waiting hopefully for a fare.

'I don't know about students in London, but us guys up north don't have the money for taxis!'

'Neither do us London boys.' Danny sighs and looks up at the sky.

'At least the weather is dry,' I say, doing the same. 'We shouldn't get wet.'

'I wasn't looking at that,' Danny says, still staring up

above our heads. 'Do you believe in Christmas traditions, Gracie?'

'What do you mean?' I ask, looking at him.

'Look what's hanging up above us!' Danny grins at me.

I look up at the station doorway and see a bunch of mistletoe hanging high above our heads.

Oh Christ!

I try and look with loathing at Danny, but I can't, he just seems to have the wrong effect on me – or was it the right one? Before I can debate that any further I see him leaning in towards me.

'Anyone want a lift?' a familiar voice asks, interrupting us before we can resurrect any old traditions, Christmas or otherwise.

I shriek with pleasure when I see who it is.

'Charlie!'

Twelve

'Hey, you!' Charlie says, hugging me. 'How have you been?'

'Hey, yourself!' I reply, delighted to see him. 'What are you doing here?'

'Your mum told me what time you were due in, so I thought I'd come and give you a lift.'

'But I'm really late, I thought I'd be on the earlier train, only I missed my first connection at Peterborough cos the train was delayed.'

'I know, I've been waiting,' Charlie says, as if it was ever in doubt that he would stay put until I arrived. He glances at Danny. 'All right, Dan?'

'Good, thanks, Charlie,' Danny says, and they both look questioningly at each other.

'I bumped into Danny on the train from Norwich,' I hurriedly explain. 'He's back for Christmas too. Quite a coincidence.'

'Yeah.' Charlie doesn't seem too impressed. 'Isn't it?'

'So what have you come to pick me up in?' I ask, looking around. 'The café's van?'

Charlie and his parents had made such a success of the café that they had expanded into lunchtime deliveries, supplying sandwiches and salads to companies in Sandybridge and the surrounding area.

'Nope, I have my own car now,' Charlie says proudly.

'You do! Where is it?'

Charlie points to a metallic blue Nova. 'She's tiny, but she goes when she needs to, and most importantly she's all mine!' He glances at Danny as he says this.

'Good for you!' Danny replies amiably. 'I'll probably wait until I finish my degree before I buy a car. Then I'll be earning enough to buy a decent one.'

Were these two digging at each other on purpose?

Of course they were.

I roll my eyes. *Men!*

And that's what the two of them are now. They're no longer gangly youths, struggling to find a way of fitting into their adult bodies properly. Both are tall (even Charlie is taller than me now), handsome young men.

Danny still has a mischievous look about him, so you can never quite be sure what he's thinking, but you get the feeling his thoughts are leaning towards the naughty side. As I'd noticed earlier on the train, he's sporting what is most likely an almost permanent dark shadow covering his chin, and his physique – which was already showing signs of becoming muscly at school – is now well toned and broad. He has the healthy glow of a person who spends a lot of time outside.

Charlie, on the other hand, has remained fair-skinned,

with a few freckles scattered haphazardly over the bridge of his nose. But his hair, which was nothing short of full-on ginger when we first met, is now a pale strawberry blond. He too has filled out, particularly in the upper body; his T-shirt – which once would have hung baggily over his narrow shoulders and scrawny arms – is taut, so you can just make out his small but well-formed pectoral muscles through the fabric, and the beginnings of smooth round biceps are clearly visible where the tight sleeves of his T-shirt end.

Boys they are certainly not.

Charlie nods at Danny's double-pronged dig, and decides not to bite. Instead he offers Danny a lift.

'Sure, man, that would be cool,' Danny replies.

So we all head across to Charlie's little two-door car, and I proceed to squeeze into the back with my suitcase, while Charlie takes Danny's rucksack from him.

'Not too heavy for you, Charlie, is it?' Danny asks, watching him swing it into the boot.

'Not at all, mate. Not at all.'

We drive back to Sandybridge with minimal conversation. What little chat there is relates to any local gossip that Charlie can recall, and our plans for the Christmas holidays.

'Maybe we can all meet up for a drink one night?' Danny suggests as Charlie drops him off outside his house. I switch to the front seat while Danny retrieves his bag from the boot.

Charlie glances at me, and sees I'm already nodding.

'That would be great, I'd like that!' I call, winding my window down.

Danny comes around to my side of the car. 'Good,' he says, leaning through the window. 'Because I'd like that too.' He glances at Charlie. 'Thanks for the lift, mate. Much appreciated.'

Charlie shrugs. 'Any time,' he says gruffly.

'Gracie, I'll see you soon, yes?' Danny asks.

I nod.

'But just in case I don't see you before the big day, would it be all right to give you a quick Christmas kiss now?'

I'm about to look over at Charlie, when I hear the crunch of a Nova being shoved rapidly into first gear.

'Sorry, gotta go!' Charlie calls and I'm thrust sharply back in my seat as the car shoots away. 'See ya soon, Danny boy ... ' he mumbles as we move quickly into second and then third gear.

I turn quickly and wave out of my window at a still-grinning Danny. Then I wind my window up and look at Charlie.

'What was all that about?' I ask, as Charlie concentrates intently on the road.

'All what?'

'You know exactly what. All that stuff with Danny.'

Charlie shrugs. 'He winds me up with all his smug talk.'

'That's just Danny, he's always been like that. But you've known him as long as me, why get wound up about it now?'

'Why was he on the train with you?' Charlie asks, ignoring my question.

'I told you, I bumped into him. Well, he found me actually.'

'I bet,' Charlie says sourly. 'Are you sure he didn't lie in wait for you at Norwich station so he could *coincidentally* be on the same train as you?'

'Don't be daft, why would he do that?'

'To get in with you again, before you got here.'

'Again, why would he want to do that? Danny and I were over ages ago. He was my schoolgirl crush, who happened to become my boyfriend.'

'They say your first love is always the strongest.'

'No they don't. They say you never forget your first love.'

Charlie nods, but doesn't look at me, because the traffic lights we've been waiting at choose that moment to turn from red to green.

'What is all this, Charlie?' I ask. 'It isn't like you to be bitter.'

'I'm not being bitter. I'm ... well, I'm just disappointed, that's all. I wanted to surprise you at the station, show you my new car, catch up on everything that's been going on in our lives. I haven't seen you since the summer, and then *he* shows up to spoil it.'

I realise now why Charlie is upset. Having this car is obviously a big deal for him; he wanted me to see it, so I'd know that he's achieving success too, even without going to university.

'I'm sorry,' I say, reaching over and resting my hand gently over his on the gear stick. 'It wasn't my plan to arrive here with Danny. It just happened.'

'I know,' Charlie says, taking his eyes off the road to glance at me. 'I'm sorry too, for being a miserable old bugger. I miss you when you're not here.'

'And I miss you too!' I pat his hand. 'But I'm here again now. I'm here to enjoy Christmas with my family and my best friend in all the world ... That's you, by the way, if you didn't already know.'

I glance sideways at him, then I wink when I catch his eye.

'Happy Christmas, you old bugger!' I lean across the car and kiss him on the cheek.

'Happy Christmas, Gracie,' Charlie says, with cheeks so red they could have belonged to Santa Claus himself.

Thirteen

Christmas is a quiet, but very pleasant couple of days, which I spend mainly with Mum and Dad, enjoying all the usual spoils of the festive season: too much food and drink, lots of naff but well-meant gifts, far too much trashy TV, and board games that only come out at Christmas.

But it's what we always do, and have done for as long as I can remember. Things have changed since I've been away at university, and I've changed too. Though I have no desire to return to Sandybridge permanently, I'm more than happy to slip back in time for a few days to temporarily become the old Grace again.

The day after Boxing Day, Mum and Dad open up the shop again, so for the first time since I've been back, I'm alone in the house.

Wilson is asleep in his basket – he sleeps quite a lot these days – so I decide not to disturb him, and keep his walk for later.

After drifting around the house for a bit pretending to tidy up, I decide to run a bath. It's a rare luxury to have a long, hot, peaceful soak; the house I live in in the centre of Edinburgh only has the one bathroom, and with four girls sharing there's always someone waiting. So a long soak seems a lovely post-Christmas treat, and also a chance to use some of the many bath salts I've been given by well-meaning relatives.

After checking on Wilson, still sound asleep in his basket, I head upstairs to run my bath. Once I've got the water temperature up high enough, I leave the bath running and go across the landing into my room in search of my old dressing gown.

I've been living out of my suitcase since I got home, and there's stuff strewn everywhere. While I wait for the bath, I make an attempt to tidy it up. As I pick up a pair of jeans and a sweater from my dressing table, I also lift the small woollen blanket that I had placed on top of the typewriter the night of the party at Sandybridge Hall. I've often thought about hiding the old typewriter in a cupboard, or disposing of it in one of the skips that Mum and Dad sometime used for house clearances. But something prevented me from doing so. Even though I'm 100 per cent sure I'll never use it again after what happened, the thought of taking the option away permanently scares me a little. What if this typewriter really can foretell my future? The letters had appeared to come from someone who knew what was going to happen in my life. But if that were so, why had they told me to do something that would result in something bad for someone else?

Still holding my clothes in one hand, I look down at the typewriter – Remy, I'd called it six years ago. Because that was what the woman ... oh, what was her name, the one we did a house clearance for at Lighthouse Cottage ... Mabel, yes that's it. Mabel had said Remy was its name. She'd also been the one who said I should have the typewriter; she'd said it might help me.

'Help me to arse up someone's life, more like,' I mutter, looking at the typewriter.

But Charlie seems happy. He's never once moaned or complained about not going to university. His business with his parents is going great guns; would that have happened if he'd gone away? Probably not. It's Charlie's drive and tenacity that has pushed their business in directions Maggie and Peter would never have thought to go. Maybe it's a good thing he's stayed.

I shake my head again, this time in frustration. No, it can't be a good thing, having to stay here in Sandybridge. All I've ever wanted is to get away.

But Charlie isn't like me, is he? All Charlie's ever wanted is to settle down somewhere. He has no urge to see the world like I do.

We're alike in so many ways, but in that one we're very, very different.

I finish tidying my room, then go to check on my bath. I'm pleased to find the water hot and topped with white frothy bubbles. So I turn off the tap, head back to my room, undress, and pop on my old dressing gown.

Gosh, that's a snug fit, I think as I attempt to wrap the fabric around me. Surely I haven't put on that much weight over Christmas? I take a look in my mirror. The dressing gown is straining at the seams in two areas: my chest, where, like the boys, I've definitely filled out since I was fifteen; and along its length. It used to sit halfway down my thighs, but now it's barely long enough to cover my bum.

'Oh well,' I say to myself in the mirror, 'so you've got bustier and taller – that's not a bad thing, is it?'

A quick double-check in the mirror reassures me it's only in those two areas I've grown. Happy I haven't filled out too much, I head for my long-awaited bath.

I've peeled off my dressing gown and I'm hovering with one foot gingerly poised to dip into the water to test how hot it is, when I hear the familiar tune of our doorbell ringing.

'Oh Lord, who's that?' I cry, as I debate for a second whether to ignore it or not. But as the theme tune to the *Antiques Roadshow* continues to play (Mum and Dad's idea of a joke), I realise I'm going to have to go downstairs to answer it.

'Hey, you,' Charlie greets me when I open the door. 'Did you have a good Christmas?'

'Hey, yourself! Yes, very good, thank you – and thanks again for your present. They're beautiful.'

'No worries,' Charlie says, blushing slightly. 'You liked them then?'

Charlie had bought me a beautiful collection of books about the progression of fashion and home decoration during the nineteenth and twentieth centuries. The gift was so perfect that I'd been quite choked when I opened it, and had rung Charlie immediately to thank him.

'Of course I did. You know me too well, don't you, to get it wrong.' I glance at Charlie's attire. 'And I can see you liked your gift too.'

Charlie is wearing what I bought for him: a navy blue cashmere scarf and gloves set from the Edinburgh Woollen Mill.

They may not look much, but they're beautifully soft, and I'd known they would not only suit Charlie, they'd keep him warm in the icy wind that often blows through Sandybridge in the cold winter months.

'They're great,' Charlie says, adjusting the scarf. 'Snug as a bug in a rug, me! Can I come in?'

'I was just about to take a bath actually.'

'Oh, I wondered why you were in your dressing gown.' Charlie deliberately averts his eyes from my cleavage, which with the tight fit of the gown is very definitely on show. 'Shall I come in and wait then? Only there's something I want to show you.'

'Can I call round for you later?' I ask apologetically. I don't want to offend Charlie, but I really want to take a long relaxing bath without having to worry that someone's downstairs waiting for me. 'I'll bring Wilson and we can go for a walk, if you like. What is it you want to show me?'

'Surprise ...' Charlie says mysteriously. 'Yeah, sure, if that suits you better. I'm free all day, cos we're still closed for Christmas.'

'About two then?' I suggest.

'OK.' Charlie turns and begins to walk away down the path. 'See you later,' he calls with a cheery wave. 'Enjoy your bath!'

I close the door and make my way upstairs again, wondering what it is Charlie wants to show me. I'm about to get in the bath when that same annoying tune rings out through the house again.

'What!' I cry. 'You have got to be kidding me!'

But the tune continues to play, so I go through the same routine of pulling on my robe as I head down the stairs.

'Yes!' I say sharply as I open the door.

'Whoa! Who's pulled your chain?' Danny says, stepping back a few paces and holding up his hand. Then he notices what I'm wearing. 'Oh, have I called at an inopportune moment?' he asks, his eyebrows raised suggestively. 'Have you left some poor unfortunate soul tied to the bedposts?'

'No, I have not!' I snap, trying to pull my robe around my chest so it's less revealing. 'I'm about to take a bath, that's all. But I keep being disturbed,' I finish in a slightly gentler tone.

'Looking like that, I'm not surprised!' Danny says, moving up the path towards me. 'I'd be quite keen to disturb you too!' He rests his hand up above me on the doorframe, the way you see men do in movies. 'What do you say, Gracie? Want someone to follow you upstairs and scrub your back?'

For all his clichéd patter, for the briefest moment the Danny effect begins to race pleasantly through me, causing its usual disruption to my heart and stomach, and for an equally brief moment I'm tempted . . .

'What do you want, Danny?' I ask, coming back to my senses.

He grins.

'Not that! I mean, what did you call around for?'

'I wondered if you liked your Christmas gift?' he asks in all innocence.

'You mean the extremely inappropriate underwear? Yeah, that was a fun few minutes on Christmas morning: unwrapping the contents of an Ann Summers shop in front of my parents!'

Danny grins. 'Yeah, but did you like it?'

I roll my eyes, and go to shut the door on him. But he puts his foot in the doorway. 'I'm sorry, Gracie, couldn't resist.

Drink later? I'd ask you out for dinner, but there's nowhere in Sandybridge I'd want to take you, and you did say we could meet up while we were both here.'

'Yes, OK,' I agree, knowing it's the only way to get rid of him so I can take my bath. 'A drink would be good. The Arms at eight?'

'Perfect,' Danny says, turning to leave, then he pauses and turns back, his eyes sparkling with mischief. 'Now you will make sure you wear my Christmas present tonight, won't you? I think it would be extremely bad taste not to!' Before I can reply, he winks at me and strides off down the path whistling.

I close the door and shake my head. Then I reach for the bell next to the door, find the control switch, and set it firmly to off.

Fourteen

I call on Charlie with Wilson as agreed at two o'clock, and we take one of our usual routes across town, over the bridge and on to the sandy beach. The weather is cold, but bright and sunny, and by the time we're halfway across the sand I'm wishing I'd worn my sunglasses, the glare from the sea and sand is so strong.

'So what is this big surprise?' I ask Charlie after we've been walking for a while. Wilson is doing his usual investigation of the sand, but I notice he doesn't stray quite as far away from us across the beach as he used to.

'In good time, Gracie, in good time,' Charlie says, smiling secretively.

'What are you hiding, Charlie Parker?' I ask, narrowing my eyes at him. 'What's going on?'

Charlie sighs. 'Well, you know how well the café has been doing?'

I do; Charlie regularly writes to me in Edinburgh and tells me all about what's happening in Sandybridge – any news or gossip, and what's going on in his own life. 'Yes . . .'

'And how we expanded into lunchtime deliveries?'

'Yes . . .'

'Well now we're expanding again.'

'How?'

'There,' Charlie says, pointing.

I follow the direction of his hand, and see the old lighthouse that we often walked towards along this stretch of the beach.

'Where?' I ask, slightly confused.

'The lighthouse,' Charlie repeats. 'It's been for sale for a while – too long in fact. So the price kept dropping and dropping, and I kept watching it while it did.'

'Why?'

'So I could buy it if the price went low enough.'

'Yes, I gathered that. But would you want to buy a lighthouse? Are you thinking of changing jobs and becoming its keeper?'

Charlie laughs. 'No! It's disused now, isn't it? Has been for some time, since the new one was built years ago. And no, I'm not going to live in it; I'll live in the cottage next door, and use the actual lighthouse as the base for my new business.'

I stand on the sand and stare in disbelief at Charlie. 'What new business?' I manage to ask.

'The Lighthouse Bakery,' Charlie proudly announces. 'The idea is to produce home-made cakes, using as many natural ingredients and as few additives as possible. I'll start small, but I hope to expand in the future if it's profitable.'

'But how are *you* going to run a bakery? Can you cook?'

Charlie laughs. 'I have picked up a few skills here and there over the years working in the café. But I'm not the one who'll be doing the baking. Hopefully, my staff will.'

I look up at the old lighthouse again; much of its white paint peels from the exterior walls, and the rust-covered metal staircase that leads up to the entrance looks extremely rickety.

'But *here*?' I ask. 'Is it practical?'

'Oh yes, I've done my research, and I know exactly how I'm going to run the place. It's a lot bigger inside than it might seem from out here. I'm looking forward to the challenge of getting it refitted, and up and running. I think it will be a great marketing ploy – a Norfolk bakery in a lighthouse.'

'Well it's different, I suppose.'

'I'd like it if you were pleased for me, Gracie,' Charlie says, turning towards me. 'I'm very excited about this. The café was always Mum and Dad's, even after I got involved and we expanded. But this . . . ' he looks up at the lighthouse again, 'this will be all mine.'

'Of course I'm pleased for you, you silly thing,' I say, wrapping my arms around him and giving him a squeeze. 'It's a surprise, that's all.'

'I told you it would be.' Charlie grins. 'Now, do you want to see inside?'

'You bet I do!' I reply. 'Is it safe?'

Charlie gives me a dismissive look. 'Do you think I'd take *you* of all people in there if it wasn't?'

'Then what are we waiting for?' I grin. 'Let's go explore!'

*

We leave Wilson tied on a loose lead to the outside staircase. He isn't quite as energetic as he used to be, and looking at the height of the lighthouse, I assume there will be a lot of steps to climb inside.

'Wow!' I exclaim, as Charlie unlocks the door and we head inside. 'This is incredible!'

My head is fully tipped back as I gaze up above me. 'And so much bigger than I expected.'

'Told you so,' Charlie says proudly as we begin to climb the long black spiral staircase that dominates the central atrium. 'It's gonna take some work to get it up and running. But I can do it.'

'I know you can,' I tell him as we head higher and higher through the individual floors, each comprising a circular room. 'It's gonna be amazing!'

We finally reach the top, the old lantern room, and Charlie takes my hand as we squeeze past the huge glass lantern that once would have shone out over Sandybridge harbour to warn passing ships of their proximity to the shore. He guides me to the seaward-facing side of the lighthouse.

'Check out this view!' Charlie says, looking out through one of the many windows that circle the top floor.

I follow his gaze, and find myself looking out over a stunning view of Sandybridge bay; the bright winter sun already beginning to drop in the sky towards the khaki-grey sea. We move slightly to the left so we can now see the whole town of Sandybridge stretching out into the distance, from the promenade right out to the school. Then as we keep moving around the top of the lighthouse, we discover the familiar warm colours of Sandybridge Hall, standing proudly in its evergreen grounds.

'It's a full 360-degree view of our home town,' Charlie says. 'What more could you want?'

'You won't get any work done if you have an office up here,' I joke. 'You'll be looking out at the view all day!'

'I know, isn't it the best though?' Charlie says. 'Why would you want to go anywhere else, when you can look out at this?' He looks at me expectantly when I don't respond. 'Look, Gracie, I know all you want to do is travel the world when you've got your degree, but this lighthouse is *my* future, *my* chance to be a success. Only, I'm doing it in a slightly different way to you.'

'It doesn't matter what each of us wants as long as we're happy, does it?' I say, resting my head on his shoulder as we both stand looking out at the view over to Sandybridge Hall. 'Are you happy, Charlie?'

'I could be,' he says quietly, as if he's reassuring himself rather than answering my question, 'if I just give it time.'

Fifteen

I decided it would be a good idea to invite Charlie to join Danny and me at the pub tonight, partly because I couldn't see why I shouldn't; three old friends – well, classmates: Charlie and Danny were never the best of friends – catching up was better than two, surely? And partly because I knew if Charlie was there Danny wouldn't try anything; as much as my body still seemed to crave Danny, my mind certainly did not.

As I'm trying to decide what to wear, I find myself staring at the old typewriter again. After what Charlie had shown me earlier, and how happy he seemed at the prospect of setting up this new business, I can't help wondering whether the typewriter had been correct with its last piece of advice. Was being prevented from attending university actually the best thing that could have happened to Charlie? I'm still not convinced, but I am intrigued to find out what the typewriter might say about his new venture.

When I open the bottom drawer of the dressing table I

find I still have some plain A4 paper in there, so I pull a sheet free and I'm about to feed it into the typewriter for the first time in six years when I hesitate.

'It better be good this time, Remy, or whoever it is that's sending these notes,' I instruct the typewriter as I feed the paper on to the spool. 'Don't be sending me any coded messages this time. Just the facts, OK?'

I stand for a moment, watching the keys of the typewriter in the hope they might feel obliged to start bobbing up and down, typing out a new letter immediately. But as always when I watch, nothing happens.

Maybe that's it, I think as I head into the bathroom to clean my teeth. Maybe the letters were only meant for me when I was a teenager. No one said they were going to keep coming. I'd thought I was in control of them, by not allowing Remy to type any more advice; perhaps the truth was there had been no more advice to give.

I finish cleaning my teeth and wash my face, then head back across the landing, still undecided about what to wear tonight. Whatever I choose, it's not going to be something that will encourage Danny in any shape or form, I tell myself. Even if I have to wear a polo—

'Whoa!' I cry as I enter my bedroom.

While I've been away, Remy has been busy:

```
Dear Grace,
   How lovely to speak with you again after
all this time.
   Sadly the advice I bring you today is not
quite as pleasant as advice I've given you
in the past.
```

146

On New Year's Eve tragedy will befall
Sandybridge. You cannot stop this, but please do
what you can to prevent as many people as possible
from being involved.

I know you've lost faith in me. But everything
I tell you is meant with the best of intentions
for you, and for your family and friends.

Please listen.

Love, Me x

*

It's around eight o'clock as I make my way to the Sandybridge
Arms, one of the town's better pubs. I've asked Charlie to
meet us there at around eight thirty, long enough to give
Danny and me the chance to catch up, but not long enough
that he could try to work his magic on me. Danny, true to
form, is late. So I sit alone at a corner table nursing my beer,
surreptitiously watching the handful of drinkers occupying
the Sandybridge Arms this evening. Not exactly original, a
pub taking the name of its town, but the Sandybridge Arms
had been part of the Sandybridge estate back in the days
when the Claymore family owned most of the local area, and
the name, if not the family, still remained.

These days Sandybridge wasn't owned by anyone, apart
from its holidaymakers! If it wasn't for our constant stream of
tourists, many of the local businesses would most likely go
under, including Mum and Dad's.

Suddenly I feel quite protective of my home town, and
even though I'm trying my best not to think about it, the
letter I found in Remy earlier bothers me as I sip on my
lonely beer.

What could Remy mean, a tragedy is going to befall Sandybridge? That's a bit dramatic, surely, even for him?

I have to admit Remy had been pretty accurate when I was younger, but he'd never predicted anything like this before. Supposing he turned out to be right this time too? And if he was, what could I do about it?

I feel my tummy growl. Before coming out I had a quick sandwich made up of leftover Christmas turkey and salad, but some of the locals are having bar meals, and there's a distinct aroma of chicken and chips wafting up into my nostrils. My stomach and I seem to fight a never-ending battle. It appears to think I need to eat much more frequently, while my brain and my size 12 jeans disagree. So much of the time it's left complaining while my willpower claims victory.

To take my mind off Remy's letter and my growling stomach, I look around the pub's interior and I notice there are several small watercolour paintings and pencil sketches of Sandybridge Hall hanging on the walls amongst the dark wooden beams. Next to me is a portrait of the third Earl of Sandybridge, Robert Claymore. By his dress I would guess the painting must have been done in the late eighteenth century. I'm gazing at the picture, mentally checking my facts, when it strikes me there's something quite familiar about the scene. *But what?* I examine the painting more closely, and realise that the earl is standing by one of the stone gargoyles that guard the front of Sandybridge Hall to ward away evil spirits and scare intruders.

'Ah, that's where I know you from,' I tell the gargoyle. 'We found a key under one of you once.' And I smile as I remember Charlie and my first trip to explore the big house.

'Are you talking to a painting, Gracie?' a voice says, making me jump. 'What are they teaching you at that university?'

'Hi, Danny,' I reply calmly, turning around. 'You're late.'

'Did you expect anything else from me, Gracie?' he grins, not in the least bit apologetic. 'I thought you knew me better than that.'

I hold out my glass. 'Get the beer in and I'll forgive you!'

'So, tell me more about this boyfriend of yours,' Danny asks after he's been up to the bar. 'Is he good in bed?'

'Danny!' I hiss. 'As if I'm going to discuss that with you!'

'I just like to know what I'm up against. Can't have someone beating me in the battle of the bonk!'

I shake my head at his use of the awful eighties slang. 'Do you ever stop?'

'Nope!' He flashes me another grin and takes a large sip of his beer. 'Most ladies don't want me to!'

'Well I do. It was over between us a long time ago, Danny, and I have no intention of starting anything up again, do you understand?'

Danny puts on his best gloomy face and looks down into his beer. Then, quick as a flash, he look up at me and winks. 'Ah, you always were a tough nut to crack, Gracie!'

'You better believe it!' I tell him, secretly enjoying his flirting a bit too much. I place my elbow on the table between us, and rest my chin on the palm of my hand. 'A hard nut with a *very* soft centre!'

'Don't I know it . . . ' Danny murmurs in a soft voice, leaning in towards me across the table so our faces are close. But this time the expression on his handsome face suggests he isn't messing. 'I miss you,' he says, to my surprise. 'There's been other girls since you and I were together, I'm not denying that.

149

Lots of girls, actually . . . ' he adds wistfully, thinking about it for a second. 'But none of them have got close to you, Gracie. Not one.'

I don't know what to say. I hadn't been expecting this at all.

'I know we're miles away from each other most of the time these days, but couldn't we give it another try? I'm sure this Johnny chap can't feel the same way about you as I do.'

'I . . . er . . . ' Come on, brain, I urge, even though my heart is racing far ahead right now in the battle of sense versus feelings. I need you to win this one!

Someone clears their throat next to us, and I spin around. *Charlie!*

I immediately jump up from my chair to embrace him. 'You made it!' I cry, sounding far too excited.

'Yes . . . ' Charlie says, peeling my arms from his shoulders. 'Did you think I wouldn't then?' He looks warily at Danny, who seems equally as unenthused to see him.

'Charlie,' Danny says, acknowledging him. 'I thought Gracie and me were flying solo tonight? We don't need a chaperone.'

'I asked Charlie to come and have a drink with us,' I tell Danny. 'I thought it might be nice if we *all* caught up, rather than just the two of us.'

'I'll go if I'm not welcome,' Charlie says, turning to leave. 'The two of you looked pretty cosy when I arrived.'

'Well, three's a crowd 'n' all that,' Danny says deliberately.

I glare at Danny.

'No, Charlie, I want you to stay,' I plead. 'Please, come and sit down with us.' I pull out a chair for him.

He looks at Danny, who shrugs in reply. So Charlie takes

the chair and sits down next to us. 'Seems like the lady wants me to stay,' he tells Danny, equally purposefully.

I have to laugh. 'This isn't the Wild West, you know,' I tell them. 'You two will be duelling with pistols over me next.'

I'm delighted when I see both of them smile.

'Right, now let's just try to get along for one evening, shall we?' I ask hopefully.

Charlie nods while Danny mumbles something that sounds like, 'I spose.'

'So, my round then?' Charlie offers in the spirit of forgiveness. 'Danny, what ya having?'

I smile gratefully at Charlie.

'No, this one's on me, mate,' Danny pipes up. 'I insist.'

I do the same to Danny.

'Mine's a pint of Adnams then,' Charlie says. 'Cheers.'

'Good choice.' Danny nods. 'Gracie?'

I look at my glass. It should be my round, but I don't want to break the truce that seems to have sprung up between Danny and Charlie. 'Vodka and Coke, please, Danny.'

'Right,' he says, standing up. 'Two pints of Adnams and a double vodka and Coke. Be right back!'

'No!' I call after him as he makes his way up to the bar. 'I only wanted a single!'

But my plea falls on deaf ears, so I turn to Charlie.

'Thanks for coming,' I tell him. 'I appreciate it.'

'Are you sure I won't be playing gooseberry?' Charlie picks up a beer mat and turns the edges around on top of the table. 'You two looked pretty cosy a moment ago.'

'No, of course not!' I insist. 'That was just Danny being Danny. I was playing him at his own game for a bit.'

'You looked like you were enjoying it.' Instead of twiddling

151

the beer mat around, Charlie now begins stacking several mats up in a sort of house shape.

'Maybe I was ... a bit. Don't tell me you don't enjoy it when girls flirt with you?'

Charlie looks at me incredulously. 'Yeah, like that happens.'

'Of course it does! Maybe you choose not to see it, that's all.'

'Grace, girls do not flirt with me. Never have. Probably never will. I'm the little ginger kid with the goofy teeth. That's how people remember me around here.'

'Are you kidding me?' I ask, amazed he actually thinks this. 'You're gorgeous now. You're not the little ginger kid any more, you're a very handsome young man with fabulous *strawberry blond* hair, and the loveliest, kindest blue eyes I've ever seen!'

Charlie looks at me with a mixture of surprise, embarrassment and something else I can't quite place. 'Don't be daft,' he mumbles, his cheeks flushing pink. 'I'm not handsome.'

'Yes, you are!' I correct him. 'You may not see it, but I've seen how the girls look at you when we're out together.'

'What girls?' Charlie snorts. 'You're imagining things.'

I try to recall a specific occasion. 'What about earlier today when we went for our walk with Wilson? There was that girl with the two Yorkshire terriers we passed on the beach – she gave you the eye.'

'No she didn't.'

'I'm telling you she did. If I hadn't been with you, I bet she would've tried to strike up a conversation. She probably assumed I was your girlfriend or something!' I grin at the thought.

'Would that be so bad?' Charlie asks, fiddling with the beer mats again. This time he flips one up from the side of the table and tries to catch it.

I look at him to see if he's joking. But he appears to be serious.

'No, of course not,' I reply, suddenly feeling incredibly awkward. I feel my own cheeks getting hot. 'Any girlfriend of yours would be the luckiest girl ever.'

Charlie stops his card game and looks at me. 'Do you really think that?'

'Of course!' I try to reply in a reassuring voice.

Charlie nods slowly. 'Good, because the thing is, Gracie, there's something I've wanted—'

'God, they're so slow up at that bar,' Danny interrupts as he returns to the table with our drinks. 'If this was London, people would walk out!' He puts down the two pints of beer. 'Back in a mo with yours, Gracie!' he says, heading to the bar again.

'What were you going to say?' I ask Charlie.

He shakes his head. 'It doesn't matter. Some other time.'

'Right, and here's your vodka and Coke,' Danny says, plonking my glass on the table in front of me. 'Christ, what's happened to all the beer mats?'

Sixteen

'So what have you been up to over Christmas?' I ask Danny later when it's Charlie's turn to go up to the bar. There's been a nice atmosphere around the table since Charlie and Danny called a truce, and for the time being anyway, they seem to have forgotten any animosity between them.

'Not much, it's pretty dull around here. It's funny, when I lived here it seemed like the centre of everything, you know?'

I nod. 'Once you've lived in a big city, Sandybridge seems very . . . ' I struggle to find the right word.

'Insignificant,' Danny finishes for me.

'No, that's not what I meant at all. Sandybridge isn't insignificant. It might be a little quieter than me and you are used to now, but it has its charms.'

'Name one,' Danny demands. 'I bet you can't.'

I think hard. 'Erm . . . oh, I know – the beaches! You can

take some lovely walks along the shingle one, and the sandy one goes on for miles and miles. It's beautiful.'

'Hmm, all right, I'll give you that,' Danny says grudgingly. 'Both the beaches are quite cool, if you like that sort of thing. Bet you can't name another though.'

I think again. 'Sandybridge Hall? That's pretty and it has a colourful history, too. I did some reading up on it. Did you know that—'

'A beach and an old house!' Danny interrupts, grinning at me. 'It's hardly Rough Guide territory, is it?'

'No, it's not, but not everyone's cut out for city living. Some people like a quieter life. Like Charlie, for instance.' I gesture towards Charlie, returning with our drinks.

'What am I getting blamed for now?' he says amiably, putting the refilled glasses on the table and sitting down again.

'Gracie says you're happy living a sheltered existence here in Sandybridge, and that you don't want to get out into the big, bad world and live life.'

'I did not say that!' I protest as Charlie looks in astonishment at me. 'I said some people like a quiet life, that's all. They're not cut out for fast-pace living.'

'Is that what you really think?' Charlie asks, looking hurt. 'That the fact I like living in Sandybridge means I don't have any ambition, any goals in life?'

'Sounds like it to me,' Danny pipes up.

And there was me thinking they were getting on well now.

'Shut up, Danny!' I tell him. 'No, that's not what I think, Charlie, you know I don't. But you have to admit you've always been happy here.'

Charlie nods. 'Yes, I can't deny it, but what's wrong with

155

that? Just because I'm not flitting off to a capital city to study at university doesn't mean I can't be successful.'

'I never said you couldn't, did I?' I respond, feeling hurt that Charlie should take this the wrong way.

Silence falls around the table as Charlie and I both take long gulps of our drinks while an amused Danny watches us.

'You two are like an old married couple sometimes,' he says, shaking his head. 'No wonder I thought the two of you were together when I first met you.'

I glance over the top of my glass at Charlie, who I find is doing the same.

'Sorry,' I say, lowering my glass and smiling apologetically at him.

'Me too,' Charlie replies, reaching out his hand and squeezing mine.

'Right, now that little tiff is over, let's talk parties!' Danny says, banging the table with his hand. 'Who's going to the New Year's Eve bash at the hall?'

'Sandybridge Hall?' I ask cautiously.

'Yeah, I hear there's going to be a big party to bring in the New Year. The dude that owns it now wants to start using it as a party venue, so my mum said. Make some money from the old place. So he's throwing a New Year's Eve party for the residents of Sandybridge as a sort of test run.'

Charlie pulls a face. 'Yeah, I heard that too. But Sandybridge Hall isn't a venue for raucous parties any more, it's a beautiful old Tudor manor. It's a shame it can't be preserved for future generations to enjoy instead of being desecrated by drunken yobs. Don't you agree, Gracie?'

Could this be what Remy had been talking about? *On New Year's Eve tragedy will befall Sandybridge . . .* was it going to be at this party? 'I have to agree with Charlie,' I say hurriedly. 'I'm not sure I'd like to see the hall trashed.'

'And even if we did want to go, I heard the tickets are really expensive,' Charlie adds.

'I'll pay for us,' Danny says, not taking the hint. 'Come on, Gracie, it'll be a laugh, and there's not much of that in Sandybridge in the winter.'

'But surely you can't afford it – we're students, remember?'

'I got a nice payout from the folks for Christmas,' Danny says. 'I'm feeling flush right now. I'll pay for you too, Charlie, if you like.'

'If I *was* to go, I'd pay my own way, thanks,' Charlie says proudly.

Danny shrugs.

'No, no one is going!' I say it so sharply they both look at me in surprise. 'I mean ... I don't think these fancy parties are worth it. Wouldn't we all be better off having a drink here to see in the New Year?'

I'm still not sure if this party was what Remy was talking about, but if it was, I don't want to take a chance on any of my friends being there in case he was right.

'Here is dull,' Danny says, looking around him at the few people in the bar tonight. 'The most excitement we'll have if we stay here on New Year's Eve is waiting to see if Cyril runs out of salt-and-vinegar crisps!'

'Gracie, I'll be happy doing whatever you want to do,' Charlie says softly. 'If you want to go to Sandybridge Hall we can, if not, then we won't.'

I nod gratefully at him.

'Danny,' I try to say in my best sexy-sounding voice, 'we could have much more fun if we stayed here.' I lean in towards him so that he has the chance to glance down my shirt at my cleavage. 'It could be just like old times ...' I whisper softly.

'Like old times, hmm?' Danny says, looking up with a knowing smile. Then he remembers Charlie. 'What, the three of us? Well, that will be different!'

'Yeah, the three of us,' I reply, pretty sure my idea of how we're going to spend New Year's Eve is not the same as Danny has in mind. 'OK with that, Charlie?'

Charlie pulls a *What are you up to now?* expression. 'Whatever you want, Gracie,' he says, looking puzzled. 'Whatever you want.'

What I wanted was for Remy to be wrong. What I wanted was for everyone I cared about to stay safe on New Year's Eve.

Remy had warned of a 'tragedy' – and it had to be something really awful if he felt the need to tell me about it – but how was I supposed to prevent people from being involved when I didn't know what was going to happen myself?

Seventeen

'What are you doing tonight, Grace?' Mum asks me over breakfast at the beginning of the last day of 1992.

'Charlie, Danny and I are meeting up at the pub for a few drinks, nothing special,' I reply as I reach across the table for another slice of toast. I've not stopped eating since I got back; the sea air is definitely giving me a huge appetite.

'That's nice,' Mum says, taking a sip of her tea. 'It's good you keep up with Charlie, he's a lovely boy, always has been.'

'Charlie is my best friend, of course I *keep up with him*, that will never change wherever we both are.'

Mum smiles knowingly at Dad.

'What?' I demand. 'Why are you looking like that?'

'I'm glad you feel that way, Grace, but life has a way of changing as we get older. New people come into our lives, boyfriends, girlfriends, we get married, have children. People that once were important to us often become distant memories.'

'Well that won't happen to me and Charlie,' I reply, wondering how they could even think that. I couldn't comprehend a life without Charlie in it somewhere. Obviously things have changed now I'm in Edinburgh, but we still keep in touch with letters and regular phone calls, and I'm always extremely happy when I know I'll be seeing him again. 'We'll always stay in touch whatever happens.'

'Good girl,' Dad says, nodding his head over the top of his newspaper. 'Stay true to who you are, love, and keep those around you that know you best.'

Mum and I both stare at Dad. He doesn't usually say much, so to make a little speech like that is quite profound for him.

'And what about Danny?' Mum asks, looking away from Dad. 'Are you two back together? I know you've been seeing him while you've been home. Such a handsome young man now.'

'*Mum!*' I almost choke on my toast. 'No, I haven't been seeing him. Not in the way you mean, anyway. We've been out a couple of times for a drink, that's all, and one of those times Charlie was there, so it was hardly a date!'

Mum purses her lips and looks at Dad for support, but he continues reading his paper.

'Well, I was talking to Kathleen the other day and we were both saying what a shame it was when you two split up. You were a lovely-looking couple, you were. Still are, actually.'

'I can't believe you were talking to Danny's mum about me!'

160

'Not about you as such, just about our children in general and how they're getting on.'

I shake my head, and take another bite of my toast.

'There is nothing going on between Danny and me,' I insist after I've chewed and swallowed. 'Nothing like that anyway.'

Although Danny had made it pretty apparent he'd like there to be. Not only in the pub with Charlie, but on a subsequent occasion too, when we'd met up for a coffee, and sat on the seawall together drinking from polystyrene cups in the sunshine. It took all my willpower to resist Danny when he was on full charm offensive. But I'd felt quite proud, and strangely a little sad, that I had resisted.

'So what are you two doing tonight then?' I ask, trying to steer the subject away from Danny. I spread more jam on to my toast and take another bite. I expect them to say they'll be staying in watching the TV, reading, or something equally quiet – that's what they usually do at New Year. My parents have never been the greatest of party animals, particularly on the biggest party night of the year.

'We're going to the do at Sandybridge Hall,' Mum says.

This time I really do choke on my toast.

Mum leaps up and begins patting me ferociously on the back.

'I . . . I'm fine, Mum,' I cough, taking a swig of my orange juice. 'Honestly.'

Mum sits down again.

'Why are you going there?' I demand, as I recover from my choking and my shock.

'We thought it would be nice,' Mum says. 'Didn't we, Bob?'

Dad tips his paper forward and nods.

'We never go out, so when we heard there was going to be a big party at the hall we thought, why not?' Mum says, looking quite pleased with herself.

'Dad?' I ask, hoping to appeal to his more stagnant nature.

'It was your mum's idea,' he says, looking up again. 'She wanted to go out for a change.'

'And so we should, Bob! We work hard at that shop, we deserve to let our hair down a bit.'

I look at Dad again; if he let any more hair down he'd be as bald as that guy from the band Right Said Fred.

'Well maybe not your dad!' Mum smiles at her joke.

'Thanks, Janet,' Dad says, rolling his eyes. 'I love you too.'

Oh God, what am I going to do? I can't stop them going – what am I supposed to say: 'Mum, Dad, a typewriter warned me there would be a tragedy in Sandybridge tonight and I think it might be at your party'? And what if they did take heed and nothing happened; how silly would I look then?

'Be careful,' I tell them. 'At the party,' I add, when they look bemused.

'Are you telling *us* to be careful now?' Dad laughs. 'I thought it was supposed to be the other way around!'

'Please, just do,' I say, as I stand up and begin clearing the table. 'You never know what might happen.'

But I knew someone that did . . .

After I've cleared the breakfast things, I head upstairs to my bedroom with every intention of asking Remy for more advice. But when I get there I'm surprised to find a typed note already waiting for me in his spool.

Dear Grace,

    I know you doubt me sometimes, but there will
be danger in Sandybridge tonight I promise you.

    I wish I could tell you what, but you know I'm
not allowed specifics, only general guidance.

    Please prevent as many people as possible
from being harmed.

    Love, Me x

*

'You want me to do what?' Charlie asks when I find him working in the café later that morning.

'I need you to help me stop anyone going to the party at Sandybridge Hall tonight.'

After reading the last letter from Remy I'd sat on the edge of my old single bed and stared silently up at the posters on my wall.

Michael J. Fox and A-Ha had made way for Tom Hanks and *Moonlighting*'s Cybill Shepherd and Bruce Willis before I'd left for university, but they were turning out to be no help whatsoever with my current dilemma.

'Tom, what would you do if this was one of your movies? How would you stop the party from going ahead?'

Probably with the help of a mermaid, a giant piano, or a slobbery dog! None of which I had. Well, there was Wilson, but I couldn't see him being much use. I looked up at Cybill Shepherd; I needed a wise-cracking sidekick like she had in Bruce Willis to help me, but where was I going to find one of those?

'Why?' Charlie is busy clearing a table, so I help him carry some of the dirty dishes back to the kitchen.

'I can't tell you that.'

Charlie finishes emptying his crockery into the dishwasher, then he stands up to face me. 'So I'll ask you the same thing again, Grace – why?'

I fold my arms. 'Can't you help me without knowing why?'

'No.' Charlie pulls a piece of paper from the small pile of orders on the counter. 'Tea for two,' he says, reading it, and begins filling a tray with cups and saucers. 'It may be New Year's Eve but we are quite busy, Grace. The mild weather seems to have brought a few people to the coast for a day out.'

'I know, and I'm sorry to bother you, but I don't know where else to turn.'

Charlie pauses for a moment and looks at me.

'You sound serious.'

'I am.'

'And you're not going to tell me why?'

I shake my head. 'Please, Charlie,' I plead. 'I know it sounds mad, but I really need your help with this.'

Charlie sighs. 'I'm not sure, Grace. It's a big thing you're asking me to do, especially when you won't tell me why we need to do it in the first place.'

'Do you trust me?' I ask suddenly.

'Of course I do. I'd trust you with my life.'

'Then help me. *Please* ...'

Charlie sighs heavily again. 'I must be mad,' he says, shaking his head, 'but OK, I'll help you. And heaven help *me* if anyone finds out what we're up to: that party has been planned by the owner for months. This better be good, Gracie!'

'*Thank you!*' I give Charlie a huge bear hug. 'You won't regret it, I promise!'

164

'I'd better not. So now you've got me to agree, just how do you plan on preventing this party from taking place?'

I screw my nose up. 'Ah, that's the thing ... I don't really know. I was kind of hoping you might be able to come up with some ideas ...'

Eighteen

'Just going, Mum!' I call from the hallway as I pull on my coat ready to head off to the Sandybridge Arms that night.

'Grace, have you seen our tickets for the party?' Mum calls back. 'Dad and I have looked everywhere for them.'

I poke my head around the kitchen door and see my parents in full party attire, desperately searching the kitchen.

'Nope. When did you last see them?' I ask innocently, knowing full well their missing tickets are safely hidden at the bottom of the bag I currently have slung over my shoulder.

'I'm sure I left them on the top of the bread bin,' Mum says, anxiously looking around the kitchen again. 'Are you sure you haven't moved them?'

I shake my head. I didn't like lying to my parents, but this was for their own good.

Mum sighs. 'We won't get in without them. Diane Lewis says it's all very formal and proper. They certainly won't let us in without a ticket.'

'Maybe it's for the best,' Dad says, removing his suit jacket and sitting down at the kitchen table.

'You never really wanted to go, did you?' Mum snaps, desperately sliding things forward on the kitchen counters, so she can look behind them. 'This suits you just fine. Maybe it's you who's hidden our tickets!'

'Don't be daft, Janet. Why would I do that? It would only be a waste of money if we've paid for them.'

Mum makes a sort of harrumphing noise.

'Gotta go!' I call hurriedly before I get dragged into their argument, or worse, searching for the errant tickets. 'Hope you find them!'

'At least someone will have a good evening,' I hear Mum say to Dad as I close the front door.

I skip happily along the street, tapping my bag. Part one of the plan complete; now I just have to hope part two goes as smoothly . . .

Not surprisingly, the pub is packed when I get there, but I soon find Charlie sitting at a table in the corner waiting with an orange juice for me, and a Coke for him. We've agreed not to drink tonight; we want to keep our wits about us.

'Everything go to plan?' Charlie asks as I sit down next to him.

I nod. 'Yup! Got their tickets right here.' I tap my bag again.

'Good, now will you tell me what it is we're actually trying to prevent happening at Sandybridge Hall tonight?'

I take a sip of my juice and look at Charlie. 'I don't know.'

'You don't know!' he exclaims, his eyes opening wide in astonishment. 'Then what are we doing all this for?'

'Shush,' I whisper. 'We don't want everyone to know what we got up to earlier, do we?'

After much thought Charlie had come up with the idea that we cause a power cut at the hall. He'd spoken to his brother, who these days was working as an electrician in Manchester, and asked him a few choice questions about electrics and old houses. Then, having found our way into the grounds in the same way we did when we were fifteen, we'd snuck inside the house in amongst all the staff busily preparing for the party.

I was quite astonished how much the hall had changed since I was last there. When Charlie and I had wandered through here with Wilson six years ago, the interiors had been quite worn and dishevelled, though much of the original décor remained. Now the house seemed completely transformed. Although the new décor wasn't modern in a way that detracted from the age of the house, it was fresh and new. There were new wallpapers and floor coverings, new light fittings, and new pictures that hung from wooden rails. It looked more like a chic hotel than a stately home.

Luckily for us, there had been so many hired helpers getting everything ready for the party that we were able to sneak in unchallenged. We'd quickly found our way down on to the lower floors of the house, where domestic staff would once have dwelled, waiting for one of the many service bells to ring, to summon them to do the bidding of their employers.

As soon as we'd located the electricity circuit board, Charlie had set about fitting a timer to the switch that controlled all the house lights, so at 7.45 p.m. the house would be plunged into complete darkness. We figured this was when most of the guests would be arriving for the party. Our hope was that it would cause as little disruption as possible, but would have the desired effect of forcing the cancellation of the party.

Everything had gone swimmingly until, on our way out, one of the caterers had mistaken us for staff and asked us to carry some trays of food from his van down to the kitchen. So we'd done as he asked, desperately hoping no one would notice us. Luckily everyone was so busy they hadn't noticed a couple of extra helpers, so we'd delivered our trays and managed to sneak away immediately afterwards, once again following the shortcut that led through the woods and back out on to the beach. Then we'd run along the sand together, laughing and smiling like we had as children.

'Do I want people to know we broke into someone's house and messed with their electrics?' Charlie whispers now as he gazes furtively around the pub. 'No, I don't thank you very much. All I want to know is *why* we did it!'

He wasn't going to let it go, and probably quite rightly so. If it had been the other way around, and Charlie had asked me to do something but wouldn't tell me why, I'd have gone on and on until he told me.

'I have a hunch something bad is going to happen there tonight,' I reply as honestly as I can.

'A *hunch*!'

I hush Charlie again.

'Yes, I get them sometimes. Sort of like a premonition.'

'What?'

'A premonition. It's like when—'

'Yes, I know what it is. But when did *you* start getting them?

'A few years ago,' I reply truthfully. 'It comes and goes but . . . ' I hesitate, 'it's usually right in the end.'

Charlie thinks about this. 'You're not winding me up, are you?'

I shake my head.

'You really think something bad is going to happen at Sandybridge Hall tonight?'

I nod. 'I don't know what specifically. I just think people will be in danger.'

'Hey up, drinking buds!' Danny says, leaning over our hunched shoulders. 'How's it hanging?' He lifts my glass and sniffs it, then he takes a sip. He pulls a face. Then he does the same to Charlie's Coke. 'And why, pray tell, are you two not drinking? It's New Year's Eve!'

'We're waiting for you, of course!' I say, springing to my feet. 'My round, what ya having, Danny?'

I get the drinks in, and when I return to our table, I find Charlie and Danny in deep discussion about something.

Pleased to see them getting on at last, I linger a few steps away from the table to enjoy the moment.

'Hurry up, Gracie!' Danny glances over and sees me dithering with his drink. 'I've got some catching up to do!'

'Danny was just telling me about the party up at Sandybridge Hall,' Charlie says quite deliberately as I arrive at the table. As Danny turns to take his drink from me, Charlie raises his eyebrows at me behind Danny's back. 'How he's glad we didn't go now.'

'Oh, why's that?' I ask, putting the other two drinks on the table and sitting down again.

'Sounds like it's only for the elderly and ancient,' Danny says, rolling his eyes. He takes a sip from his pint of lager. 'I thought it was going to be some fantastic rave, with bands and stuff, but it turns out it's a formal dinner-dance bore.'

'Tell Gracie how you know this,' Charlie says, leading him.

'My parents have gone to it.' Danny pulls a face. 'Can you imagine how humiliating it would have been, being there with them strutting their stuff on the dance floor!'

This is not what I want to hear. I know Danny's parents well, from when we'd dated. They're a lovely couple and couldn't do enough for me when I was Danny's girlfriend.

I look at Charlie. He shrugs.

'I did hear the party was almost cancelled,' Danny says, taking another slug of his beer.

'Why?' I ask, meeting Charlie's eyes again.

'Apparently someone had been messing with the electrics at the hall, nearly started a fire. If it hadn't been for some lighting guy they'd hired, who was checking out the circuits or something to see if the old place could provide the power he required, the whole hall could have gone up in flames.'

I swallow hard. That was us. We'd caused that. By trying to prevent something happening, we could have caused a disaster. It was happening again; that blasted typewriter, why couldn't it get it right!

'So the party's gone ahead as planned?' I ask as evenly as I can.

I glance at Charlie, he doesn't look happy.

Danny nods. 'Spose so. Why wouldn't it? At least I know my parents aren't going to turn up in here tonight and embarrass me, so that's something.'

'Danny, do you believe in intuition?' I suddenly ask.

171

'What?'

'Intuition, like a hunch, your gut instinct, that kind of thing.'

'Do you mean like premonitions? I've been reading this really cool book about how the ancient tribes used to rely on wise men to predict what was going to happen to them – you know, when they should go into battle, when they should move their herds, when—'

'Yes, exactly like that,' I say, interrupting him. 'The thing is, I've had one.'

Danny looks at me. 'You're having me on, right?'

I shake my head. 'No, I've had a premonition that something bad will happen at Sandybridge Hall tonight.'

'What sort of something?'

'That's just it, I don't know. But I know people are going to get hurt.'

Danny stares at me. Then he grins. 'Ah, nice one, you two!' He looks at Charlie now too. 'You really had me going there for a moment.' Still grinning, he lifts his pint glass and begins drinking from it.

'No, I'm deadly serious. Look.' I rummage in my bag and pull my parents' party tickets from the bottom of it. 'If I wasn't sure something was going to happen, why would I have stolen these from my mum and dad?'

Danny takes the tickets from me and examines them.

'I didn't want them to go to the party, Danny, any more than I wouldn't want your parents being there either. It was Charlie and I that messed with the electrics at the hall. We were trying to prevent the party going ahead.' I take the tickets back from Danny. 'I'm sure something is going to happen up there tonight, Danny, and we need to get everyone out of the hall before it does; including your mum and dad. We don't know how though. We tried our only idea earlier, and that's failed.'

Danny, his mind obviously working overtime, looks between Charlie and me. Eventually he nods slowly. 'You two may not know how to evacuate a large building. But *I* know just the thing.'

Nineteen

'Are you sure about this, Danny?' Charlie asks as we all crouch down behind a bush in the Sandybridge Hall gardens. 'It seems a bit dangerous.'

'Not at all, mate. The smoke is fairly harmless, and people aren't going to hang around breathing it in once the room is filled with it, are they? They'll head for those great glass doors. It'll be fine.'

'I'm still not sure ... ' Charlie says, sounding worried. 'Throwing flares into a room filled with people seems like a recipe for disaster to me.'

After Danny had told us his idea, we'd all left the pub and headed for the sailing equipment shop that Danny's dad ran. Charlie and I had waited outside while Danny ran to his house to fetch a key for the shop, then we watched while Danny unlocked the door and disabled the intruder alarm. We'd all crept inside, and Danny had quickly found what he was looking for – marine smoke flares of the sort carried in boats' emergency kits for use in a crisis.

Now we were hiding in the gardens at Sandybridge Hall like criminals, trying to work out how to get into the house to throw the smoke-filled canisters into the party, so the house would evacuate.

'Not as much of a disaster as will befall them if they don't leave,' I point out.

'You don't know that for sure, Grace,' Charlie maintains. 'This is all in your mind at the moment.'

'It's not in my mind!' I cry, then I slap my hand over my mouth when the other two glare at me. 'I have proof,' I whisper.

'What proof?' Charlie asks suspiciously.

The last letter from Remy was not where I usually kept his notes, safely locked up in my chest of drawers. This time I'd folded it carefully and put it in the side pocket of my bag. I didn't know why; maybe I suspected I'd need it as evidence tonight.

As I hesitate with my hand over my bag, wondering whether I should tell Charlie and Danny about Remy, I hear it.

We all hear it.

A noise that sounds like a hundred cannons going off at once. A boom so loud we automatically cover our ears. Then we slowly release them to allow ourselves the opportunity to look around the bush to see what's happened.

In front of us is Sandybridge Hall, but instead of seeing people enjoying themselves chatting, laughing and dancing through the windows of the ballroom, all we now see are dancing flames. The cosy glow of the yellow-red brickwork has become even warmer, as those same flames flicker ominously through the broken glass of the windows.

I look with horror at Charlie, who looks as terrified as I feel.

'Run down to the phone box and dial 999, Grace,' he instructs.

'Who shall I ask for?' I stupidly ask.

'Everyone,' is Charlie's chilly reply. 'We'll need everyone.'

As I stand up and stumble around the front of the bush, I see a few people beginning to stagger through the shattered French windows, looking for a way across the moat to safety. Up until a few moments ago the windows had protected the partygoers from the chilly December evening, but now, all that's left are the shards of glass that lie at the bottom of the moat and strewn all over the grass.

The people fleeing from the building have grey, terror-filled faces, and most of them are either covered in blood, more shards of glass, or both as they emerge stunned from the ballroom and make for the narrow bridge at the back of the house.

'Go, Grace!' Charlie shouts, seeing me frozen to the spot. 'Run as fast as you can.'

I look at Danny, who is silently staring at the unfolding drama in front of us.

'I'll take care of Danny,' Charlie says, waving me on. 'You have to go!'

Without another backward glance at the house I run as fast as I can down the drive of Sandybridge Hall. As I race for the gate, the thought occurs to me that I've never actually used the correct entrance and exit before, only the shortcut that Charlie and I knew. I pray that the big black iron gates at the end of the drive will be open when I get there; I don't think I'd be able to clamber over the top of them in daylight, let alone in the dark. But as I approach the gates, I notice a light coming from the gatekeeper's lodge at the entrance.

I don't stop to think, there's no time. I simply pound as hard as I can on the door, then when no one appears, I start banging equally hard on the window.

I'm turning away in search of the nearest phone box when I hear an old man's voice coming from the doorway.

'What is it, love?' he asks.

'There's ... been ... an explosion ... up at the hall.' I'm so out of breath it's all I can do to get the words out. 'We need ... ambulances ... fire brigade – everyone!'

The old man, who's wearing a long nightshirt and a night-cap, looks like Wee Willy Winkie from the nursery rhyme. He stares at me for a moment, probably wondering whether I'm high or drunk. Deciding I'm neither, he steps out of his house, on to the drive, and looks up towards the hall. Already I can see flickering flames in some of the upstairs windows, and a nasty grey plume of smoke beginning to cover the previously moonlit sky.

'Right, dear,' he says smartly, pulling his nightcap off. 'Leave it with me.'

He hobbles back inside his house as fast as he can with his stick, and I follow him to make sure.

'I need the fire brigade, and some ambulances, and probably the police too ...' the old man says into his telephone as I stand there watching helplessly. 'Yes, that's right ... There's been some sort of explosion up at Sandybridge Hall. I suspect gas. There may be a lot of casualties, there was a party on up there tonight, see.'

The man finishes his phone call and turns to me. 'I don't know what use they'll be, but there's a first aid kit in the bathroom, and some blankets in the cupboard in the hall. You'll get up there much faster than I can if you take them, dear.'

I run and fetch what he says, then with the man waving his stick at me in encouragement from the lodge, I carry them as fast as I can up to the hall.

What I find as I reach the house resembles a scene from a disaster movie. People lying on the grass covered with gashes and wounds, while other less injured people, some still covered in glass, are trying to help them.

I look around for Charlie and Danny, but I can't see them anywhere. So I begin handing out the blankets to those in shock. I end up giving my first aid kit to my old maths teacher, Mr Johnson, who seems to have survived the blast quite well. He glances at me briefly in recognition before he moves to help someone less fortunate than himself.

Then at last I see Charlie. I barely recognise him, his face is so blackened by the smoke. The white shirt that he'd looked so smart in earlier this evening is ripped, and I can see the muscles of his torso tighten and relax as he half carries, half drags a man from the house. The man is hanging off Charlie's shoulder, and they both limp along to where Charlie places him safely down on the grass. Then without a break he wipes his forehead and stumbles back towards the house.

'Charlie!' I call. 'Charlie, wait!'

Charlie turns and sees me running towards him.

'Did you call 999?' he asks desperately, his blackened hands gripping my upper arms.

178

'Yes ... well, *I* didn't but ... oh that doesn't matter – they're on their way, that's all that counts.'

Charlie nods. 'Good.' Then he turns and starts to head towards the hall again, but I grab his arm.

'Wait, you can't go in there!'

'Already have – several times. There's still people in there, Grace. Trapped by the burnt beams that have fallen. I have to go.'

'No! Not if you're putting yourself at risk you don't.'

'Have you seen Danny?' Charlie asks, looking around at the carnage.

'No. Why, is he doing the same as you?'

Charlie sighs and rubs his eyes where the smoke is getting to them. 'He ran into the house shortly after you left when he realised his parents were still in there. Haven't seen him since.'

'But I've seen Kathleen and Lionel, they're sitting over there by the tree. I gave them a blanket.'

Charlie looks towards the house again. The flames look even bigger and more aggressive now.

'You don't think ...' I gasp. 'Oh God, he's not still in there, is he?'

We both look towards the burning building. I grab Charlie's arm as he tries to leave again. 'Charlie, no! You'll die if you go in there.'

'But what about the people still trapped?' he cries, staring wildly at me through blackened eyes. 'What about Danny?'

I've never been so relieved to hear the sirens of the emergency services as I am at this moment. We turn to see the flashing lights of their vehicles tearing up the drive of

Sandybridge Hall. 'Let the experts deal with it now, Charlie. You've done your bit.'

But as I stare up at the flame-filled house, I know Charlie is wondering exactly the same thing as me:

Where is Danny?

Dear Grace

Things aren't always what they seem.

I know you think you failed in stopping the tragedy in Sandybridge, but you didn't. In fact you did just as I asked: you prevented more people from being hurt than needed to be.

Yes, your friend was injured, and I know once again you are blaming yourself for that. But please remember, Grace, life isn't always as clear-cut as it seems. Sometimes good comes from bad.

I know it will be a while before we speak again. But I'm always here if you need me.

Love, Me x

Summer 2016

I leave the station, after a kind man has helped me lift my package safely into the boot of my car, and I drive slowly towards Sandybridge High Street. Lobster Pot Alley, where our shop is situated, has been pedestrianised, so these days you can't easily park outside the door the way my parents used to in their van. I pull up as close as I can in the Range Rover, then I set off on foot, weaving as fast as I can through the throng of holiday-makers meandering about in the sunshine, to where I know Olivia and Josh will be waiting for me.

As I walk the short distance to the shop, I pass by several other shops and businesses, some of which have been in Sandybridge almost as long as we have. We've been luckier than many small towns: Sandybridge shopkeepers seem to have survived the credit crunch and the recession, and are still trading happily and profitably alongside the bigger chains that have now joined them.

'Afternoon, Grace,' several people call from their open shop doorways as I pass by. 'Lovely day!'

'Good afternoon,' I call back. But I'm not so sure it is a lovely day or a good afternoon. I know what's coming later.

As I'd hoped, Olivia and Josh are there to greet me at the antiques shop.

'Hello, Grace,' Olivia says. 'Thank you so much for doing this, I couldn't bear to risk leaving it at the station. We did that once before with a vase, and it ended up in pieces.'

'It's fine. No worries,' I lie. I make my way towards the shop door, hoping Josh will take the hint and follow me. But he doesn't.

'How're things up at the house?' he asks jovially. 'Are you busy?'

I usually have a lot of time for both Josh and Olivia, they've been a godsend to our little shop, but today I'm on borrowed time.

'Yes we are. Very busy.' I half smile and turn to the door again.

'That's great, and how's the rehab centre going?'

'It's going well. Look, I don't mean to be rude, but I didn't buy a pay-and-display ticket and I think we should get back to the car as quickly as possible.'

'Oh, of course,' Josh says. 'I'll go get the trolley.'

Josh and I leave the shop and head towards my car, Josh pushing the metal trolley that's used to move heavier objects around the shop.

When we arrive at the Range Rover, Joseph, our local traffic warden, is standing looking with interest at my ticketless car.

'Oh, is this yours, Grace?' he asks, seeing us hurrying along the path.

'Yes, Joe, I'm unloading for the shop – closest I could get. Is that OK?'

'Course it is!' Joe replies, smiling at me. 'Do you need a hand?'

With relief, I help Josh and Joe lift the parcel from the car, then Josh arranges it on his trolley. 'You two coming in for a cuppa?' he asks, as he begins to make his way slowly along the street pushing the metal trolley in front of him.

'On duty, mate,' Joe replies. 'Can't.'

'Thanks for the offer, Josh,' I call to his departing figure, 'but not today, I have to be somewhere!'

'No worries! Another time then,' Josh calls and he continues happily down the street with his latest acquisition for the shop.

'Somewhere important?' Joe enquires as I close the boot and head around to the driver's door.

'Very,' I reply, as I open the door. 'Thanks for not giving me a ticket, Joe,' I say as I climb into the driver's seat. 'Appreciate that.'

'I couldn't be giving the loveliest lady in Sandybridge a ticket now, could I?' Joe grins.

'Ah, you always were smooth, Joe!' I smile at him.

'Well you know if it wasn't for your other half, I'd be asking you out,' Joe says. 'I've told you that before.'

'You have indeed.' I feel awkward. Joe has always made it quite clear that if I wasn't happily married, he'd be right there. 'Anyway, must be going. See you soon, Joe.' I close my door, and Joe taps the side of the Range Rover as I pull out into the traffic.

But as I drive towards Lighthouse Cottage, I'm still thinking about Joe, my past relationships and how things could have been very different . . .

Part Three

2001

Twenty

'Where on earth is this place, Grace? The back of beyond?'

I look over at the man driving me through Norfolk today. He's wearing a navy suit – tailor-made; a pristine white shirt – designer-label; and a purple silk tie with matching socks – also designer; and he suits all of them. He turns to me and winks.

'It might seem like that to you, my urban, city-dweller friend,' I reply, trying to put on a stern voice, 'but Sandybridge is my home, and I'll thank you to talk kindly of it!'

I turn away from him to take in the view as we travel the last few miles through Norfolk towards the coast. Surrounding us is the greenness I always notice when I make this journey home; the never-ending trees that form tunnels for us to drive through, the farmers' fields that house crops, cattle, horses and pigs, and scattered amongst this greenness the small towns and villages filled with warm terracotta-brick houses, churches, and large open village greens. And today we are spoilt as this vista of rural Norfolk unfolds before us, because we have the added bonus of the sun shining down on it all, to make it look extra special for our visit.

'Not sulking with me are you, Grace?' Simon asks as we join the A148 and follow the signs for Fakenham. 'I was only having a joke.'

I turn to face him; Simon is unlike any other man I've dated – not that there have been an awful lot in my thirty years. For a start, he's a fair bit older than me – he'll be forty later this year – and he's a lot more sensible. But I like that; I'd needed a steadying influence in my life, a life that had been pretty wild since I left university.

I'd met Simon on an archaeological dig I was taking part in in southern France, not long after I finished my studies, and we'd quickly bonded over our despair that we weren't discovering much in what was suspected to be an early Norman settlement. We were the only ones on the dig who ever seemed to question that we might be wasting our time camping in the middle of nowhere night after night, spending our days digging and sifting minuscule areas of soil and finding very little for all our troubles. But if nothing else we gained a relationship from that miserable experience – eventually. It was years later when we bumped into each other again in New York and found out we were both working in the city. We'd agreed we must 'hang out' together sometime, and we've been hanging out in each other's company ever since.

'Of course not!' I smile. 'I'm just enjoying being back here again, it's been some time since I came home for a visit.'

Fourteen months to be precise, since the awful day that had been Charlie's father's funeral.

Peter had a stroke, a bad one, and he'd been hospitalised immediately down in Norwich. But sadly there was nothing they could do, and he never left hospital again.

Charlie had been devastated, of course, and I'd done everything I could to help him at the time. But luckily for Charlie I wasn't the only one he had to lean on, he had his new wife Louisa too.

It had all come as a bit of a surprise when Charlie phoned me to tell me he was getting married. I'd just started my job over in New York, and I hastily had to beg for time off to come home. I couldn't possibly miss Charlie's wedding, strange as it felt to think of him married. But his bride, Louisa, seemed a lovely girl, and we got on quite well in the short time I had to get to know her before heading back to New York.

Simon hadn't come with me on either of those flying visits. We had barely even started dating when Charlie got married, and a funeral wasn't the occasion to introduce him to my family and friends. But now was the right time, and I was full of excitement at the prospect.

'Well, I'm pleased you're pleased!' Simon says, his dark eyes twinkling. 'I'm always happy when you are, even if you do come from a town that's light years from London!'

Simon and I shared a flat in Chelsea. Although I paid as much as I could towards the exorbitant rent, my salary as a curator for one of the galleries at the Victoria and Albert Museum didn't pay anywhere near as well as Simon's business searching out antiques for the wealthy. Simon was a go-getter in every sense of the word; he was energetic, enterprising and a highly successful businessman.

'And here it is!' I announce as we drive past the little sign declaring we've arrived in *Sandybridge – Jewel of the Norfolk Coast*.

I direct Simon to my old house and we pull up outside. I can see Mum twitching at the net curtains before we've even got out of the car.

'Grace!' she cries, running out of the door and down the path to hug me. 'And this must be your Simon.' She stands back to check Simon out, and nods approvingly. 'Very nice, very nice indeed. Welcome, my dears!' Then to my dismay Mum reaches out to hug Simon too, but Simon just smiles and wraps his long arms around Mum, pulling her close. 'Thank you, Mrs Harper,' he says over her shoulder, winking at me.

'Oh no, dear, you must call me Janet,' Mum insists, taking Simon by the hand and escorting him into the house. 'Bob – that's Grace's dad – is waiting for us inside.'

I follow Mum and Simon into the house, and as we pass by the stairs I can't help but look. But of course the area where Wilson's basket used to be is still dog-free. Mum replaced his basket some time ago with a small set of shelves to house her collection of Art Deco pottery.

I swallow hard. I still can't get used to coming back here with no big hairy Wilson eager to greet me. He passed away in his sleep one night in 1995 when I was in Australia backpacking. By the time Mum had finally been able to break the news, in one of my rare phone calls home, Wilson's ashes had already been scattered over Sandybridge beach by Charlie – another thing I had to be grateful to him for.

Mum and Dad hadn't got another dog; much as they'd loved Wilson, I had been the reason they'd got him, and now I wasn't around there didn't seem much point getting another dog. Besides, I think they enjoyed being able to go off to auctions and house clearances at a moment's notice without having to worry about who would look after Wilson, especially since Charlie now had his own family to care for so their dog-sitter was no longer available.

'I still miss him too,' Dad says, seeing me gazing sadly under the stairs. 'The house isn't the same without his panting and snoring.'

I hug Dad. Then he holds me back in his arms to look at me. 'How are you, Grace?' he asks. 'Are you happy?'

I turn my gaze to the lounge where Mum is busy showing Simon family photographs, giving him a potted history of every person in every frame.

Simon is smiling politely, and making all the right noises in the right places, which is pleasing Mum all the more.

'Yes,' I say, turning to Dad and looking up at him. 'Yes, I am.'

'Good,' Dad says. He nods in the direction of the lounge. 'He seems like a nice fella.'

'He is. Really nice. I like him – a lot.'

'As long as he makes my Grace happy, then I'm happy,' Dad says, hugging me again. 'Now let's go and rescue him from your mum before she scares him away!'

In the lounge Mum has laid on a huge afternoon tea for us: sandwiches with their crusts cut off, a selection of cakes, and lots of tea served with Mum's best china service.

'Did you make these delicious cream buns, Janet?' Simon asks, as he finishes off his second cake.

'Oh no, Simon,' Mum says coyly. 'They're from the

Lighthouse Bakery. Baking has never been my strong point, has it, Bob?'

Dad shakes his head, and give me a rueful smile.

'Isn't that the bakery your friend owns?' Simon asks me.

'Charlie – yes, it is.'

'Ooh, he's done ever so well for himself has Charlie,' Mum says. 'That bakery is all around the country now, and Charlie was telling me the other day he has plans to go international next.'

Simon nods. 'Excellent. But Grace tells me they don't run the business out of the lighthouse any more.'

'Oh no, Charlie has a huge factory down near Norwich where they make everything now – better transportation links, see. But it's still all his original recipes the cakes are made to. That's why they're so popular, because they all taste home-made.'

'Sounds like you have your own Mr Kipling here!'

Mum nods proudly. 'Like I said, Charlie has done very well for himself.'

'And how about you, Simon?' Dad asks. 'What do you do?'

'I have my own business sourcing antiques and collectables for clients who have a need for a specific objet d'art.'

Mum and Dad both prick up their ears. 'Ooh, just like us!' Mum says, smiling proudly.

'I don't think Simon deals in the sorts of things we do, Janet,' Dad says. 'I expect most of his items are top end.'

'Well, most of my clients *are* quite wealthy,' Simon says, looking uncomfortable. 'But at the end of the day we're all doing the same thing: providing a service to people who want a piece of the past.'

Simon may as well have said he was related to royalty;

judging by the way Mum and Dad are gazing with admiration at him, his approval rating couldn't be higher.

'You'll have to come and see our shop while you're here, Simon,' Mum offers.

'Yes, come and have a look at the Harper family business, son. Maybe you can give us a few pointers.'

'Oh, I doubt that. I'm sure you're both doing very well on your own. But I would like to visit the shop. Grace has told me so much about it, and how it sparked her interest in history.'

'Another cake,' I say, thrusting the plate quickly under Simon's nose. I shake my head vigorously at Mum and Dad while Simon deliberates between a vanilla slice and a cinnamon roll, praying they won't tell him the truth.

'Talking of that,' Dad says, winking at me. 'Have you heard from Danny recently?'

I glare at him.

'That's *one* of the reasons we're here, actually.' I glance at Simon, who smiles at me between bites of vanilla slice. 'It's Danny's charity that's holding the ball we're attending tomorrow night at Sandybridge Hall.'

'Oh yes, of course it is,' Mum says, nodding. 'He's done brilliant things with that charity since the *accident*.' Mum whispers the word as if it's toxic.

'Remember I told you about Danny and the fire,' I remind Simon. 'His legs were paralysed after a beam fell on them in the fire at Sandybridge Hall, and he went on to set up a charity to help disabled teenagers have more opportunities in life.'

Simon nods. 'Sounds like a fine fellow.'

'Oh, Danny is a lovely boy,' Mum says fondly. 'But he

suffered terrible injuries that night. Dreadful, it was,' she continues, her hand pressed to her chest dramatically. 'The fire brigade got to him in time to save his life, but sadly they weren't able to save his legs. Been in a wheelchair ever since.'

'That's terrible,' Simon sympathises, as always saying exactly the right thing.

'It was. Changed him though, didn't it, Grace?' Mum looks to me for support. 'Some people said for the better! Danny was a lot ... *humbler* after his accident. A lot easier to live with, his mum said.'

Simon just nods this time.

'Did you know he was Grace's boyfriend once?' Mum asks innocently.

'Was he now?' Simon's eyes twinkle mischievously as he looks to me. 'That part you didn't tell me, Grace.'

'No need,' I reply hurriedly. 'It was a *long* time ago, and we're here because Danny's charity's a worthy cause, not because I dated him once upon a time.'

But it will be good to see him again, I think. In fact it will be good to catch up with everyone again. I never thought I'd say it, but I've come to miss Sandybridge now that I no longer live here.

'You said the ball was *one* of the reasons you were here,' Dad asks, looking between Simon and me. 'What was the other?'

I look at Simon. He nods his reply.

'Because of this!' I say, twisting the ring on my finger to reveal the rather large diamond I've had hidden in my left palm since I arrived. 'Mum, Dad, I— I mean *we* are engaged!'

Twenty-One

It seems funny, staying in the spare room while we're here, instead of my old room. But my old room only has a single bed, whereas the spare room has a double, which Simon is currently sprawled out on, taking a nap.

I tiptoe across the landing so as not to disturb him and open the door to my old bedroom for a look. It's only now that it hits me: this isn't my room any more, it's a storeroom for items my parents can't find a home for elsewhere. Where there used to be posters of my favourite bands, actors and movie stars, Mum has hung a series of quite dull botanical prints. And the wardrobe, which used to hold all my clothes, is filled with paperwork, magazines, and Dad's old cricket stuff. But what had I expected? I'm thirty now; I could hardly expect Mum and Dad to keep my room as some sort of shrine to my teenage years.

I'm just turning to leave when I notice something poking out from under a stack of old curtains on top of the chest of drawers. I go and lift the corner of the curtains, and there it is, about the only thing to remain in this room in the same place it had been when I was last here – Remy.

I carefully remove the curtains and place them on the bed with the other junk, then I turn my attention to the old typewriter that had predicted, advised and sometimes tarnished my younger years.

'Well, well, well,' I whisper, like a detective confronting a criminal. 'You're still here then?'

Remy as always stares silently back at me.

'Nothing to say for yourself today?' I ask in a mocking voice. Then I feel bad. No, I hadn't liked some of what Remy had told me when I was young. Back then I felt he'd given me bad advice on more than one occasion. But with hindsight it struck me that his seemingly dodgy advice had often led to an outcome that was good for someone else.

Charlie was the obvious case in point; it was rumoured his bakery company had made him a millionaire. I wasn't sure how much of that was true – Charlie wasn't the sort to brag about money or splash his cash around – but certainly he never seemed short of money when I saw him.

Would all that success have come about if life had taken him along the path he was on when I first met him?

And then there was Danny. He would have been nowhere near Sandybridge Hall that night if I hadn't insisted we try to stop the party. But as a result of his injuries, Danny had set up a charity that had helped countless teenagers, raising more money than even Charlie had in the bank.

A phrase from the last letter Remy sent me pops into my mind: . . . *life isn't always as clear-cut as it seems. Sometimes good comes from bad*.

'You could be right about that, Remy,' I whisper. The diamond on my finger catches the light from the tungsten bulb above. I look at it for a moment, then I look at Remy. 'What about me, Remy? What should I do next?'

Simon had proposed to me in one of our favourite restaurants in London in a very romantic way, surprising me with a ring hidden in my dessert. I did love him; I knew 100 per cent that I did. But what if I wasn't making the *right* decision, the one that would put me on the right path, the same path that Charlie and Danny now seemed to be on?

As always, Remy is quiet and still when he's being watched.

'Grace?'

I hear Simon stirring in the other room.

'I'll come back later,' I tell Remy. 'Just in case . . .'

After we'd told Mum and Dad our happy news, and Mum had used up all the tissues we had in the house sobbing, and saying how she thought it would never happen, they'd immediately insisted we go out tonight and celebrate.

'I was going to cook my speciality roast,' Mum had said through misty eyes, 'but this calls for something special. Bob, book a table at the hall!'

'Will we get in at this short notice?' Dad asked.

'We will if you remind Maurice he owes you a favour for getting Helen that Moorcroft vase she wanted for their anniversary.' Mum gave Dad a knowing look. 'Maurice is the maître d' at the new restaurant,' she told us.

'A new restaurant in Sandybridge?' I said. 'Where?'

'Up at Sandybridge Hall. These days it's not just a venue for big events like Danny's ball, there's a restaurant too with its own award-winning chef! A restaurant which your *father* can get us into if he picks up that telephone!'

Dad rolled his eyes at this, but got up to make the necessary phone call with Mum trailing after him.

When they were out of sight, Simon opened his eyes wide, then smiled. 'I love your parents,' he said, grinning.

'That's because you've only spent a couple of hours with them! Wait until you've done a whole evening, then see if you're saying the same thing!'

Sandybridge Hall looks absolutely beautiful as our taxi passes through the gates and on to the long gravel drive. There are little lights twinkling in all the trees, giving the place a magical, fairylike look.

The last time I'd been inside the hall's grounds there had been flames billowing from the windows, and the walls of the house had been veiled by evil plumes of smoke. But tonight I'm pleased to see Sandybridge Hall looking much more welcoming as we pull up in front of the bridge across the moat.

Dad pays the taxi driver while the rest of us stand admiring the hall, which tonight is cleverly lit to create a soft glow that enhances the red-and-yellow brickwork and dances playfully off the water below us.

'Well, this is a surprise,' Simon says, gazing in awe at the building I knew so well. 'I didn't expect to find such a gem of Tudor architecture here in the middle of Sandybridge.'

'I know, it is a bit at odds with the rest of the town,' I say, wondering how much the building has changed since the last time I was here. 'It looks as though the owners have done a lot of work to the place. Didn't it stand empty for some time after the fire, Mum?'

'Yes. It was on the market for years until the company that have it now came along and bought it – the cost of rectifying all the fire damage was so high, no one was willing to take it on.'

'It's magnificent,' Simon says. 'This wonderful moat lends it an almost castle-like quality – what a joy to have this here on your doorstep, Janet.'

'Yes, Simon, I've always thought so,' Mum agrees. 'We did a house clearance here once, you know,' she adds proudly. 'Didn't we, Grace?'

'We cleared the gatehouse, if that's what you mean,' I correct her, so there's no confusion. 'Didn't all the important antiques and works of art from the house go into storage?'

'Yes, I believe they did,' Mum mumbles, flushing a little. 'Ah, here's your dad!' she recovers. 'Now we can go in at last.'

The interior of Sandybridge Hall is nothing like I remember. It would seem the new owner has completely revamped the whole place to fit in with the hall's new life as a social venue. Where once there had been beautiful wooden panels covering the walls, and intricate plaster mouldings decorating the ceilings, there are now smooth, emulsion-covered magnolia walls, and flat white ceilings with tiny halogen spotlights dotted about. I gaze up at the ceiling recalling the huge crystal chandelier that used to hang there.

'What's up?' Simon asks me.

'Oh nothing, it's just there used to be a lovely chandelier up there and I was wondering what had happened to it.'

'Everything that wasn't fire-damaged was removed and is now safely in storage,' the maître d' says, coming over to us. 'Please don't worry, miss, nothing was destroyed when the hall was transformed into the culinary spectacle you see before you today.'

'What about the panels that were once on these walls?' I ask, going over to them. There's a print of one of Monet's lily paintings hanging on the bland, emulsion-covered wall now, where once intricate carved wooden panels had graced the entrance hall. 'What happened to them?'

'You seem to know the hall well, miss,' the maître d' says, smiling disingenuously at me. 'I believe the oak panels are still there, behind the plasterboard that covers the walls now. Sadly, some of them were blackened by smoke, so they weren't at their most attractive when the renovation began. But as I said before, no original features were destroyed during the hall's transformation. The present owners always take great care to preserve the history of the buildings they acquire.'

'Oh, right, that's good,' I tell him, still not too sure about Sandybridge Hall's new look.

The maître d' nods. 'Bob!' he says turning to my father. 'How wonderful to see you this evening. I believe congratulations are in order?'

'Yes, that's right, Maurice,' Dad says proudly. 'My daughter, Grace, here, has just got engaged to Simon.'

'Congratulations to both of you,' Maurice says, giving a little bow. 'Is it too early to start thinking about reception venues? We do a wonderful bridal package ...'

'Yes,' I insist. 'It is. Tonight we only want to eat, thank you.'

'Of course, miss.' Maurice nods again. 'Now if you'd all follow me ...'

'Grace, that was very rude,' Mum says as we follow

Maurice into the dining room. 'Perhaps it would be nice to have your wedding here?'

'Not tonight, Mum. Tonight is about celebrating our engagement. Wedding plans can happen later.'

Plus, how can I even think about what sort of wedding I'm going to have when I haven't even told my best friend I'm getting married?

Tomorrow morning I will find Charlie, before word gets out – as it's bound to if my mother has anything to do with it – and I'll tell him my good news.

He'll be thrilled for me, I know he will.

Twenty-Two

The next morning I arrange for Dad to take Simon to visit the shop while I go in search of Charlie. Mum had said he was in Sandybridge at the moment, because she'd seen him at his parents' tea rooms the other day.

It's funny how your parents never stop seeing you as a child. Charlie had bought the tea rooms from his mother when his father died, so she could retire and take some well-earned time off. The little shop had quickly become a part of the Lighthouse Bakery chain, and was as successful as ever, but Mum will always see Charlie as the teenager she first met when he used to walk Wilson with me, and to her the tea rooms will always belong to his parents. Mum proved last night she will always see me as a child too; when we were waiting to cross the road, she'd caught hold of my hand. No matter how old I am, I'll always be her little girl.

I decide to head for the lighthouse first. It's gone from being the place where Charlie and his staff used to bake all the goods to his company's headquarters, housing about twenty office staff over its several floors. Charlie still lives next door at Lighthouse Cottage – when he's in Sandybridge. These days the business takes him all over the country and, from what I've heard, the world too.

Instead of taking the easy route to the lighthouse along the pavements and cobbled streets of the town, I choose to walk across the sand the way I used to with Charlie. As I go, I remember our walks with Wilson, throwing his ball and watching him scrabble across the sand to fetch it.

It hardly seems possible, but I've known Charlie for almost fifteen years now. It seems like only yesterday he was the skinny ginger kid I'd hang around with. Now he's a fully grown man with his own company, and Louisa, his pretty wife, at his side. Where have all the years gone?

While Charlie was busy building his own happy and successful life, I graduated university with a first-class honours degree in history, then, just as I'd always dreamed of doing, I set off travelling around the world, seeing things I'd always wanted to, experiencing things I'd never thought I would, and living the way I'd daydreamed about since I was young. I had not only travelled the world, I'd lived it too: working diverse jobs in various countries, whether related to history or not, to pay for the next plane ticket to another country, and another way of life.

While I was in America on a working visa I was given the chance of my first proper job using my degree, working for the Metropolitan Museum of Art in New York. At first I was working in their gift shop in another of the temporary positions I took to pay my way. But then I got word the Costume Institute needed someone to provide maternity cover. So I applied and to my complete surprise was offered the position. I was initially on a six-month contract, which was then extended to a year, and it was during this time that I met Simon, also working temporarily in Manhattan, at a prestigious gallery on the Upper West Side.

How our lives have changed since Charlie and I used to stroll along this very sand together, worrying about our O-levels and then my A-level results. And how *we've* changed too ...

I've reached the lighthouse now, so first I head around to the little cottage to see if Charlie's there. Louisa has a high-powered job in banking, working mostly in Norwich but sometimes in London, so it's unlikely she'll be here on a Friday morning. I've never quite understood what Charlie sees in Louisa; he's always been a quiet, content sort of fellow, but she's a full-on workaholic. She works long days, and on top of that she commutes back and forth to Sandybridge, a journey I was used to after so many years of doing it, but one I still found taxing. Perhaps Charlie's changed more than I realised. He's quite the successful businessman himself these days; maybe that's what they have in common.

There's no one at home at the cottage, so I walk around to the front of the lighthouse and climb the steps to reception. The entrance looks a lot smarter, and the steps a lot safer than they did the first time I climbed them with Charlie. At the top I arrive to an open glass door.

'Grace!' Fiona, Charlie's ever-friendly receptionist, greets me from behind her desk as I go in. 'It's been a while since we've seen you here. Ooh, I like your new hair, very nice.'

'Thank you,' I reply, patting my short bobbed hair. 'I had it done a while ago.'

'I like the colour too – auburn suits you. It must be so much lighter than before, with all your long hair. I'd like to do the same with mine.' Fiona pulls at her high ponytail.

'Yes, it's definitely easier to style,' I agree amiably. 'You should go for it. When I was at uni I had it really short, but this is lovely in between the two.' I glance up the spiral staircase. 'So, is Charlie around today?'

'Yes, he's up in his office. I'll tell him you're here.' Fiona lifts the receiver on her phone.

'Can I surprise him?' I ask suddenly. I don't know why this seems like a good idea, but it does.

'Er ... yes.' Fiona hesitates. 'I suppose, since it's you, Grace, it'll be all right.'

'Great!' I begin to bound up the central staircase to Charlie's office. As I climb higher, passing several floors of modern open-plan offices where Charlie's staff are working hard at their desks, my pace begin to flag. Gosh, I'm not quite as fit as I used to be! I think as I move ever more slowly to the top, pausing to greet a few of Charlie's staff on the way. I'll have to make a real effort to use the gym regularly when I'm back in London, I think, as I take a quick breather. I want to be super slim for my wedding day, and that's going to take some work right now; my weight has always been an issue for me, and since Simon came along I've been steadily piling on the pounds, mainly due to Simon's love of dining out at rather delicious, but expensive restaurants.

I'm almost at the top floor now, the narrowest part of the building, so there's only the one office up here: Charlie's. I pause, wanting to catch my breath before I surprise him, but as always Charlie is one step ahead and surprises *me* by arriving at the top of the spiral staircase.

'Hey, you,' he calls, looking down at me. 'Nice hair!'

'Hey, yourself!' I call back, taking the last few steps to the top. 'And thank you, but how did you know?'

'I'd like to say it was my sixth sense,' Charlie says, hugging me. 'But Fiona rang up and told me.'

'Aw, I wanted to surprise you!'

'I know, but Fiona's a bit *too* good at her job! Come through.'

Charlie leads me through to the main part of his office, and we take a seat on a brown leather sofa opposite a large ergonomic desk on one side of the room. The sofa is positioned to give the perfect view of the sea through the huge glass window panels that extend 360 degrees around the top of the lighthouse.

'Drink?' Charlie asks. 'I've got a fridge up here with cold drinks in, or I can call Fiona and she'll bring us tea or coffee.'

The thought of Fiona climbing all those stairs balancing a tray of china cups is too much. 'A cool drink would be great – what do you have?'

'Your favourite, of course!'

My brow furrows, as I look at him.

'Fanta!' Charlie says, grinning at me. 'We always used to drink Fanta when we were together!'

'Oh … I don't drink full sugar drinks any more,' I tell him apologetically. 'Do you have a diet drink?'

Charlie looks crestfallen.

'Yeah, Diet Pepsi all right for you?'

'Lovely. Why don't you have a Fanta for us?' I suggest, not wanting to upset him.

'Nah, you're all right. Tell you the truth, I don't really drink that stuff either nowadays.' He pats his stomach, which doesn't wobble a jot. If anything, it looks even firmer under his white shirt. 'Got to watch my weight. Did you know your metabolism starts dropping as soon as you hit thirty!'

I laugh. 'Tell me about it! Yes, I did know – and do you know why? You told me!'

Charlie passes me a can of Diet Pepsi, and takes one for himself.

'It's good to see you again, Gracie,' he says, sitting down next to me. 'It's been too long.'

'I know, I'm sorry I haven't been back for a while. Life has been a bit hectic.'

'Tell me about it,' Charlie says, mimicking me.

'So, how are you?' I ask delicately, hoping he knows I mean how has he been since his dad passed.

Charlie shrugs. 'OK, I guess.'

'It takes a while to fully recover from these things,' I say, trying to sound as if I know what I'm talking about. I look towards the staircase in the middle of the office. 'Looks like everything is going well here though. Everyone looks super busy downstairs.'

'That's because they are,' Charlie says, pleased with himself. 'The business is going so well, I can barely keep up with it all.'

'I heard you were thinking of expanding internationally.'

'We are.' Charlie nods, then his joyful expression drops a little.

'Is something wrong?'

'Expanding internationally was Louisa's idea,' Charlie says after a moment.

'So? I think it's a great idea.'

Charlie looks at me oddly. 'You haven't heard then?' he asks quietly.

'Heard what?'

Charlie gets up and wanders over to the other side of his office. He stares out of the window in the direction of the cottage below. 'Louisa and I split up.'

'When?' I ask, completely shocked to hear this.

'About a month ago. She left and moved back to Norwich. She's staying with her parents until she can find somewhere to rent.'

'Why didn't you tell me?' I ask, getting up and going over to him at the window. *And why didn't Mum?*

Charlie shrugs. 'I didn't know how to. I guess I was embarrassed.'

'Why, you daft thing? I'm your oldest friend, you can tell me anything.' I reach my hand out and touch his arm.

'I'm not good with failure, Gracie,' Charlie says, looking into my eyes. 'Never have been. Remember my O-levels and how I didn't retake them after my accident?'

How could I forget?

'That was because I was scared of looking like a failure by having to redo a year at school.'

'But you haven't failed in this – it's not your fault your marriage broke down, it happens all the time.'

'But I feel like it is. Louisa and I should never have got married, we weren't suited, we were too different from the start.'

I knew it! But I try and stay calm – euphoria isn't going to be the best emotion to show right now.

'Then why did you marry?' I ask gently. 'If you knew it wasn't right.'

'She was pregnant,' Charlie almost whispers. He turns away from me and looks out of the window again. But I get the feeling from his painful expression he's not seeing the view.

'Did she lose the baby?' I ask in an equally quiet voice.

Charlie nods.

'Oh, Charlie …' I'm not sure what to say, so I put my arm around his neck and rest my head on his shoulder. I feel Charlie's head touch mine, and we just stand together in silence, looking out into the distance at the waves crashing on to the rocks below us; thinking about life, and what a bastard it can be sometimes.

'Shall we go for a walk?' Charlie asks about fifteen minutes later, when we've recovered from our melancholy and returned to our drinks. 'I could do with some fresh air.'

'Sure!' I reply brightly.

I'd felt pretty useless sitting there as Charlie confided in me, giving details about his and Louisa's break-up. I'd tried to say all the right things, but it was hard; I could only imagine how he was feeling. I'd been lucky in that I'd never suffered such loss as he had over the last few years: first his father, then his baby and now his marriage. But I wanted to make up for the fact I hadn't been here when he needed me, and I had tried to be the best listener I could.

'I have a surprise for you!' Charlie says as we descend the spiral staircase.

'What is it?'

'Ah, you'll have to wait and see!'

'The last time you said that, you'd bought this place!' I say.

'Ah, it's not quite on that scale!' Charlie grins. 'Come on, I'll show you.'

This sounds more like the old Charlie. In the last few minutes I've seen a Charlie I don't ever want to witness again: a broken Charlie, a distressed Charlie, a Charlie that life had swung a huge wrecking ball at, and it had left a very large hole.

211

We head out of the offices and over to Lighthouse Cottage. As I wait for Charlie to unlock the door, I feel a bit awkward being here. I'm not sure why; maybe because this had been Louisa's home with Charlie. But I needn't have worried. No sooner has Charlie opened the door than a bundle of chocolate fur comes tumbling out on to the step in front of us.

'Meet Winston!' Charlie says, rubbing a chocolate Labrador's tummy, as it immediately rolls over on its back in greeting.

'You have a dog!' I cry in delight, kneeling down next to the puppy. 'Another thing you didn't tell me about!'

I rub Winston's tummy like Charlie had.

'I haven't had him that long. I got him after Louisa left. She was never a dog person – a bit frightened of them actually. So the minute she was gone, Winston came to stay.'

'He's wonderful!' I say, watching Winston race madly around the cottage's tiny back garden while I wonder how Charlie ever ended up with Louisa. *Not a dog person!* What was wrong with her?

'Do you like his name?' Charlie asks.

'Winston – yes, why wouldn't I?'

'I named him after out dear departed old friend Wilson – another prime minister's name,' he reminds me. 'Churchill didn't quite suit this ragamuffin. So Winston it was.' He ruffles Winston's coat as he runs up to us and rubs his head against Charlie's jeans.

'Of course! I get it now. That was lovely of you to think of old Wilson.' My throat tightens as I think of him.

'I still miss him too,' Charlie says. 'It's like when you lose a human you love: it never completely goes away, just gets a little easier every day.'

I nod.

'So where does Winston like to go for a walk?' I ask, addressing Charlie and the dog currently rolling on my feet.

'Where do you think?' Charlie winks at me.

We walk a dog along the sand, just as we used to as teenagers. Winston, although nowhere near as big as my Wilson, behaves in much the same way on the beach: racing after a ball, then when something else grabs his attention, stopping to sniff at it before lifting his leg to add his own scent and running after the next thing.

'What time are you getting to Danny's do tonight?' Charlie asks, picking up and throwing Winston's red ball for him.

'We thought around eight? And it's not Danny's do, it's a fundraiser for his charity.'

'I know, but that's the reason you've come back, isn't it – to support him?'

I look at Charlie. Now thirty-one years old, he's a fine-looking man, tall, broad and muscular. His strawberry blond hair – which had a tendency to be a bit wild – is short and closely cropped; his face is extremely handsome, if a bit pale, but that only serves to make his bright blue eyes sparkle even more.

'What?' Charlie asks, seeing me looking at him.

'You can't still be jealous of Danny after all these years, can you?'

'Me? Jealous of Danny – no way!'

I raise my eyebrows at him. 'You used to be.'

'No I didn't ... Well, maybe a little, when you two were dating.'

'See?'

'But I'm not jealous of him now. Why would I be?' Winston has retrieved his ball; he drops it at my feet.

'Thank you, Winston. Now, fetch!' I call, throwing the ball along the sand into the water. 'Then don't say I've only come back to Sandybridge to support him,' I tell Charlie. 'I've come back for many reasons.'

'Such as?'

'Well … I'm here to support Danny, yes, I can't deny that. But I'm also here to see my parents, and catch up with a few people, and … what else … ' I pretend to think. '*You* of course, you silly thing!' I give Charlie a hug. 'I'm here to see my best friend because it's been too long.'

I can't tell Charlie that Simon and I are getting married, not after what he's just told me about Louisa.

'I'm glad to hear that, Gracie. I've missed you. Sandybridge isn't the same when you're not here.'

'Aw, that's sweet of you.' I give him a friendly nudge. 'But you're hardly here yourself these days, are you, with all your wheeling and dealing around the country.'

'No, that's true, I do spend a lot of my time elsewhere, but I always come home to the cottage, and now Winston. I can't imagine living anywhere else. There's something special about Sandybridge, something I can't altogether put my finger on. It's like I belong here. Does that sound weird?'

'No, not at all. You've always been happy here; anyone who knows you can see that. You and Sandybridge are a good fit.'

Winston has moved on along the beach carrying his ball, so we follow him.

'Unlike you and Sandybridge, eh?' Charlie asks as we walk. 'You couldn't wait to get away.'

'That may have been the case when I was younger, but now when I return I can definitely see the benefits of life here.'

'Really? I never thought I'd hear you say that.'

'I never thought I'd say it. I love London – don't get me wrong. But I can see the positives in coming to live in a place like this when I'm older.'

Charlie nods. 'That's good to hear. Maybe I can persuade you back when we're both old and grey, and we can walk along the prom together holding each other up!'

'That would be lovely, Charlie Parker,' I say, putting my arm through his. 'Perhaps we can sit on one of those benches on the seafront in the sunshine watching the world go by?'

'You have a deal!' Charlie says, smiling. 'I'll be here waiting for you.' He hesitates for a moment. 'Only problem is, what will the infamous Simon think?'

'What do you mean?'

'Come on, Gracie, when are you going to tell me the real reason you've come back?'

'I don't know what you mean,' I say innocently. 'What real reason?'

'This reason!' Charlie grabs my hand and we both look down at my engagement ring. 'Did you think I wouldn't notice?'

I look up at him, but I'm relieved to see he's smiling.

'Sorry, I was going to tell you.'

'And you didn't because ... ?'

'I didn't want to thrust my good news on you, when you were still so obviously upset about Louisa.'

'Gracie, don't be silly! Did you think I wouldn't be pleased for you just because my own marriage failed?'

I shake my head, and I'm about to apologise again when Charlie continues: 'I'm pleased for you, of course I am ...' Then he hesitates, as if he's unsure whether to go on.

'But ... ? I demand. 'There's a "but", isn't there?' I know Charlie too well. I know when he isn't telling me everything.

'Have you really thought this through properly?' he asks. 'Are you sure this Simon will make you happy?'

I stare at Charlie for a moment, puzzled by his words. 'Of course I think he will, otherwise I wouldn't be marrying him, would I?'

Charlie merely nods and begins to move away across the beach in the direction of Winston, who's strayed a bit too far.

I watch him walk away.

'Come on, say what you want to say,' I call after a few moments, as I chase him across the sand. 'There's obviously more to this.'

'Not at all,' Charlie says as I catch up with him. 'As long as Simon is the right person for you, then everything will be fine. I haven't even met him yet, so I can't comment, can I?'

'But you already have. What's bugging you, Charlie? Come on.'

Charlie stops walking and turns to face me. 'Make sure he is the right one for you, before you commit yourself to marriage,' he says in a solemn voice. 'I've been there, Grace. I stupidly rushed into marriage when it wasn't the right thing for either of us. And now I'm living alone, waiting for the inevitable divorce papers to arrive. By all means marry him, if you think he'll make you happy. But if you're not one hundred per cent sure . . . ' Charlie's pale blue eyes look straight into mine, 'then please don't, or you'll regret it, just like I did.'

Twenty-Three

I'm still thinking about what Charlie said as I make my way
back to the shop to find Simon.

Why would Charlie say that? I know he's only looking
out for me, and wants me to be happy, but he's got me
worried now. What if Simon isn't the right man for me? I
do love him, I know that because when he's away on business I feel so lonely at our flat on my own, and I miss him
a lot. But is that really enough reason to marry someone –
because you miss them?

'Come on, Grace,' I try to reassure myself as I walk. 'You
love Simon, you know you do, you both get on so well, he's
virtually your best friend!'

Virtually, that's a telling word. Shouldn't your future husband *actually* be your best friend? I have colleagues who
would describe their husband as their best friend and their

worst enemy at the same time – but they're only joking; in the next breath they'll tell me they don't know what they'd do without them.

Simon isn't my best friend, and never will be; no one could ever oust Charlie from that spot. Even though I don't see him as much as I'd like to these days, we keep in touch all the time. Charlie will always be my best friend; I can't manage without him. But could I manage without Simon if I had to?

I think carefully about this before I give myself an answer. I wouldn't like it if Simon wasn't a part of my life any more. In fact I'd probably hate it, but eventually I'd get used to him not being around, I guess.

Arrgh! This is madness! Charlie's got me doubting my own relationship now, a relationship I'd been quite happy with until today.

What is Charlie's problem? It can't just be that his own relationship broke down, surely? Does he think we won't be as close if I'm married to Simon? Yes, maybe that's it. But he should know that won't happen; nothing changed between us when he married Louisa, I'm sure of it. Then again, I was living thousands of miles away across the Atlantic, so maybe our relationship did change but I didn't notice.

Why is life never easy? I sigh. If only I had a magic ball to tell me what to do, then I'd know if marrying Simon was the right thing. I stop dead in the middle of the pavement, much to the surprise of an elderly lady carrying a wicker shopping basket who almost bumps into me.

'Sorry,' I apologise as she goes on her way grumbling – likely about me.

I turn and begin to walk in the opposite direction from

the shop. I may not have a crystal ball, but I have something almost as good . . .

There's no one at home when I get in. Mum and Dad are no doubt still showing Simon the joys of the antiques world – Sandybridge style.

I rush upstairs, and throw open the door of my old bedroom. It's already there, waiting for me:

```
Dear Grace,
   I know you're worried about your engagement,
and you are right to be so. Marriage is a
lifelong commitment. At the risk of sounding
like I'm preaching to you, it's not something
you should enter into lightly, without a great
deal of thought. Which is of course why you are
consulting me again!
   However, all I can tell you is that marrying
your current love will definitely be the right
thing for your long-term happiness.
   Love, Me x
```

I read the letter twice before tucking it safely into the drawer where all my previous letters are still hidden away amongst my old school books. Then I head downstairs and out of the front door, locking it behind me.

As I walk down the street in the direction of the shop, I feel much happier after reading Remy's advice. But there's still something bugging me, something that doesn't feel quite right, only I'm not sure what.

'Hey,' I say as I open the door of the shop. 'How's everyone?'

'Hello, sweetheart,' Simon says, looking up from where Mum is showing him an antique brass plate. 'Wonderful, thank you! I've had the most informative time in your little shop this morning.'

That's one of the reasons I love Simon: he always knows the right thing to say, even if he doesn't always mean it.

'And we've loved having you here,' Mum says, looking up at him with affection.

I haven't seen Mum look like that at anyone since the vicar of Sandybridge brought in a set of antique – and as it turned out, highly collectable – bibles to be valued and sold.

'Grace,' she says, coming over to me and taking my hands in hers. 'You've chosen well.'

Well, that was two votes for Simon in the last thirty minutes!

'It's not often your mother and I agree, Grace,' Dad says, appearing from the little room out back where he did all the paperwork for the shop. 'But on this occasion I must concur with her sentiments.' He pats Simon reassuringly on the shoulder. 'Welcome to the Harper family, son.'

And now a third ... Obviously Remy knew what he was talking about this time.

'Thank you, sir,' Simon says, shaking Dad's hand. 'It's a real pleasure to become a part of it.'

I sneak a glance at Mum: she looks like she might burst with pride, and for one awful moment I think she's going to call for a group hug, but to my relief she doesn't; instead she offers to put the kettle on for a nice cup of tea.

The invitation to the fundraising ball at Sandybridge Hall states 'Black Tie', so that's what Simon and I are attempting to get dolled up in now in my parents' tiny spare room.

'Can you help me with my bow tie?' Simon calls, turning away from the mirror on the wardrobe. 'Wow! You look wonderful, Grace.'

I'm wearing a full-length navy gown in a soft velvet fabric. One side of the dress is sleeveless; the other covers my whole arm. The dress is quite fitted, and I think exposes every flaw, so I'm a little nervous about wearing it this evening.

'Thank you,' I say, walking over to him in my bare feet. I've never got on well with heels, so I'm waiting until the very last minute to put on the gorgeous but crippling pair of red-soled delights that Simon bought me as a gift to go with this dress. 'You've made me feel a lot better,' I tell him as I begin arranging his tie into a bow. 'I thought it might be a bit on the tight side.'

Simon's hands reach around my waist while my hands are still busy at his neck. 'You look stunning, Grace, it shows off your beautiful curves to perfection.' I feel one of his hands begin caressing my skin where the dress falls open at the back.

I shiver at his touch. 'Lovely though that is, Simon,' I say, placing a gentle kiss on his lips, 'we really don't have time for that this evening, or we'll be late.' I tap his lapel. 'There, all done.'

'Are you sure we don't have time?' Simon murmurs as he begins to caress the side of my neck. 'You look so edible in that dress, I want to eat you.'

'No,' I insist, wriggling away from his grasp. 'I told Charlie we'd be there at eight.'

'Ah, the infamous Charlie. At last I get to meet this wonderful friend of yours.'

That was the same word Charlie had used for Simon – *infamous*.

'Yes, you do. I'm so pleased the two of you are meeting at last.' Pleased, and somewhat nervous after what Charlie said earlier.

'It will be good to see if I've anything to worry about,' Simon says, adjusting his bow tie slightly in the mirror.

'What do you mean?' I ask anxiously.

Simon turns around. 'Well this is my fiancée's best friend; for most men in my situation, that means a lady they've got to impress. But for me it's different, your best friend's a bloke.'

'You don't need to worry about Charlie, he isn't like normal men. He's . . . ' I struggle for the right word. 'He's different.'

'You mean he's gay?' Simon asks, surprised. 'But I thought he was married? Didn't you tell me you went to his wedding? Yes, that's right, it was soon after we met up in New York, I remember you telling me you'd just been back to England for a visit.'

'Charlie isn't gay!' I'm almost laughing. 'Anything but. What I meant was, he's not the rough, tough type of bloke – you know, drinking pints and watching footie.'

'And I am?' Simon is grinning at me.

'No, but you fit into a different category.'

'I do?' He looks highly amused by my struggle to explain myself.

'Yes, you're what I would call a smooth man. I don't mean smooth as in you've got all the chat going on – although I do remember you chatting me up on that dig! No, I mean you care about the way you look. You like expensive suits and fancy restaurants. You're happy to spend the equivalent of some people's mortgage on a car if it's what you want.'

Simon looks at himself in the mirror again. 'I guess I do like the finer things in life,' he says, brushing some fluff from his black sleeve. 'But that, my dear Gracie,' he says, spinning around, 'is why I want to marry you. You, Grace Harper, are quality! Quality with a capital Q!'

'What did you just call me?' I ask as Simon comes over to me.

'Quality—'

'No, before that, when you said my name. Did you call me Gracie?'

'Er . . . I think I might have done. Why, don't you like it?'

I smile up at him. 'No, it's not that, it's . . . someone once told me that's what the love of my life would call me one day. I thought it might be someone else for a while, but now it must mean you!'

'Then that person was a very wise man indeed.' Simon kisses me, and for the first time since I saw Charlie earlier, I feel myself relax. 'I love you, Gracie,' he murmurs in between kisses.

'And I love you too,' I reply, my doubts vanishing as if they'd never been here at all.

If Remy said it was so, it must be.

Dear Grace,

I'm so glad I've alleviated your doubts.

The one who called you Gracie is the one for you. And it is he who will make you happy in the future.

Enjoy your evening with him and your other admirers.

Love, Me x

Twenty-Four

Sandybridge Hall looks magnificent again tonight as we arrive along its pretty tree-lined drive in a taxi. We're not the only ones; ahead of us I see a steady stream of cars and cabs pulling up on the sweeping gravel drive next to the house, either dropping their passengers and heading off down the drive again, or disappearing around the back to park.

A fancy-looking doorman opens my cab door; he's wearing a military-inspired scarlet suit, and he has a matching cap with a black patent peak.

'You weren't here when we came for dinner last night,' I say, smiling.

He tips his hat at me. 'No, miss, I'm only here for the festivities tonight. Just doin' me bit for the charity!'

'Lionel!' I exclaim, recognising him. 'How have you been?'

'I'm well, Gracie, very well. Gotta help my boy out on his big night, haven't I?'

'Simon, this is Danny's father,' I say, introducing them.

'Pleased to meet you.' Simon shakes his hand.

'So this is the fella who's stolen our Gracie's heart,' Lionel greets Simon. 'When's the big day?'

'You've heard?' I ask, surprised.

'I think the whole of Sandybridge knows – your mum has been telling everyone!'

I shake my head. 'We only told *her* last night!'

'You know how gossip travels here, Grace.' He turns to Simon. 'There once was a time I thought Gracie here might have become *my* daughter-in-law.'

'That was a long time ago now, Lionel,' I cut in hastily. 'A lot of water under the bridge and all that.'

'Yes, my dear, so there has been. Oh, duty calls!' he says as another cab pulls up next to us. 'I'll see you two later. I'm losing the uniform once everyone is here and changing into my Sunday best!'

'See you later, Lionel,' I tell him and we begin climbing the stone staircase up to the main entrance.

'So, you and this Danny . . .' Simon asks. 'It was quite serious then? And there was me worrying about Charlie, when all the time there was another man I should have been watching out for.'

'Don't be silly,' I tell him. 'You don't need to worry about any of the men in my life – except my dad perhaps, but you seem to have won him over!'

'Your tickets please – madam, sir,' asks a man I don't recognise.

I open my bag and pass them to him.

'Have a wonderful evening, won't you,' he says, nodding at us. 'And spend big! It's all for charity!'

'I'll do my best!' Simon says, saluting him.

We walk through into the house, but tonight we carry on past the restaurant where we'd had such a delicious meal last night, and head for the ballroom at the rear of the house. There are a lot of people milling around in the foyer of the hall tonight, and as I check out the ladies' outfits I can't help but remember the time Charlie and I had snuck in here, and I'd imagined ladies of the past wafting around in their ballgowns, ready to dance with their latest beaux. Or even waiting hopefully to get their dance card marked by the suitor of their choice.

But tonight it was 2001 and the dresses, although pretty, had a little less fabric, and probably a lot less colour than their counterparts of the past. No one would have been seen in black at an event like this in the old days; it was seen as a colour of mourning. But tonight it seems to be the colour of choice for men and ladies.

'Drink?' Simon asks, noticing a table outside the ballroom with complimentary glasses of fizz on it.

'Yes, please. I'm parched!'

'Back in a mo then,' Simon says, and I watch him weave his way through the crowds.

I look around the room at all the guests enjoying themselves, but surprisingly I don't recognise many folk. There are more than a few locals here tonight. Most of the people standing around sipping glasses of champagne and chatting look quite wealthy, and the voices I can hear are either loud – new money – or cultured – old.

I look for Charlie but I can't see him anywhere. I don't

really know anyone else that's going to be here tonight other than Simon, and of course our host for the evening, Danny, and I haven't seen him yet either. I feel a bit awkward, standing in the busy room on my own, so I decide to head over to a large board in the corner, with a table plan for dinner pinned to it.

I look for our names, and I'm pleased to discover Simon and I will be sitting together – always a relief! Then I look to see who else is on our table: Charlie – that's good, at least that'll give him a chance to get acquainted with Simon. There's a few people I don't know, and then I see Danny and his wife Rebecca are sitting with us too – great! I haven't seen them in ages. Last I heard, Rebecca was expecting their first baby.

'Hello, Gracie!' I hear a deep, familiar voice behind me.

'Danny! How are you?' I ask looking down at him.

'Still in this old thing!' he says, rolling his eyes. 'But me and the chair are on very good terms these days.' He pats one of the wheels.

'It's so good to see you again,' I say, leaning down to give him a kiss.

'Mmm, you smell exquisite, as always!' Danny says, holding me down at his level for a moment. I look into his eyes and I'm surprised to feel a jolt as we gaze at each other.

Danny obviously feels it too so I quickly stand up again.

'How's Rebecca?' I ask swiftly. 'Is she here?'

'She's good, thanks. Yes, she's about somewhere, you won't miss her – she's the one who looks like she's wearing a huge mountain of flowers draped over her front.'

'Danny!' I admonish him. 'She's pregnant!'

'Yeah, don't I know it! She's eating us out of house and

home right now. I've warned the catering staff not to let her near the buffet in case it disappears.'

I shake my head at him. He'd never change – always the first with the funny quip or joke, usually at someone else's expense. But it was always in jest, there was no intention to hurt anyone. His accident may have rendered his legs useless, but it had never dented his spirit. If anything, I think he's got worse since being in the chair. He'd certainly used it to his advantage when flirting with the ladies in the aftermath of his accident. That is, until he met Rebecca, a no-nonsense girl from Yorkshire who'd been helping out at one of his fund-raisers. Rebecca knew just how to put Danny in his place, and frequently did so, much to his obvious delight.

'Grace?' Simon appears next to us with two glasses of fizz, and passes me one. 'Oh, you must be Danny,' he says.

'Yeah, the chair gives me away every time!' Danny says cheerfully. 'Which one is Danny? Oh, the one in the wheel-chair of course!'

'Gosh, sorry,' Simon falters, his cheeks hot, 'I didn't mean ... it's just ... Grace has told me so much about you, you see,' he finishes, sounding much more like his usual self.

'Has she now?' Danny's eyes twinkle, and I know what's coming. 'Has she told you about the time when we were seventeen and we skinny-dipped off Sandybridge beach at midnight?'

Simon looks at me, his eyes wide.

I give Danny a mock glare. 'Ooh, you don't change, do you?' I shake my head at him good-naturedly.

'Nope! Same old Danny!' He grins at me. 'Seriously, though, I hear congratulations are in order. When's the big day?'

229

'Thank you, but we don't know that yet. We've not been engaged long.'

'I hope your proposal was romantic, Simon. Grace loves a bit of romance, don't you, Gracie?'

'Er . . .' Simon is thrown again.

'Simon proposed in our favourite restaurant in London, didn't you?'

'Yes, that's right,' Simon nods. 'I had the waiter bring the ring in Grace's favourite dessert.'

'Viennetta?' Danny asks, his eyes innocently wide. 'Do they do those now?'

'Not my favourite dessert when I was fifteen, Danny! My tastes have changed a bit since then.'

'Sticky toffee pudding then?' Danny asks, trying to keep a straight face.

'It was a Belgian chocolate mousse actually,' Simon says, not seeing the joke. 'The chef baked it specially with the ring inside a tiny oven-proof box.'

'Smooth!' Danny winks at me.

'Talking about me again!' Charlie says, appearing behind Danny's wheelchair.

'Hey, man!' Danny holds his hand out to Charlie. 'How's things?' They give each other one of those cool-dude grippy handshake things.

When did those two get so friendly?

'Good, good. Looks like everything is going well tonight.'

'Yep, thanks to you!'

What are they talking about now?

Puzzled, I look between them both.

'Ah, Gracie doesn't like the fact she doesn't know something!' Danny taunts me.

Charlie looks at me now too. He grins. 'What's up, Grace? Do we have a secret you don't know about?'

'Ah, let's put her out of her misery, Charlie,' Danny says, grinning too. 'Her pretty face doesn't suit a frown. Charlie was the one who helped me get Sandybridge Hall for this fundraiser tonight. He knows someone in the company that owns the place.'

I look at Charlie. 'Do you?'

He nods. 'Yep, they owed me a favour so when I asked if a friend of mine could hold a ball here for his charity, they agreed.'

Danny lifts his hand and Charlie high-fives it.

'Sorry,' Charlie apologises, looking at Simon. 'You must be Grace's fiancé. We haven't been introduced properly – I'm Charlie.'

They shake hands much more formally than Danny and Charlie had.

'Good to meet you, Charlie. Grace has told me a lot about you.'

Charlie pulls a face. 'Ah, that's never good.'

'In this case it is. I'm quite jealous, standing here next to you two, you know? You've known Grace so much longer than I have. You probably know so much more about her.'

Charlie and Danny look at each other and grin.

'Well . . . ' they both say at the same time. And Danny rubs his hands together.

'Where shall we begin?'

Twenty-Five

Eventually, Charlie and Danny run out of embarrassing stories they can tell Simon and we part ways, ready to go in for dinner.

'Sorry about all that,' I tell Simon as we're shuffling along with everyone else feeding into the ballroom. 'I had no idea those two got on well enough to spend a full fifteen minutes thinking of hilarious anecdotes about me!'

'That's OK, it was fun. I'm old enough and wise enough to know much of that was embellished on their part.'

Actually none of it had been. Charlie and Danny had told all the stories exactly as they had happened. But Simon didn't need to know that!

We all sit down to a delicious five-course dinner, and the boys behave themselves; this has much to do with Rebecca being around to keep Danny in check. Then just before dessert is served, Danny wheels himself away from the table and up a special ramp to a small stage.

The person who has set the microphone up for Danny obviously hadn't realised he is in a wheelchair, because it's set far too high.

Danny being Danny makes a joke about this as soon as the mic is lowered, and at once puts everyone at ease.

'Welcome, everyone!' he says into his mic. 'As you all know, we're here tonight for one of three reasons. One, because your wife made you come along . . . ' A few titters of laughter spread across the room. 'Two, *I* made you come along . . . ' More sniggers. 'Or three, because your conscience did!' A few people applaud.

'Most of you will know,' he continues, 'that I set up the Lucas Foundation seven years ago in 1994, after I had my own accident in which I lost the use of both legs.'

I look around the table. Rebecca is watching Danny lovingly, willing him to do well with his speech.

'In fact my accident happened here, in this very room.' He gestures around the room. 'I was only twenty-two years old when it happened. Twenty-two. I was in the prime of my life, ready to take on the world. But the world had other ideas, and it bit back.'

I glance at Charlie; he's watching me.

'But I had news for the world, I wasn't about to roll over and give up on life.' Danny pauses and looks out into the audience; he has them in the palm of his hand. 'Becoming disabled when you've been able-bodied isn't the end; in fact, for most, it's only the beginning; the beginning of a whole new way of life. A life that is different – yes. More challenging – definitely. But also so much more rewarding than it ever was before. This, ladies and gentlemen, is what the Lucas Foundation is all about: we try to give the help, hope, and most importantly life back to those that need us, and we do it when they need us most.'

More applause.

'I won't hold up your lovely desserts any further, except to say that just by being here tonight you've already done a great thing – you've donated to a wonderful cause, and already you've helped to make someone's life that little bit brighter. But if you really want to help us; if you really want to put a smile on someone's face and give them their life back – albeit a new one – then our auction, ladies and gents, our auction is for you! You've all seen the stupendous lots we have listed in the catalogues on your tables – and if you haven't, then look now, before all the fun begins. Above all, dig deep and bid high – very, very high! Goodnight!'

Danny does a little bow, then he quickly wheels himself off the stage and back to our table.

'You were amazing, darling,' Rebecca says, struggling to her feet her bump is so big.

'Don't get up, you daft thing!' Danny says, wheeling himself into his vacant space. 'It took you long enough to get down there in the first place!' He reaches over and kisses Rebecca on the lips. 'Was I OK?' I hear him whisper. Rebecca nods and kisses him on the cheek.

'That was quite some speech,' Simon says across the table. 'Well done.'

'Cheers, mate.' Danny nods at him. 'Appreciate it.'

'You were good, Dan,' Charlie says, getting up and coming around to the other side of the table. He pats him on the shoulder. 'Very good. Back in a bit,' he says to the rest of us. 'I've just seen someone I need to talk to on another table.'

I smile at Charlie, and he smiles back, but does his smile

fade slightly as I feel Simon's hand rest on my shoulder? No, I must be imagining it. I thought Simon and Charlie had got on fine tonight; surely there wasn't still tension on Charlie's part?

'Do you think your mate Charlie likes me?' Simon whispers as soon as Charlie has left the table.

'Yes, of course he does. What's not to like?'

'Ah, only I get the feeling I'm not his favourite person in the world.'

'No ... like I said, Charlie is ... complicated. I think he's finding it difficult seeing the two of us together now his own marriage is over.'

'But he must be with couples all the time.'

'It's not only us, is it? It's Danny and Rebecca too. We all grew up together.'

'I guess ... You're sure it's not more than that?'

'No, honestly. Everything with Charlie will be fine. Just give it time.'

The auction is a great success. Danny has obviously chosen the right people to come to this ball tonight, because some of the lots go for amazing sums of money.

My donated lot of a one-on-one guided tour of the V&A Museum goes for £1,000, and Charlie's lot – to have a new biscuit from the Lighthouse Bakery named after you – goes for a staggering £3,700.

'The next item,' the auctioneer calls, 'is this beautiful late nineteenth-century oil painting of dogs in a large kitchen. It's called *Waiting for Dinner*. Can I start the bidding at one hundred pounds?'

'Oh, I love that painting,' I whisper at the same time as

Simon says, 'I have a client who would pay big bucks for that. She loves dogs.'

So do I, I think, as the bidding quickly races up; especially ones that look like my Wilson. There are a variety of dogs in the painting: as well as a Labrador, there's a King Charles spaniel and a Jack Russell, all waiting for their dinner in a Victorian kitchen. But the one that has caught my eye, and the one that looks the most likely to get first dibs on the bowl of food that's sitting on the Victorian kitchen counter because he stands higher than any of the others, is the Irish wolfhound that reminds me so much of Wilson.

It's a popular lot, and the bidding is soon well out of my league. I wish I could ask Simon to buy it for me, but I can't; he obviously has a client who will pay twice as much again as the bidding is at right now, and he'll make a healthy profit.

So I watch and listen to the painting make lots of money for Danny's charity, which is wonderful, but I can't help feeling a little sad that it will be going somewhere I will never see it again. A lot of Simon's clients are American; the dogs will probably end up in a bar in Texas.

'And at two thousand three hundred pounds, going once, going twice – oh, we have a late bidder! Is that two thousand four, sir?'

I look around the room to see who else is bidding against Simon at this late stage.

'No, it's *three* thousand.' I hear a confident voice from close by.

Simon's head turns also – towards Charlie. He regards him for a moment then simply nods.

'Three two!' Simon calls, not looking at Charlie this time.

'Do I hear three five?' the auctioneer asks Charlie.

Charlie nods.

'Three five it is – back to you, sir?' The auctioneer looks hopefully at Simon.

'Four thousand pounds,' Simon calls, and he looks across the table at Charlie. 'I can play at this all night, if you'd like to, that is?'

Charlie doesn't respond. He glances at me. 'Too rich for my blood,' he says. 'It's all yours, *mate*.'

Then he stands up and pushes his chair back from the table, and without saying another word he walks away.

'At four thousand pounds then, going once, going twice – sold to the gentleman at table three.'

'I should make a healthy profit from that purchase,' Simon says, still looking at the painting being carried from the stage.

But I'm not looking the same way. Instead my eyes are following Charlie as he leaves the room.

I excuse myself from the table while Simon is still congratulating himself, and exit through the same door as Charlie had.

'Did you seen a man – sandy hair, about six foot – coming through here just now?' I ask one of the catering staff.

'Ooh, I most certainly did!' he cries in delight. 'How could I miss him! He flashed straight by me and went out over the bridge on to the little veranda across the grass. Good-looking fella,' he adds, raising his eyebrows mischievously. 'Is he yours by any chance?'

'No,' I say, knowing full well that's the answer he's hoping for. 'But he's not going to be into you either, I'm afraid,' I add when his eyes light up. 'He's as straight as that silver tray you're carrying!'

'Ah, these trays are easily bent,' the guy says, winking,

'as are so many pretty things in life! Your guy is straight ... sadly, through those doors.'

'Thanks for your help!' I call as I leave my waiter friend, and head through the wooden doors. I hurry across the bridge and see Charlie leaning up against one of the stone pillars that supports the roof of a new arrival to Sandybridge Hall, an elegant creamy-coloured stone veranda. He appears to be in deep contemplation as he gazes out into the gardens.

'Hey,' I whisper as I approach him. 'What ya looking at?'

'Hey, yourself,' Charlie says, turning to look at me. 'What are you doing out here?'

'Came to find you. You looked a bit upset after the auction.'

'You mean after I lost the painting?'

'There was no way Simon would have let that picture go – he has a buyer already lined up for it.'

'Are you sure it wasn't because I was the one bidding against him?' Charlie raises his eyebrows questioningly.

I shake my head. 'Simon was really nervous about meeting you tonight. He probably just wanted to impress you.'

'Gracie Harper, you don't believe that any more than I do!' Charlie turns his body fully to face me. 'More like he wanted to impress *you*, and make *me* look bad!'

'No, Simon isn't like that – honestly. He takes his job very seriously though, and once he decided he was buying that painting, that was it, nothing was going to stop him.'

'Shame,' Charlie says, sighing. 'I really liked that picture. The Irish wolfhound reminded me of your Wilson, and the chocolate Lab, my Winston.'

'That's exactly what I thought,' I tell him. 'If it hadn't been so expensive, I might have been the one bidding against you!'

'That would never happen,' Charlie says, without explaining himself. 'I wouldn't allow it. Why don't you ask Simon for the painting, if you like it so much?'

'Oh, I can't do that. It's his business. He's probably already rung his client to tell her about the painting.'

Charlie is quiet for a moment. 'If it was my painting I'd have given it to you,' he says quietly. 'Without hesitation. I wish I'd bid more for it now. I could have afforded it, you know. I only pulled out because I didn't want to cause a scene with your fiancé.'

'I know,' I tell him, resting my head on his shoulder. 'I realised that was what you were doing. Thank you, Charlie.'

'Anything for you, Gracie,' Charlie says, putting his arm around my shoulder as we stare out into the gardens together. 'You know that. Anything.'

Twenty-Six

Charlie and I eventually head back into the house after we've taken a short moonlit walk around the grounds together.

He sighs contentedly as we walk arm in arm through the perfectly manicured gardens, and around the lake.

'You sound very pleased with yourself,' I remark, smiling.

'Yeah, it's odd, but I've always felt really comfortable here at Sandybridge Hall – especially when I've been here with you.'

'What a lovely thing to say,' I reply, surprised by his comment. 'But they've not always been happy times when we've been here together, have they?' I can't help thinking of what happened to Charlie at Danny's birthday party, and then what happened to Danny at the New Year's Eve bash.

'No, that's true. But lots of good stuff came from those bad things.'

'It often seems to be the way.' I sigh, thinking about Remy again.

'Who's sighing now?'

'OK, no more sighing!' I look around at the gardens. In the moonlight they look even prettier than they had when we'd arrived earlier this evening. 'Haven't they done a good job here? They've made it so pretty, the people who own the house now.'

'Do you think? I liked it much better when it was the old house, with all the original features.'

'Oh yes, the *inside* was definitely better before – it needed a bit of modernising, but all that plasterboard they have in there now, covering the original features, it's horrific! I meant the outside is pretty these days, with all the little lights guiding you around.'

'Yes, I like that too. Funny, isn't it, how we've always liked the same things, you and I.'

'Always have done, always will,' I tell him, giving his arm a squeeze.

Eventually we re-enter the house and find our way back to the ballroom.

'Where have you been?' Simon asks as I return to the table, while Charlie is waylaid by yet another colleague. 'You missed the end of the auction.'

'You didn't buy anything else, did you?'

Simon shakes his head and waits for me to answer his question.

'I was smoothing things over with Charlie. We took a walk around the grounds together.'

'Sounds romantic.'

I look at Simon. 'Don't be silly. We're just friends, always have been, always will ...' I falter, recalling that I'd said something similar to Charlie a moment ago.

But Simon notices. 'What's wrong?'

I shake my head. 'Nothing, everything's fine. Look, Simon, if we're going to be together you're going to have to get used to Charlie. I know it's unusual for a woman to have a best friend who's male, especially one who's male *and* not gay. But that's the way it is with me.'

'I know,' Simon says, leaning in towards me. 'I know, and it's fine, really. After all, it's not like we'll see Charlie all that much, is it? He's based here and we're in London. I'll only have to deal with the unique relationship you two have on the rare occasions we run into him.' He leans over a bit further and kisses me on the lips.

But as he does, all I can think about is how I don't want the occasions I see Charlie to be rare. I want him to be a regular, even daily part of my life ...

Later, the ball is beginning to wind down, and it seems Charlie and I aren't the only ones who've seized the opportunity for a walk around the gardens of Sandybridge. As I stand by the window of the ballroom watching couples taking moonlit strolls, I think about how romantic this old house can be, and I wonder what secrets it would have to tell if it could speak.

'Penny for them?' Danny says, wheeling himself up next to me. 'Or aren't they worth that?!'

'I was wondering what stories this old house would have to tell if it could talk.'

'Plenty, I bet! It would tell of the many love affairs that have taken place here – both the declared ones, and the

242

much more exciting clandestine ones. I bet there's been many more of that sort than the dull ones.'

I turn to look at him. 'Still the same old mischievous Danny! Like I said earlier, you don't change.'

'Neither do you. You're exactly the same as the Gracie I knew at fifteen. You might be older and, if I may say so, even more beautiful than you were back then. But you're still behaving in the same way as you did when you were a teenager.'

'What on earth do you mean – I'm nothing like I was back then!'

'I didn't say you were the same. I said you were *behaving* the same.' Danny nods his head out of the window. 'You're still denying there's anything going on between you and him.'

I follow his gaze and see Charlie standing, wine glass in hand, chatting amiably with Rebecca.

'What do you mean, "anything going on"? We're just friends. You should know that better than anyone!'

'And as one of your exes, I should be able to comment more accurately than anyone!'

'I'm sorry, Danny, maybe it's all the champagne I've had, but I'm really not understanding you at all.'

'Do you know how hard it is, going out with someone who has such a close relationship with another man as you have with Charlie?'

I shake my head.

'No, you don't, but I do, and he does too.' Danny looks over towards Simon on the other side of the hall; he's admiring his newly acquired painting before it's covered up for us to take away. 'It's probably worse for him. I was only your boyfriend, but he's your fiancé – and your fiancé should be the closest person to you in your life, until he's your husband.' He looks out of the window again. 'Rebecca is the closest person to me in my life – she's my best friend and my wife all rolled into one – it's the best!'

As if she knows we're talking about her, Rebecca looks across to the window. She waves when she sees us looking through the glass. Charlie looks too, to see who she's waving at.

He smiles when he sees me.

'See that smile?' Danny says, still looking through the window as if we're simply having a casual chat. 'That's how I smile at Beccy. That smile is the smile of someone that loves you, Grace. No, doesn't *just* love you, but is *in* love with you.'

'What? Don't be silly, Charlie isn't in love with me!'

'Still denying it, I see. That's exactly how we got into this conversation: you're behaving exactly the same as you were at fifteen, Grace. Completely in denial.'

'Denial of what?'

'That Charlie is in love with you – which to any casual observer is quite plain to see – and you, my darling, innocent Gracie, are totally in love with him too!'

Twenty-Seven

'I am not!' I explode in the ever-quietening ballroom. 'I am not,' I whisper, aware someone might hear me. I pull up a chair from one of the now-empty tables and sit down on it, so I'm closer to Danny's level.

'How can you even think that?' I demand of him.

'It matters not what I think, it's what you think that counts.'

'But I'm not in love with Charlie.' I glance out of the window again, but Charlie and Rebecca have now been joined by a few others, mainly people gasping for a cigarette.

Charlie won't like that! I think, and I physically jump.

'What?' Danny asks, quick as a flash. 'What were you thinking just then?'

'That Charlie wouldn't like being out there amongst all those smokers. He hates cigarette smoke. Even when it's outside.'

Danny nods knowingly as we watch Charlie make his excuses and move away from the group.

'That doesn't mean I'm in love with him though. It simply means I know him well.'

'Favourite colour?'

'What?'

'What is Charlie's favourite colour? Quick, before he comes back in to find you – which I'm absolutely positive he's going to do. It's like a test.'

'Blue,' I reply, wondering where Danny's going with this.

'Good. Favourite food?'

'Bread with cheese – preferably Stilton,' I say without missing a beat.

'Details, even better! Favourite movie?'

'*E.T.* – he cries every time.'

Danny pulls a face. 'Really?'

I nod.

'Right, Simon's favourite movie?'

'Er . . .' We don't watch many movies together. When had I stopped doing that? I used to love going to the cinema.

'OK, his favourite food then?'

'He quite likes Chinese . . . whether that's his favourite though . . .'

Danny looks knowingly at me. 'Let's try his favourite colour.'

'That's easy, it's green. No, maybe it's blue, like Charlie. Simon has a lot of blue shirts . . .'

'Case closed!' Danny says while I'm still thinking.

'What? But you haven't proved anything!'

'Case closed!' he insists, spinning around in his wheelchair. 'Ah, here he is, everyone's hero! How goes it, Charlie, my man?' He slaps Charlie's palm. 'And here comes Simon too. Ah, the gang's all here again, eh, Grace?'

I can only nod.

'What were you two discussing in such great depth?' Simon asks. 'I could see you across the hall, heads bent together like you were plotting something important.'

'Grace and I were discussing colours, actually,' Danny says. 'What's your favourite colour, Simon, as a matter of interest?'

'Red,' Simon replies emphatically, without having to think about it. 'Why do you ask?'

That night, once I know Simon is asleep, I creep across the landing to my bedroom to consult Remy again.

There's a letter already waiting for me:

```
Dear Grace,
    Marry him. You won't regret it.
    Love, Me x
```

Summer 2016

Finally I arrive at Lighthouse Cottage. I hurriedly park the Range Rover and make my way inside.

No one is home, so I quickly check my appearance in the hall mirror, then pull open the door of the cupboard under the stairs and remove the crate on wheels I'd hidden in there earlier. It's quite heavy, so I have to wiggle it about a bit to free it from the confines of the tiny cupboard.

'Right,' I say to no one in particular, 'it's time.'

I lock up the cottage and, leaving the Range Rover behind, begin pulling the crate along the path that runs parallel with the top of the beach. Usually I'd walk across the sand – I always enjoy a stroll on the beach – but there's no chance of that today. The crate, while easy enough to pull on the concrete path, would be hopeless on the soft sand.

As I walk, the laughs and squeals of holidaymakers

enjoying their time on the beach are drowned out by the rhythmic whirring of the crate's wheels spinning around, the cries of gulls soaring above me, and the ever-constant waves rolling on to the sand. The sounds soothe me, and my anxiety at being late for this very important meeting begins to melt away.

It had been funny to bump into Joe earlier. His playful flirting had made me think about the men I'd had in my life, what they'd meant to me, and how their existence had changed the course of my life.

I'm so engrossed in my thoughts that I almost don't see a bright red tricycle hurtling towards me. It's being ridden by a small girl, and chasing after her is a stressed and anxious-looking young woman, who I assume must be her mother.

'Amy, stop!' the mother calls. But the small girl riding the trike has a look of determination on her face that I've seen many times before.

I stop walking and park my crate across the narrow path.

The little girl sees it, and as I note the panic in her eyes, I also notice her legs begin to pedal that bit slower, so as she arrives in front of me she's almost freewheeling.

I catch hold of the handlebars of her trike, and pull her to a stop.

Her breathless mother catches up with us.

'Oh, thank you so much,' she says, panting. 'She's a terror once she gets going on this thing.'

'No worries,' I tell her, pulling my crate to the side of the path again. 'I know exactly what that's like.'

The mother looks briefly at my crate, then back at me, and smiles.

'Well, thanks again,' she says. 'Come along, Amy, we need

to go and find Daddy. Make sure you stick by my side this time, please.'

I watch them for a moment as they continue along the path. Then I take hold of the handle of my crate and begin walking purposefully again in the opposite direction.

Yes, I know exactly how it feels to have a toddler running away from you. The only difference is, in my case we were rarely running towards Daddy ...

Part Four

August 2012

Twenty-Eight

I look out of the window as the bus trundles its way along the often narrow and always winding road towards Sandybridge. I hate buses – they're bumpy and slow, and right now all I want is to get back to my old home as soon as possible.

This isn't a visit I've been looking forward to. In fact, I've been dreading it. The last time I was here was for my father's funeral, a day that will be etched in my memory for ever.

The service was held at the same church where I'd been christened, the one where I'd watched Charlie get married and then, a year later, bury his father. And it's the church where Simon and I had exchanged vows ten years ago.

Ten years – where had that time gone?

Ours had been a happy marriage to begin with; Simon and I were living a life many people dreamed of – both in well-paid jobs we enjoyed, a large lavish house in a prosperous part of London, and a social life that kept us busy, mixing with the sort of people who could further our careers. We holidayed in exotic destinations, and dreamed about when we would retire to live in those same locations.

I was happy, we both were, but then came the pressure of producing a new member of our family. It was fun at first; the mere thought I might soon be carrying a baby inside me was enough to propel me into spending hours wandering around Mothercare looking at cute, bunny-covered babygrows, and snuggly soft cot blankets. But after the first few months passed and I still wasn't pregnant, I started to get a bit worried.

When that few months turned into twelve and still nothing had happened, we decided to get some help. Luckily for us, we had money saved and could afford to go privately. After countless rather expensive tests, it was concluded by a very knowledgeable Harley Street consultant that I had an 'inhospitable environment', and Simon had a low sperm count. Our only option was IVF treatment, which we went through several times, with each unsuccessful attempt putting even more stress on our already strained relationship.

'I'm coming back for a visit,' I told Charlie over the phone one day in late 2006 when the stress was getting too much to bear, and Simon and I were rowing constantly over the tiniest thing.

'Great – when?' Charlie had replied, apparently not noticing anything was wrong.

'Tomorrow. I'm coming alone.'

I waited for the inevitable questions, but they didn't come.

'What time is your train?' is all Charlie had asked. And I loved him all the more for it.

*

I stay with Charlie at Lighthouse Cottage for a week, not doing much at all, just anything I find comforting, normal and not too taxing.

I take walks with Winston over the beach; pleased I've chosen December for my visit and not the height of summer when Sandybridge would have been packed out with holiday-makers. I spend time with Mum and Dad, both at home and in their shop, but their questions about my visit are rather more probing than Charlie's. Most importantly, though, I spend time with Charlie, who I haven't seen for some time, and who I've missed terribly.

'So,' Charlie asks one day when I return to the cottage from a walk with Winston, 'when are you going to tell me?'

'Tell you what?'

'Tell me why you're here.'

I say nothing for a few moments. I prepare Winston some food, then I watch while he gulps it hungrily down.

'I can't have a baby,' I blurt out at last. It comes out more bluntly than I intended.

'Ah,' Charlie replies. 'I guessed it might be something like that.'

'Did you?' I ask in a pleading voice. 'Did you really?'

'Of course. I'm not stupid, you know. You've been married to Simon for what – four years? You're getting to *that* age, and you spend all your time watching children and babies when we're out together.'

'Do I?'

Charlie nods, and I go over and sit next to him at the kitchen table.

'Do you want to talk about it?' he asks.

'Not really; there's not much to say. We've tried

257

everything. We've done it naturally, unnaturally, with herbal remedies, with old wives' tales, and we've been trying IVF.'

'And how's that going?'

I shrug. 'It's putting so much stress on our relationship, I'm not sure I even want to be with Simon any more, let alone have a baby with him!'

'It's early days,' Charlie says. 'You've got to give it time.'

'That's the thing – it's not early days, it's late days. Next month is our last shot at it and I'm scared. Very scared.'

'Of . . . ?'

I look at Charlie. 'Of it not working, of it not working and us splitting up.'

'Gracie,' Charlie says, putting his hand over mine on the table, 'I can only talk about my own experience, but it might help you. When Louisa and I lost our baby I thought it was the end of the world, I thought nothing would ever be the same again. And do you know something, it wasn't. It wasn't the same; it was different. Life became different, but eventually it's in a good way. Louisa and I were never meant to be together, and it took the loss of our baby for us to realise that.'

'Are you saying that this is being sent to test Simon and me, to see if our relationship is strong enough to survive this problem?'

'Possibly.'

I think about this for a moment.

'But how will I know, how can I tell if we're strong enough? If it's worth going through that final IVF?'

'You don't,' Charlie says. 'No one can tell you what to do for the best, only you can figure it out.'

I'm nodding, but my mind is thinking new thoughts,

thoughts of a little black typewriter. Remy would know what to do for the best. He always did.

'Mum!' I call as I use my old key to open up their house. 'Are you home?'

There's no answer, so I take a quick look around the house to make sure no one is in, then I head quickly upstairs to my old bedroom.

As I open the door, I realise the task of gaining advice from Remy about my latest problem isn't going to be such an easy one. Mum and Dad appear to be in the process of redecorating, and my old room is empty, bar a few cans of pale yellow emulsion sitting in the middle of the floor, with some unused brushes on top of them.

Damn, where have they put all the stuff from in here?

I'm about to go in search when I hear the front door open and my parents' voices wafting along the hall and up the stairs. I look at my watch: 6 p.m., they must have just come in from the shop.

I go to the top of the stairs.

'Grace! You nearly gave me a heart attack!' Mum calls as she sees me. 'What are you doing up there?'

'Where's all the stuff from my old room?' I ask quickly. 'All the junk you keep in there.'

'That's not junk, that's all my craft stuff, my knitting things, my sewing kit and—'

'What about the typewriter?' I interrupt. 'The little black one that was mine?'

'Oh, I think your dad took that to the shop yesterday,' Mum says to my horror. 'Bob!' she calls. 'Do we still have that old Remington typewriter we found in the new nurse— I

259

mean, spare room?' Mum flashes a quick look in my direction and her cheeks flush.

Oh Lord, they were decorating the room as a possible future nursery! I close my eyes for a moment. This was getting worse by the minute.

'Yes!' Dad calls back. 'Why?'

I thunder down the stairs past them, grabbing the shop keys from the table in the hall as I pass. 'I'll be back in a bit!' I call to my bemused parents.

I run all the way to Lobster Pot Alley. Unnecessarily, as Remy isn't going anywhere now the shop's closed. When I get there I fumble with the keys in my rush to unlock the door, then I burst through flicking the lights on. I frantically search through the shop, but I can't see him anywhere.

Was Dad wrong about them still having Remy? Had he been sold?

But as I glance through the door to the office, I notice a little black typewriter sitting high up on a shelf – Remy!

I lift him down, and I'm about to speak to him when I see there's already a sheet of typed paper in his spool. So I pull it out and read:

Dear Grace,

I'm so sorry you are having such a hard time right now. But please be aware everything you are going through is for a reason, and as time goes by that reason will become clear.

Keep trying; your prize for persistence will bring you much joy.

Love, Me x

*

That visit was almost six years ago. I look down at the small head fast asleep on my lap as the bus trundles along the winding road towards Sandybridge, and I gently stroke her long hair. Regardless of what followed that visit, I could never regret having my little Ava. She's my life – what's left of it now.

Twenty-Nine

Finally I see the sign for Sandybridge and I gently wake Ava.

'Ava, time to wake up and go see Granny,' I whisper in her ear.

The little girl stirs on my lap, and smiles sleepily up at me. 'We here?' she asks.

I nod. 'We need to collect all our stuff up so we can get off the bus at our stop.'

We don't have a lot of stuff, I'm not intending on staying that long, but Mum needs me. She's been struggling since Dad passed away, finding it hard to run the shop, and hard to survive in general without her partner of so many years.

Ava and I alight at the stop on the promenade, and stand with our bags at our feet, watching as the bus drives away.

I sigh as I look around at Sandybridge. The shops along the promenade are much the same as they've always been – a mixture of tea rooms, amusement arcades, food outlets and gift shops. Most of them have changed hands over the years, but some, like the Lighthouse Bakery, still remain with the original owners. The only new additions I can see are the Olympic banners and flags that line the seafront, from when the Olympic torch passed through the town on its relay across the country a few weeks ago. Charlie, as a prominent local businessman, was one of the torchbearers, and I'd been gutted when I couldn't get home to see his moment of glory.

As my eyes rest on the tea rooms that once belonged to his parents, I wonder if Charlie will be here while we are. It would be good to see him again; it's been a while.

While my life has taken a bit of a nosedive in recent years (except for Ava, of course), Charlie's has taken off big time. The Lighthouse Bakery chain has gone global – and Charlie is now conquering the States as well as the UK. Mum mentioned that she barely sees him in Sandybridge these days.

'That Charlie is always off around the world somewhere, selling his cakes.' Mum makes him sound like a nursery-rhyme baker, carrying his wares around in a wooden tray. But I know how big Charlie's company has grown; he still keeps the lighthouse at Sandybridge as a showpiece to commemorate where the bakery began, but his main offices are now in London and New York, and he divides his time between the two. Even though Ava and I still live on the outskirts of London, he's so busy that I rarely see him. On the rare occasions when we're able to meet up, I savour the small amount of time we have together.

'Come on, you,' I say, taking Ava's tiny hand in mine. 'Let's go find Granny.'

*

Mum has laid on an enormous spread for us on our arrival, and Ava's eyes light up when she sees all the cakes, crisps and sandwiches.

'Help yourself, sweetie,' Mum says, her face as happy as Ava's. 'We don't want it going to waste.'

Ava looks at me for my approval.

'It's fine; you go ahead and enjoy yourself. But don't eat too much or you'll be ill.'

I turn to Mum. 'You didn't have to do all this – honestly, a sandwich would have been fine.'

'Nothing wrong in wanting to spoil your family, is there?' Mum says, watching Ava pile her plate up. 'What little I have left . . . ' she adds sadly.

'How are you doing?' I ask her as we leave Ava munching on a jam sandwich and head into the kitchen to make tea.

Mum shrugs as she fills the kettle with water. 'Ah, well there are some good days, but then there are many more bad ones.'

She plugs the kettle in, and I put my hand on her shoulder as she moves back across the kitchen to get the tea things out of the cupboard.

'I know, Mum. I do understand. I may not be here all the time like you are, but I still feel it. Especially when I come home and he's not here any more.'

'I still get two cups out,' Mum says, stroking a mug fondly with her thumb, 'when I go to make a cup of tea. It's little things like that that hit you the hardest.'

Mum puts down the mug – Dad's favourite – and pulls out another two from the cupboard. 'But at least I have you to make tea for today. I've missed you, Grace,' she says, suddenly turning around to face me. 'You need to come home more often, love.'

'I will,' I tell her, and for the first time I see Mum the way she is now: an elderly woman of advancing years – she'll be seventy next birthday. She's no longer the Mum I remember from my childhood, rushing around between this house and the shop, bursting with enthusiasm and energy, wearing her denim dungarees with her hair tied up in a brightly coloured scarf. 'I promise.'

Mum nods. 'My offer is still open,' she says hopefully. 'For you and Ava to come and live here with me. It can't be good for the child, bringing her up in London in the area you live in, Grace. She'd do much better here by the sea with her family.'

Oh not this again, I think, but I don't say anything. Mum has been perpetually offering us a home back in Sandybridge since Simon and I split up. But I've always refused.

The joy Simon and I had shared at finally having our longed-for child soon turned to sorrow when the stress of the IVF, and then the strain of a new baby to look after, took its toll on our marriage. We split up permanently not long after Ava's first birthday. The cost of the IVF had severely dented our bank accounts, so we sold our house in Chelsea and both rented flats in new, but much less salubrious areas of London, so we could continue with our jobs and Ava could continue to have both parents as a constant presence in her life.

Now I had Ava, I could only work part-time, and the cost of childcare ate most of my salary from the small art gallery in central London. Simon was good, he gave us more than he needed to in child support, and I never had to ask him for it. But if it wasn't for the extra money I got in tax credits, we'd have had trouble surviving.

'I'll think about it,' is my reply. I haven't the heart to tell her I've no intention of returning to Sandybridge permanently. It took me too long to get away in the first place.

Mum nods gratefully. 'That's all I ask, Grace. That's all I ask.'

Tea made, we return to the table to feed ourselves and find Ava still tucking into the spread.

'So, what's the gossip in Sandybridge these days?' I ask after we've managed to polish off most of the sandwiches and we've moved on to the cakes. 'Who's been up to what?'

Mum thinks. 'You heard about Danny Lucas, did you?'

I shake my head, but even after all these years the mere mention of his name makes my stomach twitch.

'Divorced,' Mum states categorically. 'Last month. Real shame; him and his wife seemed like a lovely couple.'

'I didn't know they'd split up!' I say, shocked to hear this news. 'What happened?'

Mum leans in towards me and whispers so that Ava can't hear. 'Another woman, so I heard . . .'

'Really?' I think about this. 'It doesn't surprise me, actually. Danny was always a bit of a ladies' man.'

'Oh no, not Danny – his wife, apparently.' Mum raises her eyebrows.

'Rebecca! But she isn't gay.'

'Wasn't,' Mum corrects. 'Is now though. How does that work, Grace? Do you know?'

I wasn't going to try explaining to Mum how people changed their sexual preference, because I didn't understand it myself. At forty-one, I can't help feeling the sexual exploits of the younger generation these days are a bit beyond me. So I simply shake my head.

'I heard it was one of the women that worked with Danny at his charity,' Mum says knowingly. 'Poor Danny, one day he's happily married, the next his wife runs off with a lesbian wife-snatcher.'

I have to smile at Mum's description.

'Is Danny in Sandybridge much these days?' I ask casually.

'Oh yes, he's moved back here permanently now. Lives and works from a nice bungalow up on the coast road that leads out of town. You should pop in and see him sometime, Grace. I'm sure he'd love to see you again.'

'Maybe I will,' I reply, thinking about Danny. 'It would be good to catch up . . .'

'I hear he's rolling in it these days,' Mum continues. 'Apparently he had a bit of a win on the lottery – EuroMillions. He deserves it, though, after all he's been through, and everything he does with that charity of his. You wouldn't know he had money though; he's just the same. I don't think he has anything to spend it on now his wife's left him; only his daughter, and he doesn't see her that often.'

How Mum always knows so much about everyone else's lives is a constant source of wonder to me.

'Poor Danny,' I say. 'Such a shame for him. He doted on Emily too. I'll make sure I go and see him while I'm here.'

Mum nods approvingly. 'Oh, I almost forgot!' she says clapping her hands together. 'The *really* big news! We have another new owner of Sandybridge Hall.'

'Another one – what happened to the last lot?'

'That crunchy credit thing,' Mum says, her face screwed up. 'The company ran out of money – and customers, by the sound of it.'

'You mean the credit crunch?' I say, smiling.

'Yes, that. It's been empty a while now, but apparently it has been bought by some multimillionaire recluse.'

'A recluse? So he won't be gracing us with his presence in Sandybridge any time soon then?'

'Word on the grapevine says no, he's only bought it as an investment and he won't actually be living there.' Mum clearly doesn't approve.

'Sandybridge Hall, an investment?' I ask in disbelief. 'What's he going to do with it then, if he's not going to live there – turn it into one of those health spas for the rich and famous?'

Mum shrugs. 'No one seems to know. It's all very hush-hush.'

'Mystery and intrigue in Sandybridge, whatever next?' I grin.

'Maybe you'd know a bit more if you came back to live here,' Mum suggests slyly. 'Would you like to come and live with Granny, Ava?'

'Mum!' I hiss furiously.

But Ava has already heard. 'Yay! Live with Granny!' she calls, lifting her piece of cake up and waving it in the air in celebration.

'See?' Mum says triumphantly. 'You're the only one that doesn't know what's best for you. Even Ava is keen.'

'Ava thinks there will be cake for every meal,' I tell Mum. 'It's hardly a glowing recommendation for coming back to live here.'

But I have to admit that returning to Sandybridge this time feels a bit different to all the previous times I've come home over the years. I don't know what has changed, but something has, and I'm keen to find out what.

Thirty

We're going to spend the day helping Mum in the shop, so having got Ava ready and left her downstairs with Mum – the two of them happily playing a spelling game Mum has bought for her – I'm hurriedly getting myself dressed.

I opt for one of my favourite shirts – the white one with pretty multicoloured buttons all down the front. It's only Primark, but that's all I can afford these days; a far cry from the designer shirts I would pay a fortune for when Simon and I were together. When I think how much I used to spend on clothes, I shudder. The price of one designer shirt would feed Ava and me for a month.

But as I go to do up one of the buttons on this Primark gem, I realise the thread is coming loose. Damn, if that button is put under any pressure, my bust will end up popping into view – and that's the last thing I need today.

269

'Mum!' I call downstairs. 'Have you got a needle and some white thread?'

'There's a sewing basket in the cupboard in Ava's room,' Mum calls back. 'You should find everything you need in there. I think it's on the top shelf.'

With my shirt half-buttoned, I head across the landing. Even though I haven't slept in here for over twenty years, and it's been known as Ava's room since Mum and Dad happily finished decorating it as a nursery when she was born, I still think of it as my old room. I open the door and, ignoring all Ava's mess strewn across the floor, I head to the built-in wardrobe and scan the top shelf. There is indeed a wicker sewing box sitting up there. I lift it down and I'm about to close the door and head back to the spare room to sew on my button when I spy something black poking out from underneath a pile of old blankets and pillows.

Remy.

After the last time, when he'd ended up at the shop, I'd asked Mum and Dad to keep him here for me. Even though I've said over and over again since I first found him that I'm never going to use him again, I can't bear to get rid of him just in case . . .

I hesitate for a moment, knowing that if I pull him out of the wardrobe I'll be opening myself up to all sorts of trouble again. In one of my last letters from Remy, he'd been all for me marrying Simon – and look how well that turned out.

No, I'm not about to chance any more 'well-meaning' advice.

I close the wardrobe and I'm almost at the door when I trip over one of Ava's dolls lying on the floor. Ava has three favourite toys that go everywhere with her: Maisie – her rag doll; Bunny – her floppy-eared white rabbit; and Charlie – her golden-haired teddy bear, who she named after her favourite uncle and his strawberry blond hair.

I pick up Maisie and I'm about to place her on the bed with the others when I pause, looking down at the doll in my hands. If I hadn't married Simon, Ava wouldn't exist. My little girl, who I love so much, wouldn't even be here.

I think about this for a few seconds; if I could go back, would I choose not to marry Simon, in an attempt to prevent all the heartbreak I'd suffered during and after our break-up? But if I did that, then I wouldn't have my gorgeous baby girl ... and life without her is unimaginable to me now.

Maybe marrying Simon *had* been the best thing for my future, and Remy's seemingly incorrect advice was actually spot-on.

I look towards the wardrobe again. Mum keeps going on at me to come back here to live, and I keep saying no. But what's so great about my life in London? I live in a small flat on a questionable estate, and my rent for the privilege is extortionate, as is my council tax – and it's definitely not an area I'd choose for Ava to grow up in if I had a choice. London was great when Simon and I had money, good jobs and a social life, but these days, struggling to get by with a small child, city life isn't quite so wonderful.

Suddenly my mind's made up. I put Maisie down on the bed and go across the room to the wardrobe.

When I've freed Remy from his blanket and pillow prison, I place him on the chest of drawers where he always used to sit when this was my room, then I close the bedroom door quietly, and turn to look at him.

'So ... maybe you were right again,' I whisper, hoping

Mum and Ava won't hear me downstairs. 'Perhaps telling me to marry Simon *was* the best thing for me, because I have Ava now, and she's the most precious thing in my whole life. But ...' I look back to the door, just in case, 'that life isn't so great any more, and I want to make it better, for me and for Ava. So, Remy, I need your advice again. What should I do to make things better for us?'

As always when I ask, nothing happens. So I collect up my sewing box and return to the spare room, where I spend the next few minutes sitting on the bed sewing my button on. Then I brush my hair – now that I can't afford expensive hairdressers, it's long again and back to my natural colour, or at least as natural as I'm prepared to let it go; I rely on a box from the chemist's to colour the stray grey hairs – check myself in the mirror, collect my bag and make my way to the top of the stairs. Where I pause.

I wonder ...

I peek through the door of my old bedroom and, to my delight, it's already there:

```
Dear Grace,
    I'm so pleased you've come back to me again.
    As I've told you in the past, my advice is
always given with your best interests at heart.
And as you are now beginning to understand,
sometimes bad things have to happen before good
things can.
    My advice to you right now is to stay close
by. People who you love need you more than you
realise.
    Love, Me x
```

As always I read the letter through twice, and then instead of popping it in my bottom drawer like I used to, I fold it and place it carefully in my bag.

'Are you ready yet, Grace?' Mum calls up the stairs. 'Ava is getting a little restless.'

'Coming, Mum!' I call. Ava's never been good at sitting still for long – according to Mum, she's a lot like I used to be.

The three of us make our way to the shop on foot. Even though I've been expecting to see a few changes, I'm unprepared for what confronts us once she unlocks the door.

The once neat and tidy shelves and cabinets, crammed with antiques and knick-knacks for people to browse over and hopefully buy, are now in a state of chaos. Every surface I look at seems to be covered in a thick layer of dust. The pristine back room, where Dad kept his books and records, is a complete tip, with papers and bills – some of them in red ink – piling up on the little desk where he was often to be found when he was working in the shop.

Mum notices my shocked expression.

'It's a bit of a muddle right now,' she says, hurriedly repositioning a couple of glass vases as if that will make a difference. 'But I've not been myself lately . . . '

'Just lately, Mum? Or a bit longer than that?'

Ava runs over to a raggedy Steiff teddy bear and picks it up to cuddle. A huge cloud of dust puffs up around her, and she starts coughing.

'Don't touch anything, Ava,' I tell her gently, taking the bear from her arms. 'We need to do some tidying up first, then you can play with the bear.'

'I guess things have been going a bit awry since your dad . . . ' Mum admits, looking around her as if this is the first time she's noticed the state of the shop. 'The business is a lot to handle on your own.'

'Don't you have Nadja in to help any more?' I say, opening up a couple of the little windows at the back of the shop to let some air in. I daren't leave the front door ajar or people will think we're open, and I don't want any prospective customers to see the shop looking like this.

Mum shakes her head. 'She moved to Newcastle to be with her boyfriend.'

Nadja had been brought in by my parents last year to help out in the shop. She was Polish, and at first I'd been doubtful about her knowledge of British antiques and collectables, but there was no denying she'd been a great help to Mum and Dad as they struggled to cope with the business.

'When did she go?'

'About six weeks ago.'

'Six weeks! Have you tried to get anyone else? Ava, be careful with that!' I say as Ava begins bashing the number buttons on the till, which is thankfully switched off.

'No, it's difficult on the amount I can afford to pay anyone. The shop isn't doing as well these days. I don't have the inclination to run the place like I used to, or the energy to seek out new stock.'

'Then maybe the time has come to sell?' I suggest, knowing the reaction I'll get. Mum's always been as adamant about not selling the shop as I've been about not moving back to Sandybridge. We first discussed it shortly after Dad died, but she was insistent she wanted to keep the shop, in his memory.

'Maybe it has,' she says to my surprise. 'I certainly can't run it on my own any more. Just look at the place.' She indicates the half-empty shelves covered in dust and sighs. 'I'm ashamed of it, Grace.' Then to my horror she begins to cry. 'What would your dad have thought? This place was his pride and joy.'

Ava jumps down from the till and rushes over to take hold of a now sobbing Mum's hand. 'Here ... ' She reaches into the pocket of her dungarees and passes Mum a sweet. 'This will make you feel better, Granny Harper.'

'Aw, thank you, Ava. What a lovely, caring granddaughter I have. What it is to have family around you.' She looks up at me imploringly.

I reach into my bag for a tissue, and at the same time I pull out the letter.

... stay close by. People who you love need you more than you realise.

'OK, OK – you win! I'll help you,' I tell her, passing her the tissue. 'If you want to sell the shop, I'll help you get it ready for sale. And ... ' I glance at Ava, still holding Mum's hand, 'if you want to keep it, I'll help you run it until we can find you some new staff.'

'You will?' Mum stops sniffing and looks at me, her eyes wide behind her tortoiseshell-rimmed glasses. 'Do you mean it, Grace? You and Ava will move in with me and help me out with the shop?'

'Only temporarily,' I insist. 'Until we can sort everything out.'

'But what about your work in London – your flat?'

'I'm owed some holiday from work – they're usually quite flexible about me taking it. And the rent on my flat is paid up until the end of the month, so it'll be fine. It's not like it's a permanent thing,' I remind her. 'It can't be: Ava starts school in September, we have to be back for that.'

'Of course.' Mum nods, but she can't stop herself from smiling. 'Oh, Grace, just to have the two of you here with me for the summer will be wonderful!'

'We stay with Granny? We eat cake?' Ava asks, looking delighted at the prospect.

'Yes, Ava, as much cake as you like!' Mum promises.

'Er . . . only on special occasions,' I correct. 'But yes, Ava, we're going to have a little holiday here in Sandybridge with Granny Harper, and help her out in her shop. Does that sound like fun?'

Ava claps her hands in excitement. 'Shop, Granny and cake!' she squeaks. 'I love Sandy Bridges.'

Dear Grace,

More people love and care for you than you
realise.

I know your heart is still hurting, and
therefore is closed to new opportunities.

But watch out for them, Grace. They're coming
to you very soon.

Love, Me x

Thirty-One

'Hurry up, Ava,' I say as I wait in the newsagent's next to an indecisive Ava, who is trying to decide what sweets she wants to buy with the bit of pocket money Mum has given her for helping clean the shop. 'We need to get back to Granny's shop so she can go to the auction this afternoon.'

Since my decision to stay in Sandybridge to help Mum out, we've been working non-stop, getting the shop in order. Ava and I have helped clean and tidy and catalogue all the stock, and now we're looking to get new items in. There were a few requests for house clearances that Mum hadn't dealt with under a pile of other paperwork in Dad's old office, so I contacted the people, hoping it wasn't too late. Luckily, for a couple of them it wasn't. While Mum watched Ava, I went and cleared as much stuff as I could from the houses, keeping anything I thought might be worthwhile to be sold in the shop, listing some of the items on eBay, and giving the rest to the charity shop just up the street from us.

Ava and I have only been here a week, but already the shop is looking in better shape.

Surprisingly, I've quite enjoyed helping Mum get the business back on its feet; so much so that when I had to pop to London to pick up some more clothes for Ava and me (we'd only planned on visiting for a few days, so had travelled light), far from wishing I could linger in the city, I couldn't wait to return to Sandybridge. All the more so since this time I was travelling by train – a journey that was so much quicker than the bus Ava and I had been forced into taking because it was the cheapest option.

'Grace?' I've been so lost in my thoughts about Sandybridge and the shop that I jump at the sound of my name.

'Danny!' I cry, turning around. 'How are you?'

'Still not fully functioning, as you can see,' he says, winking and gesturing down at his legs. 'Other than that, I'm very well, thank you. How are you?'

'I'm good, thanks.'

'And is this beautiful little Ava?' he asks, looking at Ava – who's still debating between a packet of Smarties and a Milky Bar, or some Magic Stars and a packet of Cadbury Buttons. 'I haven't seen her since she was a baby!'

I nod. 'Yes, that's my daughter, the chocoholic.'

'I'd go with the buttons,' Danny says to Ava. 'Always been one of my favourites.'

Ava looks with interest at Danny. 'Why are you in a push-chair?' she asks to my horror.

'No, Ava, it's a wheelchair,' I correct her as my cheeks redden. 'I'm so sorry, Danny,' I apologise. 'She's only four.'

'Don't be silly,' Danny tells me, wheeling himself closer to Ava. 'Ava, this is a special type of pushchair – see?' He gestures to his wheels. 'I push myself around in it and, just between you and me, I go very, very fast in it most of the time when I really shouldn't!'

I smile as I watch Ava immediately warm to Danny. She's a bit of a daredevil herself, always the first to throw herself around adventure playgrounds and dive into ball pits.

'Can I have a go?' Ava asks, her eyes shining; she appears to have forgotten all about her sweet dilemma.

'I can give you a ride, if you like,' Danny offers. 'That's if it's OK with Mummy?'

I nod. 'Sure, but we have to get back to the antiques shop – Mum's waiting for us.'

'Then I shall accompany you there, and Ava can ride in pride of place, like a princess with her own carriage!'

Ava sits on Danny's lap, clutching her bag of sweets, while Danny pushes himself along the pavement next to me, and we head in the direction of the shop.

'So, how's things?' Danny asks as I walk along next to him. 'Sorry to hear about you and Simon.'

'Yeah, well … you know,' I reply, feeling my face flush. Danny had warned me not to rush into marrying Simon, and now it feels weird discussing my break-up with him.

'Yeah, I do actually,' Danny says to my surprise. 'I guess you heard about me and Rebecca?'

I nod. 'I'm sorry too.'

Danny sighs. 'It wasn't the most amicable break-up. She found someone else.'

Although Danny still pushes Ava along with brisk, strong

movements, I'm sure I see his shoulders tighten at this revelation.

'She seemed so nice, the few times I met her,' I tell him. 'You weren't to know what would happen.'

'That she would become a lesbian and run off with another woman? No, I didn't see that one coming!' Danny says wryly. 'Neither did I expect that I'd only see my daughter once in a blue moon.'

'How old is Emily now?' I ask hesitantly.

'Eleven,' he says, 'and as pretty as a picture. That's the only way I get to see her most of the time these days – in photos.'

'I'm so sorry, Danny,' I say. 'I know how hard break-ups are. But at least I still have Ava. I can't begin to imagine how you're feeling.'

'How can we ever know what's going to happen to us?' he says after a few moments. 'If only we all had a crystal ball presented to us when we're born, then we'd be able to predict our future a little better, and maybe we wouldn't make so many mistakes.'

'Yeah,' I reply cautiously, thinking of Remy, 'that would be handy, wouldn't it? But sometimes making those mistakes is necessary so we can discover something even better as a result.'

Danny looks up at me from his chair. 'Are you suggesting we've both got married and then split from our partners so that something wonderful can happen to us?'

I nod. 'Probably. No, make that *definitely*. There's always a silver lining to every problem. A rainbow after every storm. A—'

'Yeah, yeah, I get it,' Danny says, laughing. 'Who appointed you Little Miss Positive?'

I shrug. 'I don't know. I just feel quite optimistic right now, that's all.'

'Good, I'm pleased to hear it.' Danny pulls his chair to a halt as we arrive outside the shop. 'How was that for you, milady?' he asks Ava as she hops down from his lap.

'Great!' Ava says, her cheeks flushed with excitement. 'Granny!' she calls, as Mum comes to the door. 'I had a ride on a grown-up pushchair!'

Mum looks with interest at Danny.

'*Wheelchair*,' I remind Ava as she pushes past Mum into the shop.

'Is it elevenses time, Granny Harper?' I hear Ava call from the back room. 'Can we have biscuits?'

'Takes after you, I see.' Danny grins. 'You always loved your food, if I remember rightly.'

'Still do!' I smile back. 'Can't you tell?'

'No,' Danny says, looking appreciatively at my figure – now a good two sizes bigger than it was when we'd been a couple. 'I think you look great.'

I feel myself blushing.

'Danny, why don't you stay for a cuppa?' Mum asks. 'I'm off out now, but I'm sure Grace will be more than happy to look after you.' She gives me a knowing look.

'That would be lovely, Mrs Harper,' he says. 'OK with you, Gracie?'

I jump at his use of my old nickname.

'Er, yes, of course. I'll go and put the kettle on. Can you manage getting into the shop?' I ask, then immediately regret it. 'I mean ... there's a slight step and—'

'It's fine, don't worry about me. I've conquered bigger mountains than your shop step.' He smiles, and suddenly I'm cast back to my school days and the effect a Danny Lucas smile would have on me.

'Sure . . . I'll just put that kettle on then,' I say, and I hurry off to the back room, my cheeks flushing furiously.

Mum has now departed to her auction, her first in many months, and I'm pleased to see her go. It's been good to see Mum so excited about something; she used to love auctions when Dad was here, and I'm hoping this will help her get back into the swing of things again.

Danny is currently colouring with Ava; they've balanced one of her books on his lap, and while he helps her choose coloured pencils, Ava stands in front of him concentrating hard on adding colour to a picture of a teddy bear with a bunch of balloons in his hand.

I'd been quite shocked at the effect Danny's smile had had on me earlier. But should I have been? I've always had a soft spot for him, ever since our schooldays. Even when we broke up and he went away, I still thought about him every day, hard as I tried not to. There had been the time we almost resurrected our relationship when we were both home from university at Christmas. And when Simon and I had attended Danny's fundraiser soon after our engagement, I'd felt that strange twinge when I was talking to him, guiltily pushing it aside because I shouldn't have been feeling anything at all when we both had partners.

I've always felt guilty about Danny's accident, even though he seems to have become a better person as a result, helping so many people with his charity. Could it be that I'm confusing my constant guilt with feelings of a different kind?

Danny is still a good-looking man. Though his dark mane of hair has been invaded by the odd fleck of grey at his temples (which, unlike me, he chooses not to cover), his face is handsome as ever. The smooth, almost movie-star perfection of his teenage years has given way to a more rugged look. He may be confined to a wheelchair, but he obviously keeps himself fit; his upper body in particular is very muscular. His eyes are the only part of him that haven't changed in the slightest; they still twinkle like naughty sapphires when he's up to mischief. Which is most of the time.

Danny notices me watching him, and he smiles.

'Remember when I flicked a pencil at you in registration?' he asks, his eyes shining. 'And it missed and hit Donna Lewis?'

I nod. 'She screamed and said she'd been stabbed. Tried to make out she'd get lead poisoning.'

'I was only doing it to get your attention. I quite fancied you, even before that party.'

'Is that what you do now to get the girls?' I ask, grinning. 'Throw wooden objects at them? Bit caveman, isn't it?'

'Doesn't that work these days, then?' Danny asks with a straight face. 'I'm a bit out of practice.'

'Try it next time you see a woman you like the look of and see what reaction you get!' I laugh. 'But don't come ...' I hesitate. Damn, could I have picked a worse saying? 'Don't come to me if she throws something back at you – like a slap!'

'Point taken,' Danny says, winking at me. Then his face turns more sombre. 'You don't need to tiptoe around me, Gracie,' he says earnestly. 'I've been like this almost twenty years now. I'm not a delicate little flower that needs protecting from anything that might upset me.'

'Sorry, it's still difficult sometimes, seeing you like that. Even though it's been so long. I can't help feeling guilty.'

'You feel guilty – why? The fire wasn't your fault.' Danny passes Ava a blue pencil and she continues to happily colour in the bear's bow tie.

'I know, but if it hadn't been for me, you wouldn't have been there that evening.'

Danny nods, acknowledging my point. 'Perhaps, but think how many people Charlie and I helped that night. If we hadn't been there, some of those people might have died from their injuries or been trapped inside the burning building. And if you hadn't been there, who would have rung the fire brigade? These days everyone has mobile phones, but back then, Grace, someone had to run to the phone box, didn't they? If you hadn't, Christ knows how long the place would have burned before someone summoned help.'

I nod. He was right, of course. Remy had said something similar in a letter to me afterwards. But why did Danny have to suffer when he'd been so heroic that night? It didn't seem fair.

'Anyway,' Danny whispers, leaning away from Ava, 'do you know how many women I was able to bag using my chair as a pulling point before I met Rebecca? Loads! It's awesome. Best babe-magnet ever. You might even have done me a favour!'

I shake my head reprovingly. 'And there was I, thinking you still threw pencils!'

'Ah, I save that for the special ones.' Danny winks.

'You never change, do you?' I say lightly, standing up from my chair. I lift our empty coffee mugs, intending to take them to the little sink in the office. 'I think the word that

285

best describes you is incorrigible!' I call, turning away from them and walking towards the door.

But as I do, I feel something hit the back of my head.

I turn around and find Danny concentrating hard on his colouring with Ava. I look down at the floor and see a pink colouring pencil lying at my feet. When I look back at Danny, he's watching me out of the corner of his eye.

'Only the special ones,' he whispers.

Thirty-Two

We've been in Sandybridge for three weeks now, and I'm quite enjoying myself. The shop is almost back to normal – well, as normal as it's going to get without Dad. Mum seems much happier, and is taking an interest in the antiques business again, which is of course having an impact on the shop's success. The place is going great guns right now. Even Ava seems to be flourishing here. Her little face, which is usually pale when we're in London, has a healthy glow these days, and her brown eyes seem to shine that little bit more.

Ava loves the beach, just as I did as a child, and we seem to end up visiting the sandy one near the lighthouse nearly every day. Sometimes we walk, sometimes we stop and build the odd sandcastle, and sometimes we have a picnic with Mum – which is one of Ava's favourite things to do.

Every occasion we're there I look for Charlie, hoping he might emerge from the lighthouse and see us. But both the lighthouse and the cottage next door seem to be empty most of the time. The only sign of life I've seen is the occasional visitor to the Lighthouse Bakery's exhibition.

'Does Charlie never come back these days?' I ask Mum one afternoon as we're picnicking on the beach. 'I haven't seen him since we've been here.'

'Charlie comes and goes,' Mum says, passing Ava a cheese sandwich. 'He was here the day you went to London for more clothes. He called at the house to see you, but when I told him you weren't here, he said he wasn't staying. Apparently he had to rush up to Northampton that evening.'

Northampton was home to the distribution company that delivered the Lighthouse Bakery's wares around the country.

'Oh . . . ' I look forlornly at the lighthouse. 'It would be nice to see him again. I hope he comes home while we're here.'

Mum purses her lips a little. I've said the wrong thing.

Mum refuses to discuss what will happen when we return to London in September for Ava to start school. We've been here three weeks already, and I know I'm pushing it with work. The gallery had been supportive about me taking extra time off when I'd explained about Mum's problems, but we needed to go back sometime, and that sometime would have to be soon.

'I wish you would reconsider, Grace,' Mum says, casually rearranging the items on the picnic rug, 'about staying on in Sandybridge. You know how much I love having you here, and Ava loves the seaside so much – don't you, dear?'

Ava nods furiously. She's in the middle of chewing a bite of her sandwich, and she knows I'll scold her if she speaks with her mouth full.

'*Mum* . . . ' I give her a reproving look. 'You know we can't do that. I have my job, for one thing—'

'You can work with me at the shop! We're doing so well now, I'm sure we can afford a wage for you.'

I just nod. Mum's right, we could afford another wage, but I'd prefer it if that wage went to someone else. As much as I'm enjoying being here in Sandybridge and helping Mum at the shop, I don't want it to become my permanent career. I studied for too long, and gained too much experience in the field, to use my history knowledge to run an antiques shop, lovely though ours was.

'I'll think about it,' I reply, hoping this will keep her off my back for a while. 'I'm making no promises though,' I tell her when I see her face light up.

'I would have thought you'd want to stay, now you and Danny are stepping out together again,' Mum says with an innocent expression.

I roll my eyes. 'Mum, there are two things wrong with that statement. Danny unfortunately doesn't step anywhere these days.' I raise my eyebrows at her. It's as if our roles have reversed lately, and now I'm the one always doing the chastising. 'And even if a miracle did take place, and he was able to walk again, you wouldn't find me stepping alongside him in the way you mean!'

That's not entirely true. Danny and I have been out for a drink a couple of times, leaving Ava in Mum's care, and last time he'd suggested that we have a meal together sometime soon. But Mum makes it sound like we're dating, and that's certainly not the case. More like two friends catching up after a long time apart.

'Whatever you say, Grace,' Mum says, winking at Ava. 'Whatever you say.'

I shake my head and look away from her down the beach,

289

and it's as I do that I see a familiar silhouette walking towards me along the sand, with a smaller, four-legged silhouette next to him.

'Charlie!' I call, scrambling to my feet. I hold my hand up over my eyes so I can see him better. The bright sun is so strong that I can barely make him out, but I'd know that figure anywhere. Walking next to him is his beloved and now quite elderly Labrador, Winston.

I run towards them both, and as I get closer Winston barks and Charlie holds out his arms to me. We embrace as we reach each other, and that wonderful familiar feeling of being close to Charlie engulfs me, like a soft warm blanket being wrapped around my body.

'I thought that was you sitting on the beach,' Charlie says as we loosen our hold and stand back to see each other's faces. 'I was looking out of one of the lighthouse windows and I spied you on the sand.'

'Uncle Charlie!' we hear a small voice call, and we turn to see Ava running along the beach towards us, still carrying her sandwich.

Charlie reaches out his arms and sweeps Ava up in them, spinning her around in the air.

'Hello, Pumpkin,' he says, using the nickname he's had for her ever since she was born in late October. 'Gosh, you're getting a big girl now, aren't you?'

Charlie puts Ava down on the sand, and she immediately slips her hand into his, while I crouch down to fuss Winston, who happily licks me in greeting.

I stand up again and smile at Charlie. 'I didn't think I was going to see you while we were here this time.'

'I haven't been in Sandybridge that much lately,' Charlie

says. 'I've got some stuff going on at the moment – business stuff. It's keeping me quite busy.'

He doesn't volunteer any information about what that business might be.

'How long are you here for this time?' I ask, hoping I'm going to be able to spend some time with him again. It's been ages since we've seen each other properly.

'I'm here for the weekend,' Charlie says. 'Will you be around?'

'Of course I will! Oh, Charlie, we've missed you! And you, Winston!' I say, ruffling the dog's ears again. 'It'll be great to spend some time with you and catch up.'

'I've missed you both too,' Charlie says, watching me. 'More than you know.'

Thirty-Three

Charlie and I spend as much of the weekend together as we can.

We take walks along the Sandybridge beaches with Winston, both with Ava and alone. We have a pub lunch at the Sandybridge Arms on Saturday, then on Sunday evening Charlie offers to cook me a meal at Lighthouse Cottage, which I gratefully accept.

It's as I nip into the little supermarket on the high street, for a bottle of wine to take to Charlie's, that I bump into Danny.

'Whoa, slow down!' Danny laughs. 'What's the hurry?'

For some reason I try to hide the bottle of wine behind my back.

'No hurry,' I reply, smiling. 'Didn't see you, that's all.'

Danny looks at me suspiciously. 'What's behind your back?'

'Oh, this?' I retrieve the wine and hold it in front of me. 'Just some wine.'

'You and your mum fancy a tipple tonight, do you?' Danny grins. 'Nice.'

'Something like that – yes.'

'Why don't I bring round a couple of bottles and we can make a night of it? We could even order some Chinese in from that takeaway you love so much, and I'll hire a DVD. What do you say?' Danny looks up at me expectantly.

'Ah ... it sounds lovely, Danny, really it does. But I'm not actually going home right now. Perhaps another time?'

'Oh, I see ... right, yes, of course.' Danny's cheeks flush pink. 'My mistake.' He looks up at me curiously. 'So who is the wine for, if you don't mind me asking?'

I can't lie to him. Not that there's any reason why I should.

'It's for Charlie, he's cooking me dinner tonight at his cottage.'

'I didn't know he was back.'

'Only for the weekend. He's off to London on Monday for a few days.'

'Ah, I see.' Danny nods thoughtfully. 'Perhaps we can get together again next week instead then? I know from past experience that when Charlie's around he always comes first.'

I'm surprised at his tone. Danny doesn't usually make sarcastic remarks. Witty ones, yes, but sarcastic wasn't his style.

'Danny, that's not fair! I hardly see Charlie these days. It's been wonderful to spend the weekend catching up with him, and Mum said she'd baby-sit Ava tonight, so we thought we'd have dinner, that's all.'

Danny looks thoughtfully up at me, as if he's considering

something. 'I'm sorry,' he says. 'I only wish I had a friendship with someone that was as close as yours and Charlie's. We'll get together next week then? Go for that meal I suggested?'

'Yes, of course, that would be lovely.'

'Great. Well, have a good evening with Charlie, and I'll call you next week.' He nods abruptly, spins his chair around, then wheels it hurriedly down the aisle and back out of the shop.

I sigh. What was that all about? It wasn't like Danny at all.

I pay for my wine and begin walking towards the beach and the lighthouse, still thinking about Danny's behaviour.

He'd seemed almost jealous that I was spending the evening with Charlie. But why would he be? It wasn't as if we were together any more. We might have been out a few times lately, but only as friends. Danny had offered a pleasant distraction from the shop and my concerns about going back to London. I enjoyed his company – nothing wrong with that. But was Danny reading something else into it that I wasn't?

No, I tell myself. A memory flashes into my mind: the night of the auction, and Danny trying to persuade me I had feelings for Charlie! Why would he have done that if he still had feelings for me himself?

But that seems a lifetime ago, and a lot has changed in our lives in the meantime. Maybe Danny's feelings have changed too.

I shake my head, unable to deal with this now. I have too much other stuff to contend with at the moment to worry about Danny. I'll have to deal with him later. Tonight I just want to enjoy dinner with my best friend.

Instead of walking across the sand towards the cottage, I keep to the path that runs above the beach next to the woods. I don't want my pumps to be filled with sand by the time I get to Charlie's.

It had been a struggle deciding what to wear tonight. I didn't want to over-dress; after all, this was Charlie I was having dinner with – my mate. But at the same time I wanted Charlie to think I'd made a bit of an effort, since he was cooking me dinner. So I'd chosen a pair of blue cropped jeans, teamed with a white shirt and red pumps. It was casual, yes, but not scruffy, and seemed perfect for dinner with my best friend.

As I walk along the path I get glimpses of Sandybridge Hall through the trees.

'I wonder who has bought you this time?' I murmur as I pause to look through one of the gaps. 'You've known some owners over the years, eh?'

I carry on my way, thinking about the house and all the reincarnations it's had over the years, from party venue to restaurant. 'Let's hope this time the person who's bought you will look after you properly,' I whisper. Then I turn and walk towards the lighthouse and its little cottage neighbour.

Lighthouse Cottage is as pretty as it's always been. Whitewashed all over, like its bigger brother, it still has the same pink roses climbing up and over its wooden front door that I remember from when I was a girl, and came here the first time with Mum. That was the day I'd first come into contact with Remy.

I think about the typewriter now as I wait for Charlie to come to the door.

I haven't asked Remy anything else since he advised me to stay close to the people who love me. He'd been right though; my staying in Sandybridge for a while had helped Mum no end.

Maybe I should ask him whether I ought to remain here permanently.

Then there had been the second, bonus letter, the one about me watching for new opportunities. I wasn't sure what that could mean. My heart *was* closed, Remy was right about that, and I intended for it to remain so. It had been hurt far too much in the break-up for me to risk opening it up again to further abuse.

'Hey,' Charlie says, breaking into my thoughts as he opens the front door to greet me. 'You made it then?'

'Hey, yourself,' I reply, checking my watch. 'Not late, am I?'

'A few minutes, but it doesn't matter. Come in!'

I follow Charlie through into the cottage, thinking how he's always been overly punctual, where I've always been the opposite – something that used to drive him mad.

'You've decorated since I was last here,' I say as we walk through the clutter-free hall. 'And not too long ago,' I add, catching a whiff of fresh paint.

'Yeah, I thought it was time for a change,' Charlie says, heading for the kitchen. 'I'm hardly ever here now, so I was thinking of renting the place out.'

I'm surprised to hear this. I've always thought of Lighthouse Cottage as Charlie's bolthole from the stresses and strains of his international business.

'You don't approve?' Charlie asks, opening the bottle-green Aga to check his dish, some sort of pie by the look of it.

'It's not that I don't approve, I just thought you'd keep the cottage as a sort of retreat, a place to get away from it all.'

Charlie closes the oven door and looks at me.

'Do you think I should keep it then? I mean, I wasn't going to sell it, just rent it out.'

I look around the kitchen and memories of the times I've been in here suddenly come flooding back to me – the first time Charlie met Ava, the first time I met Louisa. The times Charlie and I had sat in his sitting room drinking wine and putting the world to rights. We'd talked about our lives – the good times and the bad. I'd cried on Charlie's shoulder about Simon, and Charlie had poured out his heart to me about Louisa.

'Yes, I definitely think you should keep it. There are too many memories here, Charlie – we've shared such special times here, you and I – it would be awful if some stranger came and broke into our little bubble.'

Charlie listens to me, then he smiles.

'I'm so pleased you said that, because that's exactly how I feel. I thought I might be being a bit silly or too sentimental, hanging on to a house I hardly use. But we have had some good times here, haven't we?'

I nod, walk across the red-brick kitchen floor and wrap my arms around him. Charlie does the same to me, so we're holding each other around the waist.

'We certainly have,' I tell him, looking into his eyes. 'And hopefully there will be many more to come in the future. Now, I must ask you something very important.'

'What's that?' Charlie asks, worried.

'Can you smell burning?'

Charlie rescues his slightly chargrilled dish – a home-made lasagne – from the Aga, and after I've helped him prepare a salad we sit down to eat at the scrubbed wooden table in the cosy kitchen.

'This is delicious,' I say, sampling my lasagne. 'I didn't know you could cook.'

Charlie laughs. 'Considering my whole business is based around a bakery, I should hope I can!'

'Ha ha, very funny. No, I meant cook meals. Obviously you know a bit about baking cakes!'

'Yeah, I taught myself a while ago. There's only so many ready meals you should eat in your life, and I think I've had my fair share of them over the years. Especially after Louisa left.'

I've never understood why Charlie hasn't found someone else after Louisa, but he's always insisted he's quite happy on his own, and a woman would only confuse things.

'Well, I for one am glad you've found this new skill. I can't wait to taste the pie we're having for dessert – what is it? Apple?'

'And blackberry.'

'Yum!'

'So have you given any more thought to how long you might stay with your mother?' Charlie asks, pronging some pasta on to his fork, and scooping up cheese and tomato sauce to go with it. 'You said the other day you weren't sure.'

'I'm still not. It's so difficult to know what to do for the best. Mum still desperately wants me to stay here with her, and to be honest I'm starting to wonder if it might be a good idea.'

'Really?' Charlie asks, surprised. 'I never thought I'd hear you say that. I remember when you couldn't wait to get away from Sandybridge!'

'Yes, I know, but I guess we change as we get older, and our priorities change too. Mum needs me, and Ava certainly seems a lot happier and healthier since we've been here. Perhaps moving back would be for the best.'

'Sounds as though you've already made your mind up.'

'I know, but what would I do and where would I live if I did move here? Much as I love Mum, I can't move in with her permanently – I need my own space. And I can't work at the shop forever either, so I'd need to find work. You know me, Charlie, I need a project, I need to feel I'm achieving something in life, otherwise I stagnate.'

Charlie looks at me thoughtfully. 'I may be able to help you out.'

'How?'

'Remember what I was saying earlier about finding someone to rent the cottage? Why don't you and Ava take it? I don't want any rent – you'd be doing me a favour looking after the place. Like I said, I'm hardly ever here these days.'

I stare at Charlie across the table, my fork hovering between my plate and my mouth. He's come up with what sounds like the perfect solution, but I don't want to be beholden to him, best friend or not.

'It sounds lovely, Charlie, but what would I do here? I still need a job.'

'That I can't help you with, sadly. As you know, most of my staff are now scattered about the country at our various offices. The only staff I have based here in Sandybridge are the two ladies that look after the bakery exhibition in the lighthouse.'

'Oh, I know, and I wouldn't expect anything more from you. But if I were to take you up on your kind offer of the cottage, I'd have to insist on paying rent, and that means I need a job.'

'I told you, Gracie, I don't want rent. I'd be happy to be giving you and Ava a home.'

I shake my head. 'I'd have to insist on paying you. Look, I know you don't need the money, Charlie, now you're a multi-millionaire or whatever, but I need to feel independent.'

Charlie nods. 'I understand. So you'll definitely take it then – the cottage?'

I look around the kitchen. I've always loved this little house from the first time I set foot in here with Mum. It has a lovely warm, cosy feel about it, and I know that Ava and I would be happy here.

I also know that Simon wouldn't object if I moved back to Sandybridge. He's recently taken a job in Dubai, collecting valuable works of art for some wealthy sheikh, so it's unlikely he'll want to see Ava too often while he's living out there.

'Yes, I will,' I say emphatically. 'But,' I interrupt quickly before Charlie can begin celebrating, 'on ...' I think hurriedly, '*three* conditions.'

'Go on.' Charlie takes a sip of his red wine.

'One: that I can get Ava into the local primary school. It can be a nightmare getting children into schools they haven't been signed up to for years.'

Charlie nods. 'I think you might be OK: one of the ladies that works for me also works part-time at the school, and I'm sure I remember her saying it was lovely here because the primary school was never over-subscribed, so the children all get individual attention.'

'That's good to know,' I say, warming even more to this

idea. The primary school I'd signed Ava up for in London was filled to maximum capacity.

'What's next?' Charlie asks, obviously eager to solve every problem I might find to prevent us moving.

'I must find a job. I can work with Mum for the time being, until I find her an assistant, but then I need to get something that will pay enough to support Ava and me. Preferably something that I won't be bored stiff doing!'

Charlie smiles and shakes his head.

'I'm a tough old bird to please, eh?' I say, grinning back.

'Enough of the old!' Charlie winks. 'I'm eleven months older than you, remember? So, you said three things. What's your third condition?'

'Ah, this one could be the hardest for you to solve, Charlie Parker . . . '

'Why, what is it?' Charlie asks anxiously.

'I must insist that . . . ' I pause for effect, 'you come to Sandybridge to visit Ava and me on a regular basis!'

Charlie looks immediately relieved. 'That goes without saying! I'll have every reason for coming home if you're here, Gracie.'

Thirty-Four

Charlie and I spend the rest of the evening talking about how we're going to arrange for Ava and me to move in to Lighthouse Cottage.

We've finished our main course, and now we're lounging on comfy sofas in the sitting room at the back of the cottage, both of us feeling pretty full after large helpings of apple-and-blackberry pie and custard.

'I'll have to work some notice,' I tell Charlie. 'Problem is, that might overlap with when Ava has to start school.'

'I'll help you,' Charlie says, without thinking about it. 'I'm sure that between us, your mum and I can care for Ava for a few days.'

'That's very kind, Charlie, but I don't want to impose on your time. I know how busy you are.'

'That's one of the perks of being your own boss! You can take time off whenever you want to. I can easily manage a few days off to look after Ava.'

'Oh, Charlie, what would I do without you?' I say, reaching across the sofa to take his hand. The pair of us sit contentedly watching the flames dance in the little fire Charlie has made up for us. Even though it's the middle of August, the nights are beginning to feel chilly.

'And what would I do without my Gracie?' Charlie replies, squeezing my hand as he looks across at me. 'Do you know, we've known each other twenty-six years?'

I work this out in my own head. 'So we have. I remember the first time I met you: we had on virtually the same outfit – I was horrified, but you thought it was amusing.'

'Ah, back when I was the ginger kid,' Charlie says, running his hand through his now much calmer straw-coloured hair, which unlike Danny's doesn't appear to have any grey in it yet. 'That was fun, being called carrot-top, and Duracell.'

'The joys of being young,' I say, stretching my legs out so the tips of my now bare feet sit that little bit closer to the fire. 'I think I'd rather be the age I am now than go back and do it all again – especially school.'

Charlie nods. 'Apart from meeting you, I can't think of anything I'd want to go back and do again.' He thinks for a moment. 'What about Danny?' he asks casually, lifting the bottle of wine we've been drinking, and topping up our glasses. 'Wouldn't you want to meet him again?'

I think about Danny and our time together at school.

'Danny will always be my first love – I can't change that. Nor would I want to, I guess. He's still my friend now, and not many people can say that about their teenage crush.'

Charlie nods. 'I heard you'd been seeing him again.'

'Hardly seeing him. We've been out together a few times – as friends,' I emphasise.

'That's not what Ava thinks.'

'Why, what has she been saying?'

'Ava told me yesterday when you popped into that shop to get ice creams that Danny was your boyfriend.'

'She *what*?' I ask, astonished by this. 'Whatever gave her that idea?'

Charlie shrugs. 'You tell me.'

I'm about to defend myself, when I look at Charlie and suddenly get it. I shake my head. 'When are you two ever going to grow up?'

'What do you mean?' he asks.

'This feud between you and Danny? OK, maybe "feud" is a bit strong, but there's always been a rivalry between the two of you, you can't deny that.'

Charlie looks at me with a puzzled expression.

'You're jealous because I've been out with Danny a couple of times, and he's jealous that I'm spending the weekend with you!'

'He is?' Charlie can't hide his pleasure at hearing this.

'Yes! I met him in the supermarket when I was picking up some wine for tonight. He was quite put out I was heading over to see you, and not spending the evening with him.'

Charlie looks almost smug now.

I shake my head again. 'This really has gone on for too long. Why can't the two of you just get on? I thought you'd moved on from this years ago. When we were at Sandybridge Hall for Danny's charity ball, the two of you were acting like best mates.'

'I wouldn't say that,' Charlie says, lifting his wine. 'I don't actually see Danny that often these days. We're rarely ever in Sandybridge at the same time.'

'And when you are . . . ?'

Charlie shrugs. 'We're fine, I guess. We went for a drink together one night actually.'

'You did?' I'm surprised to hear this. 'What did you talk about?'

Charlie smiles, 'All sorts. We even talked about you.'

'Me – why?'

'A common interest, perhaps? We both care a lot about you, Gracie.'

I calm down a little.

'Danny has always had a soft spot for you since you dated, everybody knows that.'

'He does?' I say, trying to sound surprised, even though Danny has made it pretty obvious.

'Of course.' Charlie pauses as if he's considering something. 'Did you know that you were one of the reasons his marriage broke down?'

'What! That's not true. Why would you say that?'

Charlie takes a slow gulp from his glass. 'Because when we were having a drink together that night in the pub, he told me. We were talking about you, and it just came up. I was pretty shocked too.'

'This is madness! I had nothing to do with Danny and Rebecca breaking up – she had an affair and went off with someone else. Danny told me.'

'That was afterwards. After she realised there was someone else in their marriage.'

'Who, me?' I can barely believe any of what Charlie is telling me. 'Are you telling me I turned Rebecca into a lesbian!'

Charlie has to smile. 'Hardly. But I think she only began to look elsewhere because she wasn't getting what she wanted from Danny. You've always been the one in Danny's mind, ever since school. Apparently no one else ever came close.' Charlie takes another long gulp from his glass, this time draining it dry. 'Pretty high praise, Gracie. We both know Danny's had his fair share of female attention over the years. More wine?' he asks calmly, while I sit completely dazed by what I've just heard. 'I could certainly do with some.'

I can only nod and watch silently as Charlie heads back into the kitchen.

How could this be? I'd kind of guessed Danny had always had a soft spot for me, as I had for him, but to tell someone it was one of the reasons his marriage broke up was insane.

And why was Charlie telling me all this now? He must have known for some time. Why had he not said something sooner?

Charlie returns with a new bottle of wine already uncorked. He pours some into his glass. Mine is still half-full.

'Why didn't you say something before?' I ask him immediately.

'I didn't think it was my place to. Plus you were living in London, I didn't think it mattered. But now you're here and dating . . . '

'We're not dating!' I insist again. I lift my wine and take a long gulp.

'Do you want to be?' he asks.

'No . . . I mean . . . yes . . . oh, I don't know!' I drain my glass dry this time, and Charlie leans over and refills it without even asking me.

I look at him. 'What do you think I should do?'

Charlie sits studying me for some time before answering.

'I think you should do whatever makes you happy,' he

says quietly. 'That's all anyone can ever ask for. You should be with someone who makes your heart leap with joy every time you see them. Someone who makes you laugh until your belly aches. Someone whose smile lights up your world, and whose mere presence makes you feel utterly alive . . . '

His gaze doesn't veer from my face throughout this little speech, and I in turn am completely mesmerised by his words.

Even now, when Charlie has clearly finished speaking, we still gaze at each other.

'Do you know someone who makes you feel like that?' Charlie whispers eventually.

'Yes . . . ' I whisper back, not understanding why my heart is suddenly racing. 'Yes, I do.'

'Then you should be with him, Gracie,' Charlie says, turning away. He grabs his glass again, but pauses before he takes a drink. 'Because he is the one who will make you happy.'

Dear Grace,

I'm so pleased you've made the decision to return permanently to your home and to those that love you. I know your choice concerns you, because you feel you've taken a step back. But please don't worry; this is definitely a decision you will not regret.

I know too that your love life is something that is bothering you. You want to know whether you've made the right choice in matters of the heart. But that's the thing about the heart; it's very good at telling you what it wants you to do. You only have to listen to it, Grace, and it will guide you, just as I have tried to do over the years.

Love, Me x

Thirty-Five

'There's some post for you on the side, Grace,' Mum says as Ava and I arrive at her house for tea one night. 'Came today – redirected, by the looks of it. Come on through, Ava sweetheart, I've baked your favourite – jam tarts!'

Mum takes Ava through to the kitchen while I pause to pick up my post. After deciding to stay on in Sandybridge, I asked for my post to be redirected to Mum's house. I haven't got around to asking for it to be changed to Lighthouse Cottage yet, even though Ava and I have been living there for almost a month now.

The first few letters are the usual – a credit-card bill, a bank statement, a catalogue – none of which I want to see right now; having worked the notice period on my old job, I've yet to find a new one, so money's tight. Then I come to a typewritten envelope with a real stamp on it. I turn it over to look at the back, but there's no return address. I go ahead and open it.

'What?' I exclaim as I read through the letter again. 'This can't be!'

'What is it, Grace dear?' Mum asks, coming back into the hall. 'Bad news?'

'No – the opposite, very good news,' I tell her. 'Have you found out yet who the new owner of Sandybridge Hall is?'

She shakes her head. 'All I know is that it was sold a while ago. No one knows who's bought it. Why?'

'Because I've been offered a job there, as chief curator. Well, it's a bit more than that, actually: they want me to be in charge of restoring the whole place to its *former glory* – their words, not mine.'

Mum takes the letter from me and reads through it. 'It says you were recommended to them by one of your former bosses. Who's that?'

'I'm not sure . . . Oh, it might be Hilary at the V&A; I told her I was looking for work.' I take the letter back. 'This is amazing, Mum, exactly the opportunity I've been looking for, something to get my teeth into, yet right on my doorstep.'

Mum gives me a huge hug. 'This calls for a celebration! I wish I'd baked one of my cakes now. How about we go out to eat at the pub?'

'It's not definite yet. They say they'd like to talk to me first, to see if we're on the same wavelength about how to restore the house and its gardens.'

'Of course you'll be on the same wavelength, you've known that house since you were a little girl, you'll know exactly how to restore it to its former glory. I'm sure when my Grace is finished with it, Sandybridge Hall will look better than it's ever looked before.'

*

'So, what did they say?' Danny asks me, as we sit at a table in the Sandybridge Arms.

I'm just back from a trip down to London to see a representative of the new owner of Sandybridge Hall.

We met at a rather beautiful Art Deco café, and I was asked to outline my ideas for the refurbishment of Sandybridge Hall. Luckily my ideas seemed to match those of the new owner: that the aim should be to return the house and gardens to their original Tudor glory, using original and reclaimed materials wherever possible.

There'll be a dedicated team of staff, which I'll be in charge of, tasked with finding as many of the original furnishings as can be traced. Any items that can't be found, I'm to replace by sourcing the closest match available.

The owner not only wants to return the hall to its heyday, but to turn it into a place where he can live comfortably. So along with all the renovation work, I'm to convert some of the rooms into modern living quarters too.

It's a huge job, but according to Sue – who it turns out is personal assistant to the new owner, Mr Braithwaite – money is no object. He's determined that this must be done properly, and I'd been highly recommended to him at a party as the ideal person for the job.

'So you've accepted the job then?' Danny asks eagerly.

'Yes. There was no way I was going to turn it down – unless the pay had been rubbish, which it isn't; it's surprisingly good, actually. I can't believe it, Danny – this couldn't be more perfect for me right now if it tried!'

Danny lifts his glass. 'Here's to you, Gracie, your new job, and your return to Sandybridge. I for one am very glad you're going to be sticking around!'

'Thank you!' I chink my glass with his.

Since Ava and I moved into Lighthouse Cottage, I've been spending more time with Danny. It still isn't anything more serious than a few dates, and I'm taking care to keep it that way.

After Charlie told me about Danny, and his possible feelings for me, I'd spent a lot of time thinking about what I should do next. But I couldn't suddenly stop seeing Danny – for a start, what excuse would I give? And anyway, I didn't want to. I like Danny, he's my friend, and I want it to stay that way.

And we're hardly lovesick teenagers any more; if we can't just be friends without anything else happening, then we have a bit of a problem.

'How's Ava getting on at school?' Danny asks. 'Is she settling in OK?'

'Wonderfully, I couldn't have asked for it to go better. It's like she's always been there, she loves it.'

The first week of Ava's new school coincided with working the notice period on my job in London, but I'd done some unpaid overtime so I could be the one to take her in on her first day. I'd anticipated Ava being the one who was tearful and upset to be leaving me and starting school, but far from it: my eyes had been the only ones shedding tears.

I replay the events of that morning in my mind: Ava, happily mingling with her new classmates, playing with some building bricks, while I exit the classroom and walk through the school playground, somehow managing to stay strong until I pass through the school gates. That's when the torrent of big wet salty tears that I'd been holding back began to well up, finally escaping from my eyes and pouring down my cheeks.

Charlie had been waiting for me at the cottage that day with a fresh box of supersize tissues, and a cup of tea already brewing in the pot. He'd allowed me to sob on his shoulder until my tears dried up, and I was ready to nurse my sorrows with a cuppa.

'She's a little star, that one,' Danny says, smiling. 'I've become quite fond of her.'

'Yes, she certainly knows her own mind. She's a lot braver than I was at her age.'

'I don't know, you were quite feisty, if I remember rightly. That's one of the things I liked about you. Amongst others, obviously!' He raises his eyebrows suggestively.

I take an uncomfortable sip of my orange juice, and try to change the subject. I don't know what it is. I like Danny, I really do, but not in *that* way any more.

'Did you hear anything back from Jonathan after your meeting last week?' I ask. 'He sounded quite keen when I spoke to him.' I'd put Danny in touch with a friend of mine from the art gallery who was looking for a new charity to support. From what I'd heard, it sounded as though they'd hit it off immediately.

'Yes, I did. I meant to tell you, but with all your exciting news I almost forgot. Jonathan's company is going to provide quite a substantial amount of new equipment for us in return for some heavy advertising on our website. They might be interested in helping us build a new rehabilitation centre if things go well. That was a good shout, Gracie; thanks for the tip-off.'

'My pleasure.' I smile at him. 'I thought you might work well together.'

'It seems I need you in my business life, as well as my personal one ...' Danny says, winking at me. 'So what are you doing now?' he asks, when I don't respond. 'Have you eaten yet? Fancy a meal here?'

'Ah, that would have been lovely, but I have to get back,' I reply, before drinking the last of my juice down. 'Mum is giving

Ava tea at her house, but she's going out tonight – WI, I believe, so I need to collect Ava from her pretty soon and head home.'

'I could bring takeaway to the cottage?' Danny suggests.

'That's very kind, Danny, but I have to prepare for tomorrow – we're interviewing for a new assistant in the shop and I need to go through the applicants.'

'Then let me help you,' Danny says, undeterred. 'I'll bring fish and chips and we can go through them together. I'm a pretty good judge of character – I must be, I've been chasing you all these years.'

It's obvious he has no intention of giving up. 'OK, but on one condition: we share some of our chips with Ava. She'll never forgive me if you turn up with takeaway and she's not involved!'

'Deal!' Danny says, looking pleased with himself. 'Shall I come round at say ... seven?'

'Seven is fine. That'll give me time to get Ava bathed and in her pyjamas. She can spend a while with us, then I'll put her to bed.'

'Great ...' Danny hesitates. 'It's only the three of us I need to buy chips for? Charlie's not around at the moment?'

'No, he's away in Belgium. He said he'll be back at the weekend though for a couple of days.'

'Good. I mean, it will be nice just the two of us.'

'Yes. Well, us and Ava.'

'Of course,' Danny says, nodding hurriedly. 'I mean when Ava goes to bed.'

That's exactly the bit I'm worried about ...

Thirty-Six

'You look like you're enjoying those chips,' Danny says as he watches Ava wolf down the small plate of chips we've shared with her. 'You have an appetite like your mum's.'

'Hey, I'm not so bad these days,' I protest, just as I'm about to enjoy another forkful of chips. 'Well, not as bad as I used to be, anyway.'

'Mummy likes food,' Ava says, smiling. 'We bake cakes at Grandma's and eat them all up.'

'Ha, I bet you do!' Danny says, grinning with delight at Ava. 'And rightly so. I bet they're delicious. Your grandma always did make good cakes.'

Danny glances across at me, and I know he's referring to the time we dated and Mum would insist on feeding him huge helpings of cake, sandwiches or whatever else she could find every time he came around.

'It was her way of showing she liked you,' I tell him.

'Would you make me some cakes sometime?' Danny asks Ava. 'I bet you make the best cupcakes.'

Ava nods. 'With sprinkles on top?'

'Oh yes, definitely sprinkles!'

'Is that OK, Mummy?' she asks, looking across the little table we're sitting at in the kitchen. 'Can I make Danny cakes?'

'Yes, I don't see why not.'

'They won't be as good as my Uncle Charlie's cakes,' Ava says matter-of-factly. 'His lighthouse cakes are the best.'

Danny flinches slightly at the mention of Charlie's name. 'Yes, his bakery do make lovely cakes, but I bet yours will be even nicer!'

Ava shrugs. 'Maybe. Are you my mummy's boyfriend now?' she asks suddenly, as if it's the most natural question in the world to want an answer to.

'Ava!' I cry, my cheeks glowing as red as the ketchup bottle that sits on the table. 'That's very rude.'

'No, it's fine,' Danny says, grinning. 'Don't worry about it. No, I'm not,' he says, to my immediate relief. 'But I was once, a long time ago.'

'Oh,' Ava says, picking up one of her last remaining chips and dipping it into her ketchup. 'But you don't want to be now?'

Oh Lord!

Danny glances at me. 'That is for your mummy to decide,' he says. 'I think it's up to her who she has as a boyfriend, don't you?'

'I think it's about time you went to bed, Ava. It's way past your bedtime and you have school tomorrow.'

Ava looks at me and is about to argue when she sees the

stern expression on my face. She considers the matter for a split second longer, then decides this isn't going to be a battle she has a chance of winning.

'*OK* ...' she says, climbing down from the table. 'Can I have some milk to take up to bed though?'

'A small glass only, or you'll be up all night at the toilet. I'll pour you one and bring it up, now say goodnight to Danny.'

'Goodnight, Danny,' she says, coming around the table to hug him.

Danny leans down a little and gives Ava a hug. 'Goodnight, Ava.'

'Uncle Charlie said you weren't Mummy's boyfriend,' she whispers, looking innocently up at Danny. 'He said you were only friends.'

Danny nods. 'And he's right, we are. Now, do girls of your age still like stories before they go to bed?'

'Ooh yes, please!' Ava jumps up and down excitedly.

'Is it OK if I read Ava a story?' he asks, looking at me.

'I don't see why not. Go choose a story, Ava, then Danny can read it for you before you go to your bedroom.'

'I'll read it to you in bed, if you like?' Danny says. 'After all, that's what a bedtime story is for, is it not?'

I hesitate, not knowing what to say – Ava's bedroom is upstairs.

'Is your chair magical?' Ava asks innocently. 'Will it fly up the stairs? That's clever, I'd like to see that.'

'Ah ...' Danny says, looking uncomfortable. 'I hadn't thought of that. Slightly awkward.'

'No, Ava, Danny can't go up the stairs,' I explain quickly. 'You go and choose a story and bring it down. It's OK – I'll let you stay up a little while longer for that.'

Ava dashes out of the kitchen and we hear her climbing the wooden staircase that's tucked away behind a curtain in the hall.

'Sorry,' I apologise. 'She didn't realise.'

'No, totally my fault. Strange as it may seem, sometimes even I forget I'm in this thing.' Danny taps the side of the chair.

'Why don't you go through to the lounge?' I suggest. 'Then you can read to Ava in peace while I clear up. Winston is through there, asleep in his bed, but he won't mind having company.'

'Are you sure? I don't want to leave you with all the tidying up.'

'We've only had chips, I'm sure I can manage! You go, Ava loves someone different to read to her.'

'All right then, if you're sure?'

'Danny! I have a story!' Ava cries as she thunders back down the stairs clutching a book in her hand. 'Hurry up!'

'There's your answer!' I smile.

Danny follows Ava through to the sitting room, which is not an easy task for him. The narrow hall of this 150-year-old cottage wasn't built for wheelchairs, but Danny is very agile in his, and manages it without making a fuss.

I quickly clear up what little mess there is in the kitchen, and I'm about to go through to the sitting room to join Ava and Danny, when I pause for a moment in the hall to listen.

Danny is reading Ava one of her favourite stories about a bear and his family. I've read this particular book to Ava what feels like a hundred times, but Danny is managing to make it sound different, giving each character in the book a funny voice. By the sound of Ava's giggles and squeals of delight, she's loving it.

I'm about to go in and join them when I hear a key rattle in the back door behind me. Winston barks and rushes through into the hall, and as I turn to see what's going on, to my astonishment I see the door open and Charlie walk through it carrying his overnight bag over his shoulder.

'Charlie, what are you doing here? I didn't think you'd be here until the weekend.'

'I wasn't supposed to be,' Charlie says, leaning down to pat Winston, 'but my meetings were cancelled. One of the guys has got chicken pox, and the other's son was rushed to hospital suddenly, so I thought I might as well come home.'

He dumps his bag down in the hall, and kneels to fuss Winston properly.

'Is it OK for me to stay a few days longer?' he asks, looking up at me while he rubs Winston's ears.

'Don't be silly, this is your home, of course it is!'

'I know, but I like to let you know when I'm going to be back. Give you some notice.'

An excited giggle escapes from the sitting room.

'It's a bit late for Ava to be up, isn't it?' Charlie asks. 'On a school night, too.'

'We have a visitor,' I tell him, suddenly feeling very awkward that Danny is here. After all, this is still Charlie's house, however much he insists it's my home now.

'Oh, who?' Charlie stands up, looking interested.

But Ava comes bursting through the door before I can tell him. 'Mummy, can Danny read me another story please? He's ever so good.'

She sees Charlie standing in the hall.

'Uncle Charlie!' she cries, running over to him. 'I wondered who Winston was barking at!'

Charlie scoops her up in his arms and twizzles her around. He looks over at me questioningly while he hugs Ava.

Danny? he mouths, raising an eyebrow.

Danny has wheeled himself to the sitting room door. 'Evening, Charlie,' he says, smiling at him. 'We didn't expect to see you this evening.'

'I bet,' Charlie murmurs. 'I came back early, Danny. Thought I'd spend a few extra days here in Sandybridge. There's no place like *home*, is there?' He stresses the word. 'And this is still my house.'

Danny nods. 'Yes, you're right, of course.' He turns to me. 'Perhaps I'd better go, Gracie. Thank you for a lovely evening. I'm sorry it didn't last longer.'

'No,' I snap, completely fed up with their bickering. 'No, you don't need to leave, Danny. I want you to stay.'

Ava, sensing something isn't quite right, looks between the three of us with an anxious expression.

'Ava, I'm going to take you up to bed now,' I say, taking her from Charlie.

'But, Mummy!' Ava protests, knowing she's going to miss something.

'Now,' I insist, putting her down on the floor and taking her hand.

'What about my milk?'

'I'll bring it up in a minute,' I say as I pull her towards the stairs. 'Now say goodnight to everyone.'

'*All right* ... Goodnight, Danny, thank you for my story. Goodnight, Uncle Charlie – will I see you in the morning?' she asks hopefully.

'You bet you will,' Charlie says, winking at her.

'I'll be back in a few minutes,' I tell the two men watching us from the hall. 'And you'd both better be behaving when I come downstairs.'

'Yes, Mummy!' Danny grins.

Out of the corner of my eye I see Charlie smile.

I shake my head dismissively at them both and continue up the stairs with Ava.

We're supposed to have got older and wiser with the passing years, but sometimes it feels like Charlie and Danny have never grown up at all.

I finally head downstairs again after settling Ava in her bed. Having the only two men in her life at the cottage on the same evening had got her a little over-excited, and it had taken me a while to calm her down enough to sleep.

I think about this as I descend the narrow staircase. Danny and Charlie are the only two constant male influences in Ava's life right now. It's doubtful Ava will see Simon for some time, unless he comes back to this country for a visit, which seems highly unlikely as, according to Simon, he's 'making a mint' over there. And money, as I'd eventually realised, is all that matters to Simon.

Ava has asked twice now if Danny is my boyfriend. Is she really that desperate to have a more permanent father figure in her life to fill the void that Simon left?

And if she is, could Danny be the man to do it?

I don't love Danny in the same way I did when I was a teenager, I know that; I don't do anything in the same way I did when I was younger. But I still care a lot for him. If Danny wants to try again, would I be silly not to give it a try? Especially when Ava seems to like him so much?

I pause outside the sitting room door to eavesdrop, as I had earlier, but this time on Danny and Charlie.

'Are you sure that's what you want?' I hear Charlie saying. 'Gracie has been let down too many times by men to have it happen to her again. And I seem to remember, Danny, that you were one of those men.'

'Charlie, you know I love Gracie,' Danny responds. 'I probably always have. Yes, I've made some mistakes in the past – who hasn't? But she's always been incredibly special to me.'

I feel my hand go protectively to my chest. It remains there while I fiddle with my necklace and continue to listen.

'But how does Gracie feel?' Charlie asks. 'Does she feel the same way about you?'

There's a pause in the conversation now, and I guess Danny is thinking about this. 'I don't know, I honestly don't. She seems to enjoy spending time in my company, as I do hers, but Gracie is quite a closed book these days. It's hard to tell what she's really thinking.'

Again a pause, before Danny speaks again. 'What do you think, Charlie? As much as I hate to admit it, you are her best friend.'

Ooh yes, what does Charlie think? I'd be interested to know that too.

'I think Grace cares about you a lot,' Charlie says, so quietly I can barely hear him through the door. 'I think, like you, she's carried a flame since you were both teenagers. But whether that's love, I don't know. Only she can tell you that.'

Silence again.

'But what if she did love me, Charlie – how would *you* feel about that?'

'How do you mean?'

'I mean, would you stand in our way?'

It's Charlie's turn to think now.

'If two people love each other, Danny – truly love each other – then nothing will ever keep them apart. They will always find a way of coming back into each other's lives until they realise their true feelings for each other.'

Charlie, that's beautiful ...

'So are you saying that we'd have your blessing?' Danny asks.

'If that's what Grace wants ... then I won't try to come between you.'

I hear Danny's wheelchair move along the wooden floorboards.

'Cheers, mate. I appreciate that,' he says, and I assume they're shaking hands. 'It's been a funny year. I know we haven't always got along in the past, but we've come together recently, haven't we? Perhaps we can continue that good will into the future?'

'Sure,' Charlie says. 'I'd like that.'

On the other side of the door my mind is whirring.

What could Danny mean, they'd come together recently? Is he talking about the time the two of them had a drink together? No, it sounds like more than that. Ah well, at least they seem to be getting on for a change; perhaps my earlier threat did some good after all!

But in forcing Danny and Charlie to make amends, I've forced myself into making a choice.

Is Danny really the one for me? Do I want to give it a

proper go with him, to see what would happen if we were a couple again?

Could he be the one who makes me do all the things Charlie had described to me on the sofa a few weeks ago?

Or is that someone else entirely?

Dear Grace,

I'm so pleased you keep coming back to me and consulting me on what to do next, as this is a very important time for you.

All I can tell you at the moment is you're doing the right thing.

I know it was difficult for you to make your decision, because as always you were trying to think what would be best for everyone, not just yourself.

But the path you have chosen is the right one for you, and for so many other people too.

Love, Me x

PS I love my new home in the cottage. It's so much cosier than your old bedroom!

PPS What about a party? It would be a REALLY good idea, I promise.

Thirty-Seven

'Morning, Grace!' Olivia, Mum's new assistant, calls cheerily to me as I enter through the shop door. 'How's it going up at the hall?'

'Good, thank you,' I say, unwrapping my scarf from around my neck where it has been protecting me from the chill wind that's blowing through Sandybridge today. 'It's early days yet, of course, but I'm really pleased at how much I've been able to do already.'

'It's such a huge undertaking,' Olivia says as she secures her long blonde hair into a ponytail. 'I don't know where I'd even start with it.'

'I felt a bit like that at first, but now we're a few months in, I can see how it will all come together eventually – fingers crossed.'

'Good. So what can I do for you today, Grace? Your mum

isn't here, I'm afraid: she's gone to oversee a house clearance with Josh.'

Joshua was the other new member of the Harper's Antiques team. In the end, after much thought, we'd decided to take on two new members of staff. Olivia and Josh were a brother and sister who had recently come back to live in Sandybridge after their grandmother had died and left them her house, and as it turned out quite a substantial amount of money.

They had seen my advert for staff and had both jumped at the chance of doing something different. Thanks to their windfall, they didn't need huge wage packets any more, so had given up their well-paid but stressful jobs in London to do something they both enjoyed. Apparently, working in a little antiques shop by the sea was exactly what they were looking for.

They were a great asset to the business, both of them keen to learn all about the trade they were now working in. And Mum was more than happy to impart her knowledge.

'Actually, it's you I've come to see, Olivia. Charlie and I are having a pre-Christmas drinks party at Lighthouse Cottage on Saturday, and I wondered if you and Josh would like to come?'

'Ooh, we'd love too. Well, I would, and I'm sure Josh will feel the same.'

'Fab! It's nothing fancy, just a few drinks with friends, but you're more than welcome.'

'I shall look forward to it. Would you like a coffee, Grace? I'm about to pop the kettle on.'

'Oh thank you, but no. I have to get up to the hall for a meeting with the architect at eleven.'

'No worries. Perhaps another time?'

'Yes, of course, I'd like that.'

As I leave the shop, I think about how lucky we were to find Olivia and Josh. They've not only fitted in perfectly at Harper's Antiques, but in Sandybridge too. Olivia is already shaking up the local WI with her ideas, and Josh has volunteered with one of the local groups that helps keep the beaches clean and tidy, and is often to be seen of an evening picking up litter with the other volunteers.

I couldn't have asked for two more perfect people to work with Mum in the shop.

There's a strong wind buffeting the town as I make my way along the main road, bracing myself against the gusts coming in off the sea as I approach the entrance to Sandybridge Hall. As always when I walk up the long driveway these days, the house in front of me is obscured by scaffolding, lorries and vans. It's been that way since the renovations began.

The project, although complex, is immensely satisfying. We're a long way from finished yet, but I'm loving seeing everything coming together.

It hasn't been an easy task, planning a complete refurbishment of a Tudor manor house, but it's given me something I'd been lacking – a project to get my teeth into. Already I've managed to track down many of the original items from the house that had been put into storage back in the eighties. My next task was to find replacements for all the furniture and fittings that had been destroyed in the fire or lost over the years. I'd been particularly excited when I managed to source, and then purchase at auction, an exact replica of the chandelier I so vividly remember hanging in the hall. The chandelier is currently sitting in a packing crate at Lighthouse Cottage, until the grand day when it can be re-hung in pride of place at Sandybridge Hall.

I'd been worried to begin with about the amount of money that would be required to complete the restoration, but Sue assured me that money was not a problem – and she's been as good as her word. I've been able to spend whatever's needed to do the job properly.

I still haven't met the mysterious Mr Braithwaite who's funding all this. Sue is my contact whenever I have any enquiries. She assures me that Mr Braithwaite is happy with everything I'm doing, and wants me to keep up the good work.

So that's what I've been doing, and I'm loving every minute of it. For me it's a dream come true, seeing the old house come back to life once more.

When my meeting with the architect is over, I check on how the builders are getting on. Once we'd finished ripping out all the nasty plasterboard that had been covering up the original oak panelling in the great hall, there had been a bit of bother when an expert had arrived to restore the wood to its original splendour. Both parties had come to me with their grievances: the builders complained that the expert was getting in their way and preventing them doing their work, and the expert said the builders were stirring up so much dust he couldn't do his restoring.

In the interests of harmony, I'd arranged for the builders to work on the ballroom until the restorer had finished his work.

It turned out to be the first of many 'disputes' that I was called upon to resolve.

'How's it going, Alf?' I ask, wandering over to the foreman of the building crew, who's currently peering at a clipboard.

'Oh hello, Grace,' Alf says, looking up. 'Yes, good … Well, it would be, if they hadn't delivered eight by four instead of ten by four.'

'In English please?' I ask. Alf has a habit of talking to me in builder's jargon. Some of which, after a few months working together, I now understand, but most of which, I don't.

'Wood,' Alf explains. 'The eejits have delivered the wrong size. Now we can't get on properly.'

'How quickly can you get replacements?' I ask.

'Oh, I've already rung them. They say they'll have more with us by the end of the day.'

'Good man,' I tell him. 'This is why I pay you to be in charge.'

'You don't pay me enough to be in charge of this lot,' Alf says, looking around at his team, but he's smiling. 'We'll get there, Grace, don't you worry.'

'Of that I have no doubt, Alf. Dominic says he'll have finished the panels by Thursday, so you'll be able to get back in the hall and carry on with that floor. The tiles did arrive, didn't they?'

'Yep, all stacked at the rear, safe and sound. Although why you'd pay all that for some floor tiles, I don't know. I saw the ticket when they were delivered; what are they made of – gold?'

'Ha, no, but they are hand-painted with an original Tudor pattern that may have been in the hall when it was built, so they're worth it.'

'Hmm, the guy who owns this place must have more money than sense.'

'Perhaps, but he pays our wages, Alf, so who are we to question him?'

'Too true. Oi, Ricky, not like that!' he calls across the huge ballroom to one of the builders. 'Sorry, Grace, I'd best go and sort this out.'

'Sure, I'll pop by in a couple of days, Alf, see how things are coming along.'

'No problem. Right, you eejit,' he yells, marching across the floor. 'Let me show you how we use a nail gun like a builder, and not like a prima ballerina.'

I smile as I head out of the house and into the gardens. The house isn't the only thing being renovated; the gardens are to undergo an overhaul too.

I'd been in contact with a garden designer, and we're meeting next week to finalise the plans for how the gardens can be brought in keeping with the new house design. Although work will not be starting until after Christmas, we want to get the plans finalised so the designer can work out a schedule of what she needs to do and when.

I breathe in the crisp December air as I step outside. The house is a bit dusty and noisy these days, so it's always a relief to step outside into the gardens, which even though they are being redesigned are still striking after all these years.

I look at my watch, and find I've a couple of hours before Ava needs collecting from school, so I decide to take a little walk around the grounds to try to imagine how they might look after their redesign.

The grass is long and damp as I leave one of the formal gravel paths and walk in the direction of the lake. The once neatly mown lawns have been allowed to run wild since the previous owner sold the house, but luckily I have my winter boots on, so the wet doesn't bother me too much as I stride over the unkempt grass.

I stop for a moment as the lake comes into view; the dank December weather has caused a low mist to hang over the water, making the lake look eerily beautiful today.

As I stand in awe of nature's work once more, I notice movement down by the water. I can just about make out a human form, standing by the lake.

Who could it be? The only people at Sandybridge right now, other than myself, are the builders, and I hardly think one of them would be pausing by the lake to gaze dreamily into the water. So I head down to the water's edge to investigate.

As I get nearer, a dog appears from behind a bush, happily carrying a stick to its master.

'Charlie, what are you doing here?' I ask, surprised to see him. 'I thought you were doing paperwork at the cottage this morning.'

Charlie smiles as I walk towards him. 'I was. Just fancied a quick walk after being stuck inside too long.'

'Here? Why not walk along the seafront?'

Charlie shrugs. 'I was heading that way and then I decided to take a detour into the grounds for a change of scenery. We're not in trouble with the boss, are we?' He ruffles Winston's fur, and reaches down for his stick. Then he throws it a little way across the grass for the Lab to fetch.

'I remember a time when Winston would have swum across that lake,' I tell Charlie as we watch him trot slowly after the stick. 'But not so much now, I guess.'

'He's getting older, a bit like we all are,' Charlie says, smiling at me. 'A few more grey hairs and a bit less energy. It comes to us all.'

'We're only in our forties, Charlie! We're hardly pensioners!'

'You're telling me you don't feel it?'

'Sometimes, I guess. But most of the time I prefer to pretend I'm still a teenager.'

'You wouldn't have been the boss of Sandybridge Hall back then. You hated everything to do with history, if I remember rightly.'

'That's true, I suppose. I've definitely changed in that respect . . . ' I think about this for a few seconds. 'But stop calling me the boss of here – that's the new owner.'

'Well, you're the boss for now, until he – or is it a she? I forget – moves in.'

'It's a he – a Mr Braithwaite.'

'Ah.' Charlie nods.

I shiver. 'It's freezing standing here. I'm having a walk around the grounds myself; shall we carry on walking together?'

'Sure, why not?' Charlie says. He calls Winston and we set off along the narrow path that circles the outside of the lake.

'Not a very regal name, is it – Braithwaite?' Charlie ponders as we walk. 'It hardly conjures up images of the lord of the manor.'

I shrug. 'Well, that's his name – regal or not.'

'What do you know of him? I mean, you've not even met him yet, have you?'

'No. Sue says he moves about a lot, but I will get to meet him when he's in the country and can get all the way over to Norfolk.'

'You'd think he'd want to see how his future home was coming along. I know I would if it was me; I'd want constant updates.'

'I do update him. I email pictures of the house and any new pieces I've picked up to furnish it.'

'You email him, or Sue does?'

'Usually Sue, but she passes them on.'

Charlie pulls a face, 'It's rather odd, isn't it, all this cloak-and-dagger stuff. Why is it all so secretive?'

'It isn't. He's a businessman, that's all. He pays other people to do things for him, and he's paying me *very* well, so I'm not complaining!'

'But why Sandybridge Hall?' Charlie continues. 'Why come all the way out to Norfolk to live? If he's this international jet-setter, why choose a house here?'

'You're full of questions today, aren't you? Maybe he wants it as a bolthole, a hideaway from the stresses and strains of his busy life.'

'A bolthole? Sandybridge Hall is hardly a bolthole. Maybe he's famous – a pop or movie star?'

'His name is Braithwaite. How many celebrities do you know with that name?'

'It could be an alias – so you don't know who he is, and the press don't get hold of the story.'

'Don't be daft, Charlie,' I say, although the thought had crossed my mind too. 'You're letting your imagination run away with you.'

'Perhaps, but until you actually meet him, I shall believe what I want to.'

Having finished our circuit of the lake, we now take the gravel path that leads around the back of the house. Both Charlie and I fall silent as we arrive by a large bush. It was the bush we'd all hidden behind the night of the Sandybridge fire many years ago. While owners of the hall had come and gone, the bush, like many other shrubs and trees in the garden, had remained and flourished.

'It never goes away, does it?' I say quietly to Charlie. 'The memory of that night.'

Charlie shakes his head. 'No, but it's only one of many memories I have about this place, and most of them are good.'

'That's true. I guess we have had a lot of good times here as well as bad over the years.'

'How're things going with Danny?' Charlie asks, looking up at the house as he speaks. 'I know I haven't been around much lately, but you two don't seem to have spent that much time together when I have been here.'

'Ah . . . that.'

Charlie turns towards me. 'Trouble in paradise, eh?'

I kick at a crisp brown leaf on the path.

'No . . . well, not exactly.'

'Do you want to talk about it?'

I look at Charlie; I still find discussing my relationship with Danny with him incredibly awkward, even after I'd overheard him giving Danny his blessing at the cottage.

'No. It's good of you to offer, but no. I need to deal with Danny myself.'

'Sounds ominous.'

I sigh. 'It's not going to be the most pleasant thing I've ever done. But sadly it's something I need to do.'

Dear Grace,
    Trust me. You must do this.
    It's for the best, I promise.
    Love, Me x

Thirty-Eight

Over the last few months Danny and I have been seeing each other a little more often. As always, I enjoy Danny's company a lot, and so, it appears, does Ava. Everything should be going fine; I'm seeing someone I know well and, more importantly, trust; someone who not only likes me, but who seems to adore my daughter too. There shouldn't be a problem – but there is.

I just don't feel about Danny the way I know he feels about me. As hard as I've tried, my feelings don't extend beyond friendship. Danny wants more from this relationship than I do, and it isn't fair to string him along any longer.

As I walk slowly to the pub where we're planning to meet this evening, my heart is pounding and I feel sick. I've never broken up with anyone before; it's always been someone else doing it to me. I know how bad *I* always felt, and I don't want to be the one to make Danny feel that way. But I have no choice.

'Hey,' I try and say as casually as I can when I arrive at the pub and see Danny sitting at a table waiting for me. 'Oh, you've got the drinks in already.'

'Is that OK? I got you your usual.'

'Sure,' I say, pulling back a chair and sitting down at the table.

A double might have been good tonight, I think.

I take a long sip of the vodka and lemonade and glance around me. I've sat in here with Danny and Charlie so many times over the years; like the rest of Sandybridge, it never seems to change that much.

'How were your meetings up at the hall today?' Danny asks, bringing me back to the present.

'Oh good, thanks, yes.'

'Is everything progressing as you'd hoped?'

'Yes, very well.'

'OK, what's up?' Danny asks, leaning across the table towards me. 'Don't deny it, I can tell something is.'

I shuffle my glass about the table, and rearrange my coaster.

'You can tell me, you know. I don't bite.' He winks. 'Not that I wouldn't want to, you understand ...'

'That's just it!' I snap, a bit too sharply.

'What is?' Danny asks with concern.

'I don't want you to – bite, that is.' I take a deep breath; this is it. 'Danny, I really like having you as a friend. There's not many people who can say their high school sweetheart is now one of their best friends, but I can, and I like that. But that's all I want. I don't want to take our relationship any further.'

My gaze, which has been fixed on the table, now turns

towards Danny, and immediately I see sorrow in his eyes.

'And it's not because of your wheelchair or anything like that,' I continue, in case he thought it was. 'Honestly, I don't have a problem with it.'

'It's me then, is it?' Danny asks calmly.

'No, not at all, I think you're great. Just not in *that* way.'

Danny nods, and his gaze drops now so he looks down into his lap. It remains there for the next few seconds.

'I'm sorry, Danny,' I tell him. 'If it could be any other way ...'

Danny's face lifts, and to my surprise it doesn't look sad or forlorn, but amused.

'Gracie, I think you're amazing,' he says, while I watch him in confusion. 'But sometimes you are a bit dense.'

'What do you mean?' I ask, still no wiser.

'We've been dating regularly for what, three months?'

I nod.

'And in that time have you ever shown me any ... how can I put this ... affection? I don't mean friendly affection; I mean lustful affection.'

I shake my head.

'So why would I think you wanted anything other than a friendship with me?'

'But ...'

'Of course I would have loved for that side of things to take off – you know how much I care about you.' He pauses for a moment and we both hold each other's gaze. 'But I'm not silly, Grace, I can tell when a woman is interested and, more importantly in your case, when she isn't.'

'I'm so sorry, Danny,' I say, taking his hand. 'I wish things were different.'

'No you don't. You're quite happy being my friend when your heart lies elsewhere.'

'What do you mean?'

'Come on, Grace. I know I said you were dense before, but you're not that bad. It's Charlie, isn't it?' he continues when I don't respond. 'It's always been him. Probably since we were kids. Charlie is the one you really love.'

Thirty-Nine

I watch Charlie as he hands drinks out in the cottage at our little pre-Christmas gathering.

Lighthouse Cottage is looking beautiful tonight; we'd bought the biggest Christmas tree we could fit into the sitting room, and decorated it with pretty lights and decorations bought from one of the craft shops on Sandybridge High Street. Then we'd hung even more tiny white lights over the archway outside the door, intertwined with the remnants of clematis and roses that grow there in the summer months. There's a roaring fire burning in the hearth, over which hang three stockings – one for each member of the household.

Tonight the cottage is filled with friends and family, all happily sipping on punch and munching mince pies as they chat and laugh with their fellow guests.

The picture I see before me is like a scene from a Hollywood Christmas movie it's so perfect, and I hug myself with pleasure at being one of the people who's created it.

Charlie winks at me as he passes by with a tray of punch – he's in his element being the host. But tonight, instead of it being industry people he's trying to impress, it's people we care about, and it's clear from the smile on Charlie's face that this is making him extremely happy. And when Charlie is happy, so am I, I've grown to realise over the years. But tonight something is different, something has changed, and I'm still trying to come to terms with what exactly that is.

After the evening at the pub with Danny, I'd spent a lot of time thinking. Thinking about Charlie, thinking about Sandybridge, and thinking about my life.

Charlie has been a part of my life since I was a teenager. Yes, we've had times apart over the years, but we've never stayed far from each other for long. I've been there for him in good times and bad, as he's been there for me. We've celebrated important occasions together, and commiserated with each other when things have gone wrong. We're even living together now; Charlie isn't in Sandybridge too often, but when he is, Ava and I enjoy our time here in Lighthouse Cottage all the more.

'Penny for them?' Mum asks, walking over towards me carrying a glass of punch. 'You look like you have the weight of the world on your shoulders standing there.'

'Oh no, I was just thinking how wonderful it is to see so many people we care about in one room tonight, and how much Ava and I enjoy living here at the cottage with Charlie.'

'Well of course you both love living here with Charlie; I was never in any doubt you would. It was you, Grace, that was the sticking point.'

I raise my eyebrows at my mother; I can feel a lecture

coming on. I make a mental note while I wait for Mum to get into full flow, never to lecture Ava in this way.

'Getting away from Sandybridge was all you ever wanted, Grace. You seemed to think life would always be better if you went somewhere else, and it probably was for a while. I would never have wished for you to stay here for ever.'

'You wouldn't?' I ask, surprised to hear this.

'No, of course not. When you were younger you needed to see the world a little, live life with no ties. But then you had Ava, and things changed.'

Worryingly, Mum is actually making a lot of sense.

'Ava is happy living by the seaside,' Mum continues. 'She gets to play in the fresh air with her new friends, and go to a school she loves and feels safe at.'

I nod. Ava does love school.

'And you, Grace, you're happier than I've seen you in a long time. Even though you fought against it, you've come back home. You're doing a job you love, and you're living with your beautiful daughter and your best friend in this beautiful little cottage. What could be better than that?'

I shrug. 'Nothing, I guess. I just never thought I'd end up back in Sandybridge living with Charlie.'

'And that's bad because ...?'

'It's not. It's ... unexpected, I suppose.'

'Life has a funny way of working like that, Grace. Sometimes the things you expect to happen don't, but other things come along instead that are better than your original plan.'

I think about this. It's a bit like the advice that Remy's given me over the years. At the time it often didn't appear to be good, but somehow it always works out for the best in the end.

I've never told anyone about Remy; it's a secret I've kept for nearly thirty years. And it isn't as if I'm suddenly going to tell anyone that I have a fortune-telling typewriter – they might have me sectioned. Remy's something I still don't understand, and probably never will. But he's been a part of my life for a long time, and I hope he always will, a bit like Charlie.

'You know what, Mum?' I say, turning towards her. 'I totally agree with everything you've just said.'

'Well,' Mum says, smiling proudly, 'that's something I never thought I'd hear you say.'

The cottage doorbell rings.

'I'll go!' I call. 'Thanks, Mum!' I give her a quick kiss on the cheek. 'For everything.'

I push through the crowd of people we have packed into the little cottage tonight, and head for the door.

'Hey, you made it,' I say as I open the door to find Danny. 'I wasn't sure you would.'

'Never miss a party me!' Danny says, wheeling himself over the small step and into the cottage. He reaches into the side of his chair and produces a bottle of wine. 'Here, I brought you this.'

'Thanks,' I say, taking the bottle from him.

'Is that mistletoe?' Danny asks, looking up.

'No, I don't think so,' I say, following his gaze.

'Well, this is!' Danny says, pulling a bunch from the other side of his chair. 'Now, you're not going to deny me a Christmas kiss this time, are you?' Grinning, he holds up his mistletoe.

'Are you talking about that time we were at the train station on our way home from uni? That was years ago, and it wasn't me that stopped you. I seem to remember it was Charlie who interrupted us.'

'Ah, Charlie – we'll talk about him in a minute. I want to hear what you're going to do about him. But first my kiss!'

I lean down to Danny's height, and aim for his cheek, but Danny quickly twists his face around so I end up kissing his lips instead, and immediately I'm transported back to the 1980s and the first time I kissed him.

My eyes closed, I allow myself to linger there for a tiny bit longer than I should, and as I pull away I open them again to find Danny looking up at me.

'Best mistletoe kiss ever,' Danny whispers.

I reach out and gently caress his face, running my fingers down his cheek.

'Be happy, Gracie,' he says.

'You too, Danny,' I whisper back.

'Grace, do you have any more coasters?' Olivia asks, coming into the hall. 'I'm worried about your lovely furnit— oh, sorry!' she apologises, her cheeks flushing pink as she sees us.

'Nothing to be sorry for,' I reply, hurriedly standing up. 'Olivia, this is Danny, a very old friend of mine. Danny, this is Olivia, she works at the shop with Mum.'

'Yes, I know,' Danny says, eyeing Olivia. 'I've seen you in there.'

'And you're the man that runs that fantastic children's charity. I've heard all about you from the WI ladies.'

'My reputation precedes me!' Danny grins.

'I'd love to hear more about it sometime … if you're ever free?' Olivia shakes her long blonde hair over her shoulder. 'It sounds amazing.'

I smile. Is Olivia hitting on Danny? Danny wouldn't be used to that, it was usually the other way around!

'No time like the present,' Danny says, raising his dark eyebrows at Olivia. 'How about we go through and get a drink, then we can chat?'

'I'd like that,' Olivia says, forgetting all about her coaster emergency, as she and Danny head through to the lounge together.

I pause for a moment alone in the hall. That was something I hadn't foreseen coming. But Remy had suggested I hold a party; obviously he knew something I didn't – as usual.

I should ask him, I think, as I stand in the hall. I should ask him the question. *The question*. The one I've wanted an answer to for a very long time ...

Dear Grace,

   You will have the answer to the question that
is troubling you soon.

   I am unable to say more at present.

   But patience is your friend right now. I
promise.

   Love, Me x

Forty

Christmas seems a long time ago, I think as I stand in the grounds of Sandybridge Hall looking down to the lake.

Eight months have gone by since that day I walked around here with Charlie, and rather than a mist hanging over the lake and my feelings, now I can see shards of light dancing merrily off the top of the water, as the sun shines down on Sandybridge Hall on this beautiful August day.

What a perfect day for the new owner of Sandybridge Hall to be making his first visit, I think as I shuffle awkwardly in my stiletto-heeled shoes. I'm dressed to impress today, I won't deny it. I've even broken a dress free from my wardrobe, so used to providing me with jeans, T-shirts and jumpers.

I don't feel all that comfortable, but I have to be content with the thought I look good. Well, good in a smart and professional sense anyway.

The email arrived just over a week ago – from the mysterious Mr Braithwaite himself this time rather than my usual contact,

Sue – announcing that he was going to visit Sandybridge Hall to see how the renovations were coming along.

I was pleased to report back that the work was almost complete, and likely to be finished ahead of our original predicted timescale of twelve months.

He seemed suitably pleased to hear this, and we arranged a time for him to come and visit.

'You're actually going to meet this mysterious Mr Braithwaite at last?' Charlie exclaimed, when I told him one morning over breakfast. 'Is he coming in a big black car with blacked out windows so no one recognises him?'

'I highly doubt it,' I reply, standing up to begin clearing the table. 'Have you finished with your cereal, Ava?'

'But it's possible?' Charlie winks. 'Will you text me and tell me if he's famous when he gets there. I could casually pop by and bump into you both while you're doing your tour.'

'No!' I insist, glaring at him. 'Don't you dare.'

'*Well!*' Charlie says, his eyes wide with amusement. 'You want to keep the multimillionaire all to yourself, do you?'

'What's a mini air?' Ava pipes up. 'Is it like Minnie Mouse?'

'No, Ava, it's a person with a lot of money,' I explain. 'That's not the case at all,' I say, turning back to Charlie. 'But if he *is* famous, he might want to keep his visit quiet.'

'So you *do* think he might be then?' Charlie grins. 'I knew it!'

I shake my head at him, and turn towards the sink. But my mind isn't on the mugs waiting to be washed; it's firmly on my mysterious millionaire.

Our emails hadn't been confined to simply arranging a time for him to visit; they'd continued into friendly chats about antiques, and collectables, then had moved on to discussions

349

about our lives and families. Although Mr Braithwaite didn't give much away, I was able to discover he had no children and wasn't married. But he declined to answer my question about how he'd made his money.

So as I stand waiting for him to arrive at Sandybridge Hall today, I'm excited to learn what this man is really like, but I'm also hoping he doesn't turn out to be some sort of gangster or criminal who's made his money illegally. It would be a complete travesty if I'd done all this work just for some loan shark to come and live here. I've grown quite attached to the old house, putting my heart and probably my soul, too, into restoring her to her former glory.

'You mean too much to me not to have someone deserving living in you,' I whisper, turning to look up at the old house. 'Fingers crossed it's going to be OK.'

I head back up towards the house, and stand at the entrance waiting for the mysterious Mr Braithwaite to arrive. I look at my watch; he should be here any time now.

As I stand waiting for the moment of truth, I think about all the work that has gone into the house over the last twelve months, and how it's changed not only over the last year, but since I'd first visited here as a child.

Charlie had once said that this house was special, and now I'd spent so much time here, I had to agree. For such an old house it wasn't cold and unwelcoming as some buildings of this age could be; it was warm and inviting, especially with all the new décor, which, even though it's in keeping with the period, is pretty special.

I only hope Mr Braithwaite likes it, I think as I stand at the end of the little bridge that leads over to the house. Or all this will have been for nothing.

'What ya looking so scared about?' a voice calls from across the grass, and I turn to see Charlie striding towards me carrying something under his arm. Winston trots along faithfully behind him.

Normally any glimpse of Charlie is a pleasant one. But today he's the last person I want to see.

'What are you doing here?' I hiss, hurrying over towards him. 'Mr Braithwaite will be here soon. I told you not to come!'

Charlie's been spending a lot more time in Sandybridge lately; he's opened up his office at the lighthouse again and has been working from there as much as he can.

Although he's never interfered in anything I've done at the house, he's often been on hand when I've needed a bit of help or advice with the renovations, and I've really appreciated that. It's been lovely for Ava and me to have Charlie around, but today he'd promised he'd stay away.

'I won't get in your way,' Charlie says, apparently determined to ignore my plea. 'I thought I'd come and take a look at the old girl before her life changes for ever. Getting a new owner is a very important time for a house.'

'What *are* you babbling about?' I ask, my eyes wide.

'A house doesn't just need an owner; it needs the *right* owner. Especially one with as much history as this one.'

I open my mouth to protest, but Charlie continues unabated.

'We've both known this house through many owners, Gracie, haven't we?'

I nod impatiently and peer down the drive in case a car might be coming.

'But I don't think it's ever had the *right* owner since we first came here.'

'Probably not.' I take a quick look at my watch. Any minute now . . .

'Do you remember when we used to talk about what we wanted in our futures, and all you wanted was to travel the world, and all I wanted was to settle down?'

'Yes, of course I do, but do we have to step down memory lane right now, Charlie? Can't we do this later? Mr Braithwaite will be here at any moment, and I don't think his first impression of me should be punching someone and dragging them behind a bush!'

'Point taken.' Charlie turns as if to go, and I'm about to breathe a sigh of relief when he turns back. 'Oh, I forgot – this package came for you this morning.' To my horror he puts a brown paper parcel down on the ground next to me, and leans it up against the bridge.

'You're not going to leave that here, are you?' I ask, astonished he's being this silly. 'Can't you take it to the cottage and I'll open it later?'

Charlie shakes his head. 'It says urgent on it, so I assumed you might need it immediately. Come on, Winston,' he calls. 'Time to go. Gracie doesn't want us any more.'

'Hey, that's not fair!' I call to their departing figures. 'I just don't want you at this very moment.'

But Charlie and Winston are already heading back across the grass.

Damn, I'm going to have to take the parcel into the house now; it can't be here when Mr Braithwaite arrives. I grab the brown paper and try to lift the parcel, but the paper is loose so it slides off, leaving two framed oil paintings propped against the bridge.

'Paintings? I didn't order any paintings,' I say, turning them over so I can see them.

The first is a painting of some dogs waiting for their dinner in a Victorian kitchen. 'This is the same painting Simon bought at Danny's auction!' I exclaim, looking at it. 'Why is it here?'

I look at the signature on the picture, and see that it is indeed the original oil painting, the one with dogs that looked like Wilson and Winston. I'd loved that painting when I saw it for the first time – both Charlie and I had, actually – but why is it here now? I've spent months tracking down paintings that once belonged to the Sandybridge estate or were in keeping with the décor of the house, but this particular painting hadn't come up in any auction or sale. So why had someone sent it to me?

I take a look at the second picture, and again it's immediately familiar, but I'm not so sure where I've seen this one before.

It's another oil painting, this time of a sandy-haired woman sitting at a writing desk; in one hand she clutches a quill pen, and her other hand is holding down a piece of white parchment on her desk, so she looks like she's writing a letter.

'Oh, I know!' I exclaim. 'This painting was in that box I found upstairs when Charlie and I went exploring all those years ago. But why is it here now in this parcel with the other picture?'

I stare hard at the painting. The woman's face looks so familiar to me, just as it had when I'd first seen it many years ago.

Then I realise why.

'Oh. My. God,' I say to no one but the house behind me. 'How did I not know? How have I never realised this before?'

Then, forgetting all about the imminent arrival of the mysterious Mr Braithwaite, I grab the paintings, tuck them both under my arm, and run.

Forty-One

'It was you!' I cry, flinging open the door of Lighthouse Cottage. 'It was you that sent these paintings to me! But why?' I ask as I burst into the kitchen and find Charlie sitting at the kitchen table with Winston by his side.

'Did you look at them?' Charlie asks calmly.

'I did.'

'And what did you see?'

'This is the painting that we both liked at Danny's auction,' I say, holding up the painting of the dogs. 'And this' – I put the painting of the woman on the table in front of him – 'is you.'

Charlie looks at the painting. 'Well, it's not actually me,' he says. 'It's one of my ancestors. Her husband was the owner of Sandybridge Hall in the nineteenth century. I must say, there is an uncanny resemblance there though.'

'One of your ancestors? But how . . . I mean, what . . .'

354

'I'm adopted, remember? I never knew my real family. But I always wondered, though I didn't get very far when I attempted to trace them myself. So last year I hired an expert, the best in the business, and I was absolutely staggered when he was able to trace my real family back as far as this lady.' Charlie taps the gilt frame of the painting.

'But ...' I still can't quite get my head around all this. 'You mean, you're related to the owners of Sandybridge – the Claymore family?'

Charlie nods. 'My real mother was a teenager at the time she got pregnant and apparently it would have brought shame on the Claymore family if she'd kept me, so I was given away at birth. That's why it was so difficult to trace my heritage: I was a secret no one talked about.'

'Oh, Charlie,' I say, my shock turning to sorrow. 'That's so sad.'

Charlie shrugs. 'I can't complain. I had a good childhood, and it wasn't like it was a big secret I was adopted. My family were completely open about it. It kind of explains why I always loved this place though, and why I always felt happy here. Sandybridge is my family home.'

'Is your real mother still alive?' I ask.

Charlie shakes his head. 'No, sadly she was killed in a road accident some years ago – hit by a car. Which is a bizarre coincidence, when you think about what happened to me outside Sandybridge.'

This gets weirder by the second. I shake my head. 'This is all such a shock, Charlie. I can't quite believe it's happening.' I think for a moment. 'So if Sandybridge Hall is your family home, was it you that bought it? Are you the mysterious Mr Braithwaite?'

Charlie shakes his head. 'I wanted to be. When I found out about my family connection to the house, I tried really hard to buy the place when it came up for sale, but I was outbid.'

'By who?' I ask, surprised. I'd been convinced Charlie must be my mysterious boss.

'By me,' Danny says, appearing from the lounge. 'I bought Sandybridge Hall.'

'*You?*' I exclaim, turning towards him. 'But why would you buy it?' I have to sit down on one of the kitchen chairs. This was all getting a bit much now.

'Because I wanted to put the place to good use this time. I didn't want to see it become a restaurant, or a party venue again. I was going to transform the house into a rehabilitation centre for my charity. Use the grounds, everything.'

I frown. 'In that case, why have I spent the last year restoring the house to its Tudor beginnings, if you're planning to rebuild it?'

Danny looks at Charlie.

He nods.

'It was Charlie's idea,' Danny explains. 'We both wanted you to stay in Sandybridge, and this seemed the perfect way of getting you to stay here permanently, by offering you your dream job.'

'You mean you concocted this whole thing between the two of you?' I stare in bewilderment at the two of them.

Charlie and Danny both nod.

'Charlie put the extra money in for the restoration,' Danny tells me. 'But we decided to keep quiet about it, because we weren't sure you'd take the job if you knew it was us.'

'We both care about you, Gracie,' Charlie says now. 'And we wanted you to be happy.'

'But why invent the mysterious Mr Braithwaite?' I ask, still trying to piece all this together. 'Why not tell me the truth?

Charlie and Danny both grin like the schoolboys I once knew.

'You tell her, Danny. This bit was your idea,' Charlie offers.

'Do you remember the name of the boy who held the football party we all first met at?' Danny asks.

'*Seriously?* You expect me to remember something that happened almost thirty years ago?'

They both nod.

I sigh. 'Right . . . ' I think hard, trying to run through all my ex-classmates' names as fast as I can.

'Duncan!' I cry. 'There, is that enough for you? Duncan Braithwaite . . . Wait!' I look with suspicion at them both as I realise. 'You are kidding me! That's how you came up with the name?'

The boys grin.

I shake my head again as the final pieces fall into place. 'So you've succeeded in keeping me here . . . and I've nearly finished restoring Sandybridge Hall. What happens now?'

Danny looks at Charlie. 'Your turn, mate.'

'Danny offered to give me the hall when he found out it was my family's home, but I insisted on paying him for it.'

'Paying my charity,' Danny corrects.

'Donating to his charity,' Charlie continues. 'In return, we're going to build a rehabilitation centre in the grounds, once the restoration is finished, somewhere away from the house so it can have its own private entrance.'

'So everyone is a winner,' Danny says, looking extremely pleased with himself. 'My charity gets a new home, and

Charlie's ancestral home is returned to its rightful owner.'

I look back and forth between the two of them. I've waited for years to see them getting on together, yet now that day is finally here I feel a bit cheated.

'Well, it seems everyone has the happy ending they deserve,' I tell them. 'But explain this to me: what will I do when the renovations are finished? My job will be over. What am I supposed to do then?'

'Time for me to go,' Danny announces. He wheels himself over and kisses me on the cheek, then as he passes Charlie on his way out, he pats him on the back and says, 'It's all yours, Charlie boy. Good luck.'

I watch Danny wheel himself out of the kitchen, and then I turn to Charlie. 'What does he mean: "It's all yours"?'

Forty-Two

Charlie comes over to my chair and takes hold of my hand. He kneels down in front of me and for one mad moment I think he might be about to propose, but he doesn't. *Don't be daft, Grace,* I tell myself. *Why would he do that? The last few minutes have definitely messed with your mind!*

'I can see you're upset,' Charlie says gently, 'but you must know we only did all this because we love you.'

'I know,' I say. 'And I should be grateful to you both – restoring Sandybridge Hall has been a dream job for me. But I can't help feeling like I've been duped. I thought I gained that job on my own merits.'

'You did!' Charlie insists. 'Of course you did. No one could have restored Sandybridge Hall with as much care and love as you have. You were the perfect person to do it, and if I may say so, the perfect person to live there in the future.'

'Whatever do you mean? Why would I live there when the hall belongs to you, Charlie? You're lord of the manor now.'

'Not much fun being a lord if you don't have a beautiful lady to share it with,' Charlie says, looking up at me.

I stare at him, not understanding.

'Don't you know what I'm trying to ask you?' Charlie says, smiling.

I still look at him blankly.

'I want *you* to be my lady, Gracie. I want you to live at Sandybridge Hall with me. You and Ava.'

'B-but why?' I stutter: the last few minutes have thrown me completely off-kilter.

'Because I love you, Gracie, of course. I always have, since we were teenagers.'

I continue to stare at him, my brain for some reason not comprehending what he's saying.

'Yes, I married Louisa,' Charlie continues, 'but that was only because I thought I'd lost you to America and then to Simon. I was lonely, Gracie, I missed you.'

I shake my head, as if this might help me understand what's happening a little better.

'I missed you when you went to university. I missed you when you went travelling and ended up in the States. I missed you when you married Simon – so much it almost broke me. That's why I closed the lighthouse offices here and moved the business elsewhere. I couldn't bear the thought I'd lost you for ever, and you'd never return to Sandybridge and to me.'

'Oh, Charlie,' I whisper.

'And then you did. You and Ava came home. Better than that, you chose to come and live with me. I felt like my life was complete there and then.' Charlie takes hold of both my hands now. 'I haven't bought Sandybridge Hall for me, Gracie – I've bought it for *us*, somewhere we can put down those roots I've always talked about.' He pauses, and his pale blue eyes search my face for an answer before he goes on: 'I know by asking what I'm about to ask, I run the risk of pushing my best friend away for ever. But I've waited a long time for this answer and I have to know. Gracie, is there any chance you could love me in the same way I love you?'

This time I nod helplessly.

Charlie beams. 'I've loved you for so long, through all your various incarnations.'

When I look puzzled, he explains: 'I've loved you with all your weird and wonderful hairstyles over the years – from brunette, to blonde, to redhead, to this' – he reaches out and gently strokes my hair – 'your wonderful, natural self. And, contrary to what you think, I've loved all your different figures too, whatever size you've been, especially the stunning one you have now – gorgeously curvy.' His other hand reaches around my waist. 'Gracie, I know this has all been very sudden, but there is something else I need to ask you.'

I nod.

'It's taken me nearly thirty years to pluck up the courage to do this, but now you know how I feel, I have to go ahead.' He takes a deep breath. 'Grace Marie Harper, will you marry me?'

I nod again, absolutely lost for words.

'Is that a yes?' Charlie asks, grinning from ear to ear. 'Only you haven't said anything for the last few minutes.'

I still don't speak. Instead I pull my hand away from his and reach into the pocket of my dress, where I retrieve a folded sheet of typed paper.

I open it up and show it to Charlie. He looks at me, somewhat mystified, then he reads it aloud:

```
Dear Grace,
    The time has come.
    The one who owns the place you love is the
one that will make you happy forever.
    Cherish him, Grace.
    And make sure you say yes!
    Love, Me x
```

'What is this?' Charlie asks. 'Who sent it?'

I take the letter from Charlie and look at it briefly before putting it back in my pocket.

'That doesn't matter now. All that matters is they were right. You're the person that owns the place I love, Charlie. You. You own Sandybridge Hall and this little cottage we're in now. You're the one that's made me happy for nearly thirty years, and now it's about time I started making you happy.' I cup his face in my hands. 'I love you, Charlie, and I always have. Of course I'll marry you. If it's possible, it would make me even happier than I am now.'

Charlie leaps to his feet and pulls me into his arms as he has done so many times before, but this time it's different, this time I feel different as I look up into his elated face.

Charlie hesitates, and I know what he's thinking: this should feel weird, we've been friends for so long we shouldn't be doing this. But it doesn't feel weird, it feels so, so right when Charlie leans forward and gently places his lips upon mine.

So perfect that I only wish we'd done it sooner.

Summer 2016

My walk from Lighthouse Cottage back into Sandybridge takes me past all the special places that Charlie and I have known over the years.

As I leave the lighthouse – and the cottage that we both continue to live in with Ava, having decided it suits us better than a Tudor mansion – I walk past the sandy beach where we've spent so many happy hours walking dogs together, along the promenade with the pebble beach on one side and the Lighthouse Bakery café, busy as always, on the other. I carry on through the town, weaving my way through crowds of holidaymakers, until I'm able to stand on the opposite side of the road to the antiques shop.

It seems important to take one last look at all the places that have meant something to me since I was fifteen. *Since you came into my life . . .*

Harper's Antiques and Collectables stands proudly in front

of me. This shop was my parents' pride and joy back in the day, and now, even though it still belongs to our family, it's run with just as much enthusiasm by Josh and Olivia – and, to my delight, Mum, who still helps out on occasion.

'Gracie!' a familiar voice calls, and I turn to see Danny wheeling himself along the pavement towards me.

'Busy, isn't it?' I say as he arrives by my side.

'Ah, it's fine, they always stand aside to let the cripple through!' Danny winks, and I shake my head at him.

'Never change, do you?' I say.

'Would you want me to?'

I shake my head and smile.

'Now, tell me why you're standing forlornly looking at your shop,' he demands. 'What's up?'

'Why do you think something is up?'

Danny pulls a wide-eyed look. 'Gracie, I have known you long enough to know when you're happy, when you're sad, and when something is most definitely up! What's in that?' he asks, peering at my crate.

'Nothing.'

Danny carries on staring at me, waiting for an answer.

'OK, it's something for the shop.'

'If it's something for the shop, why are you hanging around out here? Why not take it in?'

'I will, in a minute. I was just taking a moment ... to remember.'

Danny looks at me questioningly; he opens his mouth, then thinks better of it and closes it again.

'Anyway,' I say, realising I need to lighten the moment, 'what are you doing here? Haven't you got a rehabilitation centre to run?'

'I could say the same to you.' Danny winks. 'How is your palace coping without you this afternoon?'

'It's not a palace, it's a Tudor hall – as you should jolly well know by now. How long has your centre been on our grounds?'

'OK, touché!' he concedes, grinning. 'You know I think you do a great job of running the place. We'd be lost without you.'

'Thanks,' I reply, almost blushing. 'I only hope our success continues after—'

'After what?' Danny asks, quick as a flash.

'Oh, here comes Olivia,' I reply, relieved to see her approaching. 'I assume she's the reason you're here.'

Olivia spies her new husband waiting with me across the street, and hurries over to see us.

'Darling, this is a surprise!' she says, kissing him.

'I thought I'd take you for an ice cream, since it's your early finish today,' Danny says, gazing with delight at his new wife.

'A ninety-nine?' Olivia asks, grinning. 'With a flake?'

'Definitely!' Danny agrees. 'Let's head down to the kiosk on the pebble beach. Can I interest you, Gracie?'

'No, thank you. I've something I need to do.'

Danny looks at me, and then he nods knowingly. 'Sure.'

'Go into the shop and see the new bear, Grace,' Olivia encourages. 'That's what was in the huge parcel you dropped off earlier: a life-size stuffed brown bear! I love him already.'

'No,' Danny says, before Olivia can ask. 'We don't have room.'

'Ah, I bet I can persuade you,' Olivia coos. 'Let's talk about it over our ice creams. See you later, Grace,' she calls as they begin to make their way along the pavement.

Danny looks back at me and mouths, 'Good luck.'

How does he know I need luck? But Danny's always been able to read me so well; almost as well as Charlie.

I take a quick look at my watch. It's time.

With a sigh, I cross over the road to the shop, dragging my crate behind me.

The shop door is propped open on this warm summer's day, so I'm able to enter silently, and for a moment I stand just inside the doorway taking it all in – the smells, the sounds from outside, and most importantly all the memories. Dad in his little office going over the books. Mum behind the wooden counter helping a customer with their purchase. And me as a teenager, mooching about the place, not really wanting to be there.

Helping my parents in this shop was where it had all begun, so it seems quite appropriate this is where it should all end.

'Grace, what are you doing here?' Josh appears from the back room to greet me.

'I thought you might need someone to cover the shop for a while,' I tell him, putting part one of the plan into action.

'No, I'm fine, I shouldn't need to leave the shop until ...'

The shop phone begins ringing behind him.

'Excuse me a moment,' he says, as he darts into the office again. 'Yes,' I hear him say. 'Now? I didn't expect it would be ready until later ... OK, yes, sure, but ... oh you won't. Right then, I'll get there as soon as I can.'

Josh reappears. 'It seems I might need you after all,' he says. 'The garage say they've finished the MOT and the van is ready, but they need me to collect it now or it'll be locked up in the workshop until after the weekend.'

'That's fine, you go,' I tell him, not sounding in the least bit surprised. 'I'll be fine here for a while.'

'You're sure?' Josh says, grabbing his wallet and phone from the desk.

'Absolutely. It will be like old times.'

'OK, I'll be back in about half an hour then.'

'Perfect.'

I watch Josh disappear out of the door. Then I turn to my crate.

'Looks like it's time,' I say, removing the lid, and lifting an antique black typewriter from its carrier.

I place Remy in prime position in the window, rearranging some Clarice Cliff pottery to make him fit, then I stand behind the counter and wait. I glance at my watch again – two minutes to go.

At exactly four o'clock I see her, a young woman hurrying past the shop. But something in the window catches her eye, and she pauses to look at it, then a few seconds later she enters through the door.

'I was wondering about the typewriter in the window?' she asks. 'There isn't a price.'

I quickly appraise the young woman standing in front of me; she has long dark hair – not dyed or highlighted – she wears minimal jewellery, jeans and a plain white T-shirt, with a long crocheted waistcoat hanging loosely over them. She looks quite normal, and actually, I have to concede, quite pleasant.

I take a deep breath.

'That's because it doesn't have one,' I tell her. 'It's free to a good home.'

The woman looks at me in amazement. 'Free? Really?'

367

I nod. 'Do you like typewriters?'

'Yes, very much, I have a collection of them at home. But I don't have anything like that one – are you sure it's free?' She looks at me suspiciously, as though I might not know what I'm talking about.

I nod again. Every word pains me, but I know what must be done. It's time for Remy to move on to a new owner. He's done what he needed to with me, now it's time for him to begin helping someone else.

'Well, I'd be happy to take him off your hands then,' the young woman says, looking pleased, and excited she's found such a bargain.

'I'll fetch him from the window then,' I tell her, doing just that. 'He's quite heavy,' I say as I carry Remy across the shop. 'But you can put him in this crate, if you like. It will make him easier to transport.'

'Thank you,' the girl says, looking mystified by this strange little shop she's found herself in.

I place Remy back in the crate. It's all I can do to stop myself from patting him and running my hands over his keys one last time. But Remy and I already said our goodbyes earlier today. So I simply cover him up and hand the crate to his new owner.

'One last thing before you go,' I ask. 'What's your name?'

'Alice. Why?'

'I just needed to be sure,' I tell her. 'Look after him, won't you?'

'Er . . . yes, sure, I will,' Alice says, and she turns to leave the shop. 'Thank you again,' she says as she pauses on the doorstep. 'I've been having some real problems lately, so finding you, and getting this, has totally made my day.'

The contents of that box will not only make your day, but your life if you listen to him, I think, but I simply nod as she leaves the shop.

'Thank you, Remy,' I whisper as I follow her to the door, and watch her walk away down the street wheeling the crate behind her. 'It's been an honour and a pleasure knowing you.'

I had intended to walk straight back to Lighthouse Cottage, but instead I find myself stopping along the way to reflect on all the places that remind me of Remy.

I'm about to leave the promenade, where I've been sitting on a bench for some time gazing out to sea, when a navy blue Range Rover honks its horn at me.

It's Charlie.

'I've been looking for you everywhere,' he says as I climb into the passenger seat next to him. 'When I found the car back at the cottage I wondered where you'd got to.'

'Is Ava at Brownies?' I ask, looking at the empty seat behind me.

'Yes, I dropped her off a little while ago,' Charlie says, putting the car in gear and pulling out into the traffic again.

'I see you brought Thatcher,' I say, dodging his question. I lean over to stroke our new rescue pup, who is curled up on a tartan blanket on the back seat. 'Was she good for you today? The house seemed very quiet when I went round there earlier.'

'She's not been a bit of trouble. She's a good dog.'

'Yes, she is, isn't she? Like all the dogs we've had.'

Sadly we'd had to scatter Winston's ashes, like those of his predecessor Wilson, into the sea only a few months ago. And then, as always happens when you love dogs as much

369

as we both do, we'd missed having one in our lives. So we'd adopted a rescue pup that nobody wanted, because she was a cross between an Irish wolfhound and a chocolate Labrador. We called her Thatcher, in memory of the two dogs we'd known and loved before.

'*So*, how did it go?' Charlie asks a little impatiently as he pulls up at some traffic lights. 'You climbed into the car empty-handed, so I'm guessing everything went to plan.'

Charlie knew all about Remy now. I'd told him soon after we got together properly. And, as I knew he would, Charlie had simply accepted my story about Remy's magical letters, even though I knew he found it quite hard to believe.

That was until he saw one for himself, sitting in the little black typewriter one day, and he got on the phone and asked me to come home immediately so I could read it.

'Yes, Remy has a new owner now,' I say sadly. 'I'll miss him.'

'He did his job though,' Charlie says, to try and cheer me up. 'I'm assuming you agree his job was to get us together in the end?'

'Of course I do!' I reach over and squeeze Charlie's hand. 'And he did it magnificently! Even if it him took thirty years to accomplish!'

'I still don't understand where the letters came from though,' Charlie says. 'I'm a fairly open-minded person, as you know, Gracie, but you have to admit it's pretty bizarre.'

'Maybe we'll never know,' I reply, reaching into my pocket and pulling out the last letter I had from Remy.

Or maybe I will, I think as I begin to read it once more.

Dear Grace,

Sadly this will be my last letter to you.

Now I have successfully guided you through difficult times, the day has come for Remy to move on to a new owner, so he can help them through the challenging periods in their life, just like he did you.

At the bottom of this letter you'll find details of who you should pass Remy on to next, where you will find them and when.

But in the meantime I want to tell you what a pleasure it's been to be a part of your life all these years. I know we've not always seen eye to eye, but I hope you'll agree that everything I advised you to do was for the greater good in the end.

And now you've found the one. The one who first called you Gracie. He will continue to love you the way he's always done, and make you happy forever. Look after him, Grace.

I guess you might be wondering who has been sending you these letters all this time. Everyone that owns Remy for a short while does, it's human nature.

This is the part that is always so difficult to explain.

We all have messages sent to us throughout our lives, and everyone receives their guidance in a way that works best for them.

Me, I go by many names; some people call me their subconscious, a gut instinct or a sixth sense. The more enlightened might call me a spirit guide, or even a guardian angel.

Your guidance may have been sent to you initially using Remy — we often find physical messages are more easily accepted than random thoughts. But now you're ready to go it alone ... Except, you're not alone, Grace, you never have been. If you look deep inside yourself, you'll find every answer I've ever given you, and so many, many more for the future.

I've been there all along, and I always will be.

Love, Me x